D0098323

WHITE

Also by Christopher Whitcomb

Cold Zero
Black

WHITE

A NOVEL

Christopher Whitcomb

LITTLE, BROWN AND COMPANY

NEW YORK   BOSTON

Little, Brown and Company
Time Warner Book Group
1271 Avenue of the Americas, New York, NY 10020
Visit our Web site at www.twbookmark.com

First Edition: July 2005

The characters and events in this book are fictitious. Any similarity to real persons, living or dead, is coincidental and not intended by the author.

Library of Congress Cataloging-in-Publication Data

Whitcomb, Christopher.
   White : a novel / Christopher Whitcomb. — 1st ed.
      p. cm.
   ISBN 0-316-60080-6
   1. Government investigators — Fiction. 2. Terrorism — Prevention — Fiction.
3. Americans — Indonesia — Fiction. 4. Islamic fundamentalism — Fiction.
5. Undercover operations — Fiction. 6. Survivalism — Fiction. 7. Indonesia —
Fiction. I. Title.

PS3623.H564W48 2005
813'.6 — dc22   2004021266

10 9 8 7 6 5 4 3 2 1

Q-FF
Book design by Bernard Klein
Printed in the United States of America

To Joe Blake and Peter Berg
Everything for a reason

WHITE

PROLOGUE

The first casualty of war is truth.

— Rudyard Kipling

Sunday, 13 February
06:27 GMT
Jayawijaya Highlands, Indonesia

JEREMY WALLER STARED down the length of his high-powered rifle to where a brilliantly colored butterfly had alighted on its barrel. The creature fluttered its wings as a thin breeze drifted over the sniper's shoulder, slowly parting the bamboo shoots and elephant grass around him. Beads of sweat slipped down the ridge of his painted nose and fell silently into the furrow between his thumb and forefinger. Odd smells danced in his nostrils — the conflicting odors of broad-weave burlap, triple-canopy jungle, and something dead out there among the shadows.

"Milon's swallowtail."

It was a woman's voice, a sound Jeremy had never heard in a situation like this. Delta Force, now known officially as Combat Applications Group, referred to her as GI Jane, but sparingly and only out of sarcasm. Military SpecOps teams claimed to have no female members, though both the army and navy kept a small number for "military operations other than war." Now that the CIA had joined the game with Special Activities Division personnel, you needed a program to know all the players.

"*Graphium milon*," she continued, "a beautiful tropical fauna distinguished by a yellowish tuft of hair on the left dorsal hind wing. Probably a male with all that ventral red, though it's tough to tell with this species." Her pearl-white teeth shined from behind thick camouflage greasepaint, which she had applied in jagged green and black stripes.

Jeremy wiped sweat out of his eyes. Raindrops the size of snow peas began to fall among the broad-leaved plants around them.

"Goddamned rain," he said out loud. It fogged up his scope, obscured the target, and made Jeremy's now rancid ghillie suit stick to his skin. The garment of hemp, canvas, and local vegetation crawled with insects and had begun to torture him with a chronic and pervasive itch.

"Do all you FBI guys bitch this much?" Jane asked.

Jeremy, a six-year veteran special agent with a little more than a year on the Bureau's elite Hostage Rescue Team, saw no point in responding. They were partners in an operation that hinged on anonymity; he had no interest in becoming her friend.

■

TEN THOUSAND MILES east, two men and a woman waited in a dim corporate boardroom lined with claro walnut and silver filigree wall sconces. Three flat-screen televisions flickered with grainy images, then flashed to high-resolution pictures, clear as cable news.

"We have GPS signatures here, here, here, and here," one of the men said. He stood to the right of the monitors and pointed an infrared laser at the center screen. Red dots popped up at the four compass points around a jungle clearing.

"Where exactly is *here*?" another man asked. Dressed in a bespoke chalk-stripe suit and John Lobb shoes polished to an oxblood patina, the obvious leader of the group sat near the end of a huge table.

"Central Indonesia," the briefer responded. "The Irian Jaya province — a remote and isolated patch of primeval rain forest that is well protected by sympathetic indigenous populations. The nearest town is a Yani tribal village called Telambela."

"Telambela? That's a hell of a place for something like this to start, isn't it?" the man in the four-thousand-dollar shoes asked.

"A better place for it to end," a woman in a dated yet still elegant business suit of cashmere and silk answered. Tall and refined, she paced back and forth in front of leaded glass windows that reached all the way to the ceiling fifteen feet overhead. New York at night stretched out before her.

"Let's hope so," the briefer agreed. His voice sounded hollow, like that of a soldier consigned to a hopeless battle. Recent intelligence suggested that the strongest wave of terror in U.S. history could begin within days. If they failed to intercede in this godforsaken stretch of Third World wilderness, the ramifications would spread to places the best minds at CIA and the FBI had never even imagined.

■

"I GOT THAT sentry with the Galil coming around the bunkhouse. Call him Banjo Man."

Jeremy spoke softly and used his left hand to dial an NMARSAT phone that technicians at the FBI's Electronic Research Facility had fitted with a specially modified FASCINATOR secure voice module. A second sentry, whom they'd already nicknamed Castro, stood smoking a double corona just outside one of the huts.

"What time you got?" he asked.

The rain, which began to fall in earnest now, had crept inside his supposedly waterproof watch, rendering it useless.

"Thirteen forty," the woman said. Without waiting for Jeremy's reply, her voice turned low and guttural. A strange combination of clicking sounds and grunts filled the sodden air around them, foreign words that seemed to originate in the back of her throat and pass up through her nose.

A response came from somewhere behind where they lay at the base of a steep mountain slope. "Click hung ctock ctock oum aup," a huskier voice said.

"Quit that shit and speak English," Jeremy whispered. He craned his neck, searching for the Yani tribesman nestled in the tangle behind them. The tiny man with the penis gourd, rattan nose rings, and a string of babirusa teeth around his neck had guided them into position and then secreted himself back within an environment only a native could love.

"Be careful what you say," Jane responded. "These people are very intuitive and perceptive of tone. You know, his ancestors were headhunters."

"Yeah, I think I saw them once at the circus." Jeremy's tone left little need for intuition. "You tell him to stay where we can see him. I don't trust that little bastard."

GI Jane said nothing for a moment, then, "He says the messenger will come out of the north just before dark. Onset of evening nautical twilight is 07:37 Zulu, which means we have two hours. You want to rotate off your scope for a while?"

Jeremy shifted behind the butt of his sniper rifle. It had taken his team three days to walk into position from a helicopter insertion near a river village. A CIA case officer had met them there and introduced the eight-member task force to this tribesman, whose name Jeremy didn't even try to pronounce. GI Jane, a former Special Forces intelligence officer now assigned to the CIA, served as translator.

Why the U.S. government would train anyone to speak some arcane Indonesian dialect had never really dawned on Jeremy. Then again, he had spent enough time in the intelligence community to know that nothing ever really made sense. In the universe of secrets, you just accepted what you were told and moved on toward the objective. Unless you had a need to know, information usually ended up being little more than a liability.

"I'm staying right here," Jeremy said. He had no intention of rotating off his rifle until the "messenger" — local slang for an Indonesian bomb master named Ali Fallal Mahar — walked into the hut complex in front of them. Mahar had distinguished himself in eleven terror attacks against East Asian targets within the past year. More than 340 people had died at his hands, 37 of them Americans.

Jeremy knew that the messenger was due into the compound sometime before dark. He meant to be there when Mahar arrived . . . with a special greeting.

■

"WHERE ARE THE shooters?" The man in the John Lobb shoes rose from his chair and walked to the far end of the table. He ignored the multimedia screens for a moment as he thumbed through the news clip folio his press advisors assembled three times each day.

"Just inside the tree line," his briefer advised. The chief of staff —
a rigid former marine named Trask — pointed toward the jungle,
east of a clearing approximately one acre square. Five crude huts
rose haphazardly from the banks of a slow-running creek. A satellite communications dish rested on a flat-topped teak log just outside the largest of the shacks. Satellite imagery showed a small red
generator, several jerricans, assorted cardboard boxes, and clothes
hanging from a line between two sago trees. There were no women
or children, but a pack of mangy dogs rummaged through a burn
pile trying to sniff out lunch among the trash.

"Waller is positioned here," Trask continued. He drew a concen-
tric circle just east of the hut complex, then pointed to the south.
"The Dev Group sniper is here."

"How many altogether?" the man in charge asked.

"Eight. We have three green assaulters, two blue assaulters, one
blue sniper, and Waller." All three knew green referred to army assets; blue to navy.

"What about the Agency woman?"

"Yes, of course . . . the translator. She's cross-trained like the others, but her background is academic. If it comes right down to it,
she'll fight, but that's not her primary MOS."

The man in the John Lobb shoes closed the press clippings file
and laid it on the massive conference table. He turned toward the
screen.

"What if we don't get him here? What if something goes wrong?
Tell me about the contingency plans."

The woman stopped her compulsive pacing and stood beside the
window.

"We've poured millions of dollars and countless man-hours into
cultivating the contacts that put us here in the first place," she said
in a well-educated South Carolina lilt. The distinguished-looking
woman — perhaps the best known face in America at the time —
crossed her arms and stared out into a city she had never learned
to like.

"This is a one-time opportunity," she said. "If we don't intercept this operation here, there won't be any need for a contingency plan."

. . .

"SO SINCE WHEN is the FBI working insurgency ops with military units in Third World countries?" GI Jane asked. She had turned her attention away from the hut complex and seemed transfixed with the Milon's swallowtail on Jeremy's rifle barrel. "I mean, you guys are all about following the rules, not breaking them, right?"

"The rules have changed," Jeremy said, without elaborating. He wiped dripping rain from the brow of his ghillie hat and scanned the scene in front of him, trying to visualize just what this operation would look like if and when it finally went down. According to the five-paragraph warning order, Mahar was due into this isolated camp sometime before dark. Earlier efforts to capture or kill the terror chief had failed because of poor intelligence and corrupt Indonesian officials, but a new source had emerged. Code-named Parsifal, this Jemaah Islamiya insider had already compromised four of Mahar's associates, driving the terror group's remaining leadership into the jungle.

"You ever killed anyone?" GI Jane asked.

Jeremy shifted positions as the jungle pulsed around them. Ranked among the world's most impenetrable environments, it struck him as a land of shadows, ghosts, and misery. Without its mazelike network of tribal footpaths, this place might have forever remained civilization's last link to the Stone Age.

"I thought you CIA types already knew everything," Jeremy responded. "Don't you have some kind of dossier on me or something?"

She laughed out loud.

"Don't flatter yourself. Terrorists, despots, and radio talk show hosts are all we have time for," she said. "Besides, aren't you Feebies the ones with all the files? Or did they get pushed off into some West Virginia closet with all of J. Edgar's evening wear?"

Jeremy tried not to smile.

"Closets? You mean like the one Saddam used to hide all those weapons of mass destruction you said he had before the war?"

She stopped smiling.

"Cheap shot. What we sent up to the White House and what the politicians told the world were two totally different things, and you know . . ."

"Wait . . . ," Jeremy interrupted. "What the hell is that? Check the northwest trailhead."

The HRT sniper leaned into the reticle of his sniper scope, intent on something very unusual. GI Jane adjusted her spotting scope, trying to follow.

"Shit . . ." was all she said.

■

THEY APPEARED ON the flat-screen televisions like black dots in a field of green: a handful of bodies moving out of the jungle and stopping at the edge of the clearing.

"Who the hell are they?" the man in the John Lobb shoes asked.

A commercial satellite cruising 127 miles above Indonesia had just passed the apex of its arc, shooting video at a very steep angle. Despite the high resolution and excellent stream feed, no one in the conference room could see much except for the tops of their heads.

"I count six walkers," Trask said, stopping a moment as another emerged from the jungle. "Check that . . . seven."

"There's only one civilian I know of who has the connections and the desire to find a godforsaken hole in the jungle like that," his boss added. "It's gotta be Mahar."

"And the others?" the woman asked. "The intelligence said he'd be alone."

"Intelligence?" Trask huffed. "Even the best report is just one man's opinion — usually some tenured bureaucrat who hasn't seen field time since Christ was a corporal."

The three of them stared at the screen for a long moment, waiting for some kind of response from the fire team hiding in the surrounding jungle. Whether this was Mahar or not, the operators sent in to get him would surely react with force. This special ops team included some of the most capable soldiers on earth, and they had eyes on target.

"We'll find out soon enough," the leader said.

The others nodded. Despite technological advances in space-based imagery, there would never be any substitute for good men on the ground.

. . .

"YOU GONNA CALL this new guy into the CP?" GI Jane asked.

Jeremy shook his head. "I'm kind of busy right now," he whispered, fingering the trigger of his rifle and scouring the area through the reticle of his sniper scope.

At the north end of the clearing stood a Yani guide just like their own, sporting a hand-carved bow and prehistoric-looking body markings. He moved ahead of six taller men, then signaled to Banjo Man, who maintained his position near the bunkhouse.

"Sierra One to TOC," Jane spoke softly into the telephone receiver. "We have seven, repeat *seven* new players entering from the black/green corner, copy?"

They waited a moment for the mission planner at a tactical operations center in Bangkok to acknowledge the update. From Bangkok, these essential elements of intelligence, or EEI, would pass all the way back to a Secure Compartmented Information Facility (SCIF) at the FBI/CIA Joint Terrorist Threat Integration Center in Arlington, Virginia. Any word of a command-initiated assault would get relayed from there to NMARSAT units at each of the three ground cells. This communications plan seemed clumsy and time consuming, but the foreboding jungle terrain had rendered conventional options useless.

Jeremy stared through his rifle scope.

"I thought your headhunter guy said this wasn't going down until . . ."

Midsentence, he realized there was no more time for discussion. The targets had started to move quickly from the jungle toward the huts. The task force, which consisted of just five assaulters, would lose tactical advantage if Mahar and his buddies made it inside.

"Buckle up," Jeremy whispered. "This is going down now."

◾

"DAMMIT, THIS CHANGES everything," the woman said, focusing on the television screens.

"It's all right," Trask reassured her. "They can handle it."

Mission organizers had foreseen virtually every variable, from airborne medevac contingencies to visual triggers designed to compensate for on-site communications problems. No matter how many people showed up in that compound, rules of engagement allowed for immediate, unannounced use of deadly force the moment Mahar's capture looked tenuous.

"I don't care if there are fifty of them as long as we get Mahar," the leader growled. "He's the only one we really care about."

Neither of the others responded. They had seen enough of the war on terror to understand that no one bad guy ever shouldered all the blame.

"YOU GOT BANJO MAN," Jane said.

Jeremy knew the plan. He would take the gunman standing next to the bunkhouse. A Navy SEAL just inside the southern tree line would take Castro, the only other visible sentry. Once the two men were down, five task-force assaulters would step out of the jungle and demand Mahar's surrender. If the terrorist made any movement — any movement at all — Jeremy and his counterpart at the other side of the clearing would eliminate "targets of opportunity."

"What do we do if they get back into the jungle?" GI Jane asked.

"They're not getting back into the jungle," Jeremy answered, trying not to shake his head. If only Fritz Lottspeich, his regular HRT partner, had been there to help. He knew nothing about Indonesian butterflies or esoteric tribal dialects, but the man sure as hell could hunt.

Pffft!

Jeremy squeezed the trigger of his Accuracy International AW-SP rifle, a 7.62 x 51mm caliber death stick that fired subsonic rounds and limited muzzle blast to just sixty decibels. Although the weapon's accuracy was limited to 100 yards, anyone standing outside the suffocating vegetation around Jeremy's sniper hide would hear nothing at all.

"Sentries down," GI Jane observed.

Even before the two bodies hit the ground, a team of five assaulters from the Army's Combat Applications Group and the Navy's Surface Warfare Development Group emerged from the jungle, assault rifles at the ready. They looked like alien life-forms morphing out of the foliage, so odd and imposing in their camouflage that Mahar and his posse barely thought to flinch.

Pop, pop, pop . . .

An MP-5 erupted. The dogs dropped.

Jeremy held his crosshairs on the bridge of Mahar's nose, just in case, but there was no need to shoot. The Yani tribesman disappeared into the jungle, little more than a spirit fading into scattered light. Mahar and his colleagues lifted their hands over their heads. A clean surrender.

■

"THAT'S IT," TRASK said, back inside the walnut-paneled office. He had moved away from the screens and now stood near a normal-looking multiplex phone. "Two sentries dead. Six players in custody. Mahar is one of them."

This simply confirmed what they had just seen, of course. Now that the surveillance satellite had passed its apex, faces and clothing were becoming easier to distinguish.

"God almighty!" the woman suddenly exclaimed. "Are you seeing what I'm seeing?"

The others nodded silently. Mahar was easy to spot. FBI, CIA, and Interpol photographs had made his face familiar even to casual cable news watchers. The two men beside him looked familiar, too: Ramsi al-kir Amuri, Jemaah Islamiya's widely feared political leader, and Adnan al Shukrijuma, Mahar's chief assassin.

But the other three looked altogether different. They wore blue jeans, sweat-stained T-shirts, and ball caps. The patch above one visor read "Bass Pro Shops."

■

"WHO THE HELL is that?" Jeremy asked, turning from his scope to his partner. But she was already gone. Jeremy just lay there and watched as the short, muscular woman burst out of the jungle and ran across the clearing toward the six newest prisoners in the U.S. government's war on terror.

"I hope you're better at questions than you are at answers," Jeremy said to no one in particular. He watched as the colorful butterfly flapped its wings and drifted off the tip of his barrel in jagged, staccato-stroke flight.

. . .

AS IF ON cue, the newly elected vice president of the United States, Elizabeth Beechum, turned toward Jordan Mitchell, the country's wealthiest and best-known industrialist. It had been more than a year since the two first met in hostile discussions before the Senate Select Committee on Intelligence. Unlikely allies, the two had forged an alliance of sorts, a "new century" partnership of will that reached beyond politics or traditional boundaries of business and government.

"I see it, but I don't believe it," Mitchell said. Intelligence reports had suggested nothing like what appeared before him on the high-resolution monitor. "How can that be?"

Beechum shook her head. Everything they had worked so hard to achieve was supposed to end here in this isolated jungle. Now that had changed.

"Damned if I know," she growled. "But those three on the right sure as hell look like Americans."

Book I

OPERATIONS PLANNING

In the end, it will all come down to a war between Christianity and Islam — the Prince of Light against the gutter gods of Muhammad. The sooner we get down to it, the better off all our children will be.

— Richard Alan Sykes
Christian Identity Movement member
and self-proclaimed Phineas priest

I

Monday, 14 February
12:02 GMT
Situation Room, The White House

"ALL RIGHT, LET'S get moving. Matthew?"

Newly elected president David Ray Venable waved his hand to quiet a room that seemed to quiver with shock and nervous energy. He stood behind his chair at the midpoint of a broad mahogany table. To his immediate left sat National Security Advisor Matthew Havelock, a former University of Pennsylvania history professor who looked down his nose through Dollar Store reading glasses at a sky-blue briefing package. Havelock folded his hands around a tumbler of slowly melting ice, trying to keep it from rattling.

"You've seen the morning papers, I presume, Mr. President. I think we . . ."

"Seen the papers? Is this what I hired a national security advisor to tell me? Of course I've seen the morning papers!"

The *Washington Post, New York Times,* and several others lay neatly stacked in front of him. Headlines trumpeted the story.

BOMBERS STRIKE AT THE HEARTLAND, one proclaimed; *TERROR RAVAGES HOMELAND,* screamed another. *USA Today* perhaps said it best: *NATION'S WORST FEARS A REALITY.*

Just before 10:00 P.M. eastern time — nine hours earlier — terrorists had struck three targets: a popular Buckhead nightspot in Atlanta, Disneyland in Anaheim, and the Mall of America in Bloomington, Minnesota.

Virtually every channel in broadcast news had preempted regular programming to go wall-to-wall with on-scene coverage. Local, state, and federal emergency response crews were working frantically to deal with massive casualties. Organizations from the Red Cross to small-town fire department auxiliaries and church-based volunteer groups were streaming in to help.

Washington had awakened as well, trying to bring three years of terror response planning into action. Unfortunately, the nation's capital — the seat of virtually every federal agency from the Department of Homeland Security and FBI to intelligence gatherers like the NSA and DIA — had been paralyzed by the worst winter storm in three decades. For a city that closed its doors at the lightest dusting, this crisis could not have come at a more difficult time. The only people moving around inside the beltway had four-wheel drives or skis.

"Reports are still sketchy, sir," Havelock said, "but based on what we know, this is the most serious attack anywhere in the world since 9/11."

Venable, the former Democratic governor of Connecticut, shook his head in disbelief. He had sworn his oath to the nation's highest office just three weeks earlier. It appeared that his so-called honeymoon had come to a crashing halt.

"Here's what we know," a voice interjected. It belonged to FBI director Richard Alred, a former judge, accomplished trial lawyer, and, at forty-three, the youngest Bureau head since J. Edgar Hoover. Like his pug-nosed predecessor, Alred never missed an opportunity to exercise his authority, regardless of audience, jurisdiction, or protocol.

"Experts from our Bomb Data Center at Quantico have determined that the I.E.D.s were similar in construction and sophisticated," he said. "Well planned. They hit all three sites — thousands of miles apart — within eight seconds of each other."

Venable crossed his arms and considered the FBI chief. The man wore close-cropped hair and a properly tailored suit over an athletic build. He spoke with remnants of a Boston accent, but the clean-cut delivery was bred of military heritage and enough time in the private sector to understand imperative. Though Alred came as a holdover from the previous administration, Venable suspected that this man would serve him well.

"I.E.D.s?" the president asked. "What are I.E.D.s?"

"Improvised explosive devices, sir: Czech-made Semtex — a particular batch with additives used in the manufacture of land mines. This special compound was exported to an Indonesian factory in 1997 and is the same chemical composition found in the 2003 Marriott bombing in Jakarta. Our investigators also found evidence of unusual e-cell timers and residue of methyl nitrate, ammonium nitrate, and fuel oil — the compound Timothy McVeigh used in Oklahoma City."

"You think this was homegrown?"

"Not at all, sir. ANFO is one of the most common explosives out there, and these attacks bear all the hallmarks of Muslim extremists. They used truck bombs with remote detonators and planned the primary strikes to inflict maximum casualties. Once emergency crews and television cameras showed up, they set off tertiary explosives for even more devastating effects. These were well planned, expertly executed military operations."

"Press reports indicate they may have used ambulances," Havelock added. He still looked shaken but saw no point in letting Alred — who wasn't even officially part of the National Security Council — monopolize discussion. "Is that true? Did these animals turn vehicles of mercy into bombs?"

"It appears so," Alred said without turning his eyes from the president. "Up to thirty percent of the casualties are believed to be police, fire, and EMS personnel. I don't have to tell you what kind of impact this might have on responses to any future attacks."

Voices grumbled among more than a dozen people who had crowded into the living-room-sized space located one floor below the Oval Office. Most of the president's newly appointed National Security Council staff had been called in for this emergency session.

To the president's right sat his chief of staff, Andrea Chase, followed by the secretary of defense; secretary of state; attorney general; the heads of CIA, Treasury, FBI, and Department of Homeland

Security; the chairman of the joint chiefs of staff; the president's economic advisor; the U.S. representative to the United Nations; the council's national coordinator for infrastructure protection and counterterrorism.

"Future attacks." Venable huffed. "For God's sake, I thought we were done with nonsense like this." He placed both hands on the shoulders of his high-backed chair and shook his head. "You said Muslim extremists. Do we know that for sure?"

"We've received three separate claims of responsibility by a new group that calls itself Ansar ins Allah," Alred offered. "All came in the form of videotapes delivered via courier to local television stations in the affected markets. This is the same sort of delivery technique we've seen after attacks in Mombasa, Riyadh, and Jakarta. Standard rhetoric, suicide-ritual indicators, plenty of proprietary specifics."

CIA director Milton Vick cleared his throat. "The Agency has obtained all three tapes," he said, striving not to get upstaged by his FBI counterpart. "FIDUL is cross-referencing voiceprints and language patterns through Dominant Chronicle databases and . . ."

"Whoa, whoa, whoa . . ." The president stopped him. "The what is what?"

Vick, a short, plump former Congressman and ambassador to Chile had read this information from a piece of paper. He looked completely lost to deeper explanation.

"FIDUL is our Federal Intelligent Documents Understanding Laboratory," Alred explained "They work with groups like CENDI and NAIC in support of an interagency working group of STIs from Commerce, Energy, NASA, the National Library of Medicine, the DoD, and Interior. Dominant Chronicle is a joint DIA-FBI document analysis center."

The president shrugged and shook his head, bewildered by the endless list of agencies and acronyms. Explanations just added to his confusion.

"Bottom line," Vick said. "We don't have solid visual identification due to facial obfuscation, but our top analysts believe the claims of responsibility are credible."

"Quite frankly, Mr. President, Ansar ins Allah represents what we have most feared about the terror threat facing this country," Alred said. "A cell of al Qaeda sympathizers who haven't shown up on any radar screen. Small. Rogue. Violent. We really don't have a lot to go on."

"Don't have a lot to go on."

Venable spoke in a small voice, the falsely endearing rattle predators use to lure their prey. These were the nation's top intelligence and law enforcement officials, and they knew little more than what Venable had seen on cable news. For a man just three weeks in the Oval Office, that didn't seem possible.

"Did you say you don't have a lot to go on?"

Shoulders started to tighten around the room.

"Well, you sure as hell better come up with something! Thirteen hours from now, I've got to walk out in front of two hundred eighty million Americans and convince them that we're still the land of the free and the home of the brave. I'm going to need a little help here."

The president leered at his cast of experts. They ranged from political appointees to career professionals. None of them had ever presided over a disaster like this.

"We inherited this mess from a Republican administration," Andrea Chase pointed out. "They can hardly hold you responsible after just three weeks in office."

"This is America, Andrea," the president growled. "We hold everybody responsible." He raised his right hand over his head, palm out.

"Let's look at what we *do* have. We have at least three hundred fifty confirmed deaths, three times that number injured." Venable's voice began to rise as he curled up his index finger. "We have twenty-four-hour news outlets running nonstop images of the carnage." He tucked his middle finger beside the first. "We have panic in the heartland — places that never thought they'd experience something like this."

He paused for a moment as the blood rose in his face. A figure that had moments earlier looked like a confident commander in chief suddenly flushed crimson with rage.

"We've got the worst storm in thirty years shutting down the government, and we have nobody in custody!" He closed his last two fingers under his thumb and held a tight fist out in front of him, like some thug threatening a bar brawl.

"I haven't even arranged my kids' photos on the Oval Office credenza yet," he growled, "and Congress is going to march up the Hill with a saber in one hand and a whetstone in the other looking to cut my balls off! I don't want to hear that we don't have a lot to go on! I want to know precisely what we are going to go on, and I want to know it now!"

The windowless room froze silent except for the passive hum of fluorescent lights.

"Excuse me everyone . . . ," a voice interrupted. The conference room door closed with a loud *thunk* as Vice President Elizabeth Beechum blew in bold as the storm outside. Still pink in the face from the arctic air, she brushed snow off the collar of her heavy wool coat. "Sorry, but the air force delayed us coming out of New York."

She removed her coat and tossed it to a uniformed marine, then dropped her briefcase on the mahogany table, pulled out the last remaining chair, and sat.

"CNN is reporting a death toll over one thousand and there is talk of new explosions in Miami," she announced, oblivious to Venable's position or demeanor. "Perhaps one of you would be kind enough to read me in on what we plan to do about it."

■

SIRAD MALNEAUX LOVED New York in the winter, especially when it snowed. Storms like this painted the black city white, erasing the broken asphalt and the trash and the pollution-stained brick with an almost apologetic air. Snow pushed everyone indoors, clearing the sidewalks of tourists, chasing away the cabs and the New Jersey commuters and the double-parked box trucks; silencing the horns and the hawkers and the beggars. Storms handed New York back to its most stalwart souls — adventurers like Sirad who thrived on braving impassable expanses just for the thrill of looking back on their tracks.

And what a storm this was. More than eighteen inches of nor'easter had already fallen on Manhattan, and forecasters predicted that the worst still lay ahead. JFK, LaGuardia, and Newark International all had closed. Banks, city offices, public transportation, and retailers had barred their doors. Only the bodegas and the newsstands remained open, shining their neon ATM beacons for those who simply couldn't live without umbrellas, porno mags, and stale deli salads.

7:23 AM

Sirad's digital watch flashed as she leaned into the blizzard and ran. Slush had already leaked through her shoes, melted down the back of her jacket, and misted on her face, but she smiled just the same. Running out across Central Park's great lawn, she felt free for a moment from the stress of a job that with each passing day seemed to consume her more and more.

Up to Eighty-first Street, then around the reservoir, then back down the horse path, she thought to herself. Most days she would have completed the four-mile run in half an hour, but today would take longer. No matter — with everything she had seen on the news last night, it might be a while before she next got to run.

"Ms. Malneaux!" a voice called out. It was a male voice, muffled by the storm yet all around her. It sounded urgent.

Sirad continued running but turned her head instinctively to the right. She squinted through the clouds of her exhaling, trying to make out the dark figure who appeared to be chasing her from the east.

"Ms. Malneaux, wait up!" A young man emerged through the blinding snow, a tall junior executive wearing earmuffs, a cashmere topcoat, and those L.L. Bean boots with the rubber bottoms. He breathed deeply, trying to suck in air and cough out words in the same instant. "Mr. Mitchell . . . wants you . . . back . . . in his office. Now."

He stopped beside her as she ran in place and doubled over with his hands on his knees. Sirad guessed he had been sprinting.

"Is this about the terror attacks?" she asked. Sirad spoke calmly, with the composure of a well-conditioned athlete. "Because from what I've seen, there isn't a whole helluva lot we can do in this weather."

The man shook his head.

"It's the Quantis system," he managed to say. "Someone has . . . launched an attack . . . on our mainframes."

"What?" Sirad exclaimed. Quantis couldn't be attacked. The world's first truly secure data transmission system had been tested by the finest minds in telecommunications, both inside the government and out. It was Sirad's project — a project she knew intimately — and it was secure.

"That can't be." She stopped jogging in place, reached out, and straightened the man to standing. "What are you talking about?"

"I'm just here . . . to get you." The man heaved. He wiped melted snow and sweat out of his eyes and pointed back toward Borders Atlantic's corporate headquarters, which in better weather would have stood out clearly on the eastern skyline. "I think you'd better hurry," he said, panting. "Mitchell said the sky is falling . . . and I don't think he was talking about the storm."

■

IN A WARMER place, at the eastern edge of the sole remaining communist country in the Western world, a team of CIA elicitation experts stepped out into a brilliant Caribbean sun. They wore khaki cargo pants, polo shirts, and safari vests covered with pockets, Velcro, and zippers.

"Why do you think he has agreed to talk?" one of the men asked. He was trying to keep up with a sturdily built woman named Sarah. Two other men and a female advisor from the Army's Third Psychological Operations Group were falling in the best they could.

"Because he wants a deal," Sarah answered. She had a dark-green government-issue "wheel book" in one hand and a Skilcraft pen in the other. "He knows that information is the only ticket off this godforsaken rock, and he's going to try and play his trump card. If he really has one."

They traipsed toward Camp Four, a cluster of prefabricated buildings squared around an exercise yard of crushed rock and concrete slabs. Bearded men in white jumpsuits sat at picnic tables beneath an overhang. Guards with M-16s nodded as the elicitation team passed. The name tags on the guards' BDUs had been covered up with white medical tape to keep the prisoners from exploiting any personal identifiers.

"Good morning, ma'am." A corporal nodded as they passed. He motioned them through a subwaylike turnstile. A sign behind his left shoulder read CAMP DELTA-4, and beneath it: HONOR BOUND TO DEFEND FREEDOM.

"Fair, firm, and consistent," the group's leader responded. It seemed to be the mantra here, something the camp commander felt he needed everyone to say out loud. She heard it everywhere she went.

"Fair, firm, and consistent, sir."

Camp Delta. Built of concertina wire, chain-link fencing, and plywood, the U.S. military's Inmate Detention and Interrogation Center at Guantánamo Bay, Cuba, housed more than 650 of what some have called the world's most dangerous Islamic zealots. Held without charges, without legal representation, and without hope, prisoners from forty-two countries — some as young as fifteen — sat there, awaiting successful "behavioral modification."

Camp Four represented the medium-security section of the prison. Only about a dozen men had earned their way here in a process detainees sarcastically called "the Hajj."

The rules were simple: Provide information on al Qaeda and the Taliban and you may someday return home. Show intransigence or hostility and remain caged in a four-by-eight-foot cage until hell freezes over. At Gitmo, where humid ocean air typically reached one hundred degrees, that seemed like a very long time.

"Good morning, Khalid." Sarah stepped into a meticulously kept room, leaving the others waiting outside. Four olive-drab military cots lined one wall. Each cot came with sheets, a green wool blanket, two changes of white linen clothing, a toothbrush, plastic shower sandals, and a Koran. The walls gleamed antiseptic white.

"Good day," Khalid Muhammad said in perfect English. He had learned the language well during his undergraduate years at State University of New York at Binghamton. The son of wealthy Saudi rug merchants, he had received the finest Western education before joining the soldiers of Islam in the Afghan struggle against the Great Satan, George W. Bush.

"Why won't you call me Sarah?" the woman asked. She went by many names and preferred virtually all of them to her last: GI Jane.

"I am not your friend," he said, glancing at the others outside. "I provide truthful information though I get little in return. I tolerate your condescending American tone. I even betray my countrymen out of futile hope that it may one day win me freedom. But I will not grant any kindness to a woman who blasphemes my God by refusing to cover herself. I will not call you Sarah."

"Whatever." GI Jane shrugged. She sat down on the bed across from Muhammad and pulled out a tape recorder. He had seen the devices before, of course. The CIA used them to collect voiceprints so they could identify him if he ever got out and said anything threatening over unsecured phone lines.

GI Jane held the recorder to her lips when she spoke, then pushed it toward him for his answers.

"We recently captured a man named Ali Fallal Mahar. Do you know him?"

"Yes. Of course," Muhammad responded. "He is called the messenger. I met him once in Malta. 1999. He is a religious man — a mullah."

"We have reason to believe that Mahar has been planning attacks inside the United States," she said. Prisoners were deprived of outside news, so Muhammad had no idea that the attacks had already begun.

"He has talked of such things," Muhammad volunteered. "But his resources were small. He had great power within his own country, but I think it would be hard to imagine him gaining any real following among American Muslims. Indonesians don't have a strong community inside the United States."

"What about non-Muslim groups?" she asked.

Muhammad looked puzzled.

"Non-Muslim groups? What do you mean by this? Mahar is a jihadist. He wants to kill your people, not befriend them."

That seemed to bring Muhammad some pleasure. GI Jane made a note in her little green notebook, then turned off her recorder and laid it on the cot beside her. She paused a moment to consider her words.

"What if I told you we found him less than a week ago with three Americans? Non-Muslim Americans," she added. "What if I told you they had traveled all the way to Indonesia to see him? What would you think about that?"

Muhammad's eyebrows tilted.

"I would not know what to say."

But then the expression on his face began to change. The thick black eyebrows settled, and the glimmer of resistance in his eyes dulled to some deeper understanding. GI Jane noticed.

"Muhammad, I know you don't like me," she began. The CIA officer spoke with the confidence that comes with being able to stroll
out of the jail cell at the end of the interrogation. "I don't care. What
I do care about is saving American lives. Give me the information I
need, and you can walk out of here. Dance me in circles and you
can rot in this shithole with all the rest of your towel-headed freak
buddies."

Muhammad thought a moment. He understood the American
mindset. Their arrogance. He had seen it in Beirut and in the West
Bank and in Afghanistan and Iraq and Pakistan. But he also knew
how to turn this knowledge in his own favor. Capitalism was trade;
trade was barter, and barter was old as his Bedouin ancestors.

The Americans wanted information, and he wanted to leave this
place of empty souls. As the posters in the infirmary said, "Brother,
follow my steps; truth, cooperation, then back home." As Muhammad's personal favorite stated: "Brother, the road to return must be
paved with your complete truth and cooperation."

"Jafar al Tayar," he said. The one-time Taliban fighter spoke
softly, quieter than the ventilation fans behind him. He looked concerned that the others outside would hear.

"Jafar the pilot?" GI Jane spoke Arabic as well as Muhammad
did.

"Jafar the pilot, Jafar the one who flies, the high-flying one . . .
yes. Depends on your interpretation, of course."

"Not another airliner plot." She laughed. "You'll have to do better
than that. If I had a rial for every airliner plot I've heard about
down here, I'd be able to buy the goddamned island. Save your
breath."

"No, no," Muhammad objected. "I am not talking about planes.
Jafar al Tayar is a person of great power and respect. This is why
they call him the pilot, or the flyer. It is metaphor . . . a metaphor
for one who holds high position, one who can control things from
on high."

GI Jane picked up the tape recorder and rested it in her lap. She
had conducted dozens of interrogations in which prisoners tried to
trade meaningless information for an extra ration of bread at dinner. This sounded like something more.

"Who? What kind of person are we talking about?"

"Could be a military leader, a powerful businessman, someone in the media," he replied. "This person has earned himself a position of trust and power."

Muhammad stared out the door behind her. If he could have seen beyond the tarpaulin-covered walls, he would have looked out on more than three thousand miles of open ocean. The nearest land — should anyone get past the guard dogs and machine guns — was Florida. That was a ninety-mile swim over open ocean with little hope of friendly faces on the other side. There were just two ways out of Camp Delta: through cooperation or in a pine box.

"I do not even know if this is true," he said. "All I know is that Jafar al Tayar is hope for many of my people. It is a plan you won't hear discussed in mosques, in the bazaar, over coffee. No, it is whispered — like a legend. A myth. Maybe nothing more."

GI Jane tried to judge veracity in the man's face.

"Do you believe it?" she asked, hoping to catch something in his answer.

"I believe in Allah," Muhammad said. "I believe in his will. If it is His Will that your government shall fall, then it will happen. This is all nonsense, this business between you and me."

GI Jane stood to leave.

"Thank you, Muhammad," she said. "I'll note your cooperation in my report to the warden."

"I don't care about favorable reports to the warden," Muhammad said, now smiling. "But there is something more you need to know. Something only I can give you. If you want to save your country, you will have to offer me something in return . . . something considerably more valuable than freedom."

■

"ELIZABETH, THIS IS no time to butt heads. I need options, not power trips."

The president of the United States led a party of five upstairs from the Situation Room to the Oval Office. He was still dressed in the white shirt and pinstriped suit he had worn the previous day. One of his aides had handed him a fresh tie on the way, and he was clumsily looping it around his neck as they walked.

Unfortunately for David Ray Venable, and perhaps the rest of the country, as governor of Connecticut he had never dealt with anything more threatening than budget deficits. And like most leaders unaccustomed to true crisis, he had already violated the first rule of incident response: he had mistaken leadership for responsibility. Instead of delegating authority and going to bed at an appropriate hour, he had stayed up the entire night, obsessing over what few details he could glean from cable news. Unlike Beechum and many of his senior advisors, the leader of the free world was headed into day two of a national tragedy with no sleep at all.

"This is not a power trip," the vice president argued back. "You need to accept that the United States government worked quite well before you took the reins and will work quite well after you're gone. Let the professionals do their jobs. You need sleep."

The president stopped in the middle of the brightly lit room and turned in circles, searching for a mirror in which to check his tie.

"Can't we get a mirror in here?" he barked. "What kind of office doesn't have a mirror?"

This office, apparently. In fact, not only was there no mirror, there were no wall hangings at all. The room looked more like a construction site than an executive work space. The paint scheme was only half finished. New carpet lay in rolls along the west wall. Opposing couches offered the only place to sit, and movers had stacked them with boxes of Venable's personal memorabilia. None of this had seemed much of a problem until today, of course. Presidents get to decorate as they please, and Venable — the product of a New England lineage that traced its roots to the *Mayflower* — had shown no tolerance for his predecessor's bronze Remington horses and western scenes by Julian Onderdonk, Tom Lee, and WHD Koerner.

"If your beloved intelligence community is so good, why does the director of the CIA have to read stuff off index cards that I can get from CNN?" he demanded, trying to find his reflection in a silver Revere bowl one of the decorators had left atop a bookshelf.

"This happened less than twelve hours ago, David," she answered. "Crises are very confusing at first. It takes time to put the pieces together."

Elizabeth Beechum, a four-term senator from South Carolina,

had served three terms as chairman of the Select Committee on Intelligence. Few people in Washington knew more about the resources available in the government's war on terror.

"I don't have time," the president said. "I want the first draft of my remarks by six o'clock, understood? And I want something meaningful to say. Something promising."

The president walked to a thin wooden podium that had been arranged in front of the Rose Garden windows. Venable used the relic, which White House historians traced to Lincoln's Gettysburg Address, to write on, having years earlier sworn off traditional work spaces as breeding grounds for procrastination. Many things would distinguish his presidency, he had declared during his inaugural address, but none more than decisive action. One of his first acts had been to clear the Oval Office of its trademark desk.

"We have FBI evidence response teams and the Critical Incident Response Group on-scene with all the best technology available," Alred ventured. "We have integrated federal, state, and local law enforcement through sixty-six joint terrorism task forces. The Joint Terrorist Threat Integration Center is coordinating law enforcement, military, and intelligence resources with the CIA's Counterterrorism Center and counterparts around the world. Everyone from FEMA to DOE to the CDC and every other TLA you can name is pulling out all the stops to make sure the on-scene commanders have what they need to deal with this."

"TLA?" the president asked. "What's the TLA?"

"Three-letter agency," Alred explained sheepishly. "It's an expression we use to . . ."

"Like I told you," Beechum said. "Get some rest, David. Trying to micromanage operations from a podium in the Oval Office is counterproductive."

Venable rubbed his sleep-deprived eyes.

"How about a cup of coffee?" he mumbled. "What I really need right now is a double skinny latte."

The people around him looked at one another accusingly. Just five staff members had made the cut and been summoned upstairs from the National Security Council meeting in the Situation Room: Beechum, Chief of Staff Andrea Chase, Havelock, Alred, and the director of Homeland Security, Jim Davis. None of them felt obliged to fetch refreshments.

"DHS thinks we need to raise the terror threat advisory," Havelock announced. Davis shot the national security advisor a curious leer, guessing correctly that Havelock had made the suggestion simply to escape steward's duties.

Venable stopped rubbing his eyes.

"Oh for goodness' sake, that color crap is a national laughingstock," he grumbled. "I'm sure FOX and MSNBC will be glad to cover the press conference, but don't you think that most Americans have already gone to the highest state of alert!"

Beechum smiled. Davis leered at her too.

"What about SIGINT?" Venable asked. He had heard the term numerous times during coverage of the 9/11 aftermath and thought using it made him sound informed. "Alred, what are we hearing?"

The FBI director rolled his shoulders. What he knew about signals intelligence could be summed up with a shrug, but that didn't stop him.

"Based on the reports I have seen, sir, chatter is up," he said. "Unfortunately, our intercepts show little more than loosely defined celebration. There is a lot of confusion among terror players, from Indonesia's Abu Sayaaf and Jemaah Islamiya to Hamas, Hezbollah, and the remnants of al Qaeda. Everyone seems thrilled about the attacks, but no one seems to know anything about who is behind them."

"Chatter. Right. What exactly is that anyway?" the president asked.

"Intercepted microwave transmissions," Davis explained. He didn't want to get the coffee either. "Unfortunately, pulling actionable intelligence out of the data stream is like trying to sip water from a fire hose. We often target a geographic region — the Middle East, for example, or Central Asia — and have to draw conclusions based on generalized traffic. That's chatter."

"In other words, a bunch of Middle Easterners are ringing their phones off the hook, talking about bombings in America." Venable nodded, now satisfied with the knot in his tie. "I would hope that you don't find that surprising."

"No, sir," Alred said. "But there is something else. We have been tracking a series of odd financial transactions by ranking officials within the Saudi government. Big transactions to very obscure accounts. Our best analysts suspect that one or two wealthy Saudis have established a financial pipeline to rogue cells inside the U.S."

"Saudis?" He paused a moment. "Inside the U.S.?"

"Yes, sir. But they are using Quantis phones to conduct their business. We simply can't listen in."

The president shook his head. Even with three weeks on the job, he understood how much these new phones had hurt U.S. intelligence efforts. Borders Atlantic, the world's biggest telecommunications company, had developed a new encryption technology that rendered everything from standard telephone relays to fax, cell, satellite television, and Internet connections impenetrable to overhears. Jordan Mitchell, the company's CEO, had introduced his product in a joint venture with the Saudis, handing virtually everyone in the Middle East secure lines of communication. The NSA still hadn't broken through.

Venable walked to within arm's reach of his FBI chief. This man definitely seemed the best prepared so far. "You have names?"

"Well, yes and no, sir. We have focused our investigation on three possible subjects." He reached into a manila envelope. "Hassam Ibrahim Lnu, Ahmed Mustafa Lnu, and Fnu Lnu, also known as Ali Asar — three Saudi-born Yemeni nationals last known to be living in Spain. We may not be able to intercept their calls, but we can trace them to . . ."

"Wait a minute," the president interrupted. "Lnu . . . Fnu Lnu? Those don't sound like Arab names. Sounds Asian to me — maybe Indonesian. Are they all brothers or something?"

All eyes focused on Alred. It suddenly became obvious that he would be the one going after the coffee.

"Umm . . . no sir, not exactly." The FBI director cleared his throat. "Lnu is law enforcement shorthand for Last Name Unknown. Fnu Lnu would mean 'first name unknown,' 'last name unknown.' We know these individuals by code names, mostly. We don't have full descriptors."

The air in the room grew too thick to breathe. No one wanted to watch the president twist in embarrassment.

"Director Alred, I've been president of the United States just long enough to find the toilet paper dispenser in the Oval Office toilet. How am I supposed to make sense of all these acronyms you keep throwing at me? Speak English!"

Everyone except Beechum suddenly felt the need to check his or her watch.

"Don't worry about the details, sir," Havelock said. He had regained most of the composure he'd lacked in the meeting downstairs. "All this country needs right now is gravitas — a president who can act decisively and stand behind the tough calls. Nobody understands all that spy crap anyway."

II

Monday, 14 February
14:10 GMT
Homestead Ranch, Kerrville, Texas

ONLY THREE THINGS mattered to Colonel Roderick "Buck" Ellis. Family, God, and country. Not necessarily in that order.

"Poppy! Poppy! Look at me!" a child called out from the other side of a split-rail corral. His oldest grandchild, a towheaded six-year-old cherub named Gracie, sat atop her brand-new Shetland pony. She wore the white gaucho skirt and linen blouse her momma had dressed her in for the birthday party. Calfskin roping boots the size of teacups kicked against the pony's sides as she waved with one hand and clutched the reins with the other. A fifty-X Stetson sat proudly atop her widely beaming face. To everyone watching, she looked like a rodeo princess just waiting for a bigger horse.

"Ride 'em, cowgirl!" the colonel hollered back at his little treasure. Gracie looked every bit her beautiful momma, with the confidence and energy of her Special Forces daddy.

"Sun's gonna get hot today, Colonel. Better watch yourself."

Buck Ellis continued staring at Gracie as he wrapped his arms around the woman responsible for all this. The former Patricia

Margaret Nash — always just Pat — had given him five children. Through twenty-nine years in the military, eleven duty stations in seven countries, interminable overseas tours, and the loss of a sixth child while he was away on "business," she'd never offered anything but complete devotion.

"Thank you, darlin'," the colonel said, turning back toward the party. Dozens of children ran about, yelping and hollering beneath the colorful birthday banners, piñatas, and trestle vines. A seven-piece mariachi band filled the air with festive music. His grown children and their spouses and family friends sat at tables full of food or stood in the glow of an unseasonably warm morning sun.

"This is some spread we've built here, isn't it?" Ellis allowed himself a moment of pride.

His wife, still fit and lovely at fifty-eight, hugged him close and nodded her head. Everything around them — all that they could see in any direction — from the horses and lawn chairs to the 3,600-acre ranch they called the Homestead, meant nothing compared to the love behind it. She enjoyed the ranch, but material things didn't seem to matter. It was heritage and a cleansing faith in Jesus Christ that sustained her.

"Wonderful, Colonel." She beamed. "Isn't it wonderful?"

Native Texans, they had returned home to Kerrville a decade earlier. But not to retire. The colonel had turned what was left of his great-grandfather's spread into one of the finest facilities of its kind in the world — a tactics, operations, and firearms training facility that catered to everyone from his old friends in the military special operations community to law enforcement SWAT teams to private citizens willing to cough up tuition. The Homestead represented more than a home to him and his extended family, more than a job. It was a way of life — a vocation. A calling.

"I wish all of us could have been here today to share in it," Pat said, turning to her husband. "Have you heard from him?"

"Not yet." He smiled. The sounds of gunfire from nearby training ranges provided background they never even noticed anymore. "But he's been busy. The boy'll call just as soon as he gets a chance."

Their eldest son had always proven conscientious and responsible. He wouldn't have missed a family function like this without good reason.

"I guess you're right." She nodded, turning for a kiss. "But look at you. You are going to burn yourself red if we don't get you into the shade."

Years outdoors in the military had turned her husband's face brown and rough as tree bark, but she worried about him just the same.

"You hush now," the colonel said, wrapping her up in his arms. "I've had lots worse to worry about than a little Texas sunshine."

With that, he winked, pushed the brim of his Resistol rancher higher onto his forehead, and kissed his wife between closed eyes.

"Now you leave me be." He smiled. "That little girl over there needs her granddaddy to show her a thing or two about riding. Run on back up to the party and see to the hostessing . . . git."

He playfully spanked her on the butt, the way he would have shooed off a freshly groomed mare.

When his wife had gone, Colonel Ellis sidled over to where a handful of men stood talking quietly near the corral. The sounds of laughter, festive music, and playing children drowned out the distant gunfire. He tried to concentrate on his granddaughter's smile. This should have been a happy day, he decided, but darker thoughts filled his mind.

■

JEREMY WALLER LAY tangled in a pile of sheets, soaked through with night sweats and spilled beer. The only light in the room peeked through drawn shades in tiger stripes of neon — a false light that glowed so brightly across his bed, he could poke his fingers through the beams.

Bangkok, he decided, trying to remember himself. *Another hotel room in a long series of foreign cities.* It had been more than forty-eight hours since the Irian Jaya raid, and he still hadn't heard from his controllers.

Jeremy reached to the nightstand and pointed the remote at a small television, flipping through the channels: *Gunsmoke* reruns dubbed in Thai, Bollywood movies full of dark-mustached villains and fainting love interests, an old World Cup soccer match, women in brightly colored veils dancing to some Southeast Asian variation of MTV.

He climbed out of bed and pulled open the blinds, allowing the energy of a bustling downtown to come flooding in.

Another exotic city I'll see but never enjoy.

He'd been confined to this room, waiting for word about his exfil. There was nothing to do but watch TV and sleep, but despite the three hits of Ambien, a six-pack of Tsingtao, and endless reruns of *Magnum, P.I.,* he'd mustered nothing more than a couple yawns.

"Push-ups," he suggested aloud, hungry for the sound of any familiar voice. His head felt groggy, lost in a dull haze of pills, hangover, and sleep deprivation. "Five bucks says you can't knock out two hundred."

Jeremy got down on his knees and assumed the "forward leaning rest" position HRT had taught him so well. He elevated his feet on the edge of the bed and began cranking out protocol-perfect repetitions, counting silently in a room that seemed distant from the rest of the world.

Thermit, he thought as the push-up count passed ten. He lapsed back into recollection of what had happened once GI Jane ran out into the clearing. Only Thermit, a compound of iron oxide and aluminum with a potassium permanganate and glycerin initiator, would have caused such a lightning flash.

Jeremy had seen Thermit's aftermath during the war in Kosovo, but it wasn't until after joining HRT that he'd witnessed its real power. Delta breachers had demonstrated the incendiary during a training trip to Fort Bragg the previous fall. The grenades ignited at 2,200 degrees Celsius and burned like brimstone.

This was supposed to be a rendition, he thought. *A simple snatch of a terrorist the CIA had tracked to a jungle hideout.*

This wasn't Jeremy's first covert operation, of course. It wasn't even the first time he had killed. During a rendition in Yemen the previous year, he and his team leader, Jesús Smith, had eliminated a handful of terrorists. Unfortunately they had killed women and children, too. Jeremy still woke up some nights seeing an eight-year-old boy stumbling out from behind a curtain with a disabled AK-74 in his little hands, recoiling from the impact of Jeremy's bullets. Dead.

Twenty-two, twenty-three . . .

Jeremy shook his head, trying to clear it for more tolerable thoughts. His muscles began to pump up with blood, reminding him of the PT sessions he'd enjoyed back at Quantico. That's where all this had started of course, with the FBI's Hostage Rescue Team. He had survived two weeks of tryouts and six months of New Operator Training School, or NOTS, only to be shipped off to the U.S. Marine Corps Scout/Sniper school for another month of "specialization."

Thirty, thirty-one . . .

Then had come the Puerto Rico mission. Terrorists had kidnapped the governor's daughter and would have killed her if not for the team's brilliantly executed assault. Jeremy remembered peering down into the cellar hole where they had secreted her, a violent attack raging around him, bullets flying up from the dark space below. He remembered leaning in with his MP-5 and blowing the back of the terrorist's head off.

"Good shooting," FBI headquarters had said after the OPR investigation. *At least it was better than Yemen*, Jeremy thought. *And better than what I just witnessed in the jungle.*

Fifty.

Jeremy blew out a couple cleansing breaths, adjusted his hands on the cheap polyester carpet, then continued.

He'd seen the Americans through the magnification of his rifle scope. Three white males, thirty to thirty-five years of age, three-day beards, Western clothing. And that Bass Pro Shops hat. By the time Jeremy had mentioned them out loud, GI Jane was already running.

Americans.

Nothing unusual had happened for some time after that. The task force entry team had separated the men into two groups, knelt them with their hands flex-cuffed behind their backs, and slipped burlap bags over everyone's head. Everyone except Mahar. This was a technique perfected in Iraq during the war, Jeremy knew. Special operations teams working with CIA Special Activities Division interrogators had determined that the initial disorientation and pursuant fear yielded significant on-scene intelligence.

Sixty-one . . .

So it made sense to Jeremy that he would see the same thing

there in the jungle. GI Jane had moved first to Mahar, kneeling beside him and placing her hand on his shoulder. She talked for a few minutes, evoking an occasional nod or turn of the head, but from Jeremy's distance there was no way to tell what the terrorist said.

After a few moments, Jane stood up and walked over to the second Indonesian. The task force team leader — a Delta Force sergeant everyone called French — stood over the man with his M-4 assault rifle hanging from his right hand. French wore Vietnam-era OD fatigues with the sleeves rolled up, a Ranger hat, and black SWAT gloves.

GI Jane had knelt down on one knee, as if she planned less conversation and didn't want to get too comfortable.

Seventy-two . . .

After a few more minutes, she moved across the compound to the three Westerners. They had been arranged side by side, close enough that they could have held hands if not for the flex cuffs.

Seventy-five . . .

She spoke to the one on the left first. GI Jane pulled the burlap bag off the man's head, exposing what Jeremy now saw as bleach-white hair and skin the color of Xerox paper. GI Jane asked the man — whom Jeremy guessed to be an albino — a couple questions and jotted a few notes on a small pad she kept in the thigh pocket of her BDUs.

Seventy-eight . . .

After a moment or two, she replaced the burlap bag, walked over to French, and mumbled a few words. It was only then that everything began to unravel.

My God, Jeremy thought.

He paused his push-ups and blinked his eyes, trying to shake off images of what had happened next.

■

JORDAN MITCHELL LIVED for acquisition. From the companies he bought up through hostile takeovers and proxy skirmishes to the secrets he gathered through government sources and industry moles, everything in his world came down to spreadsheets delineating what he had and what he yet had to have. He was CEO and principal stockholder of Borders Atlantic, after all — one of the world's largest multinational corporations — a man *Forbes* ranked as number five among the world's richest men.

According to trade projections, his recent Quantis project, which included new Middle Eastern cell phone broadcast monopolies, had positioned him well to move higher.

"Is she here yet?" Mitchell asked. He sat at a massive red oak conference table with four other men, running his hands over a rare three-barreled Drilling, which he had just obtained from a museum curator in Stuttgart. The magnificent rifle bore intricate Black Forest engravings along its Brazilian rosewood stock, nickel receiver, and ivory trigger guard. It had eluded him for years, but like all great conquests, this had been worth the wait.

"Yes, she's on her way up," Trask said. Mitchell's chief of staff moved through a stack of folders, preparing for what promised to be a particularly busy day. "Should I have the weapon mounted for you, Mr. Mitchell?"

The men sat in what was known within the company as the War Room, a sanctum sanctorum defined by claro walnut paneling, Tiffany lamps, and the stale smell of fear. Floor-to-ceiling display cases lined two walls, each filled with hundreds of weapons — Henry buffalo guns in .5440, Winchester carbines, Remington prototypes, Belgian Brownings, Damascus steel Parkers, early Kentucky flintlocks, Colt Peacemakers in shiny nickel and gunmetal blue. This extraordinary collection — rare specimens that chronicled the history of war and predation — offered threatening testament to Mitchell's might. When he brought executives in for a meeting, he expected allegiance. If these rifles suggested consequence, so be it.

"I hope I didn't keep you," Sirad said, striding into the room. She wore black running tights and a bright-yellow slicker, which she had unzipped to reveal a formfitting white turtleneck underneath. Melting snow dripped off her clothing, forming puddles on the palace-sized Oushak carpet beneath her feet. "I was running in the park."

"There's a blizzard out there," Trask reminded her. He tried, as always, not to stare.

"I know," she said. "Beautiful, isn't it?"

Sirad dabbed her face with a towel as Mitchell carefully laid the beautiful three-barreled rifle on a velvet serviette. The only sound in the room came from steam radiators hissing against the frigid air outside.

"Did they tell you why we brought you in?" Mitchell asked. He looked elegant as always, resplendent in custom-tailored wools and hand-tooled wing tips.

"Something about an attack on the Quantis system," Sirad said. She nodded to the others at the table, all Borders Atlantic executives. They shared troubling history — this unlikely assembly — but Sirad managed to put it out of her mind.

"There's a possibility that our algorithms have been compromised," Mitchell told her. "That someone has discovered the existence of a trapdoor."

"Impossible," Sirad argued. "Quantis is a hard system, impervious to intrusion. We're certain of that."

She walked across the room, pulled out a chair, and sat. Under normal circumstances, she would have used her thinly clothed physique to improper advantage, but here in the boardroom, beauty actually worked against her. Power at Borders Atlantic revolved around intelligence and wit. Standing there in a film of moistened Lycra rendered her naked in an oddly uncomfortable way.

"We're certain that it is impervious to every intrusion *we* could think of," Mitchell agreed, "but impervious is a relative term. Someone apparently thinks it worth the effort."

"Where did you find it?" Sirad asked. She ran the towel over the back of her neck, then draped it over her shoulders, covering nipples that had hardened conspicuously from the cold. "Are they trying to tap our data streams or going after the encryption rubrics themselves?"

"Neither," came the reply. Sirad turned toward Dieter Planck, the company's chief security officer. The squat, dimple-cheeked German sat just across the table from her, wrinkling his nose beneath frameless oval glasses.

"They haven't completely shown themselves yet," a second man said. Sirad knew the mathematician by his first name only: Ravi. "One of the systems auditors discovered a suspicious shadow about four o'clock this morning."

"A shadow?" Sirad shrugged. "Systems auditors find probes all the time — everything from wiseassed kids hacking in from Encino to European competitors. All futile. What makes you think any of them can legitimately compromise our system?"

"They made it all the way to the mainframe firewall," Ravi said. The soft-spoken Indian wore a sky-blue Members Only jacket and a cheap oxford shirt buttoned to the top. No tie. "This shadow suggests a very sophisticated cloaking protocol that is designed to look like one of our own audit incursions. It's no kid from Encino."

Sirad ran the towel over her face.

"To get to the firewalls, they must understand our encryption protocols," she said. "That means it's possible that they know our ability to tap consumer data streams."

"That's right," Mitchell said. He opened the breech of his Dremmel and looked down the pyramid-stacked barrels. "Unfortunately, there's something else. You haven't heard the worst."

■

NINETY-TWO . . .

Jeremy's arms had begun to burn with the push-ups. The pain gave him focus, but nothing could keep his mind from traveling back to that Irian Jaya jungle.

Once GI Jane turned toward French, things had happened very quickly. The Delta sergeant stepped up behind one of the Americans, pushed the muzzle of his Mark IV up behind the man's head, and pulled the trigger.

BOOM! The .223 caliber rifle had echoed through the clearing.

One of Mahar's Indonesian buddies jumped up and ran as if his feet were afire, stumbling with his hands cuffed behind his back and the burlap bag over his head. He took four or five steps before slamming into the satellite dish and knocking himself back to the ground. One of the SEALs walked over and grabbed him by the arm, but the man struggled, pleading in a language that made no sense to Jeremy.

One hundred five . . .

The SEAL dragged the man back to his original position. Jeremy could see through his scope that the captive had wet himself. A dark splotch spread out through his crotch and down his pant legs.

"Caleb?!" the American on the left called out. There was no mistaking his nationality now. Jeremy recognized the accent as Deep South, Alabama or Georgia.

"Sit still, Frank," the albino said. He spoke calmly, almost indignant.

"I think these bastards are gonna ki-ll us," Frank squealed. "You gotta do somethin', man! They're gonna kill us."

GI Jane knelt next to him and said something too quiet for Jeremy to hear. The man shook his head violently back and forth and tore at his flex cuffs.

"Run, boys! They're gonna kill us all!" Frank yelled. He tried to gain his feet but tripped and fell facefirst into the dirt.

One hundred twenty . . .

One of the Indonesians leaped up, too, but he made it just a couple of steps before tripping over one of the dead dogs and crashing back to earth.

BOOM!

French shot Frank where he lay on the ground. Then all hell broke loose.

■

"THE WORST?" SIRAD lifted an eyebrow. "What could be worse?"

"Our inner perimeter firewall is a quasiphysical backstop," Ravi reminded her. "Deliberately discrete from other fail-safes. In order to get to it, the intruders must already have compromised our keystone algorithms, which means they have cloned or stolen blueprints for our number generators."

Sirad sat back in her chair. Algorithms — the armor that protected Quantis's entire encryption system — were based on what in the past had always been randomly generated prime numbers, very large prime numbers of up to 155 digits. Until recently, randomness — the great limitation of encryption theory — had been "made up" by computers using stochastic variation in physical noise from sources such as office keyboards, city traffic, and wind. Despite their best attempts, however, no computer had produced true randomness. Borders Atlantic's new "number generators" had changed that.

"It's possible that someone may already have tapped our data streams," Planck suggested. "That means outside interests may understand the truth about our interactions with the Saudis. That, of course, could prove catastrophic."

The truth. Sirad knew that the real point in offering the world secure communications was to let Mitchell listen in. Though everyone from rival corporations to foreign governments believed their conversations and data transmissions safe, Borders Atlantic rummaged freely through their most intimate secrets like a burglar in the panty drawer.

"How?" Sirad asked, turning to Ravi. "Quantis has been up and running, commercially, for just twelve months. Your mathematicians calculated that it would take the most powerful computers several years just to map it."

Jordan Mitchell answered for him.

"Only one thing matters at this point: we've been compromised."

"Fortunately, they don't have everything they need to get in," Ravi added. "So far, we've identified four separate intrusions . . . none of them terminal. They seem to be probing the system's parameters, kind of like stumbling around in a dark room, looking for the light switch."

"Who?" Sirad asked. "Is this corporate?"

"We don't think so," Dieter said. "Conventional hacks target peer-to-peer networks, like the Sober.c or Bizex worms. Intrusions of this sophistication would have required equipment and science we know to exist only among governments."

"And few of those," Ravi agreed. "The U.S. has it, of course, as well as the UK, China, and India."

Sirad nodded. She knew that U.S. intelligence agencies had shared technology with the Brits. India wrote the majority of the world's computer software. China stole it.

"We fully expected tests of our firewalls," Mitchell said, "but nothing this extensive, well camouflaged, or sophisticated."

The room seized quiet for a moment before another man — Hamid — raised his hand as if in an elementary school classroom. As the company's chief financial analyst, he better than anyone knew the downside of a successful compromise of the Quantis encryption system.

"There's something you haven't considered," he offered. "As of yesterday, Borders Atlantic held nearly sixty-seven percent of the world's cell phone market. Even *rumors* of a successful intrusion could jeopardize market dominance and cost this company billions. We need to keep any investigation very close to the vest."

Sirad looked troubled, and not by the malicious look from her former lover. First the terrorist attacks on the Mall of America, Disneyland, and Atlanta, and now cyberattacks on America's highest-profile commercial encryption technology. It had been more than three years since 9/11 without a single domestic incident. What was going on?

"We need to find the people behind these intrusions, and we need to do it now," Mitchell said. His voice sounded firm but neither accusatory nor panicked. "Sirad, this is your program, but you'll need to coordinate closely with the seventeenth floor."

Sirad nodded. All security operations ran through what was known within Borders Atlantic as the Rabbit Hole. Dieter Planck's cadre of scientists, mathematicians, and former special operations specialists rivaled most governments in terms of assets and sophistication. The fact that Planck had proven a nemesis to Sirad would complicate matters, but no more than she could handle. He struck her as a tense, incomplete man. A nuisance.

"Yes, sir," Sirad agreed. She caught Dieter's threatening smile and held it.

"I want to know the instant you have something," Mitchell said, standing. Trask had already started toward the door, reinforcing Sirad's belief that the officious chief of staff really could read the boss's mind. "I want to know immediately if you get any unusual questions from our overseas contractors. And I want you to use all means necessary to end this. Do you understand? *All* means necessary."

With that, Jordan Mitchell walked out of the room.

"Meet me in my office: twenty minutes," Dieter said, standing to leave as well. Ravi, the systems engineer, gathered his stack of papers and shoved them into a cracked vinyl folder.

Sirad nodded, dismissing his authoritative tone. This had been a morning full of news, nearly all of it bad. At least she had the blizzard to cheer her up.

. . .

ONE HUNDRED THIRTY . . .

Jeremy watched through his mind's eye as the second Indonesian starting yelling, making no particular sense through his fear and the burlap mask. He managed to run farther than the others had before taking two rifle rounds in the back. The first Indonesian tried again to escape but met a similar fate as GI Jane barked out orders to French and his assaulters.

Seizing on the confusion, Caleb wrenched violently, shaking the burlap bag off his head before jumping to his feet. A SEAL moved to within arm's length to stop him, but the pale-white captive kicked out with his right leg, a well-practiced martial arts move that dropped the SEAL in his tracks. Caleb quickly knelt down, picked up the rifle with his hands still cuffed behind his back, and fired a half dozen rounds.

Jeremy just stared at first, unable to believe his eyes. It looked as if the albino had practiced this move a thousand times. He was no amateur.

The rest of the task force dove for cover as Caleb lay down suppressive fire and ran for the jungle. By the time Jeremy could draw his crosshairs, the American had already disappeared through the vegetal wall.

Shit! he scolded himself. This operation had been weeks in the planning, with input from at least half a dozen agencies. No one would want to report back that someone had escaped. Especially an American.

One hundred forty-three . . .

French and one of the SEALs ran after Caleb as Jane walked over to Mahar. She knelt directly in front of him and barked out something in the terrorist's native tongue. By inflection, Jeremy understood it to be a question.

Mahar said two words, obviously not what she wanted to hear. GI Jane pulled a semiautomatic handgun out from under her BDU blouse, placed the barrel right between his eyes, and *Pop!* shot him dead. The terrorist fell backward, folding grotesquely over his legs. A stream of blood spurted straight up out of the wound, then eased to a dribble.

GI Jane wasted no time moving on to her next gruesome task. She reached into the right thigh pocket of her BDU trousers and produced a pair of black steel pruning sheers. While the assault team watched the jungle for any sign of Caleb, she walked from body to body, kneeling down, spreading open the fingers of each man's right hand, and expertly clipping off their index digits.

All fingers — excised between the second and third knuckles — went into a Ziploc freezer bag, which she tucked back into her BDUs.

"Burn it!" GI Jane called out, motioning toward the huts. The assault force dragged the bodies to the larger of the huts and tossed the corpses inside. Each shack got a Thermit grenade, which flashed white against the new rain.

Within seconds, the entire compound vanished into a conflagration that caught the generators, gas cans, even the aluminum satellite dish, in its grip. Jeremy heard a couple rifle shots from the jungle, and then French and the SEAL emerged empty-handed. Jeremy watched as the task force gathered around GI Jane, then . . .

Brrring . . . brrring . . . brrring . . .

Jeremy stopped his push-ups as a phone interrupted the jungle flashback.

"Hello?" he answered.

"No names," a voice said on the other end of the line. "Do you know who this is?"

Jeremy did. He sat on the edge of the bed breathing heavily but said nothing more.

"We are bringing you back in," the voice advised. "Tonight. The concierge has a ticket for you downstairs."

Back in? Jeremy wondered. His initial instructions called for him to fly out the next morning to Ramstein, Germany, for a debriefing, then back to his TDY duty station in Baghdad.

"I trust you've seen the news?" the voice asked.

Jeremy swallowed hard, trying to slow his heart rate and breathing. He grabbed the remote and flipped to BBC World.

Images of broken, mangled bodies. A bomb. Devastation. The slug line said Atlanta.

"Don't miss your plane," the man said. "We need you stateside as soon as possible."

Jeremy heard the phone go dead, then turned back to televised images of the carnage. Something had gone terribly wrong; something more than what he had just seen in the jungle. The pit in his stomach told him they had to be related.

III

Tuesday, 15 February
00:55 GMT
Reagan National Airport, Alexandria, Virginia

NO ONE PAID any attention to the Merry Maids cleaning van that appeared out of the snow and pulled up to a high-rise luxury apartment building at 21789 Madison Road. The driver — a dark-skinned Indonesian working illegally on a student visa — parked in a handicapped space. He yanked the collar of his jacket up around his neck and walked around the back of the van. A passenger joined him at the rear doors, a white man who called himself Ralph.

"I take da cart," the driver said, pointing out what he wanted the other man to accomplish. He spoke only broken English and weighed little more than the brooms he pushed, but everyone at Merry Maids marveled that this man could clean toilets like a world afire. "You carry shoulder bag."

The passenger wrapped a scarf around his face against the cold and snow, then did as he was told.

"Cold as a witch's tit, out here, ain't it," Ralph said, less a question than small talk. He waited for the driver to retrieve his rolling workstation and followed him inside to the reception desk. A uniformed doorman sat near the back of a grand marble foyer.

"Sign the book an' list yo' place o' destination." The doorman pointed to a loose-leaf binder where other visitors had scribbled indecipherable scratch.

The Indonesian attempted to show his company ID, but the doorman couldn't have cared less. He looked past his visitors to consider the snow piling up outside. He had two hours left in his shift and did not look forward to what would surely be a miserable commute.

The passenger left the scarf around his face, clapping his hands together and shuffling his feet to regain some warmth.

"You gonna have ta move that truck," the doorman said. "I ain't care, but Ms. Embry in 1411 always watching those handicapped spaces. She'll call the po-lice and they write yo' ass up."

The driver smiled and nodded. "Not worry," he said. "Company pay ticket."

"Suit yissef." The doorman shrugged. They were all like this, these cleaning people. Never cared about what he said, even if they spoke English, which they seldom did. Most of the time, they were Chinamen or Mexicans or Puerto Ricans, jabbering in their own tongues. And Russians; lots of Russians lately. Shame to see a brother stooping.

With that, the two sanitation professionals pushed their work cart to the elevators and stepped inside the farthest to the right. The driver pressed twelve and waited as the car shot upward.

"How about I go get started on 2110," the passenger said when the doors opened.

"I start twelve floor," the Indonesian agreed. He nodded once, then held up the Nextel phone Merry Maids gave all their DC workers. "Call me when ready. I come up."

"Yeah," the passenger agreed. The Indonesian pushed his cart off the elevator and disappeared down the corridor, seeking his appointed toilets.

Once the doors closed, however, the passenger rode up eight more flights. When the doors opened, he walked out of the elevator and down the corridor to a service entrance. He opened the unlocked door and hurried up a few more steps to another door that opened out onto the massive building's snow-covered roof.

Within minutes, he had found himself a lee on the roof's northwest corner. He knelt down behind the waist-high parapet.

RRRRRRRRRRRR . . .

An unsettling rumble grew on the northern horizon and filled the air around him with a hoarse, deafening noise. The passenger looked up and out toward Washington DC, which lay out there someplace in the waning storm. Within seconds, he saw it. Due north, looking like they might fly directly into him, came two enormous headlights, then the distinctive nose cone of a 747-400.

Air France flight 176 from Charles de Gaulle International seemed to hang in the air as it approached, traveling more than 150 knots but almost stationary relative to his position in the flight path. It looked as though it might fall out of the sky with the snow.

The Merry Maid showed no expression as the plane roared just to the right of him, off the building's eastern shoulder. He watched until the red and green warning lights disappeared; then he reached down and unzipped the case.

He pulled out three heavy steel rifle components: a gas-operated receiver group, a black polymer stock assembly, and a massive fluted barrel tipped with a quatro-ported muzzle break. Even to an experienced shooter, the Barrett .50 caliber sniper rifle was a formidable sight to behold. With a maximum effective range of 1,800 meters, a ten-round magazine, and bullets the size of pinccones, this semiautomatic doomsday device was the only low-signature, hand-portable weapon capable of penetrating the windscreen glass of a 747 airliner. Topped with a decent scope, it could accomplish irrevocable harm.

Now all I've got to do is keep from freezing to death, the passenger thought. He checked his watch and hunkered down behind the rifle. Snow descended quietly around him, covering the rooftop and the sniper with more of its anonymous coating of white.

■

"HAVE YOU TIMED this out?" the president asked. He led the way down a broad corridor that seemed to sag with the gravity of his presence.

"The computer clocks it at eight minutes," Andrea Chase answered. She read as she walked, trying desperately to keep up with the president's exaggerated stride and the "Blue Thing" — a twice-daily summary of incoming cable traffic and key reporting. Chase still hadn't read a second package distilled from highlights of the CIA's Presidential Daily Briefing, the State Department's INR summary, and White House Press Office media clippings.

"This speech is full yet succinct; firm yet compassionate," Chase said. "That's just what we want to project to the American public right now."

The former CEO of a New Haven insurance company, Chase had never handled anything more intense than hurricanes and hailstorms, but that didn't stop her from rising to the challenge. A number cruncher by trade, she felt more than capable of making the transition from insurance claims to body counts.

"Good." Venable nodded. "We need to reassure people without getting too dramatic. Don't want to overstate our downside."

"Best if you stick to the script, Mr. President," Chase suggested. David Ray Venable was a brilliant executive, but his mouth sometimes found it hard to contain a stream of consciousness that flowed like the Niagara. "Get in and out quickly."

"Spineless cowards," he growled, practicing the high points of his speech. "Unrelenting commitment to justice . . . will not stand . . . track them down wherever they hide . . . national resolve . . . individual integrity . . . renewed vigilance . . ."

The president practiced his hand movements as he walked. He had worked as a speech coach during the early days of his political career and considered the public demonstration of emotion one of his greatest strengths.

"You tell whoever is operating that teleprompter that I pause a lot for effect, understand? Long pauses sometimes. They need to pay attention so I don't look like I'm reading this thing, especially when we get to the part about individual integrity."

"I'll supervise it personally," Chase said. She continued highlighting salient features of the intelligence reports, prioritizing and organizing.

"Matthew?" the president asked. "Anything new I need to know?"

Matthew Havelock struggled to keep up. He gave up more than eight inches of leg to the six-foot-three commander in chief and had made the mistake of changing into brand-new shoes for the speech. The leather soles slipped so badly on the slick wool rug, he had to shuffle on his heels to keep from falling.

"Uh, yes, sir," Havelock said. He forced his natural tenor down a couple stops to lend his voice substance. "Homeland Security apparently has a good lead on a radical Islamic group associated with a Columbus mosque. They have been under surveillance for some time, and the FBI is working on a FISA warrant for their . . ."

"FISA warrants? Goddammit, I told you to speak English. I don't have time for . . ."

"Foreign Intelligence Surveillance Act," he spit out. "A secret sneak-and-peek warrant. No notification of service. They think this group may be related to our bombers, and we don't want to tip our hand."

"Good."

The president suddenly looked a little less exhausted.

"Pencil in 'cautiously optimistic' where I talk about the best efforts of our law enforcement and intelligence communities," Venable said. He carried no copy of the speech; years of campaigning had refined his near photographic memory to a keen edge.

"To place our trust in a just and righteous God!" He cocked his head, trying to decide on the proper inflection, then said it again. "To place our trust in a just and righteous . . . where the hell is Alred, anyway? He should be here in case we get anything at the last minute!"

Chase shook her head. She had intentionally winnowed the president's immediate circle down to Havelock and herself. Now almost forty hours without sleep, Venable had fallen a bit too susceptible to suggestion. Reducing the number of voices in the president's ear allowed her to control a few more variables. If she could just get him through the speech and into bed, the national security staff would manage the details of this crisis while he slept.

"We have him in constant contact, sir," she said. "Vick as well. Anything happens, you'll be the first to know."

"Good," Venable said. "How's my color?"

He stopped abruptly to consider himself in a gilt-framed mirror that dated to the Taft administration.

"Color's fine, sir." Chase nodded. She lied, of course. He looked sallow and spent despite a healthy application of pancake stage makeup.

"All right." Chase changed the subject. "I've just gone through the latest intelligence estimates, and we have one issue that didn't make the speech."

Venable adjusted his tie, listening.

"Ali Fallal Mahar, the leader of Jemaah Islamiya, has been found in a jungle somewhere in Indonesia. He was killed during an arrest attempt along with two other senior terrorists."

"That's good news, right?" Venable said. "Gotta be. Jemaah what?"

Chase wrote Jemaah Islamiya in large letters on a yellow legal pad. "Here, I wrote it down for you. Adlib no more than two sentences near the end as confirmation that we're onto these guys. Got it?"

"Got it." He adjusted his lapels and lifted his chin to properly position the tie knot.

"Good. Let's do this."

Chase stopped outside the Roosevelt Room. Inside, a lone broadcast-feed camera faced a mahogany partners desk and a Federal parlor chair. Venable had argued that he should stand for the speech, but Chase prevailed. Sitting made him look more relaxed.

"The country is ready for you, Mr. President," Chase said. She offered up a look of complete confidence.

Venable nodded and started toward the chair.

"Is it Islameeeya or Islamiiiiya?" he asked, taking his seat.

"Remember what I told you," Havelock answered. The national security advisor swelled up with pride at standing second to a statesman about to face his country. "America wants gravitas . . . a president willing to make the tough calls and stand behind them. Stay away from that spy crap; it will just confuse them."

■

JEREMY LEANED BACK into his chair, staring at a perfectly acceptable plate of chicken cordon bleu served with steamed asparagus, fennel, and an arugula salad. The meal sat on bone china, with a cloth napkin, leaded glass goblet . . . and a plastic fork.

What a difference nineteen men with box cutters have made, Jeremy thought. He turned his head out the window and looked down on a sea of storm clouds, which seemed endless from where he sat. The slow drone of the 747's four monster engines coaxed back toward what would have been twelve hours of sleep without the connection in San Francisco.

How different the world seemed since 9/11.

It wasn't the grandmothers spread-eagled at airport magnetometers that shocked him; not the color-coded terror alerts, the massive new spending, not even the broad indifference with which most Americans considered the threat.

No, what amazed Jeremy was the sea change in his government's willingness to get dirty. Things only whispered in years past were now discussed openly in strategy sessions. Renditions that once had depended on host-country approval now occurred without so much as notification. Torture had become routine. Warlords were bought outright; shot when they reneged.

Assassination, the nasty-sounding administrative action outlawed by Gerald R. Ford in executive order 12333, had gained a new sparkle. Now called "neutralizing targets of military importance," the deliberate execution of individuals fell within a rubric known as "military actions other than war."

What struck Jeremy most of all was the lack of oversight and interest. No one seemed to question rule of law in the war on terror. Not Congress, not the media, not even average Americans. It signified a revolution in matters of state, a shift in the collective will of a wounded democracy. Some things needed to get done; better to beg forgiveness than ask permission.

This new philosophy reached all the way from the White House to the shielded analyst pods at Fort Meade and Boling Air Force Base; from coffee shops in Enid, Oklahoma, to the seventh floor of the Justice Department in Washington. When the military dug up anyone they deemed a "terrorist," the CIA conducted the interrogations so the FBI wouldn't have to look the other way. When the FBI fingered a suspect, they turned evidence not to a grand jury, but to a Joint Special Operations Command mission-planning cell, which meted justice from a Cobra gunship. What had been handled in open court now shuffled quietly through a maze of FISA warrants, "material witness" detentions, and national security obfuscation.

Lethal covert operations, Jeremy thought. The world had become a place he poorly understood anymore, a world of ambiguous allegiances and trapdoor truths where the most difficult job was figuring out how the hell to add it up.

"Ladies and gentlemen, the captain has illuminated the fasten seat belts sign," a soothing young voice interrupted. "This signals our initial descent into the Washington DC area. FAA regulations require that passengers remain seated during the last thirty minutes of flight, so please do not get up or we will be forced to divert to an alternate airport."

Jeremy checked his belt. A flight attendant walked over and gathered up his untouched meal.

"Not hungry?" the petite woman asked. She wore little makeup and her hair pulled back so tightly it left a permanent smile. A Singapore Airlines badge above her tiny left breast read Minge.

Jeremy shook his head. It wasn't the meal that took his appetite. It was the plastic fork his government had given him to eat it with.

■

LOS ANGELES SCOFFED at the inability of the nation's capital to function in inclement weather. An unfair accusation of course: it barely rained in Southern California. But the entertainment industry held little respect for Washington's censor-hungry bureaucrats. Washington was a city of narrow-minded politicians; the Left Coast had its own agenda. Which meetings had more impact on the world, after all, those held in stuffy Senate hallways or those in Beverly Hills over glasses of designer water?

The man with the pistol in his hand was unlike most Californians, however. To him, Washington was an objective. A target. Though it may have been three thousand miles away, he felt intimately connected to its people and their immediate future.

"There's no point in calling out," the man with the pistol said. A frightened-looking Saudi cleric named Ashar al Bayad sat beside him with his hands secured behind his back. Drool ran out of the Arab's mouth at the corners, where the rubber ball stuck in it left gaps. "These walls are insulated. No one will hear you."

The man with the pistol double-checked the ligature — simple hemp cord at the wrists and ankles. It might not hold as well as the triple-bar police cuffs he carried in his day job, but it would burn completely in a fire. There would be no trace of bondage.

"I apologize for this disrespect, Brother," the man with the pistol said. "But it is all for the good of our cause. God is great. You will see."

The captor opened a four-by-four-foot wooden box filled with fifty pounds of Czech-made Semtex — a special batch designed for use in land mines. He adjusted the detonator to make certain it would fail to function as designed. Under normal circumstances, this massive I.E.D. would devastate everything within two hundred feet, but that was not the plan. This device would "squib," or explode in a low-order detonation. There would be flames, but little boom.

When he felt certain that all details had been checked and double-checked, the man with the pistol picked up a long red-and-white Snap-on toolbox, pulled a California Electric cap onto his head, and stepped out of his box truck.

The work order in his pocket called for service on a transformer atop the LAX Radisson. The sun shone brightly in the late-afternoon sky. Santa Ana winds blew down from the mountains, ruffling his shirt and filling his nose with desert smells.

"*Allah huakbar,*" he mumbled under his breath. A 767 wide-body inbound from some destination east roared over his head as Ibrahim hefted the thirty-pound toolbox.

Heavy but effective, he assured himself of the .50 caliber Barrett inside. No matter. It was just a short trip to the elevator and then an effortless pull of the trigger.

■

"FASTEN YOUR SEAT belt, please," Minge the flight attendant politely coaxed one of the other first class passengers.

Always someone, Jeremy thought. *Shouldn't the wealthy, successful, and well traveled behave a little better up here in the good seats?*

He wouldn't have known, of course. Only the unexpected generosity of a sympathetic ticket counter clerk in Bangkok had saved him from a 10,000-mile ride in coach.

"Well, hello again, folks, this is your captain," a voice announced over the intercom. He sounded Midwestern, to Jeremy's surprise. Singapore Air with an American crew? "We're about to start our final descent into the Washington DC area, and as I said before, they have a pretty significant storm down there."

Jeremy had seen nothing but darkness and streaks of snow in his window for the past fifteen minutes. Modern planes could land in anything, right? Surely they'd divert if it were too dangerous.

"The tower has cleared us for landing, but it might be a little rough. Tighten up those belts, if you will, and we'll have you on the ground in just a few minutes. And thanks for flying Singapore Air."

Tighten up those belts? Jeremy laughed quietly to himself. It had never occurred to him, waiting there in that Bangkok hotel room, that the most perilous part of this mission would be flying home.

■

THREE NETWORKS AND all the cable news channels pre-empted regular programming for the president's address. Most of them simply integrated it into nonstop coverage of the terrorist attacks, anyway, providing an eight-minute respite for threadbare producers, anchors, reporters, experts, and bookers who hadn't had so much as a coffee break since the first bomb exploded.

Vice President Beechum watched the speech from her West Wing office, a relatively bland space distinguished by low ceilings and a view of the Washington Monument. Despite early resolutions to add color and a little feminine flair to the nation's second-most-exclusive suite, she hadn't gotten around to so much as new curtains.

"That man scares the hell out of me," the vice president said, leaning back into a cordovan leather chair that weighed as much as her Mercedes.

"Brian Williams or the president?" James asked. He punched up the volume.

"Take your pick." She laughed. The NBC anchor sat behind the traditional desk on the network's *Nightly News* set in New York. General Monte Derak flanked Williams to the right; two of their so-called terrorism experts on his left.

"It's all such a spectacle, you know?" Beechum said. "This is exactly what they want . . . the terrorists. They'd be nothing but a bunch of Third World thugs if we didn't pump them up with round-the-clock coverage. The richest corporation in America couldn't afford this kind of advertising."

"Ladies and gentlemen, the president appears to be ready to . . ." The anchor started an introduction, but the president interrupted him.

"My fellow Americans," Venable began. "I speak to you tonight with a heavy heart . . . but with a mind bent on justice."

"Well, he's off to a good start," James said. "Gotta give him that."

Beechum nodded. Speeches had always been his strong suit.

"Less than twenty-four hours ago, spineless cowards attacked us in our heartland. They murdered innocent women and children. They brazenly took credit for these barbaric acts. They demonstrated the depravity, the evil, that some will stoop to in the name of religion."

The president looked troubled yet resolute. Chase had been wrong about his color; from the healthy vigor in his cheeks to the tone of his furrowed brow and the firmly knotted tie beneath his jackhammer Adam's apple, Venable looked as telegenic as any Hollywood actor. Prime-time perfect.

"He's good, but I just don't get the feeling that I can trust him," Beechum observed. "I'm not sure what it is, but something just strikes me as wrong."

"The only things I trust are you and the good Lord." James smiled, only half kidding. "But whatever bothers you has nothing to do with his looks. This guy's hair is perfect."

■

THE WASHINGTON SNIPER felt the plane before he saw it, that disembodied roar sneaking out of the north. It grew quickly, filling the air around him like the echo of some mountain beast, raising goose bumps on the back of his neck. Or was that the cold?

"God's will," he said in English. The roar grew louder; thunder rolling down the frozen Potomac.

Every detail had been covered. The snow-draped sniper sat cross-legged behind the rooftop parapet, hidden by the night. A Barrett .50 caliber rifle rested on a matte steel bipod, tight against his shoulder. He'd just called the Indonesian up to the roof under ruse.

"God's will."

He placed his eye against the cold rubber bellows of his scope reticle.

What do the other shooters have in their sights right now? he wondered. But then the nose cone appeared in his crosshairs and all other matters of this world left him.

. . .

JEREMY HAD NOTHING to read, so he sat and stared out his window as the 747 descended into the teeth of the storm.

Daddy's home! Jeremy could hear his kids yelling as he played out the homecoming in a slow-moving daydream. *Daddy's home!*

Caroline and the kids would be there at the front door when he walked in. He'd called them with a flight number and an ETA, hoping to make it somewhat close to on-time. He'd missed so many of these welcome-home parties, flying off from one mission to another without even stopping for a hug and change of clothes.

Daddy's home! he heard himself calling out. The 747's landing gear whistled as the pilot alternately throttled up and back, trying to gauge the miserable conditions.

Jeremy watched snow streak his frosted window, imagining that his suburban DC home lay out there beneath him. The roads would be a nightmare, he knew, but that would barely slow him down. Tonight, nothing was going to come between this endlessly traveling FBI agent and a family that still found ways to love him.

■

VENABLE LOOKED BRAVE yet caring; angry yet composed. Like the best of politicians, he made up for in appearance what he lacked in ability, but according to the FBI and CIA, the government, this series of bombings may be just the beginning of something much worse.

"You know, it's damn scary to sit here behind the curtains, watching the Wizard pull the levers," James said as he and Beechum watched the speech. "You want to believe in your government and all its resources, but then you see what really goes on behind the scenes and wonder what in hell keeps it all together."

James had worked in Washington long enough to understand that no one person ever had all the answers. The "big picture" was a myth; to chase it, folly. "He looks good, but when it comes right down to it, this guy is way out over his skis. We're in trouble here, aren't we?"

"There's something you need to know, James," Beechum said. She stood up from her chair, still focused on the television screen.

"Something that stays between us. Something the president himself doesn't know."

This man had served her for more than ten years and had led her through a scandal that almost ruined her life. She knew no closer confidant.

"Mahar is dead."

James lifted his shoulders.

"I know. I saw that in the Blue Thing forty minutes ago. I'm sure the president plans to announce it during the speech."

"Hear me out," Beechum said. She began to pace as she so often did. "There's more that you're not going to read in any intelligence briefing."

"Are you sure you want to tell me this?" James asked. He well remembered his boss's iron-fisted adherence to security protocols. "I don't have the proper clearances for matters this sensitive."

"There are no clearances for matters this sensitive," she said in a soft but direct tone. "It happened Sunday morning near a little hut compound in the jungles of Indonesia."

"Agency?" James asked. "The CIA seems to get most of these gigs, nowadays."

"They had an element in the assault team, but several different entities played a role. None of them will ever admit to it, but . . ."

"A black op," James assumed. He decided to let further inquiry pass.

Beechum nodded. She looked deep in thought.

"Mahar had three Americans with him when he died."

She spit out the words as if they tasted bad in her mouth.

"Americans?" James reacted. "Are you sure?"

"Good ol' boy, Wonder Bread white, catfish jiggin', tobacco-chewing Billy Bob rednecks. Saw them with my own eyes."

"My God."

"I know. We've never seen any intelligence suggesting that al Qaeda or any of its surrogates had recruited American players. Not Anglos, anyway."

"Who?" James asked. "John Walker Lindh types?"

"No." Beechum shook her head. "Something more . . ."

Her voice trailed off.

"Have we interrogated these men? Surely we can get some answers out of them."

Beechum stopped pacing and turned toward her top aide.

"What we've seen in Atlanta and California is not the end of our problems; it's just the beginning," she said. "One of the Americans with Mahar escaped, and he's . . ."

"What the hell is this?" James interrupted her.

Without warning, the president of the United States disappeared from their television screen and Brian Williams appeared.

"Ladies and gentlemen, we interrupt the president's address to bring you this breaking news bulletin." He grimaced. The anchor's face filled the screen in a closeup so tight that you could see the brushstrokes in his tan.

"NBC news has learned that three commercial airliners have crashed" — he looked down at a piece of paper — "three international flights, apparently . . . almost simultaneous crashes . . ."

Williams held a finger to his ear, pausing for a producer to read him the very latest information from reporters at scenes of horrific carnage. The television pulsed with a sense of impending doom. The seasoned journalist looked shaken.

"We have live footage from Los Angeles International Airport . . ."

Images of flames, smoke, and emergency crews racing down an empty runway.

"Reports of similar crashes at Miami International and . . . yes, at Reagan National. Reports are just beginning to come in," he recited from behind his characteristic scowl. "But NBC news has confirmed that three separate airliners have crashed in Los Angeles, Miami, and Washington . . . are we certain about this?" he asked someone offscreen. This was live television, after all, and he had just upstaged the president of the United States. He wanted to get it right.

"All right." He nodded. "Sources in a position to know confirm eyewitness accounts." He cleared his throat. "NBC news is reporting that at least two of those planes appear to have been shot down. I'll say that again . . ."

Beechum just shook her head.

"I never thought you'd hear me say this, James," she said, in words just loud enough to turn the veteran A.A. away from footage of an L.A. plane crash. "But we're dealing with a threat unlike anything we've seen before. Something truly evil."

James stared at his boss, a woman he considered a hardened, almost impenetrable good.

"Quite frankly, I don't know that we're good enough to beat it."

IV

Tuesday, 15 February
01:17 GMT
Bunker Alpha-2, Central United States

SIX MEN SAT in chairs facing each other. There was no other furniture in the windowless room — no paintings, floor lamps or decorative moldings. Two wire-caged industrial lamp fixtures provided the only illumination. Their dark red-lens glow painted the space in a hushed, claustrophobic light — a light common to emergency exits, bomb shelters, and crack houses. The door had been bolted shut, from the inside.

"Almighty God, you are the one true and righteous God," a voice spoke in heavily accented English. He stood before the others and read from a thick religious text. "You are the fear and the hope. We declare your glory as the thunder declares your praise. You smite our enemies; you sate our need."

The speaker wore white robes that wrinkled at the floor. A linen hood covered his head and face, open at the eyes and contoured to his dark and weathered brow. The robes bore no markings, symbols, or other raiment.

"Only to you, o magnificent God, do we bow our heads," he continued. "For our strength, for our guidance, for our salvation. There is no other God. Those who pray to idols fall the way of all those who deny You. For You are the Lord of all heavens and earth. You are the guardian. You are the creator of all things, the one God. The Supreme. The Just."

The speaker closed the book and sat down with the others.

After a moment, another man spoke, also in English. Though he wore no visual markings to identify himself as the group's leader, his presence spoke for itself.

"Thank you, Brother," he said. "We have business today. Ishmael, you have an update on operations?"

Ishmael, the heaviest of the six, sat directly across from the leader. He spoke with a deep, resonant voice but no airs.

"Cell Three has successfully completed this stage of operations," he said. "As planned, brothers in Los Angeles, Miami, and Washington DC have engaged three airliners. One British Airways 777, one El Al Airbus 300, and one Singapore Air 747. All three planes were brought down. There are no known survivors."

The leader nodded. He saw no need for congratulations. This loss of life was necessary work, not something to gloat over.

"Logistics?" he asked, turning to the man sitting at Ishmael's right.

"Everything is moving forward as planned," he said. "Cell Six has operators prestaged at the rallying points. Time line remains the same."

He spoke with military precision, which made perfect sense. Like the others in this circle, he had bravely fought the infidels in Afghanistan and Iraq.

"What about our diversions?" the leader asked.

"Bodies have been recovered at two of the sites. The third was arrested a short distance from the Los Angeles shooting, just as planned."

"And everything has been backstopped?"

"Yes. Police will be busy with them for days."

"What about our claims of responsibility?"

"Videotapes have been sent to the proper media. In fact, they have already hit cable news. Everyone in America has heard of Ansar ins Allah by now."

"Intelligence?" the leader asked. He turned to a man sitting next to him, who spoke in a small, academic voice.

"Our assets remain confident that Jafar al Tayar has not been compromised in any way. There will be no further contact, of course. Not until the final stage. But that doesn't matter. We have clear and constant access should the need arise."

"Good," the leader said, finally acknowledging that things had progressed as planned. "Unfortunately, we have one other matter to take care of. Unpleasant business." He breathed deeply. "Bring him in."

The sixth member of the circle — the one who had said nothing to this point — stood and walked stiffly to the bolted door. He slipped open the lock and disappeared for a moment. When he returned, he had another man by the arm. This man wore street clothes and a blindfold. His feet were bare. His wrists and ankles had been shackled and looped together beneath his knees. The poor wretch had to shuffle along, bent double at the waist, staring at the floor.

"I hereby convene a Council of Will," the leader said. The prisoner was pulled inside the circle, where he waited, forcibly bowed before the others. "Read the charges."

The sergeant at arms pulled a piece of loose-leaf paper from his pocket and adjusted his hood to better read in the dim red light.

"That this man, a Phineas priest, entrusted with the work of a just and almighty God, has betrayed that confidence, endangering the well-being of his brothers and the success of the mission. That this man, a Phineas priest, entrusted with the work of a just and almighty God, has betrayed an oath by disclosing information outside the scope of his cell. That this man, a Phineas priest, entrusted with the work of a just and almighty God, has needlessly placed in doubt the sanctity of this Council."

The man in shackles began to weep. The tears came softly at first, obscured by the blindfold, but within moments, he began to cough as the phlegm of regret clogged his nose and backed up in his throat. Soon, sounds of his sobbing filled the room.

"Do you have anything to say in your own defense?" the leader asked. Only the sergeant at arms and the accused stood. The others remained in their chairs.

The helpless prisoner bucked up and down a bit, trying to catch his breath. Then, as if resigned to his fate, he offered a deep sigh and spoke.

"I told my wife I was going out of town and that if she was concerned about me, she should watch TV to know that I was doing God's will," he said. "Is that my crime? She was eight months' pregnant, and she was scared. I was just trying to reassure her."

"Questions from the Council?" the leader asked.

"You told your wife, and your wife told others," the operations manager said. "What if she also compromised us outside the community?"

"She didn't. She wouldn't. Ever."

"That's what we thought about you," the leader said. His voice changed within the course of a sentence from calm authority to an accusing hiss. It was a voice that even in brighter light would have sent chills down the other members' spines. "We lost good men in that Indonesian jungle on Sunday. Who's to say it wasn't because of your reckless tongue?"

The man began to tremble. To visibly shake.

"Please," he begged. "I have a new baby. My wife . . ."

"By will or negligence you have betrayed us," the leader said. "Motivation really doesn't matter now, does it?"

The leader nodded, and the sergeant at arms wasted no time. God was the only true power, they all knew, but their leader wielded the sword of vengeance.

With no further discussion, the sergeant at arms drew an eight-inch-long Tanto fighting knife. He rested the tip just below the now-condemned man's right ear, and then, with a twisting motion, plunged the razor-sharp blade into the base of his skull.

Death came instantaneously. There was surprisingly little blood.

"That concludes our enclave," the leader said. "Burn him on the cattle pile."

One of the men stood to get the door. The other three helped carry the body. When they had gone, the leader walked down a hallway past several other doors. He stopped at a flight of concrete stairs leading up and shed his hood.

"Thank you, Lord, for sparing us Caleb," the leader prayed in his heavily accented voice — that of a Texan. The light of a bright Kerrville moon spilled down the staircase, over his heavy shoulders. Word from overseas sources indicated that his son had sustained an awful wound out there in that Indonesian jungle, but had survived and would return to continue with the mission.

Clang! Clang!

A bell rang above him, the call to evening meal.

Colonel Buck Ellis folded his garments under his arm and started up the stairs. Work never ended here at the Homestead, and he was hungry.

■

"DADDY! DADDY! DADDY!"

Jeremy arrived home in Stafford, Virginia, to banners, balloons, and hugs. He hadn't showered, slept, or shaved in more than three days, but that seemed to have no impact on the three little kids who met him at the front door.

"Where's my present?" Christopher, the five-year-old, immediately wanted to know. Every time Dad left, he came home with something in his bag. It had been more than two months this time. "I want something big!"

Maddy, the oldest, held on tightly as Jeremy bent over at the waist to wrap his arms around them. All three of his kids had grown since he left. Maddy had lost another tooth, and the boys had both gotten haircuts.

"Easy kids," Caroline said, standing just outside arm's reach. "Give your dad some room to breathe for goodness' sakes."

Jeremy looked up at her with the best smile he could muster. Though he had thought about this homecoming nearly every day since he'd left, the actual event, as usual, left him feeling lost and empty. It wasn't that seeing his family again didn't thrill him. No, it was the reentry. It was the deceleration of a violent life suddenly colliding with innocence.

"Hi, baby," Jeremy said. He reached out with one hand and pulled his wife close for a kiss. She offered a cheek and wrapped her arms around him.

"My God, I thought that was you on that plane," she whispered so the kids wouldn't hear her. "I was so scared. How horrible."

Caroline fought the tears. *Not in front of the kids.*

"Wasn't my time, I guess," Jeremy responded. He kissed her forehead and held her tightly against his chest. "It could have been Dulles just as easily as National." He'd flown into both so many times.

"I missed you so," Caroline said. She had said those words so often since moving here, they barely sounded sincere anymore.

"I know, baby. I missed you too."

And there they all stood for a long moment, five Wallers tangled in the doorway of a split-level rambler, a builder's model in the Hampton Oaks subdivision of Stafford, Virginia. Though home for more than a year now, it felt as odd and foreign to Jeremy as the hotel he'd just left in Bangkok.

"OK, OK, OK," Jeremy said, finally. He broke up the hug, moved everyone inside the entry foyer, and pulled the door closed. "You want us all to freeze or what?"

Weather had been unseasonably cold in the DC area for the past week. It felt even worse to a man who had spent the previous week in the jungles of Southeast Asia.

"What did you bring us, Daddy?" Maddy asked. She and the two boys dragged Jeremy's duty bag across the floor and tugged at its thick nylon zipper.

"Hey, you guys!" Caroline called out. "I told you to ease up. Give your dad a chance to relax a minute before you go tearing through his stuff."

She managed a smile for her husband. Caroline had been through these decompressions before. Sometimes the smallest things set him off: toys lying around the house, rearranged furniture, something he didn't like for dinner. Reentry wasn't easy on any of them.

"The kids got you cake and ice cream," she ventured. That seemed like a safe beginning.

"Sounds great." Jeremy smiled. He leaned down to help the kids with his bag. "But before anybody starts opening presents, there's something I want from you," Jeremy said. Maddy and Christopher erupted in smiles.

"Not . . . the force?" She giggled.

"The force, Daddy?" Christopher squealed. They knew what was coming.

"Prepare for the force!" Jeremy yelled, throwing his arms wide and assuming an auditorium-sized smile. "The force suplex!"

With that, he executed the signature move of one of professional wrestling's most popular stars. He wrapped all the kids up in a bear hug and rolled them to the ground in a tumble of laughter, tickles, and Bronx cheer kisses.

"Uncle! Uncle!" Maddy called out, trying to get away long enough to open her presents. "Give him the knockout hug, Christopher!" she yelled.

Jeremy allowed the little boy to press his trademark maneuver and rolled over, faking unconsciousness. The kids jumped up and dug back in after their presents.

"Take those into the other room, please," Caroline ordered as they pulled out poorly wrapped parcels. She stared down at her husband, wondering what terrors he had endured. His hair looked matted and longer than she'd seen it in years. Bruise-colored rings clouded his otherwise brilliant blue eyes. A dark stubble covered his cheeks.

"You always get lost in the shuffle," he said, sitting up after they had gone. "Well, almost always." Jeremy reached into his bag and pulled out a gift for her.

"Wow," she said. Maybe this reentry would be different.

Jeremy watched her face as she unwrapped it, but all he could see were the fires back out there in that jungle. Even through the flash of the Thermit grenades, he could see the men inside the huts, burning up. The pools of blood where they had died washed away in the thickening rain.

"It's beautiful," Caroline said. She slipped the glass-bead bracelet over her arm and held it up for him to see.

"It was made by local tribesmen in . . ."

Jeremy stopped. All of a sudden, the circles under his eyes seemed darker. This mission, like so many of the others, was classified. There would be no places, dates, or times. Not even for his wife.

"I'm glad you like it."

Jeremy tried to rid his mind of the images: Americans falling forward where French shot them. He saw the survivor — the albino called Caleb — running across the clearing, passing through Jeremy's crosshairs, disappearing into the jungle.

"Bastard," Jeremy muttered before realizing that the jungles were behind him. Caroline stood there in front of him, helpless against the voices she could only guess at.

"Are you OK?" she asked. Though Jeremy had returned home, her husband remained somewhere farther away than she could reach out to. Killing had changed this man. It had taken him from her.

"Yeah." Jeremy nodded his head and stood up from the bag. "Yeah, I'm just really tired is all. I haven't slept much in . . ."

But then the phone rang. Caroline turned toward the sound but didn't dare answer. They both knew who was calling.

■

"WHAT IN HELL is going on out there?" the president demanded. He burst into the Situation Room, where his vice president had already taken command. Neon clocks glowed with times around the world. Wall monitors broadcast time lines, news reports, flash traffic. Landlines rang. Keyboards chattered. Voices rose.

"Three planes down, all foreign carriers," she said. Beechum held one phone to her shoulder and another to her ear. If anyone found it odd that the vice president was placing her own calls, they didn't say so.

"L.A., Miami, and National," the shift commander added. "The FAA has grounded domestic flights. They are in the process of checking all carriers for reports of in-flight emergencies."

Venable nodded, trying to decide where he wanted to stand.

"Were these planes shot down?" he demanded. "Is that possible?"

"We don't yet know where NBC is getting their information about the shooters," his press secretary said. The man looked surprisingly calm, considering the onslaught his office now faced. "None of the other networks have gone with it, and we have very little good intel yet from the crash sites."

"Alred!" the president yelled. Of all the agency heads he had met during the past three weeks, this FBI director seemed the most capable.

"Sir?" Alred responded. He hurried in from outside, where he had been conferring with a runner from the National Joint Terrorism Task Force.

"I thought you had these people under surveillance. How the hell are we losing airplanes all over the country if you have them under surveillance? Goddammit, how?"

Alred glanced down at a briefing paper he had just been handed, then shook his head. "We're still working on document exploitation, Mr. President. These things take time. Our surveillances have shown nothing that makes us . . ."

"David!" the vice president interrupted. She had dropped one of the phones but held the other up in the air. "Looks like we can confirm that NBC story. I have the DC police chief on the phone. He says they have a suspect in custody."

The room went quiet.

"An Indonesian male. Twenty-seven. Here on a student visa." Beechum paused for more information. "They found him on the roof of a building in Alexandria. He had a rifle."

"Well, where is he now?" the president asked, staring at Alred. The embarrassed FBI chief shrugged his shoulders.

Beechum repeated the president's question into her phone and waited for the answer.

"DC General," she finally said. "The morgue. They tell me the shooter is dead."

WITHIN AN HOUR of the first plane crash, credible and actionable leads had begun to flow in to crisis coordinators.

The FBI's Strategic Information Operations Center — a state-of-the-art command post on the Hoover Building's fifth floor — served as a clearinghouse for all local, state, and federal agencies involved with any of the attacks. The CIA's Counterterrorism Center, on the third floor of the new headquarters building at Langley, took care of all foreign assets and leads. The Joint Terrorist Threat Integration Center in Bethesda, Maryland, served as a clearinghouse, classification collaborative, and data-processing hub for thousands of international intelligence and law enforcement entities.

Elsewhere, the U.S. government's list of specialized task forces, squads, and units loosed a cascading deluge of intelligence unlike any other in history. The Secret Service's National Threat Assessment Center in Beltsville, Maryland, began poring over every known individual, group, and government who might merit further scrutiny. The Centers for Disease Control mobilized its jump teams in anticipation of potential health emergencies. The Department of Energy's Nuclear Emergency Search Team geared up in anticipation of radiological contingents. The FBI's Critical Incident Response Group in Stafford, Virginia, called in profilers from its National Center for the Analysis of Violent Crime to produce behavioral assessments, and to provide logistical support technicians from the Crisis Response Unit and negotiators from the Crisis Negotiations Unit.

SWAT teams, bomb squads, evidence response techs, EMS crews, hospital staffs, and Red Cross volunteers raced around in a maelstrom of flashing lights, sirens, and screeching tires. The National Transportation Safety Board got to crash sites any way it could. Above it all, the Domestic Emergency Support Team circled the empty skies over West Virginia in a rapid-deployment platform — a specially configured 737 called Gatekeeper — awaiting orders on where to land first.

None of this mattered to Jeremy Waller.

By the time he arrived at the Hostage Rescue Team's compound, tucked away in its corner of the FBI Academy on the Quantico Marine Corps Base, one detail had risen to the top: three men had been discovered in connection with the airliner crashes. All three were Muslims; all three had been caught with or near Barrett .50 caliber rifles. Unfortunately, only one of them was still alive.

"Hey, buddy, when did you get back?" Fritz Lottspeich was the first to greet Jeremy. They met in the parking lot, which had become a congested mess of vehicles, snowdrifts, and running men.

"About an hour ago," Jeremy said, tossing him a knuckle knock. "I leave the country for a few weeks and look what happens."

Lottspeich laughed his haphazard chuckle and badged his way through the front gate. Inside the single-story industrial-shell building, they found a hornet's nest of activity.

"All team leaders in the classroom," Billy Luther said, grabbing Jeremy before the door had fully closed behind him. "Why do you always look like shit when you roll back into town?"

Jeremy smiled and followed Billy into the HRT classroom. It wasn't the first time he'd heard comments like that.

"Waller, glad you could make it," the man at the front of the room said. Les Mason had run HRT for three years. As one of the team's plank holders, he had mounted out on more missions than any other operator.

"Been kind of busy, boss." Jeremy smiled. "Miss me?"

The HRT commander smiled. Rank meant little inside this room. At times like this, it all came down to mission.

"All right, what do we got?" Mason asked, turning to the team's S-2 intelligence officer. The former Hotel Team assaulter had received the job after recuperating from a gunshot wound he received in Kabul, Afghanistan.

"What do we got, boss?" the S-2 repeated. "Well, according to HQ, I'd say we've got us a situation."

■

"I DIDN'T ASK you if you wanted a lawyer! I asked you your goddamned name!"

Whack!

Ashar al Bayad recoiled from the open-hand blow. His head snapped backward, then down onto his chest as he tried to recover his senses.

"I-I am an A-American citizen," he stammered. He could no longer feel his fingers or toes. Mist rose from his mouth when he spoke. "I have done nothing wrong."

Whatever conviction his voice once held had left him. That hardly mattered. These people did not believe him, whatever his tone.

"Give him some more water," a male voice spoke out. The hose coughed a couple times, then squirted liquid ice.

Bayad shook his head back and forth, trying to avoid the water long enough to gasp what little breath his lungs would allow. Second- and third-degree burns covered 25 percent of his now naked body, and they hurt beyond comprehension.

"What's next?" another voice demanded. None of these men had given names. None of them had offered ID or read him his rights. This looked nothing like what he had seen on TV. Some foolish show.

"Where is Ansar ins Allah? What are you planning to do next?"

The water stopped long enough for him to answer, but he didn't. What was he to say? Bayad tried to clench his jaw against the relentless shaking. Los Angeles was warm with the Santa Ana winds, he thought. They must have put him in some kind of industrial cooler.

"Listen, you motherfucker," the first man said, "you are going to tell us what we need to know. Sooner or later, you're going to talk; take my word for it."

"Aaaaaahhhhhhhh!" Bayad yelled, trying to cleanse it all from his mind. This had to be a nightmare. How could he wake up?

"I don't know nothing!" he yelled back. His voice had grown small for a time; gut yelling seemed the only way to make his vocal cords work. "I was working at my job when this man steals me at gunpoint. He holds me in his van, and then the van blows up and burns me. I am victim, here. I do nothing wrong. I am naturalized citizen, sworn in by George W. Bush. I love USA."

This was the truth. Why would they not believe him?

"Fuck you, skinny," one of the men said. "You deserve what you got coming."

With that, they stopped the beating, opened the door, and left. Bayad sat in the chair by himself, scared and hungry and cold.

What will my family think? he wondered. *They must be worrying sick about me by now.*

He let his head hang down on his chest. The room smelled of urine and mold.

God is good, he promised himself. *A just and mighty God. Allah huakbar.*

■

PRESIDENT DAVID VENABLE had only been there a handful of times, but he already hated the Situation Room. All the noise, the frenzy of information — he hated the way it fed his claustrophobia, how everyone looked to him, demanding answers.

Answers? He hadn't even come up with any decent questions!

"So let me get this straight," he said. His immediate circle of advisors followed him up the stairs toward the Oval Office. The cadre had grown and shrunk in the past twenty-four hours, but a core seemed to be emerging. "We have found Islamic fundamentalists at all three sites? Two of them were dead when we got there, but one is still alive. Is that correct?"

"Correct," Alred agreed. "He was a local cleric, badly burned when a bomb he planned to set off malfunctioned. He's undergoing interrogation as we speak."

The FBI Director, Havelock, Chase, Beechum, and now the press secretary, a polished former CNN reporter named Noah Engle, encircled the president.

"Two were found lying next to .50 caliber semiautomatic rifles made by Barrett Manufacturing Company," Alred continued. "I'm told these guns are capable of piercing the windshield of a 747, which is supposed to be pretty tough. Only someone with specific expertise would know that."

"How the hell did they use a rifle to shoot something moving three hundred miles an hour?" Venable asked. He walked deliberately, but slower now. Beechum had begun to think of him as a shark moving relentlessly through the water. He looked menacing and strong as long as he kept moving, but threatened to drown if he stopped.

"Planes move considerably slower on final approach," Havelock said. He'd held a private pilot's license for twenty years.

Alred spoke up again.

"They selected buildings that lined up at very steep angles relative to the glide path," he explained. "That gave them an almost straight shot, which took speed out of the equation. People I talked with on our Hostage Rescue Team say it would not have been really difficult for a competent shooter."

Venable led them into the Oval Office. Workmen had brought in couches and were wrestling with an electric pump organ the president had insisted be brought down from the governor's mansion in Connecticut. He had spent many an introspective moment at its dual-level keyboards and expected to need it in the nation's corner office.

"You be careful with that!" he barked at the workmen. "That's an 1890 Estey reed harmonium my great-grandmother bought new in Brattleboro, Vermont." The president walked over to show them a thing or two, then remembered himself and turned back to his staff. "That's a family heirloom."

"We need to consider courses of action," his chief of staff said, once the workmen had departed.

"What are we supposed to do, put guards on every building?" Venable's voice trailed off as he wandered over to his podium. "I mean, there are only so many things you *can* do in a free society. We've already got guards inside the planes. Really — what are we supposed to do?"

"You're right, sir," Noah said. "I think the American people understand that. They want to know we're going after the people behind these attacks. They're not interested in details."

Havelock seemed to puff up, empowered by the press secretary's validation of his "spy crap" theory.

"Who's interrogating this suspect?" Venable asked.

"Defense Department people," Beechum said, hoping he wouldn't ask for more detail. There would always be things the president didn't need to know. "We're holding him as a material witness, which means we don't have to divulge his location, file charges, or even acknowledge that we have him."

Alred seemed fine with this, which surprised the president.

"Why would the Defense Department have a criminal suspect? Doesn't the FBI want him for prosecution?" Venable asked.

"Not at this time, sir," Alred said, looking at Beechum for guidance. This was a new president. A Democrat. How would he react to fundamental changes in judicial process that had been ushered in by a Republican predecessor?

"The FBI has to abide by the rule of law," Beechum said. She walked to the window and looked out into the snow. Windows seemed to draw her. "That means Miranda warnings, booking procedures, court hearings, public disclosure. It means civil rights scrutiny."

"Civil rights . . ." Venable trailed off. He seemed to get her meaning. "Yes, well this is war, right? I guess I don't need to know the details."

His lack of a desk seemed to confuse the others in the room, who didn't know exactly where to stand.

Havelock stepped toward the podium.

"If I may, sir," he said, "we have a matter that we need to address before we go much further. This country maintains what is known as the 'continuity of government plan.' You probably haven't been briefed yet, but . . ." — he waited for the president to interrupt. "FEMA administers a set of crisis response protocols. They provide for a smooth transition of power should something happen . . . frankly, if something should happen to you, sir."

"This involves that secure location they always talk about on the news?" said Venable.

"Yes, sir. We need to consider moving the vice president out of NACAP — excuse me, sir . . . that stands for national capital region — along with a number of congressional leaders, cabinet secretaries, and members of the judiciary. They will have full communication with the White House, of course, but will be protected in the event of further attacks."

"Right," was all the president said. He looked questioningly at Beechum, then asked, "When?"

"As soon as possible." He turned toward the vice president, as if her experience in these matters might enforce his authority.

"My place is here," she said. "I need to stay."

"Why?" Venable asked. He was president, after all; she little more than an insurance policy.

"David, I'm going to speak frankly." She looked confident, almost condescending. "You've presided over two of the worst domestic tragedies this country has ever suffered, and yet, despite the best advice of your staff, you haven't slept in nearly two days."

No one backed her, but she felt strong in her conviction.

"I'm the leader of the most powerful country in the world," Venable responded. "The commander in chief. You think I can just walk upstairs, kiss the wife good night, and call it a day?"

His incredulous smile made the room even more tense. This was a new administration, a White House fracturing between two very strong personalities.

"Yes," she said. There was no doubt in her voice. "That's exactly what you need to do. How long will you stay up? Three nights? Four?" She turned to the others, but they had no intention of sticking their noses in this. "You may be president, David, but you're still just a man. Don't forget that."

Venable's smile fell flat. He should have gone with his gut and refused Beechum as his running mate.

"Call the vice president a helicopter," he ordered. "She'll be going to that secure location as soon as possible. It seems the continuity of government protocols demand it."

V

Tuesday, 15 February
02:33 GMT
Albemarle Building, New York, New York

VIRTUALLY THE ENTIRE seventeenth floor of Borders Atlantic's corporate headquarters had been set aside for security operations. From satellite transmissions to computer interfacing and
product development, Borders Atlantic depended on high technology for its very existence, and it seemed that everyone, from com-
peting corporations to foreign governments, had tried to probe its
secrets. The seventeenth floor represented its innermost ramparts.

"So it's the algorithms?" Sirad asked. She stood beside Ravi, who
she had gotten to know quite well in the past twelve hours. "That's
our vulnerability?"

"That's just what Dieter thinks, but he doesn't really understand
the problem," Ravi answered. Despite access to some of the most
powerful and sophisticated computer mainframes in the world, the
diminutive New Delhi native had opted to test his theories on an
old-fashioned blackboard.

"Here's the real issue." He began with two boxes and a circle in
what to Sirad looked like a simple isosceles triangle. "Code-making

is simple in theory. Borders Atlantic wants to pass information from one cell phone to another."

He pointed to one of the boxes, demonstrating his point.

"That information is relayed in microwaves, which travel line of sight. Because of the curvature of the earth and physical obstructions, we need to raise our repeaters up high on towers, or in the case of our Quantis system, launch them into low earth orbit."

Ravi drew lines and arrows, connecting the cell phone boxes with the circular satellite, filling in the slanted walls of his communications pyramid. Sirad considered all of this rudimentary, of course, but saw no point in disturbing his thought process.

"The problem for cryptographers is twofold. First, the microwave is easy to intercept anywhere in the transmission/reception conduit; microwaves cannot be shielded from intrusion like hard lines. Second, you need keys to encrypt the transmission and decrypt the reception. Those keys are based on algorithms, which rely on random numbers. It's all mathematics. If you can figure out the codemaker's math, you can figure out and break his code."

"Simple enough," Sirad said, folding her arms. Ravi knew she oversaw the entire Quantis project. Why was he offering her a tourist-level orientation?

"Yes, of course."

He wiped his chalk from the board, moved to the upper left-hand corner, and began to write. Letters. Numbers. Greek symbols. The chalk tapped and scratched against the slate surface with such speed and force, Sirad stepped back to avoid the flying shards.

"Without giving up too many system eccentricities," he said, "let's begin with our random number generator — the true soul of Quantis, its key base. Conventional computer-model generators produce 'pseudo' numbers based on statistical randomness. Cryptographers can't rely on these because they too easily yield replication, so they try to find true physical sources that cannot be predicted, such as device latencies, utilization statistics — keystroke intervals, say, on a thousand different PC keyboards."

Ravi spoke one language while writing another on the board. Where he made mistakes, he swiped his hand across the equation and wrote through the smudges.

"This noise is then distilled by what is called a 'hash function' to make it all interdependent in a cryptographically strong way. The point, remember, is to generate unpredictability — to make your code confusing to external observation. You don't want the intruder to guess your root.

"Until recently, that meant at least one hundred twenty-eight bits of true entropy. To achieve this, number generators have relied on very large pools of information, cycling data through a hash function to protect the pools' contents. When you need more bits, you simply stir new chunks of the device latencies or utilization statistics into the pool, using a random key to maintain interdependence, of course."

Sirad nodded her head. *Of course,* she thought.

"All right. Now . . ." — Ravi's chalk really began to tap — "random number generation is typically the most overlooked and weakest part of the system. Our mathematicians have achieved a breakthrough in random number generation. We don't rely on these old systems because we have found a wholly different way to generate randomness. It is a major breakthrough — the kind that certainly would have won us a Nobel in math or physics if we could ever divulge it in open-source literature. Of course we can't."

"That's the famous Nguyen cornerstone I hear about?" Sirad asked. She had heard talk of this but never asked for details. All she knew was that Borders Atlantic had hired a twenty-two-year-old mathematician named Hung Il Nguyen away from the National Security Agency. He was the first-generation American son of Vietnamese immigrants. A prodigy. He apparently had done something extraordinary.

"No," Ravi said. He finished three last swipes of his chalk and stood back from his blackboard. "*This* is the Nguyen cornerstone."

The man pointed to the equation and beamed with childlike awe.

"What's it mean?" Sirad asked. She had taken her share of theoretical math classes in college but understood little of Ravi's quixotic hieroglyphics.

"It means money; more than thirty billion dollars in revenue this year alone," he said, crossing his arms. "It means security, power, beauty, a fundamental change in the way we look at the physical universe. And to most people, of course, it means nothing but a bunch of white symbols on a dirty blackboard."

"Humor me," Sirad said. "I'm afraid we don't have time for metaphor."

"Yes." Practicality returned to Ravi's eyes. "There are two primary kinds of code-making — secret, or *symmetrical*, and public key, or *asymmetrical*, encryption. Symmetrical codes use the same key to encrypt and decrypt, whereas asymmetrical use two different keys. Quantis relies on a combination of the two. We stay symmetrical from transmission to the satellite, then go asymmetrical from the satellite to the receiver. You understand that part, right?"

Sirad nodded her head. Borders Atlantic owned all satellites in their system, allowing them to depend on well-established stream cipher techniques. The company's system was very fast and, coupled with Borders Atlantic's new random number generation process, extremely secure.

"Well, the Nguyen cornerstone involves the second stage of the data stream, from the satellite to the receiver. Our problems always boiled down to message authentication codes for individual subscribers: key agreement protocols. If we integrated keys in each of the Quantis phones, for example, an attacker might reverse engineer our technology and clone it. Couldn't have that, could we?"

Sirad shook her head, then checked her watch.

"We need to get moving, Ravi," she said.

"Public-key cryptosystems — the second stage of the Quantis data stream — have always faced vulnerability to what are known as 'hard problems.' There are several, but the one Nguyen went after involved problem solving and validation in polynomial time . . ."

"Polynomial time?" Sirad asked.

"That's where the execution time of a computation does not exceed the polynomial function of the problem size itself."

Ravi pointed to his equation.

"Here," he said. "Simply put, any problem solvable in polynomial time, we'll call *P*. Any solution that can be checked in polynomial time we'll call *NP*. By definition, every problem in *P* must be *in NP*, but prior to Nguyen's groundbreaking work, we could not show that *P equals NP*."

"That's simply put?" Sirad asked. He had lost her, despite the movements of his hand through the length of his chalky equation.

"The Nguyen cornerstone forms the basis for Quantis," Ravi said. "The $P = NP$ conundrum was one of the most important problems in mathematics. Now we have solved it."

"That helps us?" Sirad asked.

"Oh, yes." Ravi smiled. "This is not the cornerstone of some academic equation. This is the basis of a whole new world."

■

HRT MOUNT-OUTS MOVED with the efficiency of a finely tuned engine. While the duty section — either gold or blue, depending on rotation — saw to personal equipment and rapid-action supplies, the training section scrambled to load team gear. Everything from beans to bullets went into the back of stake-bed trucks for immediate delivery to C-17 transport aircraft at Andrews Air Force Base, forty-seven miles to the north. HRT took pride in being completely self-sufficient, so supplies necessary to maintain fifty operators and twenty-five support staff had to move with them. Box trucks and stake-beds quickly piled up with MREs, medical equipment, communications gear, shelter, ammunition, weapons, helicopter rigging, and personal bags.

By simple process of luck, Jeremy's Xray Snipers today fell within the duty section. He and the six other members of his team quickly stuffed their backpacks with two days' worth of rations, night vision and surveillance optics, ammo, cold weather gear, an encrypted radio, and two extra batteries.

"Sixty-five pounds of lightweight gear," the guys always joked. Jeremy had read that the Spartans had carried the same battle load at Thermopylae. Whether swords and shields or assault rifles and thermal imaging scopes, warriors had always toted the same load.

"Let's move!" Jeremy called out as the rest of Xray hustled out toward their cars. As team leader, he functioned as something more than special agent and something less than supervisor. HRT had its own rules, and this paramilitary responsibility existed nowhere else in the FBI.

"You got a warning order for us yet?" Lottspeich asked, following his friend and former partner out of the garage and into the now blinding snow. They had endured selection, NOTS, and the Marine Corps Scout/Sniper School together. Jeremy considered Fritz one of his closest friends.

"On the record or off?" Jeremy asked. He wore camouflage Gore-Tex pants and a parka over polypro long johns, but the driving wind and snow bit through just the same.

"The real shit," Lottspeich said. He sidestepped the communications van as it drove up from the tech shed in what had been the team's original sniper tower.

"We've arrested one of the shooters. The military is interrogating him, but the CIA has HUMINT from a source down at Gitmo who says this is part of some bigger plot. They think this is just the first stage of an attempt to bring down the government."

"Holy shit . . ." Lottspeich lost the rest of his sentence in the howling wind.

"The team is prestaging in a hangar up at Andrews, but I don't know what the hell good that is going to do," Jeremy said. The cold wind helped clear his overburdened mind. "There's no way we're lifting off in this weather."

"Stand by to stand by — that's our motto, right?" Lottspeich yelled. He couldn't think of much else to say at the moment. Terrorism was their business, but fifty men in a snowstorm seemed a pitiful response to what Jeremy was describing.

"You driving or me?" Jeremy asked. Their assigned parking spaces were side by side.

"You drive," Lottspeich said. "All you do is complain about my . . ."

"Waller!" a voice called out behind them. Jeremy turned to supervisor Billy Luther, who had run across the parking lot in his shirtsleeves.

"Hey, didn't your mother tell you . . . ," Lottspeich started, but Billy cut him off.

"We just got word that WFO's SOG has a possible cell under surveillance in an Anacostia warehouse," he yelled over the storm.

Jeremy could feel this ratcheting up very quickly. If the Washington field office's Special Operations Group had run this Ansar group to ground, HRT might get to play in this after all.

"They think these assholes are cooking ANFO," Billy said. "Our objective is to close down the perimeter so no one gets in or out. Get your men on the road; we'll relay more information as we get it."

Billy turned and started back inside.

"Make sure you maintain a safe standoff," he called over his shoulder. "That shit can make a big hole!"

"ANFO," Lottspeich said. He opened the rear doors of Jeremy's Suburban and threw his pack inside. "That don't sound right. Anyone capable of splashing three airliners isn't likely to be messing with fertilizer and fuel oil, are they?"

"That's what I'm thinking," Jeremy said, tossing in his gear after Fritz's. "From what I heard in the team leaders' meeting, this thing goes a helluva long ways beyond some guy cooking bubba bombs in Anacostia."

He climbed into his truck and started the engine. For reasons that made no particular sense, all he could think of was that butterfly in the jungle.

Graphium milon, GI Jane had said just before everything went to hell. Odd that something so beautiful could send shivers down his spine.

■

JORDAN MITCHELL SELDOM traveled for meetings, but this was one of those exceptions. Twelve years earlier, just after the fall of the Berlin Wall, a soft-spoken midlevel-management type had walked up at a conference and asked to have a word with him. The man had offered no business card, came with no introduction, and managed to insert himself in Mitchell's day precisely at a time when his defenses were down. Ten minutes later they were talking in Mitchell's suite. Within a week they were partners.

Mr. Hoch was all he had ever called the man, but that seemed appropriate for a wraith who came and went with no contact numbers or corporate affiliation. He spoke with spare economy, a trait Mitchell had always sought in his own employees. Most interesting of all, Mr. Hoch talked about a new program, developed within the CIA, to cover young intelligence operatives inside American business. The program was run out of the Directorate of Operations — the dirty-hands-and-broken-bones side of the house — and it was so secretive Hoch introduced the concept with a question Mitchell would never forget.

"I love my country enough to die for it, Mr. Mitchell," he said. "Do you love yours enough to keep a secret?"

It had sounded like the perfect pitch. Mitchell felt compelled to hear the man out, to listen to what this otherwise completely forgettable person had to say. It felt like duty.

Hoch started by telling Mitchell that he represented a government agency and that his employer collected intelligence on other governments, agencies, businesses, and people. The intrigue alone would have compelled Mitchell to give this man a chance, but what really captivated him was the part where he talked about money.

"We have come to understand that the war on terrorism is all about money," he said in explaining the link between intelligence and business. "National security is no longer a question of keeping the seething communist hordes out of Southeast Asia and sub-Saharan Africa. It's an issue of protecting the strongest, most far-reaching financial empire in the history of the world.

"If we want to maintain the freedoms that allow people like you to accomplish their dreams, we have to adopt an entirely new attitude about national security. Our success as a world superpower is going to come down to leaders who understand the validity of the dollar."

Nothing this man or any other could have said would have seized Mitchell's attention any more fervently. All his life, he had believed that bombs and tanks were little more than a Stone Age excuse to avoid more complicated issues. If the United States ever wanted to protect itself from foreign threats, it had to accept the new reality: *pecunia vincit omnia* — money conquers all.

Deficit spending, not military action or the threat of mutually assured destruction, had won the Cold War. Ronald Reagan crippled the Soviet Union by taunting it into bankruptcy. The war on terror would be won the same way.

Mitchell had gone so far as to include a chapter in his new book about the potentially calamitous dangers of foreign acquisition of U.S. corporations. When Daimler-Benz bought Chrysler, he wrote, they didn't simply purchase a bunch of assembly lines, sheet metal, and hood ornaments; they bought a huge chunk of America. They gained access to labor contracts, research and development secrets, personnel folders, and virtually every black-walled program Chrysler ever worked on.

Corporate raiding by companies like Ford, Viacom, and GE threatened to change the global power balance more than all the bombs in Iran, Iraq, and North Korea combined. This new shadow war was being waged with a whole new kind of soldier — one armed with pinstripes and a BlackBerry. Guns and bombs were simply window dressing for the morons at cable news.

"Hello, Mr. Hoch," Mitchell said. He had agreed to meet his enigmatic partner at a tiny SoHo café called Twelve Seats. There was just one large room with an espresso bar. Two women sat talking in the back. A man on Rollerblades fought his way out the door, wrestling a venti latte and two feisty pugs.

"Nice to see you, Jordan."

It was just the two of them. Trask sat outside in the Mercedes. Hoch always came alone.

"You, too. How have you been?"

Neither man had any interest in small talk, but a mutual respect had grown between them.

"I feel well. Coffee?"

"Just water."

They ordered and sat at the window.

"So, we have business?" Mitchell asked. He could see Trask in the car, wrestling with two cell phones, trying to juggle and cancel meetings to accommodate this last-minute tryst.

"We do." Hoch looked casually around the room to ease any concern about overhears. "Jafar al Tayar."

"I don't speak Arabic. I think you know that."

Hoch watched Mitchell's face, trying to decide whether or not the phrase had surprised him.

"It means Jafar the pilot, or the high flier — one who controls things from a position of power or influential standing. We have developed a source in Guantánamo Bay who talks about an operation called Jafar al Tayar. A terrorist operation, it seems, but more troublesome than that."

"What would be more troublesome than a terrorist operation?" Mitchell asked. "Particularly in light of recent events?"

"Jafar al Tayar was developed by the United States government," Hoch said. The Borders Atlantic CEO held his eye with no change in expression.

"Go on."

"In the mid-1980s, the Pentagon was getting itself involved in all kinds of crazy schemes called 'asynchronous warfare.' I'm sure you remember the stories — everything from ESP and telepathy to subliminal suggestion and mass hypnosis. Well, one of the more rational projects involved the possibility that communists or terrorists might infiltrate our government from within."

"From within? What do you mean?"

"By getting themselves elected. The CIA and FBI had always been looking at spies, of course, but no one had ever considered the possibility that a foreign power might simply front a candidate in a general election."

Mitchell nodded. America was a free and open society. Despite lingering vestiges of prejudice, men and women from all different ethnic, religious, and cultural backgrounds had achieved high office.

"Interesting," Mitchell said. Hoch had garnered his full attention.

"To test this possibility, DARPA — the Advanced Research Projects Agency at that time — came up with an idea. What if the U.S. military found a handful of high achievers, altered their backgrounds, and gave them a mission: to get elected. It would be an off-line project, of course — something almost no one knew anything about."

"They did this?" Mitchell asked.

"Twelve people." Hoch nodded. "The best and brightest the army could find. They called it Civil Defense Scenario Four: Project Megiddo. It was run out of a Special Forces unit within the Fourth Psychological Operations Group. Very small footprint. Total autonomy. Very black."

Hoch looked around again. No one had spoken aloud about this in almost twenty years.

"The army took these twelve soldiers and for two years sculpted them into the best possible political candidates. Education, charm school, distinguished military record — all backstopped, of course, with the full resources of the Department of Defense."

"And sent them out to get elected?"

"Yes. Discharged them back to their hometowns. Dogcatcher, mayor, state assembly, U.S. Congress: their only mission was to rise as high as possible through the political system."

"So, what happened?"

"We don't know."

"What?" Mitchell asked. "How do you not know?"

"For one thing, the project was compartmented and diffused. There are no records. For another, the project was run by a colonel named Ellis who has apparently retired. Project Megiddo and anything we know about it went with this colonel when he left."

Mitchell leaned back in his chair. If America allowed business to function like government, the whole country would be bankrupt and behind bars.

"How does an Islamic holy warrior at Guantánamo Bay, Cuba, know more about Project Megiddo than the CIA?" Mitchell whispered.

"We're not sure he does." Hoch shrugged. "But the similarities between his Jafar al Tayar plot and our Megiddo project are too close to ignore. The only way to find out is to go back after this project and see what happened to those twelve candidates."

"Which means this Colonel Ellis is still around and that you know where to find him, I assume?"

"Yes." Hoch nodded. "The problem is selecting the right person to send after him."

Mitchell thought for a moment. He could see in Hoch's eyes that the CIA boss had already come up with a name.

"Waller?" Mitchell asked.

Hoch finished his coffee and signaled for the check.

"We have very little time to spare. Our analysts predict that the next wave of attacks could start at any time."

"How?" Mitchell asked. "Putting Waller on a plane to some Third World hellhole for a few days is one thing. Sending him undercover for an operation like this is quite another. We can't tell the FBI what's involved here, and they'll never let him go without full disclosure."

"They will if the right person makes the request," Hoch said. He pulled cash out of his pocket to pay the check.

"Beechum," Mitchell confirmed.

"This is a time of national emergency," Hoch said. "I would imagine that the vice president of the United States has special authority, wouldn't you?"

"She'd better." Mitchell smiled. "That's why we put her there."

■

DAVID RAY VENABLE hadn't lived in the White House long enough to take its history for granted. Each room he wandered through carried the indelible stains of American conflict — the Red Room's fireplace where Harry Truman had contemplated the nuclear attack on Hiroshima and Nagasaki, the library where John F. Kennedy prayed for strength during the Cuban missile crisis, the bedroom windows through which Lincoln saw Arlington Cemetery filling with the corpses of a nation falling upon itself.

And now it was his — this house, this country, this sacred trust. He settled in the Green Room, where a couch and two wing chairs offered ample comfort. The black velvet rope used to close it off to tourists still blocked the door.

"Is this private enough for you, Elizabeth?" he asked. It had been his only choice since the vice president had decided to make her stand. Had he decided to fight inside the Oval Office, the impact on his staff could have been devastating.

"Lose the suits," she said. Beechum meant no insult to the Secret Service agents who had followed both her and the president's every move since the first bomb exploded in Atlanta. But this was bound to get nasty, and her daddy had always told her not to quarrel in front of the help.

"Please," the president said. He nodded toward the shift commander and motioned him away with his hand. "Close the door and give us a minute, will you?"

The agent, a veteran of two previous administrations, thought for a moment, then backed out of earshot. This was the Secret Service, after all; sometimes what you didn't see was just as important as what you did.

"You need me here, David," Beechum said when they were alone. "Don't try to turn this into something it isn't. I'll stay completely out of sight. I'll banish myself to the goddamned Situation Room if it makes you happy, but this is a brand-new staff you've brought to Washington and they have never been through anything like this. I have."

Venable saw no upside in arguing that point. Beechum had served as chair of the Senate intelligence committee before, during, and after the 9/11 attacks. Few people in Washington had better sources, connections, or reputation.

"It's not that I don't value your experience," the president fired back. "It's just that we need to protect the government should something else happen. Like Havelock said, we will have full communications with . . . with wherever the hell it is they are taking you."

"Maryland," she informed him. "They call it Site Seven."

"Site Seven? I guess that sounds like something the military would come up with, doesn't it?"

The name seemed to distract this commander in chief, who had served one tour late in the Vietnam War. He quickly regained his train of thought.

"I guess there are a helluva lot of names I'll be learning the next couple of days."

"Not if you don't get some sleep. David, this is the first thing they teach you in crisis management training. I've heard it so many times: leaders get caught up in the adrenaline of the initial event, then feel they have to stay involved. The longer you stay up, the harder it is to break away. Sleep deprivation leads to faulty decision making, and that leads to . . ."

"Don't preach to me, Elizabeth. I've fought in combat, and I've overseen states of emergency during two terms as governor. I feel fine."

"Flash floods and a windstorm," she reminded him. "We're talking about thousands of lives lost in six states. We're talking about an economy that will curl up and die if we don't . . ."

"Enough." He waved at her. "I get your point."

"All right, then, let me run a hypothetical by you." Beechum reached a hand to the bridge of her nose and began to rub. She was already beginning to feel the fatigue and she'd had a good night's sleep. "Let's say this is the first stage of a much larger terror plot. Let's say our intelligence shows an imminent threat to critical infrastructure including energy, ground transportation, financial markets . . . even the Internet."

"A hypothetical?" he asked. "Or do you have information I haven't seen yet?"

"Let's say that we have reason to believe that Islamic terrorists have forged inroads with a group of Americans. Non-Islamic Americans. People who look just like you and me."

"This is no hypothetical, is it?" he asked. "I need to know, Elizabeth. Like it or not, I'm still your boss."

"That arrest I told you about earlier. Mahar's capture in Indonesia?"

The president nodded.

"He wasn't alone."

Now he stared.

"He had three Americans with him. Three Christian Americans."

"How? Why? Have we interrogated them?"

Beechum walked over toward the windows, which looked out over Pennsylvania Avenue. Snow obscured everything beyond the driveway.

"What I'm about to tell you is not written in any intelligence briefing. It falls within no particular security classification. In fact, it doesn't really exist at all. You — even with all your power as president — will never be able to penetrate the mechanism that uncovered it. It is a black program authorized by the past administration to work outside the parameters of bureaucracy."

"What are you telling me? You have started some supersecret agency to fight terrorism?" He sounded incredulous and slightly angry. "I won't have that in my administration, Elizabeth, I'll tell you that right now. Everything we do will be aboveboard and open to congressional oversight. I will not stand for . . ."

"Do you want to know about the Christians or don't you?" she asked. Beechum didn't sound the least bit impressed with his threats.

Venable crossed his arms and waited.

"The FBI has tied a Saudi charity working inside the United States to a group of white supremacists in Idaho. There have been numerous financial transactions, some of them fairly sizable. Alred says his Terrorist Financial Tracking Group has drawn clear lines of collusion directly to senior members of the Saudi royal family."

"The Saudis?" Venable exhaled a breath of resignation. "We've always worried about them, haven't we? I mean, from what I've read the past few years, they seem to turn up every time someone mentions terror."

"That's correct," Beechum agreed. "Saudi interests have invested more than one and a half trillion dollars through our financial institutions. They are one of our most important Arab allies in the Middle East. They have large and prominent communities in most of our largest cities. And yet, all our intelligence suggests they remain a critical threat."

"What about Borders Atlantic?" he asked. "Jordan Mitchell sold the Quantis system to the Saudis before he even launched it in his own country. That, despite the fact that your own committee identified it as one of the greatest threats to the intelligence community in decades."

This all made sense to him now. The gears in his Yale-educated mind began to turn in earnest.

"We don't know of any ties at this point, but yes, that certainly is a concern," Beechum answered. Lying to the president of the United States should have bothered her, but it didn't. Matters of national security seldom truly hinged on politicians. In her universe of secrets, only those with a clear sense of mission had a need to know.

"This goes all the way back to 9/11, I suppose?"

"Yes. The Saudis supplied fifteen of the nineteen hijackers, with clear financial support of causes ranging from al Qaeda to pro-Palestinian groups. Now we have significant evidence that they are backing a whole new type of threat inside the U.S."

"Who?" Venable asked. "Why work with a Christian group? What would either have to gain from something like this?"

"We don't know that yet," Beechum lied again. It would all make sense to him in the end.

"Oh, I get it." Venable nodded, a look of cynicism wrinkling his forehead. "This is your trump card. You are part of this little group that I can't know about, and you need to stay here in order to trade your shady little secrets. That's why you don't want me to stick you out there in that site . . . whatever it is."

"Site Seven." She turned back toward the windows. "And they're not dirty little secrets. They're the difference between freedom and the end of America as we know it, David. You need me here. You need me more than you can possibly know."

VI

Tuesday, 15 February
18:19 GMT
Camp Peary, Williamsburg, Virginia

ELM COTTAGE SAT at the edge of a five-acre clearing. A one-lane road led up to it, through a forest of loblolly pines and sycamore trees. Deer roamed freely, undisturbed by anything more dangerous than an occasional jogger. Dozens of species of birds enjoyed sanctuary in the wetlands preserves. If not for the occasional sounds of screeching tires and gunfire, this magic hideaway would have seemed an almost poetic idyll.

GI Jane arrived at the isolated cottage among the scattered flurries of a storm that forecasters saw slowly drifting north. A Gulfstream G-V had just dropped her off at the facility's airstrip, a single runway in the middle of a vast 10,000-acre Department of Defense installation known since World War II as "the Farm."

She had spent lots of time here over the past decade, first as a young CIA case officer learning tradecraft and then as a journeyman operative honing her trade. It had been several years already since she attended the facility's lengthy "elicitation" in-service — Agency jargon for interrogation school. But that had all been academic. This was the first time she'd come back to the Farm for anything real.

What a place, she thought, peering out through the smoked glass windows of a black Yukon as it pulled up to the cottage. There was a swingset, an above-ground pool, a satellite dish, and children's toys, all quietly gathering snow in the yard. It appeared to be just another two-story vinyl-sided home with a gambrel roof on a pretty country lot.

Except for the razor wire and security cameras, of course. Elm Cottage was surrounded with a ten-foot chain-link fence and a shoulder of concertina wire that someone had strung little white Christmas lights through, lending the whole snow-frosted scene a demented sort of Yuletide cheer.

"This shouldn't take long," GI Jane said. Two heavily armed guards sat in the front seat but said nothing. The driver nodded and shifted into park.

The CIA interrogation expert opened her door and passed another guard at the gate as she walked through the snow; she kicked off her boots after entering through a nicely ordered mudroom.

"How do you do, ma'am," a guard greeted her inside. He saw no point in checking her ID. If she had gotten this far, she had to have passed someone's scrutiny.

"Where is he?" she asked. The guard led her through a well-used kitchen, into a dining room. A very tired, very frightened-looking man sat at a nicely polished Chippendale table topped with brass candlestick holders and a dark blue Koran. The holy book had a paperback cover and was inscribed at the bottom: *Property of the U.S. Government.*

"I'm Jane," she said in English, offering a smile and the first name that fell into her head. That business in the jungle had stuck with her. "You are?"

"Ashar," the man said. He sounded hoarse. Empty. Bandages covered his arms, neck, and part of his face.

"Ashar. Of course."

Jane opened one of the little wheel books she had made a habit of carrying and turned to a dog-eared page.

"I trust you are comfortable here?" she asked.

The man stared at her. Since his arrest, he had endured a true nightmare. Kept in a constantly and brightly illuminated room with no windows, he was drugged to sleep, then drugged awake.

They made him watch bizarre pornographic movies, forced him to endure music played backward at high volume. They questioned him for hours, beating his naked body, spraying him with water. They froze him in a walk-in meat cooler, then made him sweat in a room hot as a sauna. They had fed him nothing but bread laced with something that inspired dire physical cravings, headaches, and vomiting; he thought it might be nicotine.

"Look at me," he said. Ashar thought the answer must be obvious. "Nothing is comfortable. They treat me very badly. These burns are very painful. They don't even change my bandages."

"Yes, well . . ." GI Jane leaned forward on her elbows and spoke in a clear, resolute voice. "I can't help what someone else has done to you, but I'm not here to cause you any pain."

Ashar tried not to look scared, but someone had flown him a long way from Los Angeles. This woman looked harmless enough, but he did not believe her for a moment.

■

JORDAN MITCHELL'S OFFICE, like his management style, struck his immediate circle as anachronistic but true. From the expansive weapons collection displayed on every available wall to the antique rugs, dark hardwood paneling, and richly upholstered furniture, Mitchell's space spoke of old-world heritage. Bolder decorators periodically upgraded the building's public areas, but no one dared change a thing about his office. Mitchell's taste, like his business acumen, was not open to discussion.

"The FBI has found some interesting eccentricities in the original bomb designs," Trask said. Though the former marine's title read chief of staff, he enjoyed power and access beyond anyone else in the company.

"Really. What did they find?" Mitchell asked. The CEO sat at his desk, glancing through a Helmut Lange retrospective his publisher had sent over as a courtesy. Mitchell's business hardbacks had three times proven him their biggest seller, after all; the occasional coffee-table book seemed a small but welcome gesture.

"Signature," Trask said. He had served as an artillery officer in the first Gulf War and understood plenty about the report in his hands. "The materials were commonly available, but every improvised explosive device is a three-stage mechanism: detonator, initiator, accelerant. Both the detonator and the initiator stood out."

Most executives mistook Mitchell's efficiency as disinterest. The most common mistake, Trask had discovered, was that midlevel managers would skim over important details, infuriating the boss. Mitchell wanted information — all of it.

"Go on," Mitchell said. He lay the book on his desk and stood.

"They used what are called 'e-cell' timers, a device that was developed by U.S. Special Forces for Third World insurgents. The initiator is called 'shock tube,' a lead sulfinate powder inside a flexible plastic conduit. When the e-cell is triggered, it transfers a pyrotechnic spark to a blasting cap. The whole process is mechanical, so radio interference won't cause premature detonation. It is reliable, easy to assemble, and cheap."

"These people had military training," Mitchell assumed. "Were they U.S. military themselves? Or were they *trained* by our military?"

"FBI says there is no way to tell. The universe of people with this kind of expertise is pretty big. We apparently churn out lots of bomb makers."

Mitchell walked toward a credenza and lifted a photograph showing young men and women gathered around him. Children — grandchildren presumably — tugged playfully at each other's hair and arms. It was a beach scene full of madras prints, red sailcloth khakis, and white, perfectly aligned teeth. A portrait Jay Gatsby would have expected.

"Yes, I imagine we do . . ." Mitchell nodded. His voice trailed off to other thoughts. "You know, I never have liked this woman," he said, pointing to what appeared to be his daughter in the photo. "My progeny would never have hair quite this color. Even if she did, no daughter of mine would wear an engagement ring less than three karats. Wouldn't be right."

Mitchell held the photo at arm's length as if to consider it in a different light.

"You want me to schedule another shoot?" Trask asked. It had been just over a year since he had called a casting company to find suitable faux lineage for a man who had never found time for a family of his own.

"Yes. Something seasonal. Let's simulate a ski holiday at Stowe," he said. "I want sons this time. All sons. Five of them . . . four married. Doctor types, mostly, with maybe an artist in there somewhere for a little color. Wholesome wives dressed in Burberry."

Then, turning as quickly back to the matters at hand, "Who do we think is behind this?"

Trask shuffled through a pile of manila folders, then punched a remote and flashed a PowerPoint slide presentation on the one wall not covered with guns.

"Roderick 'Buck' Ellis. Colonel, U.S. Army retired." Trask considered the photo of a man between two chaparral bushes. Though he wore civilian clothes, there was no mistaking his military bearing.

"I know this man," Mitchell said. He set the beach photo back on his credenza.

"Yes, you do," Trask remarked. Nothing escaped the chief executive.

"Chile, 1972. During the coup. Ellis claimed he worked for ITT, but I made him for DoD in about three seconds. He attended all the embassy functions. Always seemed to be looking for information about Allende's business schedules and motorcade routes as I recall. Serious bugger."

"Fifth Special Forces, Fourth Psychological Operations Group — military operations other than war," Trask advised. "He cut his teeth with MAC-V-SOG and the Phoenix program, training Montagnard hill people to fight our guerrilla war in Vietnam. During the 1970s, he developed and coordinated CIA-led insurgencies in Chile, Nicaragua, and El Salvador. After that he moved to the Defense Advanced Research Projects Agency to work on a highly classified, long-lead operation known as Project Megiddo."

"I knew he was black, even then." Mitchell smiled. "He wasn't one of our Agency guys, but he had that quality, you know? Part of the community. Couldn't fake it by reading a bunch of le Carré novels in those days. We still had secrets that seemed worth keeping."

Mitchell took the remote from Trask and flipped through a series of surveillance shots. Most looked at least a couple years old.

"Where is he?" Mitchell asked.

"Texas," the chief of staff said.

Mitchell returned to his desk and picked up a newspaper. The headlines screamed of murder in the heartland. The death toll kept climbing as new bodies were discovered in the wreckage of planes and buildings. Though initial stories had focused on the new terror group Ansar ins Allah, the finger-pointing had already begun. Some accused the new Democratic administration of complacency. Others argued that the Republican war in Iraq had inspired anti-American hatred. And then there were stories about Borders Atlantic and its Quantis phones. Why this technology? Why now? Why sell it first to the Saudis? The uniquely American contagion of blame had started to spread, and Jordan Mitchell could feel the first symptoms of a very dangerous ague.

"We're sending Waller in after them," Mitchell said. "Maybe he can find out what the good colonel has gotten himself into since our days planning revolution in Chile."

JEREMY AND FRITZ turned off I-395 at the Pennsylvania Avenue exit, the only vehicle on the road. Billy Luther had radioed directions to a block of old brick warehouses along the Anacostia River. As he'd said down in Quantico, the Washington field office's surveillance group had tracked a suspected al Qaeda sympathizer to some kind of meeting in a burned-out section of DC's worst remaining ghetto.

"Nice place," Lottspeich observed as they drove to within a block of the crisis site. Snow had covered the worst of it, but abandoned cars littered both sides of the road. Garbage stood in piles higher than some of the surrounding buildings; graffiti covered broken brick facades; worn-out mattresses, rat-infested couches, and piles of twisted, rusting steel provided the only contrast.

"I think the Realtors would call this a transitional neighborhood in a parklike setting." Jeremy laughed.

"Yeah." Lottspeich chuckled. "Plenty of wildlife: stray dogs, rats, and a flock of Safeway sparrows."

Plastic shopping bags drifted like winter birds on the gusting winds. The dogs and rats had gone into hiding.

"At least the snow is keeping everyone inside." Jeremy spotted one of the WFO surveillance vehicles parked behind an abandoned outbuilding and used his four-wheel-drive traction to pull up beside it. "Amazing what a little weather will do for drug interdiction efforts."

Lottspeich rolled down his window once Jeremy had parked. He turned toward a middle-aged black woman in the other car. She wore a white North Face parka, gold-framed Givenchy glasses, and a nose ring.

"How's the sledding?" he asked.

"Sledding?" She laughed. "Honey, this here is the ancestral home of the crack rock. Only winter sports we got is shooting up, whorin' around, and sleepin' in."

"Good thing I brought a gun." Lottspeich laughed back. He liked her immediately. "I understand you guys are looking for a couple highly trained long-range precision rifle specialists."

The woman's radio crackled, and she held up a blue-and-gold lamé fingernail. Had to be at least an inch long.

"Ten four," she said, responding to something neither HRT sniper could hear. "Like I said, you boys better get you asses up there." She turned back to Lottspeich. "Our source just got a call from the principal, said they looking to move within the hour."

She pointed to a three-story building distinguished by a bell tower and a couple hundred broken windows.

"That's your rooftop over there. We got a couple guys on top can show you around."

Neither man said much as they climbed out, pulled their collars up around their necks, and pulled shooting rucks and rifle cases from the back of the truck.

"Hope that wise ass o' yours is waterproof, honey," the woman called after them. "'Cause its gonna get both wet and cold up theya."

Jeremy and his partner trudged off through the snow. They could hear her laughing all the way to cover.

◼

"I DON'T EXPECT you to believe me," GI Jane assured Ashar. "Not after the way you have been treated. But I really have no interest in causing you further discomfort. I think you don't know a single thing about what brought you here. Is that true? Do you even know why you have been arrested?"

Ashar shook his head. This woman sounded sincere, but he didn't dare trust her.

"I was kidnapped, held in the back of a truck, and then blown up," Ashar said. He had told the others the same thing, but they did not believe him. "I am an American citizen. My family will be very worried about me."

"Of course they will. But we're going to let you go as soon as you help us with a few very important matters." Jane tried to sound sympathetic and sincere, but she had been thinking too much and sleeping too little for false sentiment.

"I need you to tell me exactly what happened yesterday in Los Angeles."

Ashar tried to decide whether or not she was baiting him.

"I was on my way to work," he said. "A white man in a van drove up beside me to ask directions, and then he pointed a large hand-gun at me."

"You work at a clothing store?" she asked. She had read his dossier and knew its details well. "The Gap."

"Yes. I was walking because my car was in the shop for brakes and the store is just a short distance from my apartment."

"But you had come from your mosque, is that right?"

Ashar looked surprised.

"Yes, I teach religious studies there on Tuesdays. I go to work after classes."

"What happened next?" Jane asked. "Tell me about the white man."

"This white man, he had a full beard and sunglasses beneath a ball cap. I could not see much of his face, which made me wonder when he rolled down his window to ask me directions. And then I saw the gun, and I felt sick at my stomach. There has been so much violence against Arab Americans, especially since the bombings."

"What happened next?" Jane asked.

"He got out of the truck — and it was a very busy street, but no one stopped. He got out of the truck and forced me into the back. He climbed in after me and secured my hands and legs with tape."

"Did he say anything to you?" she asked.

"Nothing at first. But he drove me somewhere, by the airport where I was arrested, and then he told me not to run, that he wouldn't hurt me."

Jane nodded and jotted something in her notebook.

"Would you recognize this man if I showed you a photo?" she asked.

Ashar shrugged his shoulders. "Yes, perhaps. The glasses and the beard, I'm not so sure."

GI Jane reached into her pocket and produced a Palm Zire. She touched the screen three times with its stylus and turned it toward Ashar.

"Look at these photos. Do you see the man who kidnapped you?"

Ashar looked closely, allowing himself a moment of hope that this woman might believe his story. He scrolled through dozens of photos. They were all white men, some with beards, some with glasses, some in color, some in black and white.

"I don't know," he said. "These pictures are so . . ."

Something caught his attention. His eyes sprung open.

"Wait . . . wait. Yes, that's him!" A rigid smile broke out across his face. "This is the man who took me! You see, this is him."

GI Jane turned the PDA back for a look.

"Thank you, Ashar," she said, tucking the Zire back into her pocket. "See, I told you that I believed you."

"Does that mean I can go now?" he asked. Ashar felt hope for the first time since this awful experience began.

"I'm afraid that's not going to be possible for a while," GI Jane said. There was no point in explaining. She had what she had come for.

"But when?" he pleaded. "When can I return to my family?"

"That's way above my pay grade," Jane responded, standing and moving back toward the kitchen. "But I wouldn't hold my breath."

■

COLONEL BUCK ELLIS had been born into a life of violence. Literally. His mother had given birth to him in the passenger seat of a car wreck. There, amid the gnarled chrome and torn cloth wreckage of a 1947 Ford, Ellis had summoned his own first breath and screamed bloody murder. The first man on the scene had been a Baptist minister who felt so moved by what he saw that he drafted the next Sunday's sermon in homage and preserved it in a cellophane sleeve so the miracle child would have it as a keepsake when he got older.

Both parents had died that night on a slick patch of Houston asphalt, leaving him to an alcoholic uncle and his regularly beaten wife. The sermon had gotten lost in the constant moves and revolving foster homes of a throwaway youth.

"Two-man entry, two-room clear!" he called out. Bone hard and superbly fit at sixty-four years of age, the colonel wore his hair in the same flattop style he'd adopted in grade school. He stood outside a cinder-block structure called the House of Horrors and counted down a checklist of safety issues. People from all over the world paid $1,785 a week to visit the Homestead, and as lead instructor, he wanted to make sure they walked away healthy enough to reflect positively on his preachings.

Two-man entry, two-room clear. He remembered the first time he'd heard those words, working with the Brits' Twenty-second Special Air Service back in 1980. He'd been passing through their garrison at Hereford when Iranian terrorists took over the Iraqi embassy at Princes Gate. *What a hell storm that had turned into.*

So many hell storms. Thirty years in the military, all but three of them in Special Forces. He had been there that August day at Fort Bragg in 1961 when President Kennedy handed Colonel Donovan the reins. After that, it was war, both preparing for it and fighting it. Vietnam: He'd served so much time in Southeast Asia the army actually moved his young family to Thailand so he could visit them every couple months when he cycled out for debriefings.

It had all been war, it seemed. Cambodia, Laos, Chile, Panama, Afghanistan, El Salvador, Chechnya, Philippines, Colombia. The countries ran together sometimes in an endless swirl of police actions, invasions, insurgency suppressions, and peacekeeping missions. "Domino games," he called them. Always somebody else's.

No matter. The mission remained the same: protect America from all threats foreign and domestic. Communism, terrorism, hedonism, don't-give-a-damnism, whatever they called it at the Pentagon, he knew the truth. What kept America free and secure was a fundamental belief in the one Lord and savior Jesus Christ. The Jews and Muslims and the rest of the nonbelievers would rot in hell with all those who doubted.

Soldier, spy, or savior, Colonel Buck Ellis had devoted his life to making that so.

"Door breach on one," he called out.

Two men in black Nomex flight suits and body armor hugged the wall, MP-5 submachine guns trained on a door. Ellis had affixed a C-4 "slap charge" just below the knob, simulating what the unit's explosives expert would have done in a full-team entry.

"Stand by, I have control."

Control? he wondered. *What man ever has control?* Only Yahweh, the one true and almighty God had any power in this world. Only Yahweh had delivered him from an impossible youth to a military career of great distinction. Only Yahweh had shown him the power of faith, the one way. Only Yahweh had led him to a life worth fighting for.

"Five . . . four . . . three . . . two . . . BOOM!"

Ellis touched off the charge, tossing the door like a corn husk in a hurricane. The two men rode the overpressure through a cloud of smoke, entered, and ran their assigned routes.

"Two steps in, two steps off the wall," Ellis had told them during classroom instruction. "Get through the door in a hurry. Avoid the 'vertical coffin.' Crisscross to confuse anyone not injured in the initial blast. Key on weapons. Multiple shots on every target."

He'd become quite a legend within the community. During the past decade, the Homestead had grown from a small facility with just two instructors into a nationally recognized training facility with uniformed weapons experts, bunkhouses, two helicopters, a mile-long racetrack, and shooting ranges capable of handling anything short of ICBMs.

"Even got a gift shop," his aunt had proudly said the one and only time she visited, years after that mean old alcoholic husband of hers had disappeared without a trace.

Pop, pop, brrrrrrrp, pop . . .

Ellis followed his students into the House of Horrors, watching over them as they moved, making mental notes that he would use later to make them better warriors. That was the point, after all — to teach these students the fine art of war.

Close-quarter battle — CQB — this afternoon, tactical handgunning tomorrow, unstable platform shooting the next day. Each basic five-day course included the essentials of small-unit tactical maneuvers. Anything more than that required a letter from some law enforcement agency and a larger check.

"Clear!"

"Clear!"

The two shooters finished their assigned routes and lowered their muzzles just enough to show they were done. Ellis had taught them to cover their targets until God had finished sorting the dead. These two seemed to understand his point.

"Strong shooting," Ellis called out. He removed his ear protection but left his Oakley sunglasses in place. "Smooth movement through the breach, clear communication." He checked his stopwatch. "Seven seconds to the hot zone. No friendlies down. Good work, fellas."

The two men ducked quickly out the door. They knew Ellis ran an all-business range. No high fives or self-congratulation allowed.

"Colonel, you in here?" someone called out. Ellis knew the voice.

"Back bedroom," he responded. Elijah had worked for him since Kuwait. The former captain had risen quickly in the Homestead's affairs, from overseeing tactical operations to marrying Ellis's oldest daughter.

"Coming in!" Elijah yelled. It was standard practice in the House of Horrors to announce one's unexpected appearance.

"News?" the colonel asked. He couldn't imagine any other reason for his son-in-law to lay down his other responsibilities.

"News of Caleb," Elijah said. He looked relieved. "He's been shot. The other two killed."

Ellis hung his head.

"How? That wasn't the plan."

"Well, the plan apparently changed," Elijah told him. "Caleb lost an eye. Says he's OK to travel."

Ellis thought for a moment.

"That means a delay on the next phase," he said. "How badly will that hurt us?"

"Not a problem, Colonel." His son-in-law shook his head. "We built a certain amount of flexibility into the timetable anyway. It's more important that we get Caleb back here in one piece than it is to rush things along."

"Right," Ellis said. He pushed past the news bearer, headed back out to his students. "See to it that we do. It would be a flying shame to jade things this early in the process."

■

"AFTER FURTHER DISCUSSIONS, I have decided to hold off on invoking all of the contemplation of government protocols until we get a better handle on things," the president said. He strode into the Oval Office with all the authority his beleaguered mind could muster.

"But, Mr. President . . . ," Havelock began, not daring to point out that the president meant *continuity* of government protocols, "these provisions were put in place specifically to ensure . . ."

"Darn it, I know why they were put in place!" he yelled. All eyes turned toward Beechum, clearly the force behind this sudden change in tack. Havelock, the press secretary, the president's chief of staff, and Alred had been joined, now, by the secretaries of defense and state.

"Flying helicopters in this weather would put us in more danger than these terrorists," Beechum said in a firm voice. "Besides, I doubt . . ."

"I don't have time to argue," Venable said, returning to his podium. Even through the fatigue he knew better than to let them think Beechum had coerced this decision. "We'll reassess once the storm clears. What's the latest?"

"Saudis, Mr. President," the secretary of defense barked out. "Let's get right down to the problem at hand. The FBI has found compelling evidence that Prince Abdullah, a potential heir to the House of Saud, has channeled significant amounts of money into accounts used by suspected fundamentalists here in the U.S."

"Where?" the president asked. "I want names, locations, dates, amounts."

His mind seemed to flow quickly all of a sudden, leading everyone in the room to believe his "contemplation" reference had been a mere Freudian slip.

"Atlanta, Los Angeles, Miami, New York, and DC," Alred spoke up. He had the information on a briefing paper but never even glanced at it. "Financial transfers from accounts attributable solely to him. All transactions came in ninety-five- to ninety-nine-hundred-dollar increments, thereby avoiding mandatory disclosure regulations. We have tracked eleven transfers so far — a grand total of one hundred six thousand seven hundred dollars. Movement began three weeks ago. The most recent occurred last Tuesday."

Venable looked impressed. Beechum too.

"Richard?" Venable asked, turning to his secretary of state, Richard Crabb.

"I wouldn't have believed this had I not seen the transactions myself," said the former ambassador to the United Nations. Venable had picked him for his level head and conciliatory nature. After the last administration, he had hoped that his White House would extend a hand of goodwill to the rest of the world.

"Despite our religious differences, they've been one of our strongest allies in the Middle East. I mean, haven't they? It certainly seemed like that based on what I saw on the news and read in the papers." Venable threw his hands up in the air. "I mean, you've had the briefings on this. What do you think?"

"I think the Saudis have always played us for personal gain," Beechum said. Of all the people in the Oval Office, she knew the most about the House of Saud. "Until the Riyadh bombings two years ago, they always dealt to us from the bottom of the deck, trying to placate our intelligence services without antagonizing their Middle Eastern allies. They talk a good game against al Qaeda, but there's no denying their sponsorship of pro-Palestinian groups: Hezbollah, the Al-Aksa Brigades, PIJ. Who's to say some of that money hasn't slipped into pockets of people who mean us harm?"

Everyone nodded.

"Why haven't we taken a stronger position with them?" Venable asked.

"Oil," Havelock said. "Why else?"

They all shook their heads until Beechum spoke up again.

"Don't get too cynical, gentlemen," she said. "Taking shots like that may work at fund-raisers and stump speeches, but the reality is undeniable: oil represents a way of life in this country. We may be the most powerful nation in the world, but it's the Saudis who fuel our engines. Energy, manufacturing, transportation . . . hell, you want to heat your house, brush your teeth, or go out for groceries, you got a Saudi to thank."

"Why now?" Venable asked. "Why are they backing terrorist attacks on this country? They have to know we can track their money. Surely they're that smart."

Beechum again.

"It's not that simple," she said. "The Saudi royal family is as dysfunctional as it is large. Too many profligate princes, too little money. There's power at stake, a sense among the ruling class that they'd better stake their claim now while they still can."

More nods.

"Look at the outrage over Jordan Mitchell selling them those Quantis phones," Havelock interjected. "You've got to admit that they take one helluva beating in the media over here. And they're scared. I've seen several intercepts suggesting that the Crown Prince himself fears that this administration has turned against them."

"Maybe there's a good reason for that," the president thought out loud. "I'll tell you what, I'm not going to stand around while they shoot down commercial aircraft!"

"Wait a minute," Alred cautioned. "We have a list of money transfers. I don't mean to imply for a second that we can tie anyone in the Saudi royal family to these specific acts of terrorism. This is an investigation, not an indictment."

"And we all know that where there's smoke, there's fire," Venable said, rubbing his itching eyes. "I want to know the minute you find something, understand?"

He walked toward the door, mumbling.

"Why the heck can't we get a pot of coffee in here? Is that too much to ask for the leader of the free world?"

He disappeared into the West Wing calling out, "Can't someone get me a goldarned cup of coffee?"

■

"SIERRA ONE TO TOC, we have movement in White Bravo Three," Lottspeich spoke into his radio. He and Jeremy lay behind a parapet, looking down through a storm drain.

"Wish we could tell them what the hell that movement might be,"

Jeremy complained. "This goddamned snow is dicking up every-thing."

More than two feet had fallen since the storm began, and the skies showed no signs of reprieve. All the HRT snipers could see through the thick flakes was five multipane windows on the second story of a building across the street. Frost had obscured all but plate-sized openings, blurred by refracted light from incandescent bulbs inside.

"You got any more lens paper?" Lottspeich asked, trying to defog the front lens of his 40x spotting scope. "I can't keep this damned thing clear."

Jeremy reached under a poncho and rummaged around until he found a pack of the nonabrasive paper.

"That's all I got," he said. "I hope they decide to take these ass-holes down in a hurry. I'm shaking like a dog shitting razor blades."

Lottspeich laughed.

"I'd say you might get your wish."

He pointed off to their left, at a convoy of black SUVs. The assault force was moving in to prestage for the hit.

"Probably playing cards and polishing up their boots, complain-ing about having to run all the way to the front door," Lottspeich groused. "Did I miss something when they decided we were going to be snipers? I mean, did anybody tell us up front that this lying-in-wait business really sucked?"

Both men had learned quickly that sniping was not the glam-orous, door-kicking hostage rescue business depicted in the HRT poster. This was a grueling art defined by discipline, attention to de-tail, and opportunity along the tiniest of margins. Sniper school taught men how to kill others at great distances without getting killed themselves. Staying miserable just came with the trade.

"You guys still bitching?"

A man crawled up behind them.

"Jesus," Lottspeich said. "Sneaking up on us is gonna get you killed."

"Jesus as in 'Hi, Jesus, it's nice to see you again' or 'Jesus Christ you scared the hell out of me?'" the man said.

Jesús Smith, their former Xray team leader had never known ex-actly how to respond to various pronunciations of his name. Most guys used the hard *J*, New Testament version, but he never knew if they were using his name in sport or the Lord's name in vain.

"As in 'Oh, Jesus, why is it that every time you show up I end up hating myself in the morning?'" Jeremy smiled, but both men knew he wasn't kidding.

"Hey, I'm a suit now, remember? I don't shine shoes anymore."

Jesús had been promoted to supervisor and moved to the FBI/ CIA Terrorist Threat Integration Center. Jeremy hadn't seen his former partner and team leader in more than six months.

"Right," Lottspeich grumbled. "You'd give your left nut to be out here shivering yourself dizzy like the rest of us."

"Yeah." He slapped Lottspeich's leg. "Hey, Jeremy, can I talk to you for a minute?"

His tone changed. He hadn't come to chat.

"Told you," Jeremy said, elbowing his current partner.

"Hurry back, boys," Lottspeich said, rubbing condensation off the lens of his spotting scope. "People are starting to talk."

VII

Wednesday, 16 February
05:05 GMT
Harvey Point Defense Testing Activity, Hertford, North Carolina

JEREMY TURNED LEFT off New Hope Road just after midnight, trying to decide whether or not to call home. It had taken him a little more than an hour to drive the sixty-one miles from Norfolk, Virginia, to Albemarle County, North Carolina — more than enough time to ponder events that had once again turned his life upside down.

"You have been selected for a new assignment," Jesús had told him just hours earlier. "A Group Two undercover op relative to the Irian Jaya mission."

How the two related, the former HRT team leader didn't say. But that seemed typical of assignments Jeremy had received since joining HRT. Life there felt like an ill-defined, undulating, often nonsensical series of impromptu journeys to places that were never explained with people he'd never get to know.

"You'll be gone for several weeks," Jesús had said, "but this is a highly classified mission. You can't say anything to Caroline, of course. She'll understand."

Understand my ass, Jeremy thought, driving past a sign that read WELCOME TO HISTORIC HERTFORD, NORTH CAROLINA. Caroline had put up with a year of unexplained disappearances followed by unexplainable reunions. She had always been a strong and loving wife, but every relationship had its breaking point. He had pushed this one to where it was starting to crack.

That's it up there on the right, Jeremy told himself, shaking off daydreams of Caroline and the three little kids who were growing up without him. He pulled up to a normal-enough-looking checkpoint. This was a military installation, after all — at least on the surface. Though he had never visited Harvey Point, other guys on the team had talked about the secret facility the way they talked about Camp Peary.

"The Point," as they called it, occupied the easternmost portion of Perquimans County township, a stubby thumb jutting out into the Albemarle Sound. Named for one of North Carolina's first governors, the Harvey Point Defense Testing Activity served as a paramilitary training center for second-stage CIA officers, high-risk political operatives, and some of history's most secretive groups. Yasser Arafat's security detail had trained here, as had Russian intelligence agents, Cuban Bay of Pigs insurgents, and numerous other organizations Middle America might not want to know about.

Guys on the team had told Jeremy not to bother asking for directions. This shy neighbor provided much-needed jobs and financial support to the backwater village. Besides, there was a war on. All curious visitors could expect to hear from Hertford residents was "What point?"

Jeremy pulled up to a drive-in-style talk box, where a stoic voice asked him to dim his headlights, turn off any portable electronic devices, and identify himself. *So much for a call home.*

"Jeremy Waller. FBI," the HRT sniper announced at the gate. He dimmed his lights but could see clear as day beneath the scouring wash of mercury vapor lamps. A modern-looking guardhouse stood at the other side of a heavy steel trap-gate. Three men in black SWAT gear waited nearby, M-4 assault weapons at ready arms. Another man held a regal-looking German shepherd on a short tether.

"Present your ID to the camera, sir," an authoritative voice commanded. Jeremy held up his credentials, and after a few moments, the gate dropped. He was directed to a second building, where he presented his ID again and then signed mandatory nondisclosure forms. They took his cell phone and handed him a badge, a map, and a copy of base security protocols.

"Do you want my gun, too?" Jeremy asked, but one of the guards just laughed.

"Not as long as you HRT guys are as good as you say you are," he said. "You've been billeted in bachelor officer's quarters. Just follow the map and check in at the front desk. Wear your visitor's pass at all times, observe posted speed limits, and have a nice day."

Jeremy nodded and did as he was told. It had been a long trip, and the only thing in the world he wanted at that point was a flat place to lie.

SIRAD STEPPED INTO an empty elevator and pressed seventeen. Though virtually everyone in the building had gone home for the night, she had assembled a cyber SWAT team of sorts to try to get to the bottom of what Jordan Mitchell assured her could mean the end of Quantis. The team of mathematicians, programmers, technicians, and engineers had already set up shop in the company's security center, and she looked forward to a long night among their eccentricities.

Soon after starting down from twenty-six, the elevator stopped.

"Dammit," she mumbled under her breath. Only one person would get on at twenty-four this time of night. It had to be Hamid.

"Mind if I get in?" he asked.

Sirad offered a polite smile and shook her head as he stepped aboard. The handsome Iranian-American oversaw Borders Atlantic's financial operations, but she had known him on a whole different level. Sirad's position at Borders Atlantic had always presented unique problems, and Hamid, unfortunately, had fallen among them.

"Look, Hamid," she said. "It's been a year. Are you ever going to let this pass?"

"How do you get over losing the love of your life?" he asked. "Does anyone ever get over that kind of betrayal?" He provided a smile that looked brave yet tortured.

"Please. We've been over this."

Hamid reached out and hit every button between them and the seventeenth floor, delaying their descent.

"You've been over this," he argued. "And only to tell me I wouldn't understand."

"You know I have work to do," she said. "This is not the time or place to be having this discussion."

Sirad reached into her purse for a lip gloss.

"Always work," he lamented. "I've never known a person so incapable of love for anything but a career."

The elevator finally stopped on seventeen, and Sirad stepped off without responding. Hamid followed.

"Evening, Ms. Malneaux, Mr. . . ." the door minder started to say, but Hamid grabbed Sirad's arm and turned her toward him.

"When is the right place and the right time?" he asked. "All I ever wanted to know was why."

Sirad cocked her head a bit, then pulled her arm from his hand. She looked genuinely puzzled. *What is it about the male ego that makes men so vulnerable to rejection?* she wondered. *Love is just something victims use to justify underlying weakness. Sex is the only truly honest and mutually beneficial element in any lasting relationship. Why can't I find a man who understands and accepts that?*

"Are you OK, Ms. Malneaux?" the minder asked. Like everyone else at Borders Atlantic, he would have done just about anything to curry favor with this extraordinary beauty.

"Everything is just fine," she said, shining a glossy smile while holding Hamid's stare. "But could you be a dear and card me in? I seem to have forgotten my badge."

The door clicked open as the magnetic dead bolts disengaged. Sirad turned away from the jilted lover and walked off ahead of him into what she knew would be a long night full of even less-pleasant engagements.

■

THE VICE PRESIDENT was sound asleep on the couch in her Old Executive Office Building suite when a Secret Service agent alerted her to a call from the Oval Office. The president had requested an emergency briefing in the Situation Room, he said. The

FBI had come up with new information that could impact national security, and further discussion simply couldn't wait until morning.

Beechum splashed water on her face, brushed out her hair, and hurried into James's office, where she found him sleeping under an overcoat beside his desk.

Forty-four hours, she thought, leading the Secret Service caravan on a speed walk through a tunnel to the West Wing. *Two days the president has been working without sleep. How long can he function before fatigue causes serious lapses in judgment?*

"All right, I'm here," she announced, storming into the crowded and increasingly foul-smelling SITROOM. "What's so damned important that we couldn't wait to consider it in the morning with clearer heads?"

No one said a word at first. Havelock turned toward the secretary of defense, who looked to CIA director Vick, who deferred to Alred.

"Body count," the president answered finally.

"Body count?" she repeated. "What do you mean, body count?"

"The body count is up to three thousand one hundred and twenty-seven," Andrea Chase said. "The cable channels are running it nonstop. It's official: we've exceeded the number of people killed on 9/11."

Beechum raised her eyes and let out a coughlike laugh.

"That's what we're here at two o'clock in the morning to discuss?" she asked.

"This is a big number," Venable said. "The American people are going to wake up in a few hours, and we need to be ready with a response. Andrea, why don't you break it down for us."

"One thousand seventeen killed in the three plane crashes — about eighty percent of them foreign nationals," the chief of staff said. "Two thousand one hundred and ten in the three bombings; almost eighty-five percent Americans. You want individual counts by crisis site?"

"No, no . . . that's quite sufficient." The president sighed. He stood with his hands in his pockets. The vast amount of coffee he had consumed in the past two days made him tremble so badly, it embarrassed him.

"What can we say about the investigation?" Beechum asked. The fact that they would all lose a night of crucial sleep for something like this seemed too much to deal with at this point.

"As you know," Alred answered, "we took down what we believed to be a safe house in Anacostia earlier this evening."

"Believed to be?" Havelock asked accusingly. Personality clashes had begun to show.

"We're still exploiting documents and hard drives that we recovered on-scene," Alred continued, "but it looks like a bit of a dry hole at this point."

"What?" Venable barked. "You said they were terrorists. You said they were . . ."

"We said they were suspects," the FBI director snipped. At this hour, everyone felt more than a little raw. "Unfortunately, what we thought was a bomb-making operation turned out to be a credit card scam."

"Oh, for Chrisakes!" Havelock tossed his pen onto the table in what everyone judged just a bit too much theater.

"This group appears to have had strong ties to radical mosques in Detroit, Los Angeles, and New York," Alred explained, "but it turns out that they were just trying to steal money. This was all about trying to rip off Muslims, not avenge them."

No one said a word.

■

JEREMY AWOKE TO a ringing phone. The early morning skies remained dark through polyester shades. Sky-blue wallpaper, simulated wood grain, and pine picture frames lent the room a certain trailer-park feel. The exhausted traveler thought for a moment that he was floating in some mildly pleasant dream, but then the phone rang again, and he reached to answer.

"Hello?" he asked on reflex. Jeremy had no earthly idea where he was.

"Mr. Waller?" someone asked. Male voice. Official.

"Yes."

"Good morning, sir, this is Mr. Taylor. The base commander asked me to give you a call and brief you on today's schedule."

"Right," Jeremy answered. He propped himself up on one elbow and reached for a pen and paper. "Yeah, go ahead."

"We've got an all hands meeting in fifteen minutes at building twelve seventeen. We've got an EEI briefing set for zero-four-hundred, a walk-through at zero-six, psych workup at zero-nine, and chow at noon. Your people will be here at fourteen hundred for a UC ops scenario, then at seventeen hundred we're back in the simulator until the evening meal at nineteen hundred. After that, we've scheduled in some study time."

Jeremy managed to jot down the times. He'd figure out the rest once his mind flicked back on.

"Got it," he lied. The clock read 2:29. He'd slept just an hour.

"A driver will be waiting downstairs," Mr. Taylor said. "He'll take you over to the officers' mess. Coffee's strong, black, and hot. You sound like you could use some."

■

SIRAD WALKED DOWN a hallway flanked on both sides by break-out rooms, technology pods, and secure compartmented information facilities. Jordan Mitchell had hired most of the seventeenth floor's top administrators away from military intelligence agencies, and they had designed the Rabbit Hole by combining the best aspects of NSA, CIA, and DIA operations.

"Are we going to be able to work through this?" she asked. Hamid stayed a step behind her, fuming about her actions outside, but remaining professional.

"Like you said, Sirad, there's a time and a place for everything."

"Good," she answered. "And this is neither."

The two executives turned left, into an odd-looking section of the hallway that had been lined with highly sensitive electronic sensors. Originally designed for CIA and NSA facilities, this Z-shaped "wave path" worked like an electromagnetic shower, scouring incoming workers for anything that might serve as a receiver, transmitter, or microphone. Rabbit Hole designers had shielded the seventeenth floor with lead and other acoustic buffers, but there was no point in taking chances. Tape recorders, PDAs, laptops, even the company's own encrypted Quantis cell phones, were prohibited.

"Why do I always feel like someone's trying to peek up my skirt when I walk through here?" Sirad smiled. "Good thing I wore panties today, huh?"

Hamid shook his head as they emerged at the other end of the twenty-foot hallway and stepped into a large operations center built of teak, green glass, and chrome. Television monitors lined three of the octagonal room's walls. White boards, projection screens, time line organizers, and world clocks covered two others. The rest of the space opened through smoked-glass windows into executive conference rooms.

Computer pods and cubicle work spaces covered much of the central floor space. Elaborate sound baffles hung from the ceiling, fifteen feet overhead. The floor itself was rubber.

"Project managers in Suite A!" Sirad called out.

Hamid, a numbers man at heart, counted twelve analysts in the Rabbit Hole's main chamber. There should have been twice that many.

"Where is everyone?" he asked. And then a door opened, and he knew the answer. Suite A, one of the glass-walled break-out rooms to his right, was already full. The experts Sirad would rely on for answers had apparently already gotten down to business.

"What do we have?" Sirad asked, striding into the room. A nicely dressed "watchman" closed the door behind them. "I want to start at the beginning and work our way up step by step."

"That may be difficult," Ravi said. He had already covered an expansive white board with more of his equations, marks, and drawings. "Things have changed a bit since our last meeting. The analysis indicates something a bit more troublesome than we first thought."

Sirad pulled out a chair beside an Asian man sporting a white lab coat with the name Lin embroidered over the left breast. He wore a crew cut that exposed numerous scars on his scalp, some partially obscured by his red Nike headband. A dozen other attendees had settled in behind stacks of paper and mechanical pencils. Sirad recognized none of them.

"What we seem to have is a symbiotic feed ingest," Ravi continued. He directed a laser pointer at one of his drawings and reached for a can of Fresca. "This appears to be more a surveillance effort than an actual intrusion. The people behind this seem to be casing our system, probing the armor, if you will, for chinks."

"Which means they haven't actually broken in yet?" Sirad asked.

"That's right," Ravi conceded. "It's kind of like a train robber riding alongside the money car. They are tracking the data stream, monitoring aspects of our infrastructure without actually exposing themselves as thieves."

Sirad wondered about the Wild West analogy but found that it gave her a sense of the threat.

"Well, that's good, isn't it?" she asked. "If they haven't actually made an attempt on the system, perhaps they haven't compromised our codes. Do they know we're onto them?"

"I don't think so," Ravi said. "We built hypersensitive counter-surveillance mechanisms into the Quantis conduit."

"Meaning we might have seen them before they see us?" Sirad asked.

"Precisely."

"So if they haven't broken in and they don't know we're watching them, what's the bad news?"

Ravi pointed to a thin young black man sitting directly across from Sirad. What most impressed her was not his poorly shaped Afro, his "I Can't Dunk" T-shirt, or the pencil that flipped rhythmically between his long, thin fingers. What really stood out was the intensity of his stare. Sirad actually felt a chill.

"This is a secret sharer probe." The black man spoke firmly with a refined British accent. "In any coded exchange, both the sender and receiver must have a key. With the Quantis system, however, we're talking about millions of subscribers, which requires a whole new way of looking at protocol."

"You can't give each user the key," Sirad agreed. "You have to build it into the system."

"Correct. That limits key access to a very small universe of system gatekeepers."

"How small?" Hamid asked.

"In an ideal world, one," I Can't Dunk said. "But this is not an ideal world. I'm sure that Jordan Mitchell wishes he alone could control access to Quantis, but that's just not possible. If something happened to him, the system would eventually die, suffocated within its own hermetically sealed skin."

Sirad held up her hand like a grade-schooler. This man was right, of course: Jordan Mitchell had entrusted three others with portions of the key. She was one of them.

"So you diversify," she said. "You divide the secret into sections and share it among a small group of principals."

"That's it, isn't it?" the Afro-clad scientist affirmed. "But how do you keep them from collaborating against you?"

He stood up, walked to Ravi's white board, and began to draw.

"Let's call it the 'Rabbit Hole paradox.'"

The man drew a crude representation of the seventeenth floor facility's front door.

"Let's say access to this room is based on a secret word instead of a cipher lock. And let's say you want to prove to the security guard that you know that secret word without actually telling him what it is."

Sirad nodded. She had just faced a similar situation. If not for her stunning smile, she might not have gotten in without her badge.

"What you need is a zero knowledge, interactive proof protocol that will show the security guard that you know the word without actually disclosing it. You send him into a control room where he can watch on CCTV but cannot hear. You simply call out the code word, the door opens, and in you go. He sees this and accepts the fact that you know the code."

"What if I simply guess the proper word?" Sirad asked. "Or what if someone opens it from the other side without the guard seeing?"

"Precisely. There are any number of ways you could defeat a system like this. So you set up enough doors and enough repetitions that the tester can feel confident of a very small statistical likelihood for folderol."

Hamid and Sirad understood at the same moment.

"This is someone from inside the company?" Hamid asked.

"As one who deals in probability and statistical likelihood, I would have to assume that, yes," Ravi said.

Sirad thought hard about what to say next.

"That puts us in a very tough position, doesn't it?" she asked.

"And you also have to consider the possibility that one aspect of the key has simply been stolen," Ravi added.

Sirad looked around the room. These faces were all new to her. She needed their expertise, but whom could she trust?

"Rather sticky, isn't it?" the I Can't Dunk man said. "And now you see the first theorem of secrecy: in a closed system, the universe of principals is inversely square to the probability of compromise."

"The toughest thing about secrets," Ravi explained, "is deciding who gets to keep them."

■

A POLITE IF firm E-5 met Jeremy downstairs and motioned him into a blue Navy van.

"Welcome to the Point," he said. A bright gold-capped tooth punctuated his broad smile. "First time down here?"

"Yes." Jeremy rubbed sleep out of his eyes. He hated the flat gray reality that followed overseas gigs, when your mind gives up its refusal to sleep and suddenly demands it.

After a quick cup of coffee and a ride to building 1217, Jeremy thanked the sergeant and climbed out of the van in front of what looked like a western European row house. An air force major met him with a handshake.

"Morning," the perfectly creased officer greeted his guest. He offered no name. "Sleep well?"

"Slept fine, sir," Jeremy lied again. He tried to concentrate on pleasantries, but the surroundings distracted him to the point of mention.

"You'll have to forgive me, Major," Jeremy said. The driver had dropped him off at the edge of what looked like a massive Hollywood studio lot. "But I didn't get much of a briefing before coming down. Where the hell are we?"

The major started laughing as if it were the funniest thing he'd ever heard.

"Welcome to MOUT facility, Harvey Point," he said. "Military Operations Urban Terrain. Sixteen square blocks of any damned city in the world. This morning's briefing will be in Munich. Head three blocks down Menkestrasse and you'll find yourself in a little Basque village called Guillermo. London's a couple blocks that way. We can design, engineer, and rough out virtually any interior you

can imagine within twelve hours. Even less time in simulation —
that's primarily where you'll do most of your preparation."

"You build fake cities?"

"Just blocks, really, and it depends on what you call fake. Come
on up and I'll show you."

He led Jeremy inside the row house, up an elevator, and into an
open room filled with closed circuit television monitors, recording
equipment, giant wall maps, computers, and blueprints. Digital
clocks on the wall covered every time zone on earth, with Green-
wich perched in the middle and labeled ZULU.

A big sign on the wall read, THERE'S NO BUSINESS LIKE SHOW
BUSINESS.

"Welcome to postproduction," the major said. "We've got monitoring capability that allows us to stage up to four scenarios simultaneously. That's just on-property. We've got about ten thousand
acres of woodland and rural training grounds, too, but that's run
from a separate facility."

"Scenarios for what?" Jeremy asked. He immediately regretted
the question. The major gave him the same look Jesús had during
the Yemen mission. Then he started laughing. "Oh, right . . . good
one. You Agency guys are always so big on your opsec."

Agency guys? Jeremy thought.

"You ready to get started?"

Jeremy shrugged his shoulders. He remembered one of the questions on the Minnesota Multiphasic Personality Inventory HRT had
given him during selection. "Have you ever read *Alice in Wonderland?*" it asked. Suddenly it made perfect sense. Life on the wet side
was a whole lot like chasing Alice.

"Sure," Jeremy replied. "Lead the way."

The major took him to a warehouse just outside "London." Inside, he met four men, all white and all between the ages of thirty
and fifty.

John, who offered no last name, said he was a theologian at the
Yale Divinity School. Paul introduced himself to be a clinical psychologist from Johns Hopkins. George claimed he was an army intelligence analyst assigned to Boling Air Force Base. Fred offered
no background but promised to give Jeremy a thorough rundown
on telltale signs of chemical and biological weapon production.

"I'm not going to try and make you a molecular biologist," he said. "Just want to teach you the subtle differences between phosphate-based fertilizer and WMD nerve agents. We might cook us up a little beer in the process, too."

Hollywood back lots? Postproduction facilities? Cooking beer? Jeremy wondered to himself. All Jesús had told him was that he was going on a little trip.

"I'm Jeremy," Waller said. "I work for the Justice Department."

"Good cover." John chuckled. "First time I've heard that one."

■

BEECHUM STOOD AT the end of the table, obviously shocked. The president of the United States, if she had heard him correctly, had just proposed taking military action against a long-standing Middle Eastern ally.

"You cannot launch a preemptive strike against the Saudis based on stereotypes and speculation!" she exclaimed.

Whether it was the hour, the location, or the simple lack of reason on the president's part, she felt compelled to intervene.

"We have credible and actionable intelligence here, Elizabeth," the president shot back. "I know you feel that your time on the Senate Intelligence Committee gives you some kind of cloak-and-dagger insight, but you're not in the Senate anymore. You work for me, and this president smells Saudi."

"We do have some positive developments," Havelock said, trying to ease the tension. "The NSA has intercepted four separate openline communications that you might find interesting."

Havelock held out his hand, and Vick passed him a half-inch-thick stack of overhear transcripts.

"These are more than casual conversations," he said, waving the documents in the air. "Specific times, dates, locations. Two regional government ministers talking with what we believe are operatives inside the United States. The calls were on Quantis phones, but we are trying to trace them."

"The NSA can't track domestic calls," Beechum objected. "That's illegal."

"So is blowing up Wal-Mart!" Havelock bellowed. The stress had apparently begun to wear on him too.

"What do you mean we can't track domestic calls?" the president asked. "Why not?"

"Something called the Fourth Amendment to the United States Constitution," the vice president told him. "The NSA surveys international calls indiscriminately, because noncitizens are not protected against unreasonable search and seizure. If we want a wire intercept in-CONUS, we either obtain a Title III warrant or FISA authorization."

Venable looked confused.

"This is war, Mr. President," Havelock said. Vick seemed to agree. Alred shook his head and sighed.

"I've got to agree, David," the secretary of defense joined in. "If the Saudis are financing terrorist operations against U.S. civilian targets, I don't see how listening to their phone calls is going to violate anyone's constitutional rights."

"Alred?" the president asked. He had come to rely heavily on the FBI director's judgment.

"That's a question for DOJ lawyers," he said. "Quite frankly, sir, I think the bigger issue is trying to stop the next round of attacks."

"Yes," Venable agreed. "Good point. I don't want to hear any more of these legal conundrums, understood? If there is an issue for general counsel, straighten it out before it crosses my desk . . . my podium . . . before I . . ."

The president seemed to drift from his train of thought.

"What about the issue of taking preemptive military action against the Saudis?" the secretary of defense asked. "You'll forgive an old war horse for saying so, Mr. President, but I'd rather exercise a little muscle now than pull out another truckload of body bags later."

"Muscle?" Beechum asked. She had tried to remain silent during the meeting but really didn't like what he was suggesting. "Saudi Arabia is a longtime ally — strategic and financial. They control OPEC. If we try any muscle flexing with them, we're going to be paying seven bucks a gallon for gas."

"Richard?" the president asked. Richard Crabb, his secretary of state, had said nothing to this point.

"By definition I advocate diplomacy," he said. "The options as I see them are to go public with intelligence, appeal to the UN Security Council, launch special operations attacks against specific tar-gets, or simply to offer the Saudis the same courtesy we'd hope for: if we have enough evidence to flex muscle, as you call it, we cer-tainly must have enough evidence to confront the ambassador. Has it occurred to anyone that the Crown Prince may be as surprised and outraged as we are?"

"That's a darned good point," the president agreed. He seemed to swell up with optimism again. "Objections?"

Havelock looked at Vick, who looked at the secretary of defense, but no one spoke out.

"Good!" Venable exclaimed. "Make the call."

"It's three in the morning," Havelock pointed out.

"Damn the hour, man," came the response. "The ambassador is a practical man. I'm sure he's going to prefer an early morning face-to-face more than war."

■

JEREMY'S WORLD HAD spun again. First, and most important, he had learned that his mission was to infiltrate a little-known shadow arm of the Christian Identity Movement called the Phineas Priesthood.

Small, violent, and diffuse, the Phineas Priesthood had operated for more than a decade under an organizational rubric known as "leaderless resistance." With no formal membership or organiza-tion, true believers gained priest status by committing Phineas "acts" — violent attacks against a society they saw as corrupt and morally bereft. Most targets were nonwhite, but they drew no race distinctions when it came to homosexuals, mixed marriages, and abortion. The group's inherent lack of structure had prevented law enforcement from penetrating its cells, but it had also restricted mission effectiveness.

Until now.

Recent intelligence suggested that a former Special Forces colonel named Ellis had brought a number of these domestic ter-rorists together and trained them at a central Texas ranch called the Homestead. Jeremy knew of the place, ironically, because several HRT snipers had attended schools there.

The job sounded simple though not very easy. Jeremy had to infiltrate the group by registering as a student and then convincing Ellis that he was in fact a Phineas priest. Because there was no formal membership, anyone could claim that status, but Jeremy would have to demonstrate provenance: proof of some act of violence committed within the past few years. The only problem was that a real priest may already have listed the crime in question on his own curriculum vitae.

From what Jeremy had seen during the day's intelligence briefings, the slightest misstep could lead to a very violent and sudden end to this operation. And his life.

"Are you familiar with the program?" the latest in a series of briefers asked.

Jeremy actually recognized the man as a supervisor with the FBI's Undercover Safeguard Unit back in Quantico. Sergei Andropov had carved himself a place in the Bureau's history books by infiltrating the Russian mob in New York, but not without cost. He'd lost his left hand to a "fixer's" knife just prior to taking the whole thing down. And he'd become addicted to heroin. Undercover work definitely had a downside.

"Not really," Jeremy said. His overseas missions had come with no formal training.

"Well, then we've got twenty-four hours to whip you into shape," he said, clinging to the remnants of a Gorki accent. "First we get settled into your new identity."

Andropov pulled a manila folder out of an old Samsonite briefcase — the kind Jeremy had seen Hoover-era veterans carrying in his first office.

"Your new Lambda Chi name is Jeremy Walker." The big Russian laughed at the reference to his favorite American movie.

"Walker? Isn't that a little close to home?"

"Supposed to be. It is better to stick with a name close to yours in case someone recognizes you and calls it out in a public place," Andropov advised. "Is always best to stick close to the truth. That way you don't trip up so easy."

Andropov handed Jeremy a folder that held details of his new identity.

"What about this Colonel Ellis and his group?" Jeremy asked, flipping through the dossier. "I'm going to need some background on these Phineas priests, as well as their . . ."

"All in good time," Andropov said. "For now you study your own life. After that, we will concentrate on others."

VIII

Wednesday, 16 February
10:05 GMT
Jefferson Room, The White House

THE SAUDI AMBASSADOR arrived in a black Town Car with diplomatic plates. Two uniformed Secret Service officers escorted him into a formal sitting room where the president waited in an overstuffed wing chair, sipping a glass of ice water.

"Mr. Ambassador," Venable said. He stood before realizing his shoes were undone. He had taken them off to ease the pain in his overworked feet and forgotten to retie them. "Nice of you to come over at such an early hour."

The ambassador shook Venable's hand and accepted a seat beside him. A pleasant wood fire glowed in a Rumford fireplace, but neither man felt cozy.

"I must assume something dire," the ambassador said. He had attended Harvard, undergraduate, then Oxford. Some would argue that his English surpassed the president's.

"Dire." The president knelt forward to tie his shoes. "*Dire* might be the right word, actually."

"Does this involve the terror attacks? Because the Crown Prince has asked me to convey our sympathies and assure the complete cooperation of my . . ."

"I've been up since this whole nightmare began," the president blurted out. "I've been president of the United States for three weeks. Three weeks."

He stood up and walked around behind his chair. The ambassador had to crane his neck unnaturally to look him in the eye.

"Yes," the Saudi said, trying to understand the president's subtext. "I know this."

"Then you know that the people behind these attacks are trying to play on my inexperience, perhaps to expose me as vulnerable. They would try to take advantage of the fact that I haven't been in office long enough to feel fully in control of our armed forces, that I might be ill prepared to fulfill my duties as commander in chief."

"That's certainly a possibility, I suppose," the ambassador conceded. He looked genuinely concerned. "I hadn't thought that myself."

"No, of course not," Venable agreed, somewhat facetiously. "You're a diplomat. A student of tact and protocol."

"Why have you asked me here, sir?" the ambassador inquired. As a diplomat, he felt well tuned to inflection.

Venable walked to the fireplace and tossed a birch log into the blaze. The bark caught immediately with sparks and a hiss.

"This government has solid evidence that interests inside your government have channeled money into the United States with the specific purpose of funding terror."

Venable's advisors had admonished him to broach the subject carefully, but Americans had died in these cowardly attacks. It was time for action.

"That's preposterous," the ambassador said. He looked confused, as if the hour were playing tricks on someone's mind — either his or the president's. "Saudi Arabia is your closest Arab ally. You cannot seriously imagine that . . ."

"We have concrete evidence: wire transfers, phone transcripts, corroborating data from several different investigations. We even have one of the men responsible for shooting down the airliner in Los Angeles — a Saudi. He is being interrogated as we speak."

The ambassador did not know what to say.

"I asked you here to relay a message to your government," President Venable announced. "You will have three days to provide us the names of those responsible for these terrorist crimes. We demand full disclosure of any threatening parties still inside the United States. We demand immediate cessation of financial support for terrorists. And we demand complete cooperation in an investigation to determine who in your government might have knowledge of these crimes."

Venable pounded the back of the chair, but his drama seemed lost on the ambassador, who just sat there gazing blindly into the fire.

"I d-don't know w-what to say," the Saudi stammered. "This is absolutely outrageous. Are you threatening us?"

"Threatening you? Threatening you!" Venable's voice rose. "No, I'm not threatening you, but if my country suffers so much as a falafel fart, you are going to understand the full breadth of my commitment!"

The fire crackled. The ambassador rose.

"I'm sorry that our first meeting couldn't have been more conciliatory," he said. "My government had great hopes for your administration."

The ambassador started toward the door, then remembered himself.

"Forgive my rudeness," he said, reaching out to shake the president's hand. Venable held tightly the damask back of his chair.

"You just relay my thoughts to the prince," Venable growled. "I think this situation has already moved past courtesy."

■

"*THERE ARE THOSE who obey God's law and those who don't. Those who obey are the Lawful. Those who disobey are outlawed by God. God has specified the outlaw's punishment.*"

Colonel Ellis sat in a leather-padded morris chair and read by the light of a wrought-iron floor lamp. The mounted heads of exotic game stared down at him — ibex, bork, water buffalo, polar bear, lynx — more than a dozen rare, even endangered, species from around the world. Knotty-pine paneling gave the room a stolid prairie-manor feel.

He held a worn hardback and read without glasses. The words

danced in his mind, sharp and clear to eyes that had seen more than most would believe.

Vigilantes of Christendom, by Richard Kelly Hoskins, had always struck him as a well-intentioned though limited treatment of fact. Books like it and *The Turner Diaries,* by William L. Pierce, were held up to ridicule by those who poorly understood the underlying passion of Christ's remaining disciples. To the true believers who served this cause, however, these pages inspired hope of a better world.

Better world, Ellis thought to himself. The irony almost choked him.

For thirty years he had served his country, a patriot in search of ways to prove it. First there was Vietnam. He'd arrived in Hue-Phu Bai just after Christmas 1965, a brand-new baby lieutenant in charge of a Special Forces "spike" reconnaissance team assigned to the Military Advisory Command, Vietnam, Studies and Observation Group — better known as MAC-V-SOG. The army had only recently taken over black and covert operations from the CIA, leading Montagnard, Hoa, and Nung tribesmen against Vietcong in Laos, Cambodia, and Southern China.

The Phineas priests administer the judgment, and God rewards them with a covenant of an everlasting priesthood.

From there he moved on to the CIA's pacification program, code-named Operation Phoenix, and served under Lt. Colonel Frank Barker in 1968. Ellis was initially assigned to the Census Grievance cadre in Quang Ngai Province. Though still a Special Forces officer, Ellis reported to a CIA Special Branch advisor.

It was then that he had seen and done things he didn't think possible with MAC-V-SOG. In fact, his time in the Phoenix program had changed the way this eager young officer felt about war. He learned that infliction of terror through torture, rape, and extermination worked far better than any conventional weapons at stemming resistance. The air force could defoliate the jungles with Agent Orange and rattle the countryside with Arc Light strikes, but the enemy simply disappeared into the sprawling cave networks or melted back into rural villages, waging a guerrilla war U.S. forces were ill prepared to fight.

What worked best was degrading the enemy's will to fight.

Let the soldiers hide in tunnels, the thinking went. *We'll kill their families while they're gone. Let Ho Chi Minh preach sacrifice; we'll spread fear of rape, torture, and assassination until sacrifice becomes too horrifying to use as a political slogan.*

In July 1966, he got a visit from a man in civilian clothes. Ellis was told that his successes with MAC-V-SOG had drawn the attention of superior officers. A CIA sponsored Roles and Missions Study, he was told, had concluded that only a "pacification" effort would achieve what conventional military operations had failed to do. Run through what was called the Revolutionary Development cadre, this program sought the destruction of the Vietcong infrastructure, followed by a campaign to secure the support of the Vietnamese. Propaganda and psychological warfare were becoming the new weapons in this guerrilla war. The CIA needed foot soldiers.

Ellis bought in immediately.

First there was My Lai. Then Quang Nam Province, Phuoc Tuy, and a half dozen other places no Westerner would want to know about. Ellis worked with small teams of Montagnard hill people, coordinating a campaign of terror that reached up and down the Laotian and Cambodian borders. In the early stages, they directed their efforts against suspected Vietcong and their immediate support structure. Soon, however, the list of targets degenerated to collaborators, supporters, sympathizers, anyone who lived in a particular village. Eventually, the target barely mattered at all. Cutting off a couple dozen heads and sticking them on stakes at the entrance to villages made a statement, regardless of political affiliation.

What Ellis saw in his first months in the Phoenix program changed the way he looked at war. At America. At humanity.

The rape, the torture, the kidnapping and sheer depravity. Soldiers within his immediate command began "counting coup," an old Native American custom of taking body parts after a kill. Men wore strings of ears, tongues, fingers, and scalps like service medals. They eschewed any respect for rank, believing correctly that orders from a CIA Special Branch civilian carried the same weight as those from a four-star. The only thing that mattered was killing. It became a currency of sorts, a rank structure all its own. Those who excelled survived. Those who didn't died. Simple. Poetic.

After three years in MAC-V-SOG and another three with Phoenix, Ellis knew that he had to make a choice. Despite his time in-country, the now captain had sired three children. His wife was doing her best to raise them in a diplomatic compound in Bangkok. If he wanted to save any aspect of the last thing in the world that mattered to him, he would have to escape the jungles of Southeast Asia and learn something other than murder.

The answer had come one night in a rice paddy near map coordinates he remembered only because they were all threes.

The mission was classified, of course, like everything they did in those days. They wore black "pajamas," with special soles sewn onto their jungle boots so the footprints they left behind would resemble native sandals. They ate native food so they'd smell native. They carried American weapons because the dinks did too. No rank insignia or signs of conventional military allegiance. Ellis had two South Vietnamese Special Exploitation Service noncoms, three Nung scouts, and a Fourth Psychological Operations Group communication expert to augment his A-team regulars.

They made an air insertion into what was known as the Prairie Fire AO — one of the hottest areas of operation in Vietnam. Two Vietnamese-piloted H-34 helicopters dropped them into an area that looked more like the White Mountains of New Hampshire than a Southeast Asian jungle.

Within a couple hours, they had descended into a marshy lowland: rice paddies and rain. No moon. The only sound came from the hypnotizing patter of water splashing into more water.

One of the Nung tribesman — a tiny but vicious scalp toter named Seu — was walking point. Ellis remembered staring at a string of hairy skins around Seu's neck when the man's head suddenly disappeared from his body. Ellis had seen every kind of death and wounding, but he had never seen such a clean excision, as if the rain itself had simply dissolved it.

Then came the "Stranger" — that's what his men called the bogeyman — and the moment of accountability they all knew would one day come. None of these men knew fear anymore, but they understood reckoning.

Mortar rounds, AK rattle, the smell of sulfur, fire, spitting air, body parts splashing into the rice paddy, that silence of battle when incomprehensible violence factors down to a slightly distracting hum.

That's when Ellis found Him. Badly wounded, fighting desperately through the pain and the hopelessness and the sheer justice of dying by the sword, Ellis had felt something inside that he'd never felt before.

Faith.

He mistook it for adrenaline at first, a natural physiological reaction to imminent death. So much light, so much darkness roiling around him. Tortured faces. Blood and entrails leaching into someone else's homeland. The Stranger laughing, just farther than he could reach.

Faith.

Ellis knew he was dying, that he couldn't survive this firefight, that he would never see the wife and children he had just weeks ago decided to save. Yet something gripped him, something he had never felt before — not in his alcoholic uncle's house or the foster homes or college or even in the army. He felt filled up with something, the way he had always filled up full of rage. Only different. This time he filled up with an unmistakable sense that this would mean something someday. That he would survive. That he had other battles to wage.

When they found him, Ellis had three life-threatening wounds. His left lung had collapsed, his skull was fractured, and flesh literally hung from one thigh. The corpsman who saved him initially passed him for dead but came back after finding only two other bodies still breathing. Another lay concealed beneath Ellis, who held tightly to a bloody entrenching tool.

The Medal of Honor citation said he had killed nine enemy soldiers with that shovel. The two surviving witnesses claimed he had fought like a man possessed. Possessed of what, they couldn't say.

"Colonel?" his wife's voice interrupted. Pat knocked on the open door but did not come in. "Colonel? Aren't you ever coming to bed?"

She hated to let her beloved husband sit there in his office all night, but she also knew how the voices came for him.

"Just catching up on a little reading," Ellis reassured her.

He laid the book down on a side table, forgetting to mark his place.

"You go on back up, darling. I'll be right there."

That's when God had come for him, Ellis knew. That's when he'd been saved. Every breath he'd drawn since that impossible night had been in homage to His holy calling and the belief that one day this orphan of faith might prove worthy.

■

"THIS IS CRAZY," Jeremy announced. He made no effort to hide his humor at standing in an empty room wearing a green Nomex flight suit and a video game–style headset over his eyes. The Buck Rogers contraption was attached by a thin wire to a two-inch belt around his waist.

"Nothing is too good for the Justice Department!" John joked. He still seemed to find Jeremy's assertion of an FBI "cover" amusing.

"You should try pimping this in mall arcades. You'd make a million."

"I'd certainly hope so." The technician harrumphed. "It cost more than that to develop!" He made a couple final adjustments, then flipped a toggle switch.

"Holy shit!" Jeremy exclaimed a little too loudly.

"Turn down the contrast if it's too bright," the technician said. He sounded annoyed that Jeremy didn't like the default settings.

Once properly adjusted, the headset changed Jeremy's view from four blank walls to an open expanse of chaparral, mesquite, and ankle-high cactus. The virtual reality simulator transported him through time and space to a brilliant cerulean sky drifting over broad horizons. A bright midday sun shone down on his T-shirt-clad shoulders.

"Amazing," was all the FBI sniper could say. Any direction he looked provided realistic, high-definition video of a place far and away from Harvey Point.

"I'm adding audio now," the technician advised. "It's fully inter-active, but you may hear a very brief time delay on some questions. The software runs off a binary logic program, but we still have a few kinks in some of the 'Y' diversions."

With that, Jeremy's link to anything he remembered as real disappeared into a Zane Grey novel. There was the rush of a desert wind, the sound of horses whinnying; gunfire nearby. Dry fragrances of the open range drifted through his nose, though John would later explain them off as psychosomatic.

"Mr. Walker?" someone said.

Jeremy turned to his right and there in front of him stood a fifty-seven-year-old former Special Forces colonel known in retirement as the last of the old-school spooks — a black ops warrior who had never hidden behind diplomatic cover.

"Colonel Ellis," Jeremy responded. "An honor to meet you, sir." He was making things up as he went along, of course, but a certain amount of respect seemed appropriate.

"Nice to meet you, Jeremy," the colonel said. He wore a para-ordnance Combat Special in a DeSantis speed-draw holster on his right hip. A Rolex GMT II with a black face and a two-tone red-and-blue bezel glistened on his wrist. His boots looked perfectly polished, despite a light coat of Texas caliche.

"I've read so much about you," Jeremy fawned. Andropov had taught Jeremy the importance of sticking closely to his carefully backstopped résumé and not adopting false airs with the new persona. Still, anyone in Jeremy's position would have kowtowed to Ellis's pedigree. Few had accomplished what he had during a military career.

"Yes, well, don't believe everything you read," Ellis responded.

Jeremy tried to decide where to steer the conversation. John, the Yale theologian, had briefed him on Christian Identity Movement dogma and various perversions of Biblical teachings that he could expect to hear from Phineas priests. Paul, the Johns Hopkins psychologist, had done everything possible in forty minutes to warm Jeremy up to the colonel's particular psychopathy. George had briefed him on what Army intelligence knew of this man's thirty-year career: fitness-for-duty reports, postings, personal background, even details of highly classified operations he had conducted overseas. Fred still hadn't gotten to the WMD rundown, but Jeremy assumed that could wait until the end.

"I assume you're settled in the bunkhouse," the colonel said. "Why don't I just show you around."

"Appreciate the tour, Colonel," Jeremy said.

And with that, Jeremy dove into virtual reality preparation for a mission that any normal man would have paused to fear.

· · ·

SIRAD LEANED BACK in her chair and considered the real problem confronting this team of experts. If one of Jordan Mitchell's secret sharers really had decided to attempt a run on the other key subsets, it also meant that person might have compromised Borders Atlantic's true intentions: intelligence gathering. The fact that Jordan Mitchell's company had served as an incubator for the CIA's Nonofficial Cover Program would prove very lucrative, either as blackmail or as a secret for sale to foreign interests, particularly the Saudis.

"What's our time line on this?" she asked.

"No way to tell," Ravi said. "It depends on how much of a chance this intruder is willing to take. They could simply sit back and watch us for a response. They could move boldly forward. There is no way for us to predict what they'll do if we do not understand their true intentions."

Sirad pointed at the man in the I Can't Dunk shirt.

"I'm sorry, what's your name?" she asked.

"Does it matter?" He shrugged.

"I guess not." Sirad shrugged back. "I'd just rather not say 'Hey, you.'"

"Ray."

"OK, Ray . . . what would we expect next?"

The man barely took time to think.

"I'd guess a lattice algorithm-based attack. That's if these guys are real pros and not some high school hackers."

"I agree," Ravi said. "They're going to use lattice approximation algorithms to try and break in. That's what I'd do."

"Anyone else?" Sirad asked. She realized that eleven other people in the room hadn't said a thing.

"I don't know how long it will take for these people to attempt an intrusion," said a Korean woman with short hair the color of coal. "But I have a pretty good idea of how to find them."

Everyone looked at her. They had all focused so squarely on defense that no one had even considered turning the tables.

"Go ahead," Sirad encouraged her.

"A poison pill. When an oncologist wants to track down rogue cancer cells, he gives the patient a radioactive isotope. I suggest that we offer a lure, something they will swallow and take home with them. Something we can track."

Sirad nodded. It made perfect sense.

"We suspect a lattice-based attack, so let's tease them a little bit," the Korean said. "I say we unlock one of our ports and see who pops in for a look."

Ravi nodded. I Can't Dunk folded his arms across his chest. He liked the idea but felt diminished for not thinking it up first.

"I like it." Sirad spoke with all the conviction one could muster at such an hour. If this attack really did come from one of Mitchell's secret sharers, the outcome could prove devastating, not just for the company, but for the country as well. "Any reservations?"

"Not as long as we act very carefully," Ravi cautioned. "Anyone smart enough to get this far might not go for a transparent ruse."

"Then let's not make it transparent," Sirad said. She stood and pointed to I Can't Dunk.

"I don't have to tell you how important opsec is at this point," Sirad admonished. Government employees swore oaths to God and country, but Borders Atlantic had to rely on careful employment screening and money. Corporate secrets were hard to keep.

"I'm going to talk to Mr. Mitchell about this. He's the only one outside this room who will know."

"Not necessarily," another voice piped up. Sirad turned toward a tall, thin man sitting at a laptop. "I just got flash traffic from our White Plains off-site. They say our peeping Tom has shown himself."

The man typed a quick response, then read a reply.

"And?" Sirad hurried him.

"And you'd better read this yourself, ma'am," he said, turning the keyboard to face her. "'Cause I don't think you'd believe me if I told you."

■

MORNING DAWNED WITH a bright, midwinter eye on the Holiday Inn outside Englewood, New Jersey. By 6:30 AM, its restaurant was already filling up with hungry travelers.

"Don't point!" one of them barked. A heavyset black woman in a pink velour sweatsuit grabbed her son by the arm and yanked him back toward his scrambled eggs.

"Easy, girl!" the man of the family exclaimed under his breath. He sat facing the big-screen TV but turned again to look at the appalling sight behind them. "It ain't the boy's fault. Nobody should come into a dining room looking all busted up like that."

The object of this family's distraction sat three tables away, near the front windows. He appeared oblivious to curious eyes, staring out onto Route 4 where it stacked up with commuters just west of the George Washington Bridge.

"Hush an eat yo meal," the woman in the sweatsuit scolded. "How'd you like someone starin' at you?"

"Damn . . . if I looked like that I'd expect it!" The man exaggerated a shiver, then faced his meal and did as he was told. "That's one ugly white man."

If the ugly white man heard them, he didn't show it. The pain in his head shut out everything but the mission.

"I wish you'd told me you were hurt this badly," a female visitor said, pulling up a chair and sitting next to him. "I would have gotten here sooner."

"I'm all right," the man lied. "Looks worse than it is."

"I doubt that," she said. "I'm sure you're in agony. But from what I hear, you probably like that."

The woman checked for signs of surveillance but saw nothing of particular interest. A black family sat in front of a big-screen TV. A table of men in cheap suits talked near the salad bar. Most people didn't try to hide their understandable interest.

"Where are we?" the man asked.

The woman got up and slipped a five-dollar bill into the jukebox. Beyoncé Knowles gave their conversation some cover.

"I think we're right where we need to be," the woman said. She sat on his left side so he could see her without straining.

"What about the rumor?"

"It's no rumor," she answered. "There's a detainee in Cuba. Guantánamo Bay. Told me he knows about Jafar al Tayar. He said he'd heard talk on the Arab street — that he knew more but wanted a deal in writing from the Agency before he'd give out any more details."

The woman grabbed a menu from between the salt and pepper shakers and pretended to read.

"Did you bury it?" he asked.

"Of course. My report said nothing about Jafar al Tayar."

"What about the prisoner?"

"Suicide and violence among the prisoners is a real problem at Camp Delta, you know? He's not going to be a threat for long."

She motioned for a waitress.

"What about the witness in Los Angeles?"

"They flew him back to the Farm, but he doesn't know anything. No one believes him anyway. The Bureau is running down everyone he ever worked with or knew. The Agency is pulling out all the stops, trying to tie him to something . . . anything. Those morons will be fixated on him for weeks."

"Good," the man said. This was going better than he'd dared hope.

"Look . . . I'm sorry about what happened over there," the woman said. "It wasn't supposed to . . ."

The man held up his right hand.

"OK." The woman nodded. "Are you going to be able to finish your mission?"

Her companion adjusted a wide swath of bandages that covered the entire left side of his head. Translucent white hair flopped down at the edges, almost indistinguishable from the sterile gauze. One almost iridescent pink eye looked out from the dressing of a horrific wound.

"The right eye is gone," he said. "The bullet took out part of the socket, but they put in a small plate. I can get fitted for a prosthesis once everything heals a little bit."

He paused for a moment. The pain stopped him cold at times — a bright electric chill that felt tantalizingly close to orgasm.

"It was a complete accident," he continued. "French's shot ricocheted off something and grazed my head. Wasn't anyone's fault."

"It's not for us to question, Caleb," the woman said. "God has his own ways. This had to happen for a reason."

The albino tilted his head ever so slightly. God did have his own ways. If not for His providence, none of this would have been possible to begin with.

"What do you want me to tell my father?" Caleb asked.

"Tell him I have learned of nothing that jeopardizes the project. If anything turns up, I'll be one of the first to know. The time line remains the same. From my perspective, we're good to go."

Caleb shook his head.

"You've done a fine job," he said. The Beyoncé song ended, and he waited a moment for the next to cover his words. "I'm sure the colonel will be very proud of you."

"We'll save the pride until this is done," she said, standing to leave. "Good to see you, Caleb."

"Good to see you, Sarah. Or is that what you want me to call you now?"

"Try Jane." She laughed. "GI Jane. The Delta boys seem to like that."

WHEN JEREMY HAD finished his virtual tour of the Homestead and bid farewell to the virtual Colonel Ellis, he flipped the On/Off switch and removed the headset.

"Well?" John asked him. "What do you think?"

"I think this is amazing," Jeremy said.

"What you just saw is precisely what you should expect at the Homestead," said the technician. "At least visually."

"How did you do it? How did you get video like this?" Jeremy noticed that he had begun to sweat, though the room remained a comfortable seventy degrees.

"It's not video," the technician claimed proudly. "It's all simulation. Computer-generated imagery based on stuff we culled from promotional materials, Internet sites, and sources who have attended schools there. Some of it came from satellites — two-dimensional pics that we augmented in a process called photogrammetry."

"Well, it's impressive, whatever you call it," Jeremy said. "What's next?"

The major, who still had not introduced himself by name, pointed to the door.

"Briefings until after dinner, I'm afraid," the major apologized. "Psychology, theology, microbiology, and organic chemistry . . . that sort of thing."

He started toward the door, and Jeremy followed him. They walked downstairs, talking about time lines, Jeremy's new identity, and why he had come to the Homestead. Like the total-immersion linguistics courses taught at the Defense Language Institute in Monterey, this program demanded complete reliance on the under-cover identity. From the time Jeremy had received his identity pack, his old persona had ceased to exist.

After a short walk outside, the major turned to what appeared to be an elegant London row house. The two men climbed up a flight of limestone stairs and entered through double doors to find a character right out of central casting.

"Jeremy Walker, meet Redbeard," the major said.

Jeremy tried not to look shocked at the man in front of him. A long, tightly braided ponytail poked out from under a leather skull-cap. ZZ Top facial hair cascaded down a white-on-black "Fuck Authority" T-shirt that looked full to bursting with the behemoth's barrel chest. Tattoos covered both tree-trunk arms. Sterling studs poked through his septum, lower lip, and left ear. A bright red, green, and yellow serpent curled menacingly out the neck of his shirt and across his throat.

"Pleasure to meet you," the man said. His voice sounded kind, respectful. "I'm all set up in the other room if you're ready."

"Ready for what?" Jeremy asked.

"Damn. Didn't they tell you?" the man asked. He turned toward the major, but the officer simply smiled and left.

"Come on in here."

The six-foot-six biker led Jeremy into a side room that had been decorated like the tea parlor in a proper Kensington bed and break-fast.

"Nobody told me anything," Jeremy said. But then he saw the equipment and understood.

"Shoulda said something to a clean-cut guy like you."

The giant sat down at a mahogany Edwardian card table.

"Scones?" Redbeard asked. Someone had taken the time to put out refreshments.

"You're going to tattoo me?" Jeremy asked. The tea and crumpets barely registered.

"That's what they told me." Redbeard nodded. His bear-paw

hands dwarfed the silver tea strainer as he poured hot water from a steaming porcelain pot. "You ever get inked up?"

Jeremy shook his head. He had done crazy things for his country, but so far none of them had left indelible marks.

"I know what you're thinking," Redbeard said. He poured black ink into a disposable plastic thimble and broke a ten-gauge outline needle out of a plastic autoclave sleeve. "But don't worry, buddy; ain't many people ever gonna see what I'm gonna give you. Sit down right there."

Jeremy did as he was told.

Redbeard stretched plastic surgeon's gloves onto his monstrous hands, then picked up a Q-tip.

"The downside is that this is gonna hurt."

"I've got friends who have tattoos," Jeremy said, trying to cover his doubt with bravado. "They said it wasn't too bad."

Redbeard reached out with his free hand and then raised the Q-tip.

"That may be, but ain't none of 'em ever been through anything quite like this," Redbeard said. The artist reached out toward his unmarked human canvas and Jeremy understood.

Oh my God, he thought. *This guy can't be serious.*

"Don't feel self-conscious about yelling," the tattoo artist said, getting down to his unique expertise. "As a matter of fact, I'm gonna waive the no-cry rule."

Jeremy heard the buzz of the tattoo needle.

"'Cause like I said" — Redbeard bit the sterling lip stud between his nicotine-stained teeth — "this motherfucker is gonna hurt."

Book II

INSERTION

Whoever fights monsters should see to it that in the process he does not become a monster.

— Nietzsche

IX

___

Wednesday, 16 February
18:02 GMT
1701 Coopers Lane, Stafford, Virginia

CAROLINE WALLER LOVED her husband. That had never been the problem. She'd willingly followed him into the FBI, giving up a well-paying job with the Department of Health and Human Services for a four-year excursion to the Ozarks. When it came right down to it, Caroline recalled, she had been the one to phone the Washington field office recruiter and request an application. All Jeremy had to do was fill in the blanks.

But that seemed like a long time ago as she sat at the top of a sledding hill watching a gaggle of neighborhood kids yelling and screaming in the joyous throes of a day off from school.

The nor'easter had dropped a record-setting twenty-eight inches of snow on Washington DC and its suburbs, shutting down everything from the Capitol to the Quantico Marine Corps Base and the FBI Academy. The timing couldn't have been worse for a new president facing an awful string of terror attacks, but at this very moment that seemed far away and superfluous to Caroline and her three kids. As with many Virginia storms, the furious snows and winds had given way to bright sunshine and forty-five-degree skies. It was time to play.

"Hey, Mommy! Look at me!" Maddy called out.

Their only daughter had inherited her dad's spirit of adventure. At the ripe old age of seven, she had already pleaded for a chance to go parachuting. Not content merely to ride her bike up and down the street, she had built a ramp and persuaded her younger brothers to let her jump over them. When the X Games came on ESPN, she decided to "board" a sterling-silver tea tray — a wedding gift from Jeremy's parents — down the staircase. Fortunately for Maddy, the tray had suffered the worst of the crash, leaving her bent but not broken.

"Sorry, Mommy," the little girl had cried, lying in a heap on the landing. "I tried to get technical and ended up in a total yard sale."

"Hold on to your brother!" Caroline called out. Christopher, their middle child, could hurt himself brushing his teeth. Just a week earlier, she'd run him to the emergency room after a close call with a dresser. On a dare from his sister, he'd tried using the drawers as a ladder to reach his piggy bank. The resulting crash cost him four stitches above his left eye and her ten years off an already stress-shortened life.

"Where's Daddy?" Patrick asked, panting deeply while he waited for his turn on the sled.

"He's busy saving the world, honey," Caroline said. It was a line she used all the time now.

"When is he coming home?"

"As soon as the world's safe, silly."

"Just like Johnny Rocket, right?" the little boy asked.

"I'd say more like Power Rangers," Caroline replied. She often relied on the Cartoon Network to illustrate complicated points. In the age of Tipping Point marketing, child psychology came down to knowing which action hero to cite in building a frame of reference.

"Patrick, zip up your coat before you freeze blue," she added, bending over to brush the snow off his sweater. "If you want to stay out here, you're . . ."

"Mama! Christopher's crying!" Maddy called out from the bottom of the hill.

Caroline looked down the hill to where Maddy stood over her little brother, tugging on the sled rope and trying to pull it out from under his prostrate body.

She hurried down the slope, past a mob of older neighborhood kids who had barely even noticed.

"Get offa my sled!" Maddy scolded her brother, who was hollering earnestly now, holding his breath between sobs. Caroline counted seven seconds between bleats and knew it must be serious. Anything more than a three-second breath hold usually meant trouble.

"Leave the sled alone," Caroline called out. Where the hell was Jeremy, anyway? The last she had heard from him was an answering machine message in her office.

"Something came up," he'd said, relying on the same three-word excuse he used to explain every disappearance. *Something came up* never shed any light on where he was going or when he'd be back. She never knew anything about the missions — how dangerous they'd be, whether they'd take him outside the country, whether they'd render him insufferable among the raging mood swings.

"It's all right, sweetie; Mommy's here," Caroline cooed, trying to calm the injured little boy.

"I think it's his arm, Mom," Maddy said. Doctoring had never been one of her aspirations, but she knew plenty about crashing.

"Is it your arm?" Caroline asked.

"I . . . think . . . it's . . . broke . . . Mom . . . ," the little boy managed to say between lung-clearing sobs.

Damn the FBI, Caroline thought to herself, kneeling down over her son, reaching into his snowsuit for signs of trouble. *The Bureau has ten thousand agents they can call on to fight their war on terror. Why does it always have to be my husband?*

■

JORDAN MITCHELL LOVED the Berkshires for their peace. Having spent most of his professional life in New York, he relished the quiet passage of seasons, the way Mother Nature moved relentlessly on in spite of man and all his efforts to harness her. He'd never been a religious man, but he understood some greater power in the first buds of spring, the way frost glistened in a morning sun, the last calls of geese flying south.

Neighbors might have argued that Mitchell's Bell Jet Ranger helicopter seemed somewhat incongruous to their Norman Rockwell idyll, but that would imply he had neighbors. And he didn't.

Mitchell's South Egremont estate — a stone great house and out-building cluster called Longpath — covered nearly seven hundred acres. The nearest house stood almost a mile away.

"Your lunch, Mr. Mitchell," the housekeeper announced, toting a wooden tray of salmon over watercress with pine nuts and cous-cous. The Borders Atlantic CEO always ate more heartily at Long-path, where he felt infused with vigor.

"Thank you, Mrs. Hartung." Mitchell looked up from the new Alexander Calder biography and pointed toward the corner of his desk. Rich sunlight poured in through windows whose leaded glass had sagged with age.

The stiff, heavyset woman set the tray down and shuffled out. Anna Hartung and her husband, Gerhardt, had lived and worked more than forty years at Longpath. Mitchell's father had hired them right off a merchant ship from Argentina. Any suggestions that they might have been hiding from a darker past would have fallen on deaf ears. The Mitchell patriarch valued allegiance over all else, and Nazis were known for that.

"Good afternoon, Mr. Mitchell," Trask said, nodding to the housekeeper as he entered. The old woman shuffled right on by, not interested in a newer generation of servants.

"Is it?" Mitchell asked, laying down his book. "I've been too busy to notice."

"So have I, for that matter," Trask replied. He knew when Mitchell would tolerate retort and when he wouldn't. "Thought you might want to see what I've been up to."

Mitchell knew, of course. He had heard the helicopter arrive half an hour earlier. His only question was why Trask hadn't arrived sooner.

"Well, open it, then!" Mitchell barked. Though hungry, he had completely forgotten about the rapidly cooling repast.

The chief of staff carried a brightly polished mahogany box, inlaid with fruitwoods, white gold, and birch. A large circle in the middle of the top bore elaborate engravings, including the initials AWH.

"The box alone is worth the trouble," Trask said, twisting the case in filtered sunlight and watching the wood grains dance. "It's mag-nificent."

But Mitchell had no interest in the box, and Trask knew it. He lifted the top to expose .56 caliber English horseman's pistols — two pristine examples of eighteenth-century European gunsmithing, cut from black walnut and turned Damascus steel.

"Magnificent," Mitchell gasped. He held them in his gaze for a long breath before reaching out to handle them.

What Trask had delivered were the very weapons Alexander Hamilton and Aaron Burr had used to settle a dispute over honor. On July 11, 1804, the two political enemies faced each other on the dueling ground in Weehawken, New Jersey. One of these pistols had ended Hamilton's life and Burr's career in office. Now both of them had found their way to Mitchell.

"Now to answer a question I've always wanted to find out for myself," Mitchell said. "Which one is it?"

"The one on top," Trask answered. "That's what the family says. There's no way to be certain, unfortunately, because the weapons have been outside the family for almost four decades."

Mitchell knew their provenance. After more than 160 years, a descendant had sold them to Chase Manhattan Bank. The Borders Atlantic CEO had leveraged the sale only after considerable effort.

"How many times do you think someone has pulled this trigger since that fateful day?" Mitchell asked. He lifted the stout weapon from its red-velvet resting spot.

"The family says they never did," Trask told him. "And I doubt the corporate owners ever did."

Mitchell paid meticulous attention to the history of the weapons he bought. Guns only interested him if they came with a story.

"So it was the other that killed Philip," Mitchell said. Hamilton's nineteen-year-old son had been shot down in an 1801 duel with the same set of pistols. Family lore held that the man on the ten-dollar bill had not wanted to take a chance on dying by the same barrel, so he chose it against Burr.

Mitchell held the pistol in his hands for a minute, turning it back and forth to drink in every visual detail. He raised it to his nose and inhaled, trying to detect remnants of the powder or lead ball.

"Present!" Mitchell called out the words Hamilton's second had uttered that fateful morning. He pointed the gun toward the window — his own father had demanded great attention to firearms safety — and pulled back the hammer.

They stood just ten paces from each other, the executive thought. *Close enough to spit. Hamilton's heart must have been racing as he raised his gun hand, then settled it on his adversary's heart. Could he hear the echo of the shot that had taken his Philip on that very spot? Did he expect death to come for him? Did he really intend to miss on the first shot as he had told his son an honorable man would do?*

Mitchell looked down the barrel and touched the trigger, which discharged immediately with a bright metallic click.

"Hair trigger. Just like the books say," Mitchell observed. Some said Hamilton missed on purpose. Others argued that improper handling of the hair trigger caused the gun to discharge before Hamilton took effective aim.

"They were his pistols," Trask argued. "He would have known their individual personalities." This was an important yet unanswered question of history, after all. Had this founding father died for honor or fallen to poor aim?

"He was also a politician," another voice interrupted. It was a woman's voice, a sound Trask had never heard in a situation like this. "Ready, aim, fire — right? I mean, what the hell do politicians know about gunfighting?"

Mitchell turned toward a tidy woman with short hair and bloodshot eyes.

"Pleasant trip?" he asked. The visitor had just driven up from New Jersey.

"You wanna play with guns all day or get down to business?" she asked, ignoring his courtesy. This woman wasted no time on small talk. Mitchell liked that.

"Tea for the lady," Mitchell said to Trask.

"Black," she added.

"Of course." Mitchell smiled. How appropriate for a woman everyone seemed intent on calling GI Jane.

■

BREAKING AND ENTERING had never struck Satch as something he'd be very good at. Working at the Home Depot had kept him happy the past few years. It was steadier work than roofing and a whole lot cooler during those summer months in Little Rock.

He'd fallen into the work honestly, however, and it had treated him well. The money stunk, but the rewards of eternal salvation seemed worth the risk.

"It's a bloody keypad," his partner whispered. Ollie spoke with a British accent and swore too much for Satch's liking. *Bloody* may have been a reverent allusion to Christ's blood, as Ollie claimed, but it sounded base and disrespectful to the hulking former roofer. God's name was not to be taken in vain, even during burglaries.

"Use the sequencer," Satch urged in a muffled voice.

Ollie reached into a large duffel bag and pulled out a device the size of a calculator. They'd been told to expect a card swipe and had brought an appropriate magnetic access badge. The keypad would pose no significant hindrance, but it would slow down an operation that hinged on extremely tight tolerance with regard to time.

"Five bucks says I take it down in less than thirty seconds," Ollie said, expertly attaching the device to a black keypad next to a steel-casing door.

"Just open it," Satch responded. He didn't care for gambling, either.

Click.

The door opened, and both men silently thanked God for speeding things along. Once through the door, Satch and his London-bred partner moved quickly down a wide corridor lined with classrooms. They turned right at a T intersection, then right again to a door marked HENRY VOGT CANCER RESEARCH INSTITUTE, LAB 4. Beneath the room indicator blazed two warning signs: BIOHAZARD and the yellow, black, and red sign for radiation hazard.

To the right of the door sat the card swipe they had expected to find earlier.

"We got five minutes," the Londoner advised, moving quickly past it into a university research lab. The place smelled of industrial disinfectants, stainless steel, and stale coffee.

Intelligence indicated regular physical patrols by a seventy-year-old former cop who used the seven-buck-an-hour job to pad his retirement check. He would pose no real problems, but neither burglar wanted to hurt the old codger if they could avoid it.

"Southeast corner," Satch said. "Let's go."

He pulled a red-lens penlight out of his right front pocket and twisted the head until it illuminated their path in a foreboding glow. Both men's hearts raced with adrenaline as they crossed the dark, windowless room. It wasn't the difficulty in this black-bag operation as much as the consequence. Discovery would compromise the larger . . .

"Ssshhhh!" Satch whispered louder than most men talked. Something had caught his attention   someone else's noise.

He tucked the penlight into his armpit, stranding the two men in the middle of the room. When nothing happened after a few seconds, he turned his light back on and started toward the vault.

"Don't be so paranoid," the Brit said. "We don't have time to . . ."

Creeaak . . .

The lab door opened, spilling in fluorescent light from the hallway outside.

"Somebody in here?" a curious voice asked. He sounded more annoyed than alarmed at first, as if he was used to having students steal in after class.

When the lights flashed on, however, the man's curiosity quickly turned to fear. There in the middle of the lab stood two men dressed in custodian's uniforms. Under normal circumstances, this might not have bothered him, but the semiautomatic handgun coming out of the short man's belt line made this anything but normal.

"Lab four! Break-in!" the security guard yelled, raising a handheld radio to his mouth and keying the mike. He had no gun of his own; it was the only thing he could draw.

"Doggone it, old man," Satch growled. "You hadn't oughta done that."

■

JORDAN MITCHELL PLACED the instrument of Alexander Hamilton's death back into its red-velvet resting place and motioned for Trask to leave them. Ordinarily the senior aide would have thought fetching tea beneath him, but not today. Despite Trask's intimate access to his boss's personal and professional lives, there were still some areas that both men respected as off-limits.

"I'll be back shortly," was all Trask said. He took the gun box and pulled the door closed when he left.

"You didn't answer me about your trip," Mitchell reminded his new guest. She stood in front and to the right of him, just inside the shadows of a pleasant sun. "It's not small talk I'm after. I want to assess your mental state."

"My mental state is fine," the woman said. She looked up at the stuffed animal heads above them.

"You have been busy, with little sleep."

"Yes. I don't need much."

"Well?"

"Well what?"

"Well, how is he?"

Mitchell reached for his lunch. Mrs. Hartung had served it peppered, with fresh Hollandaise, the way his father had always liked it. Mitchell had told her a dozen times that he preferred salmon neat, but she paid no heed.

"He lost an eye. Sounded weak and kind of disoriented."

GI Jane brushed hair away from her face. She looked road weary despite her claims to the contrary.

"What did he tell you about the plan?" Mitchell asked. "Do we know where they will strike next?"

"No," she lied. GI Jane was a master manipulator, but this was a delicate line she had to walk. "He is going back to the Homestead while field operatives set up the next wave of attacks. That's all I know at this point."

"What is your next objective?" Mitchell asked. He slowly scraped Hollandaise from his salmon, then tasted it, without taking his eyes off her. Strange how much like Sirad this woman should have been and how different they had turned out. GI Jane seemed even more manipulative, despite her lack of beauty.

"My next objective . . ." GI Jane paused for a moment. "My next objective is to write up a false confession for the Guantánamo prisoner and submit it to Langley with a report of my findings. They want to cover any trace of Jafar al Tayar or the Megiddo project."

"I don't believe you," Mitchell said. "There's more."

"Colonel Ellis is a very bright man. And very careful. He has to suspect that someone — some agency, some threat — is waiting out there to stop him. Why would he give me a larger role?"

"The same reason I do," he said. "Because he needs you." He paused to watch her face. "But you're not going to tell him. I know that, you see, because I'm better at this than you are."

Mitchell rested his fork on the lunch tray, got up, and walked to within two feet of her. His voice dropped to little more than a whisper.

"That's why I hired you. That's why I hired each of your colleagues. But don't ever forget that one thing: I'm better than you will ever be."

He loved this, the seduction inherent in the dance. He savored the grace of the steps, the posturing, the tease, and the rebuff. This is what had drawn him to the trade in the beginning.

"I know you don't believe that," he told her, "because you are full of ego. You work well without reference. You thrive on uncertainty. You can't wait for someone to corner you because you so love the threat of impossible odds."

He leaned in close. Close enough to smell the way the moisture on her skin was turning from perspiration to sweat.

"Never forget," Mitchell said, "that I'm the one who lifted you out of that bleak little world you used to wallow in, and I'm the one who can put you right back in. You are a cog in a mechanism you just think you understand."

Mitchell reached out with a bony finger and traced the bags under the woman's eyes. He wanted her to feel his weight.

"It's a mechanism so complex, you won't even see it coming to crush you. Your next objective is something considerably more audacious than a false report to the CIA. I knew that before you did."

Mitchell lowered his hand and leaned in close enough that GI Jane could feel his lips against her ear.

"But I don't care about your relationship with Ellis at this point. All I care about is what you are going to do for me."

GI Jane fought an overwhelming urge to tremble. Mitchell's breath smelled of pepper and heavy cream. His eyelashes slowly opened and closed against her cheek.

And then he told her what she had to do.

Knock! Knock! Sharp knuckles tapped against the door.

Trask entered after a beat, holding a pale-blue cup on a matching china saucer.

"Earl Grey, black — just like you requested," he said.

Mitchell had moved to his desk; in his hand was the Alexander Calder biography.

"I'm afraid our guest has changed her mind about refreshments," he told Trask. He seemed amused, filled up with rare good humor. "She needs to go."

Mitchell didn't bother to look up as GI Jane hurried past him on unsteady legs. He lifted a finger to his cheek where one of her tears had fallen against it. The liquid tasted salty but pure.

■

SATCH HAD NO particular interest in guns. They hardly seemed worth messing with — especially considering the physical strength God had given him.

"Please . . . ," the guard squeaked out before the brute of a man crossed the floor and grabbed him by the throat. The radio fell to the ground, sending a clatter echoing through the lab, but the man died silently with a quick snap of his neck.

"We better move," Satch said, motioning toward the locked vault. He dragged the body out of sight, picked the radio up off the floor, and hurried over to catch his partner, who had already attached his electronic sequencer to yet another cipher pad.

"Lab Four, disregard," Satch spoke into the radio, hoping it might cause enough confusion to buy them more time. He pulled out two six-sided Luxel radiation exposure badges from his pocket, broke them open, and tucked one inside his breast pocket.

"Got it," the Brit said, bouncing open the storage vault door even more quickly than the one outside.

"Here." Satch handed his partner the second Luxel badge and followed him inside a stainless-steel vault. They moved quickly from shelf to shelf, selecting cylindrical shipping containers marked *Caution: Radioactive Materials* above the orange-and-black hazmat symbols. They took only the containers marked Amersham 60-C, 137-cesium, 133-xenon, 192-iridium, and 99-technetium — all highly toxic gamma emitters: radioactive research isotopes bound for the university's nuclear medicine facilities.

The two men pulled large expedition-built backpacks from the duffel bag and took turns stuffing them with bulky transportation containers. Satch guessed his pack weighed at least 130 pounds and wondered how well his partner would handle the load.

"Time," Satch ordered, pulling the top flap over his partner's pack. He turned toward the door and started as quickly across the floor as possible. Even with his huge strength, Satch felt the pack shorten his stride, test his balance.

They made the door just as the first campus police officer rounded the corner from the elevators. He looked annoyed more than alarmed. But then he saw the enormous Satch lurching toward him and knew this was no idle call. The giant hurtled down the hallway, an expedition pack swaying behind him with every labored stride.

"What the hell are you . . . ?" the guard started to ask, but Satch's forward momentum buckled the man like a linebacker anticipating the run. The guard landed on his back, his hat tumbling across the floor, his pepper spray breaking off his Sam Brown belt, his black shoes and white socks flipping up over his head.

Satch's boot caught him in the temple, ending any further resistance.

"Darn it, that's two," he said, regaining his feet. He didn't relish killing, though he knew that's what he'd signed on to do.

They got to the elevators without further interference. It made sense that campus police wouldn't waste more than one officer on the call.

"This stuff is heavy," the Brit said as they stepped out of the elevator. He had trained hard, but the load added up to almost 70 percent of his body weight. No matter how much he'd prepared, it still felt like a sizable hump.

They said nothing else until they got outside to the van. The vehicle — marked on each door with a University of Louisville logo — had been easy to steal. No one would even know it was missing until long after they'd made the switch.

"CP to twenty-seven," someone said before Satch remembered he still had the night watchman's radio in his pocket. "Are you clear at the scene?"

Satch shrugged off his pack and lowered it carefully into the back of the van.

"Clear in Lab Four," he said, holding the radio away from his mouth and trying to emulate the police officer's voice.

"Copy, twenty-seven," the dispatcher radioed back. "See the man at twelve seventy-seven Maplehurst about noise coming outa the Alpha Omega house. Looks like they got a big party over there."

Satch clicked the Send key twice, offering the universal police shortcut for "understood." Then he grabbed Ollie's pack and laid it in the back of the van beside his own.

"You'd better drive," the smaller man said, trying to straighten up. "I think I tore somethin' in my back."

"I'm a better driver anyway," Satch said, taking the keys and moving to the front door. He smiled at the relative ease of their success as he climbed in. "Better-looking too."

X

Thursday, 17 February
15:01 GMT
The Homestead, Kerrville, Texas

JEREMY DOWNSHIFTED INTO third gear and eased out the clutch as the driveway came into sight. Wrought-iron columns rose from the far side of a mailbox cluster. A ranch banner spanned the columns, reading THE HOMESTEAD in foot-high letters painted white. The ranch looked just like the one he'd visited during the Harvey Point simulations.

Jeremy Walker, date of birth 7/22/1971, favorite color . . . hunter green, he reminded himself, trying to concentrate on anything besides the thick, spiny ball rumbling around his gut.

Stagehand with a roving Folger Shakespeare Library–based road troupe. Who the hell had thought that up?

The 80-series street-racing tires on his 1970 Nova SS chirped brightly as he turned right into the gravel drive and passed over the cattle guard. Mesquite trees and prickly pear cactus spread out as far as he could see in any direction. Wire fencing lined both sides of the road, divided every few miles by a gate like Ellis's.

The undercover job history had to be something they couldn't track down easily, he realized. Ellis likely would not have many contacts in the theater world, and even if he did, stagehands came and went like carnival workers. This job came with all the anonymity the road could offer and suggested just the right amount of distaste for an ordered world.

The Homestead's newest student tried to focus on the arrogant growl of the car's souped-up L78, 396-cubic-inch engine. Jeremy's FBI handler had arranged to borrow the boisterous muscle car — a drug seizure — from the local field office. It fit Jeremy Walker's psychological profile, they said, and it would quickly announce his presence to Ellis.

All Jeremy cared about was the thrill he got in driving it. The owner had installed a 417 rear end with a limited slip differential, Hooker headers, Edelbrock intake, Accel ignition, and furry red dice hanging from the rearview mirror. The steroid-enhanced power plant turned mid-elevens in the quarter mile, but here on the rutted driveway, it made the car lurch and buck despite Jeremy's attempts to feather the throttle.

"That's it, baby." Jeremy smiled, trying to keep rpms between three and four thousand. "Let's let him know we're coming."

There was little doubt of that. The road ran straight as a rifle shot for about three quarters of a mile to a cluster of single-level buildings painted ocher. Sound traveled well across the tinder-dry countryside, and the high-pitched whine of the SS would have awakened the dead.

Jeremy swallowed the lump in his throat as he pulled up to where a Ford Dually and two late-model Dodges sat parked near a carport. He caught himself in the car's rearview mirror and wondered if a day of preparation would be enough. They'd cut his hair close to the scalp then taken away his razor, giving him the look of a man who'd trimmed off the outside world, then been too lazy to stick with the commitment.

Divorced. Twice. Three kids: Patrick, Maddy, and Christopher. Stick as close to the truth as possible, they'd told him. The proximity to reality would keep him centered when all other reference fled him.

Jeremy shifted into neutral and raced the engine a couple times. *That's what Jeremy Walker would do,* he thought to himself. *Bold, self-centered, righteous.* Then he caught himself again.

"Don't *think* about your new identity," the FBI undercover expert had told him. "They'll see right through that. You've got to *live* it. Don't act. *Become* the new man. You have to believe it yourself before you can expect anyone else to."

Jeremy raced the engine a third time.

"Fuck it," he said, stomping on the throaty Holley four-barrel. The man he left behind would have raced the engine too.

■

ELIZABETH BEECHUM ARRIVED at the Capitol on the Senate side, up Constitution Avenue, past the makeshift Jersey walls and the dogs and the men with submachine guns and thigh bags stuffed full of gas masks.

She remembered not so many years back to when anyone could drive in off the street and cross the big lot of crushed rock and shale. Tours of grade-schoolers and Gray Panthers used to picnic on the East Lawn before queuing up in the rotunda for public tours. You could go all the way up to the top of the dome in those days, venture down into the crypt, maybe even get a member to show you the tunnels or point out the bullet holes left behind after Puerto Rican radicals had shot up the place in 1954.

But those were the old days, gone forever. No more open tours, no more public access to the viewers' galleries or Statuary Hall, no more sense that the People's House was still a place for the very Americans who had built her.

"It's a crying shame," she said out loud.

"Different world," James agreed, reading her mind.

The motorcade of black SUVs, marked Metro police cars, and decoy limos pulled up to beneath the south stairs and Beechum climbed out. Secret Service agents in their bulging suits and cuff mikes ushered her in for a handoff to plainclothes Capitol police officers.

Turf wars, she thought. Just another reason the United States would always be playing catch-up with people who answered to just one leader: Muhammad.

SR-220, a committee room reserved for closed hearings, was already full when the vice president led her administrative assistant in. She carried a worn leather briefcase in her left hand and a rolled-up battle damage assessment in her right.

"I want to read into the record that this is a meeting of the Senate Select Committee on Intelligence," the chairman said. Beechum had always liked the right, honorable, and distinguished senior senator from Florida, one of the more open-minded Republicans she'd worked with. His ascension to the chair had surprised no one. A senior member of the committee during Beechum's tenure, Radford Baines Beauchamp knew the intelligence community and he knew Washington. Few had ever succeeded in pushing rot past his discerning nose.

"This is a closed meeting," he droned. "All minutes and discussions are classified top secret."

With that, he nodded to his not-so-former colleague.

"Good day, Madam Vice President. Good of you to come. I think we all appreciate how busy you must be."

"Good morning, Mr. Chairman." Beechum nodded back. It felt odd to sit there among the witness seats. Just over a month earlier, she'd walked out for the last time with a bittersweet taste in her mouth. "Nice to be back. I have to admit that I never thought I'd find myself in the cheap seats, but I must be moving up in the world, because Evelyn actually said hello to me in the elevator this morning."

Everyone laughed. Evelyn had operated the members-only elevator for twenty-seven years. She never said hello to anyone.

"Well, cheap seats or no, it's so nice to have you back," Beauchamp said. "I want to say how proud this old Republican is to see you moving down Pennsylvania Avenue, especially with everything that has happened. This country would be hard-pressed to find a better second in command."

He held up a cautionary finger and pointed to the other Republican members.

"And I don't have to remind you that everything said within these walls is classified," he admonished them. "If that leaks out to the whip I'll deny it!"

Everyone laughed again. What might have been a very tense atmosphere loosened considerably.

"Thank you, Mr. Chairman." Beechum smiled up at the courtly gentleman. Though Washington crawled with all manner of backbiting parasites, Beauchamp was honest to a fault. "Why don't we get down to it then."

She reached for the briefing book James had carried in. West Wing staffers had prepared a redacted version of the CIA's Presidential Daily Briefing. It outlined information the president felt comfortable handing to this notorious sieve of secrets.

"As you may have seen on cable news, a new Islamic fundamentalist group has claimed credit for both sets of attacks. They call themselves Ansar ins Allah, and though we don't have a lot of information about them, the FBI is working closely with the Department of Homeland Security and the CIA to follow up on literally thousands of leads."

"There is talk of a connection between Saudis and radical Islamic cells here in the U.S." A committee member from Alabama spoke up. "Do you believe these people infiltrated this country illegally or are they naturalized Arab Americans?"

"First of all, we don't even know that they are Arabs," Beechum explained. "The State Department has identified dangerous Islamic fundamentalist groups in at least eleven countries around the world. It would be entirely premature to ascribe this to any one geographic region."

"Oh, come on, Elizabeth," another member said. "Everyone is reporting that the FBI has an Arab in custody. They're saying he is a Saudi by birth. Is that not true?"

"It's true that we have detained a naturalized American of Saudi birth," she admitted. "But we haven't determined that he had anything to do with the airliner plot."

"Has he been arrested?" the chairman asked. "Is he being interrogated?"

"I'm not at liberty to discuss his status," Beechum said. She knew how this would sound. She well remembered White House stonewalling during the 9/11 aftermath. "All I can tell you is that we are looking closely at several countries with a history of state sponsorship, and . . ."

"Including Saudi Arabia?" the senator from Alabama interrupted.

"Including Saudi Arabia. It's no secret that the House of Saud has questionable ties. They've come to this committee's attention in the past. Remember, though — we have to exercise due diligence in all aspects of this investigation. It would be negligent to focus on a single group or country at this point."

The member from Alabama slapped the table in front of him.

"Knew it!" he exclaimed. "I'll tell y'all what . . . the Saudis have been playing us for fools way too long now. I highly recommend, Madam Vice President, that you stand up down there in the Oval Office the way you stood up before this committee. Somebody needs to make sure politics doesn't stand in the way of justice."

"Follow the money," another committee member agreed. "Somebody had to cough up financial support for this. There's bound to be a trail."

"What about SIGINT?" another member asked.

"I told you we should have upped appropriations for domestic security!"

"Where do we think they'll strike next?"

The questions came fast and furious, absent the traditional decorum. The chairman banged his gavel.

"Order," he said in a firm, even tone. "I'll have order."

"Please" — Beechum held up her hand, trying to keep the others from piling on — "the veteran members of this committee know as well as I do that things aren't always what they seem. In fact, they seldom are what they seem. I assure you that our intelligence community is wearing the shine off their shoes, turning over rocks from here to Damascus. We believe these attacks have run their course now, and that . . ."

The door opened behind her, and a Secret Service agent marched deliberately toward the witness table. Beechum felt a cold chill up her spine just looking at his face.

"Excuse me," the agent said, approaching the vice president. He was a bodyguard, not an expert on Robert's Rules of Order.

Beechum turned in her chair as the man leaned in to tell her something. This was the shift commander. He wouldn't have interrupted with anything less than a summons from the Oval Office.

"I'm sorry, ma'am . . ." The agent spoke softly now, just louder than a whisper. "The president has requested that you return to the White House immediately."

She nodded gravely.

"Did he tell you why?"

"Not really, ma'am, but there's a story all over the news. Somebody broke into a research lab down at the University of Louisville.

A significant quantity of radioactive material is missing. Two security guards were killed. Ansar ins Allah is claiming credit."

Beechum gathered her papers and stood.

"Please forgive me, Mr. Chairman," she said. "I'll send someone with an update just as soon as we have more answers. Until then, I suggest you confer with leadership. Based on what I've just heard, things may not be as stable as we had hoped."

To an eruption of questions, accusations, and outright demands, the vice president of the United States got up, turned toward the Secret Service shift commander, and left without so much as a good-bye.

■

NEW YORK SAGGED under the weight of its worst blizzard in decades, but the snow had already begun to melt by the time Sirad emerged from the Albemarle Building. Three nights she had slept inside the building, popping out of the Rabbit Hole only for an occasional shower and catnaps on her office couch.

The fresh air felt wonderful on her face as Sirad stepped onto Fifth Avenue and turned south. Any other day, she would have called for a car, but not this morning. The bright midmorning sun warmed her face; the smells of new snow and empty streets filled her nose.

No point in fishtailing through the streets in a car, she had decided. *The subway will serve me better.*

It took twenty minutes to work her way down to Grand Central, where she picked up the seven train to Times Square, then the three downtown to Christopher Street. From there it was a short walk to the Soho House on Ninth Avenue. A pretty receptionist greeted her just inside the door to New York's only private membership hotel.

"I'll ring his room," the clerk said in a refined British accent. Sirad imagined it something around High Street, Kensington.

Moments later, a tall black man in a camel-hair blazer and dark gray slacks emerged from the elevator. He nodded to his visitor without further greeting and held the door until Sirad climbed aboard. They took the car up to the fourth floor, where Sirad followed him to a two-top in a nearly empty restaurant.

"I got here as quickly as possible," the man said. "What's the matter?"

He looked somewhat put out by the trip.

"We have a problem."

"You just noticed that?" he asked. "Please don't tell me I flew up here just because we have a problem."

A delicate waitress drifted up on three-inch heels. She hovered beside them somewhere between arrogance and grace.

"Hi, guys," she said, failing to turn the man's eye. "Espresso?"

Sirad nodded.

"Water," he said. "With gas. Bring a large bottle."

The woman smiled and turned, leaving a light scent of almond talc.

"Someone has launched an attack on the Quantis system," Sirad said when they were alone. "It's more a survey at this point, but a sophisticated effort nonetheless."

"Don't you think I know that?" he told her. The CIA program manager saw no point in elaborating on his sources or methods.

"Did Mitchell tell you we've identified the intruders?" she asked.

Mr. Hoch folded his fingers and rubbed his long thumbs against each other.

"Go on," he said.

"The programmers and mathematicians who designed the Quantis encryption software added a trap-and-trace aspect. They described it to me as a sort of cyber radar that detects intrusion surveys before they become all-out attacks."

"I don't like suspense," Hoch said.

"Early this morning, we tracked what was supposed to be a passive surveillance rider to a no-tell server in Delhi."

"Wouldn't you expect that?" Hoch nodded. "They're trying to wash themselves."

"We tracked the inquiry to an e-mail address in Vancouver: a Hotmail account accessed from an Internet café. Totally anonymous."

"Well, that makes sense, doesn't it?" Hoch asked. The waitress brought his water and her espresso, then walked away.

"Hardly. You're not going to find the horsepower necessary to accomplish a no-show surveillance like this in a coffeeshop."

"So how did they do it?"

"They didn't," she answered.

"Please . . ."

"They used a decoy. Very clever . . . but that's not the point. The point is in the subtext."

Sirad sipped her coffee, then pulled a pen out of her pocket. She opened her hand, wrote five letters across her palm, and showed it to him.

"Impossible," Hoch said. There was no faking the shock in his eyes. Sirad, a liar of well-documented heritage, knew this man who had seen everything truly couldn't believe his eyes.

"Possible." Sirad slowly licked the ink off her skin and rubbed it clean with a napkin. "Fact. Now you know why I called you. I need to talk with . . ."

"She won't talk to you," Hoch said. "There's just too much downside."

"And what about the downside if she doesn't?"

Hoch thought for a moment. Another couple entered the dining room but sat outside the sound of his voice.

"I'll try," he said. "What about Mitchell? How much does he know?"

"You're asking me?" Sirad said, perplexed. "This is the sonofabitch who tortured me for information he already had . . . who hired me for my ability to seduce and then alienated me when I used it. This is the man who brought me into Borders Atlantic as a NOC only to tell me later that the whole goddamned company was a cover!"

She was talking a little too loudly now, but Hoch did nothing to quiet her. Nobody would believe her anyway.

"Jordan Mitchell's whole life is a black hole of secrets." She stopped long enough to collect herself. "That's why I called you. If you want to find out where this leads, you're going to have to start with Mitchell."

■

"YOU MUST BE Mr. Walker," the man said. Jeremy sensed him before he saw him.

"Colonel Ellis. It's an honor to meet you, sir."

"No *sirs* around here, son. Not unless you've come to date my daughter or sell me a horse."

"Neither." Jeremy laughed. He liked the easy-mannered Texan

immediately. "I'm here for your high-intensity tactical course. Name's Jeremy."

He reached out and shook the colonel's hand.

"Buck Ellis," the man said. "Most call me Colonel. I'll answer to just about anything. Come on, I'll show you around."

Ellis looked taller than the six feet listed in his dossier. The darkly tanned legend wore sharply creased khaki pants, a sky-blue denim shirt with pearl buttons, and a Homestead ball cap. Earplugs dangled from a fluorescent-yellow tether around his neck. A stainless-steel Les Baer .45 comp gun rode high in a DeSantis speed-draw holster just behind his right hip. Jeremy noticed an oversized slide safety, custom backstrap paddle, Pachmayr grips, and tritium night sights. The hammer was cocked for combat carry. No thumb break.

"Should I get my weapon?" Jeremy asked. It seemed like an obvious enough question considering the colonel's status.

"Up to you. We encourage students to wear their sidearms at all times while on the property," Ellis said. "One of the first rules of gun ownership is responsibility."

"Fair enough," Jeremy said. "I'll get it after I check in."

"Where you from?" the colonel inquired without asking for further explanation. He walked away from Jeremy's Nova, around the first building, and up a gravel path.

"Washington DC. I live out west in Virginia — what's called the horse country."

"Sure, know it well. I spent lots of time out there during my years at the Pentagon," Ellis said. He walked with a bit of a limp in his right leg. Jeremy had seen his Purple Heart citations and wondered how the man could walk at all. "You like horses? Like to ride?"

"Nah, I never really had much time for it," Jeremy admitted. "I live out there because I like the country. Quiet, you know? I gotta work in the city, but I don't have to live there."

"I understand," Ellis said.

The two men climbed two steps onto a slant-roofed porch. Bare-limbed rockers lined the front wall, four to each side of a windowed door. Ellis opened it and led Jeremy into a gift shop full of T-shirts, ball caps, and coffee cups. A display case by the cash register held an impressive assortment of custom and competition handguns.

Pump shotguns with extended magazines and assault rifles in fluorescent powder-coated finishes stood in racks along the back wall.

"Impressive arsenal," Jeremy commented. He walked to a display rack full of holsters, magazine holders, and hand-tooled belts.

"Big toys for big boys." Ellis laughed. Pictures covered available wall space around him: men in camouflage clothing and stern faces. A country artist had lettered several plaques with inspirational sayings and passages from the Bible. "Are you a long gunner?"

"I like just about anything that goes bang," Jeremy confessed. He bent over the handgun case and eyed a magna-ported para-ordnance .45 with a double-stacked magazine. "Man, is that a beauty."

"That's a Homestead edition they make just for us," Ellis said. He stepped into the back room and emerged with several sheets of paper. "It runs three thousand four hundred and ninety-five dollars plus tax, if you're interested. I throw in a box of ammo and a tune-up at the end of the week."

He laid the papers out on the cabinet's glass top.

"A little rich for my blood," Jeremy admitted. "Sure is pretty, though."

Ellis pushed the paper between Jeremy and the gun.

"Sorry to bother with this, but you know what they say — it ain't over 'til the paperwork's done. Gotta get your John Hancock on these liability waivers." Ellis held up a pen.

"Hey! Are you trying to put me out of a job, Colonel?"

The door closed behind them, and Jeremy turned toward a strikingly pretty blond woman in her late twenties. She looked fit and neatly ordered in an outfit that closely matched Ellis's, right down to the .45 on her athletic hip.

"Ah, the boss is here!" Ellis said. "Jeremy Walker, meet my daughter, Heidi. Heidi, Mr. Walker here was just signing in."

"First of your class to show up this morning," she said. Jeremy tried not to look surprised at the strength of her grip or the radiance in her smile as they shook hands. "I've got you billeted in Cabin B. You'll find linens and a blanket on your bunk. Chow hall is out near Range One."

Heidi walked around the display case and stood next to her dad. They looked striking together, a hardened badger of a man and his trophy-to-proper-breeding progeny.

"I'll just get my things, then," Jeremy said, signing the requisite forms. "What time do we start shooting?"

"We assemble in the classroom at eleven," the colonel told him. He pointed to Jeremy's map. "You'll find all the ranges, training areas, and facilities on there. I should point out that all thirty-six hundred acres of our ranch is open to students, except for the shaded area. That's personal space. Off-limits."

Jeremy followed the colonel's finger to a distinctly marked section of the main compound. There was no mistaking the man's intentions.

"Now would be a good time to look over that map and find your way around," the colonel said. "Don't forget to hydrate yourself and wear some sun block. That Texas sky looks friendly, but it will bite you if you let it."

"Thanks." Jeremy nodded. He took one last look at the .45 in the display cabinet and turned toward the door. It took all his self-control to avoid ogling the woman.

"What do you think?" she asked when Jeremy was gone. The woman watched their newest student disappear off the porch and around the corner.

"Nice enough fella," the colonel said. He reached under a counter and pulled out a manila folder. Inside sat everything his S-2 had discovered about one Jeremy Andrew Walker of Burke, Virginia.

"Handsome rascal," his daughter noted. "He married?"

"Not according to this," Ellis read. "But you know the rules."

"Rules." She sighed. "I'm a grown woman now. You gotta stop treating me like the farmer's daughter."

"See to the paperwork, sweetie," he said, kissing her sun-ripened cheek. Though he would gladly have thrown down his life for Heidi, the rules he mentioned had been put in place to protect something a whole lot more precious.

■

CALEB HAD ALREADY driven more than four hours south from New Jersey when he exited I-95 just north of Washington DC, at exit 27. Though the pain in his head throbbed with the force of a rock drill, he had one stop to make before starting his long trip back to the Homestead. His father had entrusted him with the very foundation of his Megiddo project, and nothing of this world would keep him from laying its cornerstone.

Caleb merged right through heavy traffic, exited the highway, and turned left at the bottom of the ramp. He drove east a little more than a mile on Route 117 and then right onto a rural though busy two-lane access highway.

His silver-colored Ford Taurus blended in nicely with everything else on the road. Washington was a city of bureaucrats, after all, a GS-12 wasteland of midlevel managers conditioned by government employment to ignore everything but lunch and the car pool.

Thank God for indifference, he thought to himself. Rush Limbaugh and Mike Savage and Bill O'Reilly had been brilliant in their ability to prey upon it. People in this country had lost God; they had lost their sense of family, of a country that meant anything more than a welfare handout and a blank check for foreigners. Americans had lost their sense of belonging — a belief that anything mattered enough to die for. And when you lost a cause great enough to die for, you lost the point in living.

Caleb knew by the searing pain in his forehead that he was living. *Embrace it,* he told himself. *Pain is just weakness leaving the body.*

He drove until he saw the blue-and-white military reservation markers. Andrews Air Force Base was a twenty thousand-acre facility surrounded by a suburban Washington DC sprawl. No one would bother him if he pulled off at the side of the road. It was just woods out here at the far end of the tarmac, anyway. Security had concentrated their resources on the airfield itself, protecting critical infrastructure and the crown jewel of American air travel: the Presidential Airlift Group.

Air Force One. Gatekeeper. The Doomsday Plane. The planes used to ferry the president around the world counted among the most secured airframes on earth.

Use the enemy's weight against them, Caleb reminded himself, trying not to let the pain distract him. *Focus on the mission.*

He pulled off at the side of the busy two-lane suburban road, threw the shifter into park, and hit the hood release.

Car trouble was the perfect cover, he knew. Nobody stopped for motorists at the side of the road anymore. Not in this part of the country. They looked the other way, trying to pretend they didn't see so they wouldn't feel guilty. They buried themselves in the *Washington Post*, paperback novels, shortsighted administrative memos — anything that took their minds off other people's hardship.

Caleb got out of the car, walked around front, lifted the hood, and reached in as if checking for something wrong with the engine.

How ironic that the best way to hide is to stand right out here and wave for people to look.

After a couple minutes, Caleb walked around to the back and opened the trunk. He lifted a heavy duffel out of the well and set it in the gravel bar ditch. He watched passing motorists with his good eye, trying to find a single driver who would look at his heavily bandaged head. They stared straight ahead, more intent on passing the car in front of them than on helping someone who looked like an emergency-room runaway.

When he had gathered enough strength for what lay ahead, Caleb hoisted the duffel onto his shoulder, and with no concern for passing commuters, he slipped down the bank and into the tree line.

XI

Thursday, 17 February
17:18 GMT
Oval Office, The White House

"WHAT IN THE name of God is going on?" the vice president demanded to know as she stormed past two uniformed marines and burst into the Oval Office.

Venable stood behind his podium, leaning forward with both hands on the front edge. He looked unsteady, his skin pale and moist, like a crackhead craving another fix.

"Seventeen kilos . . . almost forty pounds of radioactive material," Havelock answered. He leaned against a painter's scaffolding that hadn't been there when she left.

"From the University of Louisville?" She'd heard that much from the Secret Service.

"Research isotopes, mainly," Alred explained. He, Vick, and Chase stood scattered at various parts of the Oval Office as if the lack of a desk had eliminated the president's gravity. "Cesium, iridium, mostly gamma emitters, which pose the greatest threat."

"Explain that to me again," Venable said. He raised his left hand in the air as if trying to conduct some sort of information symphony.

"Radiological materials fall into three primary categories," Alred continued. "Alpha, beta, and gamma emitters. The body's natural immune system can best handle alpha and beta particles. Gamma is a different story. My people tell me that anyone interested in building an RDD would want to . . ."

"RDD?" the president interrupted. "I told you, no acronyms!"

"Radiological dispersion device," Havelock interjected. The others nodded as if they knew.

"A dirty nuke," Alred clarified further. "Though we have always worried about the bad guys getting a nuclear weapon, the most likely scenario is an RDD. It is much cheaper, easier to build, and easier to transport without detection."

"And not nearly as deadly, thank God," Beechum said. She pulled off her coat and threw it on the couch. "We're talking about a conventional explosive wrapped in glow powder, David. Could be just about anything from isotopes used to calibrate manufacturing equipment to medical implants to spent fuel rods from a power plant."

"The concept is that the blast from the explosive would disperse the radioactive material into the environment," Alred added. "If you listen to the cable news experts, they'll tell you that the surrounding area will be irradiated and rendered useless for thousands of years. That's not true. Most of these isotopes have brief shelf lives and will disperse to nonthreatening levels within days . . . perhaps even hours."

Venable's expression showed signs of relief.

"Why doesn't the media ever mention that?" he asked.

"Fear sells," Havelock answered. "Why let reality get in the way of ratings?"

"So, what's the problem?" he asked. "Sounds like the initial blast is the biggest issue."

"True from a crisis response point of view," Beechum said. "But that's not the most important consideration."

The president waved his hand again. He wanted the denouement.

"Panic," his chief of staff chimed in. The others understood crisis response; she understood politics. "You mention the word *nuclear* and people go nuts. It's the news shows; they've gotten this thing blown completely out of proportion. Joe Six-pack couldn't tell you the difference between REMs and an RC cola, but he'll whoop up holy hell if some FOX News talking head mentions the phrase 'dirty nuke.'"

"Terrorism is about destabilization through fear," Beechum agreed. "We don't call them *bombists,* we call them *terrorists.* The psychological impact of a successful detonation will completely overshadow the previous attacks. Regardless of casualties."

Venable walked toward the West Wing door, then turned left as if he'd decided to stay after all.

"How many devices?" he asked. "If they have forty pounds, are we talking several different bombs or one big one?"

"They've hit multiple targets with each of the two prior attacks," Alred reminded everyone. "We have to assume that they'll follow the same mode of operation."

No one said anything for a moment. Alred spoke up again.

"I want to point out, however, that making one of these things is not going to be easy. This RDD concept is a paper tiger. No one has tested this sort of bomb because it has no military application and law enforcement doesn't want to deal with cleaning up after test explosions."

"What's so hard about it?" Venable scolded him. "You just told me that you wrap some nuclear waste around a stick of dynamite and set it off. How hard is that?"

"Pretty hard, actually," Beechum said. She had seen this briefing before her committee after the 9/11 disasters. "The amount of explosive has to be very carefully calculated. Too much and the radioactive material will be diffused to the point where it is not even threatening. Too little and you end up with a small area of contamination that hazmat teams can quickly contain. And like Mr. Alred said, there's no real data out there; the assholes behind this may have bitten off more than they can chew."

"Where?" the president asked. He was walking in circles now. Beads of sweat glistened on his pasty forehead. He had undone his tie and taken off his coat, exposing a wrinkled shirt that stuck to his skin.

"We have to assume high-profile targets," Vick spoke up for the first time. He tried not to notice that the president had shaved poorly. Patches of heavy black whiskers stood out on his sinking cheeks.

"New York, Los Angeles . . . here inside the Beltway."

"That's what they want us to think!" Venable stopped his pacing as if transfixed by the ghost of some president past. "They know we know about the theft. They know that we're pulling out every stop trying to prevent another attack. We know that they know that we know, but we don't know what we don't know and that's . . ."

Venable started to drown in his own stream of consciousness. He sat down at his Gothic-looking harmonium and played with the keys, pressing them one at a time with his index finger. Beechum shook her head, praying to herself that he wouldn't turn it on.

"We need to be more creative in our thinking," Beechum opined.

"Right," Venable agreed. "We need to look back to the heartland, where they struck in the first place. That's where they'll hit us next . . . Kansas City, New Orleans . . ."

"Mr. President," his chief of staff tried to interrupt him.

"Chattanooga, Ojai, Portland . . . don't you see? They just want us to think . . ."

"David!" Andrea Chase called out. She fully knew the peril in letting him ramble. "We have to assume that you're the next target. Which means you have to consider evacuation options."

David Ray Venable, the forty-fourth president of the United States, nodded ever so slightly, as if her words were no more significant than the steward announcing dinner. He looked distant, sad that things had all turned out so badly.

"Yes, of course. Well, see to it, then."

He turned square to the harmonium's keys, fiddled with a half dozen stops, and flipped the On switch. The organ's ancient electric bellows began to whir.

"Thank you. That will be all."

Beechum thought for a moment about whisking them out and staying for a chat with the leader of the free world. But then she changed her mind.

Better to deal with the cabinet members in private, she thought to herself. *Something has to be done about the president before the next crisis strikes.*

Beechum followed the equally conflicted chief of staff out into the reception area.

"A word, please?" Beechum asked.

The president's closest advisors turned to listen. Behind them rose the competently played melody of "All Creatures of Our God and King." Then David Ray Venable began to sing.

■

"READY ON THE right, ready on the left, all ready on the firing line!"

Jeremy turned to face his target, an FBI-style Q silhouette he had lined up on literally hundreds of times before. The cardboard approximation of a human head and torso faced ninety degrees to him, offering just the blade edge.

Clank!

The mechanical range sprang to life, "fronting" the target.

Smooth is fast.

Jeremy drew his handgun, the web of his right hand pressing firmly down into the backstrap, wrapping his fingers around the soft rubber grips. His right index finger fell gently against the well-oiled frame.

Balance the grip sixty-forty to the outside palm.

His hands came together six inches in front of his sternum. They folded atop each other, the thumbs aligned and pointed toward the threat.

Concentrate on the front sight, squeeze the trigger — don't jerk it.

He saw the tritium dot on the front ramp, big as a tractor trailer bearing down on him. The muzzle lowered flat as he pushed the heavy steel weapon forward, his elbows slightly bent, weight forward on the balls of his feet, knees shoulder-width apart, shoulders slightly hunched, both eyes open.

Make each shot perfect, then let it go. You can't get it back. Don't bother looking.

He watched the business end of his barrel bob up and settle back down. He saw smoke spitting out the end, the front sight gleaming in the crisp blue air. He felt the shock of recoil and caught the elegant flight of the spent shell casings drifting off to the right as he poured round after round into the target. Jeremy watched it all play out in slow motion, as if directed by the Wachowski brothers. All he needed was Neo and Agent Smith to drop in and the moment would be complete.

Follow through with a cleanup sight picture. Three shots . . . four.

Jeremy held the weapon on target an extra two count, then lowered it just below line of sight and pulled it back toward his chest into what handgunners referred to as "ready gun." Everything flashed back before him, like the video HRT used to show operators where they made mistakes.

It was all over before he knew it, of course. Shooting combat courses required an empty mind. But whatever he had learned in NOTS stuck with him much deeper than conscious thought.

"Damn, son, you look like you've done this before!"

Jeremy tuned back in to his surroundings. The man standing next to him sounded impressed. The colonel stood somewhere behind them, but Jeremy didn't bother looking to see his reaction.

"You trying to show me up, or what?"

Jeremy had fired four shots from the draw in less than three seconds, yet the cumulative imprint of his bullets amounted to a single ragged hole.

"Practice," Jeremy said, turning to a wiry Hispanic with a man-sized dip of Skoal protruding from his lower lip. The wintergreen smell carried well in the dry desert air. "That's what it's all about, right?"

"Yeah, I guess," the man said. He spoke with no discernible accent. "How come I practice all the time and my target looks like shit?"

Jeremy didn't argue. There were no fake compliments on a firearms range.

"Line's cold!" one of the instructors called out. They had been shooting for about forty-five minutes in a sun Jeremy hadn't fully anticipated. Like the colonel had said, it looked friendly but could wear a man out.

The "line," as they called it, amounted to a flat gravel lot facing ten-foot-high earthen berms. A string of pneumatically operated target stands ran twenty yards from left to right. On command, students could turn, run, roll, or crawl their way toward the targets and engage them from up to fifty yards away.

Three instructors stood behind the students as they ran the drills. The colonel hung back, quietly assessing this plenary session.

Nine shooters had signed up for the high-intensity tactical, or

HIT, course — all men. As far as Jeremy could tell from their gear, he was the only civilian.

"Juan Emmanuel Javier Subealdea," the man with the bad target said. "Everybody calls me Shotgun cause I'm a breacher. Or maybe because of my shooting, huh?" He stopped loading his magazines long enough for a quick shake. "Do I know you? You look real familiar to me."

Great, Jeremy thought.

"Doubt it," he said. "Not unless you like Shakespeare. I work for a traveling company out of Washington." He followed the rest of the students as they walked down to pull their targets. Shotgun followed him back to the bleachers.

"You sure I don't know you?" the man asked. He spit a sinew of Skoal juice at a passing scorpion. "I worked dope for years. Got a real good eye for faces."

"Sorry," Jeremy said. He walked over to a case of .45 ammo and filled his pockets for the next round of shooting drills.

"Oh, shit, now I . . . ," the man started to say.

Jeremy felt a shiver.

"Look, I'm real sorry, dude," Shotgun said after looking around to make sure no one was listening. "I hope I didn't scare you, but like I said, I don't forget a face."

Jeremy didn't know how this man recognized him but guessed that he was about to find out.

"You must be here UC, right?" he asked.

"UC?" Jeremy looked puzzled. "What's that mean?"

Shotgun smiled knowingly.

"I won't say nothing. I was back at Quantico a couple months ago at the National Academy. One of our instructors was a former HRT guy. He gave us a tour of the building. I saw your picture up on the wall. That was some amazing shit you pulled down in Puerto Rico. They gave you the attorney general's Medal of Valor."

The two men walked quietly for a while.

"I'm sorry to bring it up," Shotgun said. "I just got a lot of respect for you is all. I just wanted to tell you."

Jeremy felt a knot rise up from his gut and stick in the back of his throat. This was a Group II undercover assignment with no backup. It was an operation with distinct national security implications — a mission he knew carried life-or-death consequences. He hadn't been here three hours and he'd already been compromised.

"Really, man," Shotgun assured Jeremy. "This ends here. No shit."

Jeremy pulled out his handgun and loaded a fresh magazine. If the slide slamming shut offered punctuation, he didn't mean it.

"My name's Walker," he said. "Like I told you, I'm just a fan of the Bard."

■

"MOMMY, DOES DADDY still love us?" Christopher asked. The little boy lay curled up in his mother's lap on the couch in their family room. A lime-green fiberglass cast ran from the knuckles of his left hand halfway up to his shoulder.

"Of course Daddy loves us," Caroline reassured him. "Your daddy loves you more than the earth and the moon and the stars combined. Isn't that what he always tells you?"

"Well, yeah," their middle child said, "but why would he love the moon and the sun and the stars anyway?"

Caroline paused for that one. The kid had a point.

"It's just an expression," she said. "You know, like you hold your arms out as wide as you can and tell me you love me this much."

She demonstrated.

"Yeah, but that's all there is," Christopher said. "That's a lot more than the sun and the stars and the moon. That's more than anything there is in the whole wide world."

They sat there for a while trying to calculate matters too complicated for moments like this.

"Does your arm hurt, sweetie?" Caroline asked. She had gotten up with him when he couldn't sleep. Now they sat together in a quiet house as the other two kids slept.

"Nah, not that bad," Christopher said. His dad may not have been very good at explaining love, but he had instilled a strong aversion to tears. "Dad would be proud of me, huh?"

"Very proud." Caroline stroked her son's hair. She wondered about her husband — what danger may have befallen him, whether he was comfortable, what country he had disappeared into.

I killed a man, she remembered him saying right after the Puerto Rico mission. Caroline had no idea why a thought like that would pop into her head as she held her son in her arms. The words had sounded just as out of place then, though. Jeremy had always struck her as a peaceful man. A kind man.

Before HRT.

The team had changed him, slowly but surely, the way a beard grows in and changes a man's face. It had started during New Operator Training School, or NOTS — all the endless days that left him beaten, exhausted, and too full of course work for idle chat. Then he had made the team and gone off to Puerto Rico.

The nightmares, she reminded herself, *and the rage.* Jeremy seemed to have just one emotion now. Living with him was like walking through a minefield. You never knew when a false step was going to set him off and leave the day in ruins.

"You think Dad's a superhero?" Christopher asked.

"I don't know. What do you think?" Caroline kissed the top of his head. Jeremy had remarkable talents; there was no question about that. If he could only learn to appreciate those gifts.

"I think he is," Christopher said. "He disappears whenever somebody's in trouble. He has a gun. He under arrests people."

"You've got a point there," his mom said.

"He never tells us about his missions. Well, not really. I know he makes up a bunch of stuff 'cause we're kids and he thinks we don't know."

"Could be," Caroline said. "But that would make you a junior superhero, wouldn't it? Do you think you have special powers?"

That one required a little thought.

"Nah," he said finally. "Superheroes don't break their arms."

Caroline smiled at the gifts Jeremy had given her: three wonderful children, a fine home, trust. Maybe life didn't make sense at times like this, but what life always did? HRT wouldn't last forever. One day, Jeremy would come home for good, and whenever the kids had questions about how much he loved them, the FBI Superhero could answer them himself.

■

SIRAD ARRIVED BACK in her office feeling refreshed though no better prepared to deal with a daunting challenge. If what I Can't Dunk had shown her was true, the people trying to break into Borders Atlantic's deepest secrets presented enormous complications. Dealing with the physics and math of the Quantis encryption was difficult enough. Dealing with the hair-trigger complexity of the powers behind it scared the hell out of her.

"Where have you been?" Hamid asked. He entered her office without knocking and plopped himself in one of her overstuffed chairs. "That geek, Ravi, from the Rabbit Hole has been calling all over town looking for you."

"What's he want?" Sirad asked. She pointed a remote control at a bank of televisions and flipped on the cable news channels.

"He won't say. Claims it's for your eyes only."

Sirad tossed the remote onto her desk as the monitors erupted with FOX, MSNBC, and CNN loop footage of airliner crash sites, bombed-out buildings, and body parts in high-definition flat-screen color. The top right corner of each screen read, WARNING: GRAPHIC IMAGES. The upper left read TERROR ALERT: OR-ANGE — HIGH. A slug line across the bottom offered world opinion, White House response, the growing death toll, and stock quotes. The screen — what you could see of it behind the graphics — was split between two "experts" and the respective network's host du jour.

"It's a goddamned circus," Sirad pronounced. "A whole new psychological phenomenon where the networks lure in viewers by preying on some reptilian reflex to fear. Las Vegas meets Anderson Cooper. The news according to Dr. Phil. Only in America could we replace drama with reality in entertainment and replace reality with drama in news. Absofuckinglutely amazing."

Hamid saw no point in encouraging her. He preferred CNBC.

"What do you know about the Mind Lab?" Sirad asked, changing the subject.

"Just what I've been told. Never been there."

"Ravi wants to sequester a small team there. He wants to close our cell to work in isolation until we resolve this."

"Why?" Hamid asked. "The Mind Lab is an R & D site an hour outside the city. The seventeenth floor already has access to their mainframes and software."

"I think he's afraid," Sirad said. She stared across the desk at her former lover. It had been almost a year since they'd last enjoyed each other's flesh. For some reason, that suddenly felt like a very long time.

"Afraid of what? The Rabbit Hole is well protected; impenetrable, really."

"Did you really love me, Hamid?" Sirad responded, changing the subject again. She didn't want Hamid to know the truth about Quantis. Not yet.

"I love you still," he said. He couldn't hide the pain in his eyes.

"I'm sorry, you know," Sirad told him. "I never dared to tell you that."

"If you're sorry, why have you never explained?" Hamid asked. "Why did you walk away without so much as a good-bye?" All he had ever wanted was a reason.

"It's not as easy as an explanation." She turned back toward the televisions. The past wasn't something she spent much time pondering. "It wouldn't have been enough."

"You have never trusted anyone, have you? You've never felt secure that one person would give or do anything for you just because they loved you?"

"So Ravi wants me to go with him? How soon?"

"You don't like it when something hurts, do you?" Hamid asked. "You act tough, but you don't like pain."

"I'm sorry about what happened between us," she said. "It wasn't your fault."

"Are you sorry that it happened or that it had to end?" he asked. Hamid spoke timidly, the way a lover talks when he still holds hope for something more.

"I'm sorry . . . ," she mumbled, "that I don't know the difference."

DINNER CAME NONE too soon for most of the Homestead students. Colonel Ellis had always shied from being labeled a "dude ranch" and ran his schools hard, the way he had run them in Special Forces. By the time the dinner bell sounded at seven o'clock that night, most attendees wanted nothing more than a thick steak and all the fluids they could guzzle.

"You didn't tell us you were such a prodigy," Heidi said, setting her tray next to Jeremy's at a trestle table made of cedar logs. Instructors ate with the students, as did the colonel and his family.

"The brochure said this was an advanced course," Jeremy said. He shuffled a bit to his left, giving her room. "I assumed everyone could shoot."

Ellis looked up at him from a conversation across the room, but Jeremy pretended not to notice.

"They don't shoot like you." Heidi smiled. "Pass the pepper, please?"

Jeremy handed her a set of plastic spice dispensers. They ate off trays, but the tables had been arranged with condiments in a family-style setting. The dining hall had open walls, and a cool evening breeze began to rearrange their napkins.

"Ooops!" she said, reaching out to grab a stack of napkins before they blew away. "Derned Texas wind never seems to hush. You spent much time out here, Jeremy Walker?"

He smiled at the way she pronounced his name. Words seemed to roll off her lower lip in little droplets, all moist and glittery.

"I've been to Dallas a couple times, with work," he said. Jeremy felt the colonel's eyes on him and concentrated on his buffalo steak and beans.

"I hope it's the colonel you're shying from and not my company," she said. "I know he's eyeing you pretty hard right about now, but that's 'cause he's a daddy and a military man. He doesn't know much about a girl's taste in men. In fact, I don't think he ever noticed a cute butt in his whole life."

Jeremy almost spit out his food. Heidi laughed too, banging her knee against his under the table. Her free-spirited humor felt as big as the country around them.

"You going to get me kicked out of here the first night?" Jeremy asked. Some of the other men had begun to look his way. Heidi stood out to all of them, even in a setting of stunning natural beauty.

"Naw, I want to let you get your money's worth before I get you to do something really stupid," she flirted. The woman's perfume of lilac and honey blended oddly with Hoppes No. 9 gun solvent and barbecue. Dry wind whispered across the room, filling Jeremy's nose with an intoxicating scent. "You're not married, are you?"

Jeremy shook his head. The word *no* just wouldn't escape his lips. "Girlfriend?"

"If I didn't know better, I'd say you were hitting on me." Jeremy flirted back. The steak tasted good. His skin glowed from a day in the open air. He felt happy for the first time in a long while.

"Nothing gets by you now, does it, Romeo?" She forked a bite of beans between beautiful lips. Jeremy fought the urge to stare.

"The colonel raised no timid children," she said after swallowing. "I figure I've got one week to work my magic on you, and we're nearly through with the first day already. If you're gonna stick to that timid 'aw shucks, Miss Daisy' routine, it's gonna go hard on you."

Jeremy laughed a slow, easy release. The past few weeks had wound him into a spring-tight ball of confusion, apprehension, and fear. Between the situation at home and the mission ahead, he felt trapped in one of those dreams where you try to run and just can't lift your feet.

"Is this the part where I stand up, pistol-whip all those guys staring at you, and throw you on the back of my horse so we can ride off into the sunset?" he joked. Jeremy Walker was single, right? He had a cover to maintain.

Heidi checked her watch.

"Well, the sun's almost set, and I don't ride on the back of nobody's horse," she said, completely deadpan. "But I got a couple hours before bedtime. If you know even half as much about women as you do about shooting, I'd say you ought to pull out that hog leg of yours and commence to whipping."

XII

Friday, 18 February
01:00 GMT
Vice President's Ceremonial Office, Eisenhower Executive Office
Building

"DAMMIT, ELIZABETH, DO you know what you are saying? You're talking about treason."

The vice president sat with her hands folded solemnly in front of her. The chairman of the joint chiefs of staff, the national security advisor, the president's chief of staff, and the attorney general sat in a small cluster around a massive conference table in an office typically reserved for photo ops.

"I do know what I'm saying," she calmly replied to the attorney general, Andrew Hellier. "And it is nothing of the sort. I'm merely pointing out that the president of the United States is demonstrating behavior that may become a liability to the national security of this country should we face another terrorist attack. As proctors of constitutionally prescribed rules of government, we have a sworn duty to consider all contingencies."

"Including mutiny?" Havelock asked. "I'll have none of it."

"I don't feel comfortable talking about this," Andrea Chase agreed.

"I do," the only uniformed member of the reluctant cabal announced. The chairman of the joint chiefs was a marine corps four-star named Oshinski who had never shied from conflict. "In fact, I want to remind everyone that the man playing hymns in the Oval Office right now has full authority to unleash the most powerful military forces in the history of the world. At present, he is about thirty feet from the football, and dammit, from what I've seen, that strikes this old soldier as troublesome."

The president's chief of staff would have none of it.

"He's tired, for Chrisakes," she said. "Are we really talking about invoking some arcane provision of the Constitution and altering the chain of command because David Venable needs a goddamned nap?"

"Three nights with no sleep at all," Beechum argued. "He doesn't remember what you tell him from one moment to the next."

"Would you allow him to go on television in this state, Andrea?" General Oshinski asked. "Would you want the American people — or the people of the world for that matter — to see him like this?"

The air stilled as various sets of eyes drifted around the magnificent William McPherson–designed room. Originally built for the Navy Department, the space had been renovated in the 1960s and now served as a dramatic backdrop for important meetings and press conferences. Ornamental stenciling and maritime scenes covered the walls. Mahogany, white birch, and cherry formed a testament to American woodworking underfoot. Grand fireplaces carved of Belgian black marble with gilded overmantels and green marble hearths stood at the north and south walls.

"This is not an easy conversation we're having here," Beechum argued. "I am well aware of that. But who the hell said it was supposed to be? We have been entrusted with the care of two hundred and eighty million citizens, and we're being attacked by enemies we can't even identify. I'm not playing Alexander Haig. I'm trying to do what history expects of us."

No one reacted at first. Beechum caught the eye of a Christopher Columbus bust that had been commandeered from a Spanish cruiser after the Battle of Santiago in 1898. The decorative bronze figure stared back at her with the same posed intransigence she saw in Havelock and Chase.

"What about the White House physician?" Oshinski asked after a long moment. "Perhaps he could prescribe a sedative — something to give David the rest he needs."

"Good idea," Havelock said. "David got caught off-guard by all of this. He's only had this job for three frigging weeks. Who can blame him for trying to keep up with everything?"

"This isn't about blame; it's about responsibility," Beechum pointed out. "I think the general has an excellent idea."

"What does the Constitution say about that?" the general asked. The finger on the trigger always struck him as a crucial consideration. "We have to remember that any sedative will render him ineffectual as commander in chief. Do you inherit the wind, so to speak, Elizabeth?"

Attorney General Hellier turned to the vice president, who pulled a copy of the Constitution from her case. She had studied it well but wanted text to read for effect.

"Twenty-fifth Amendment, section four: 'Whenever the Vice President and a majority of either the principal officers of the executive departments or of such other body as Congress may by law provide, transmit to the President pro tempore of the Senate and the Speaker of the House of Representatives their written declaration that the President is unable to discharge the powers and duties of his office, the Vice President shall immediately assume the powers and duties of the office as Acting President.'"

She looked around the room.

"We've got to put this in writing?" Havelock asked.

"Not so easy to talk about now, is it?" the attorney general reminded everyone. "This is action in extremis we're discussing. I know of no precedent."

"This will pale in comparison with what might happen if we don't," Beechum said. "No one in this room has more to lose politically than I do; we might as well get that out in the open. This discussion alone could give me the shortest tenure of any vice president in history — you all know that. And yet I accept that risk because I don't want to wake up tomorrow and try to explain to the American people that we let a growingly psychotic man play church music because no one wanted to hurt his feelings."

"It will leak out," Chase said.

"We have to assume so," Beechum said. "Unless . . ."

"Unless we don't tell Congress." Andrea Chase beat her to the punch. "I mean all presidents sleep, right? Who is going to know whether or not he had a little pharmaceutical help?"

"I'm not sure I want to hear this," the attorney general said. "We're talking about drugging the president of the United States! As top law enforcement official, I have to warn you that this is very . . ."

"The Constitution mandates that if we go to Congress with a no-confidence vote, the president will have to argue in writing that he deserves to get his job back," Beechum noted. "Do any of you want to explain that to the president when he wakes up?"

Uneasy smiles rippled around the table for the first time.

"I think we owe it to David," the chairman of the joint chiefs said. "I mean, we gave him coffee to keep him up. Why can't we get the White House doc to slip him a little something to help him sleep? He'll wake up tomorrow night a new man, and no one will be the wiser."

"We're talking twenty-four hours," Chase reminded them. "What about the radioactive materials that were just stolen? We've already faced two attacks, and . . ."

"And the alternative?" Oshinski asked. "Do we wait until somebody actually uses them? I don't want to think about what that man might do after another sleepless night."

Beechum stood. The woman had never shied from tough calls.

"I think we have no choice here," the vice president announced. "The president's current mental state poses a clear and present threat to the security of this country. Unless you all take action to stop me, I plan to speak with Dr. Hernandez immediately."

No one objected.

"General, you make sure we're covered at the Pentagon," she continued. "Andrea, you handle inquiries from the staff. We run tomorrow's press gaggle as scheduled, but we cancel the two-o'clock briefing due to security concerns . . . leak a story that we've got something positive cooking. Hellier, we need you to talk with your counsel — discreetly — to make sure we don't have any legal problems here. I'll take the political heat, but I've already had one brush with jail, and I didn't like it."

There were no objections.

"Twenty-four hours," Oshinski said. "We've got our work cut out for us."

"It's one day," Havelock chirped. Beechum's resolve had buoyed his optimism. "How much could go wrong in that?"

■

JIMMY BREEDLOVE SAT at a desktop computer terminal in the middle of a perfectly round 15,000-square-foot bunker. A 160-foot-long, 12-foot-high video mosaic map board circled him, flashing information across 230,076 Lucite tiles. From where he sat in the California Independent System Operator, or Cal-ISO, Folsom Control Center, he could monitor every electron moving through the United States western power grid.

"Hey, Bo, we got a load indicator caution in Santa Barbara," he called out to one of his fellow operators. It was a routine alert, a sampling of more than four thousand locations every four seconds. Nothing to consider troubling.

"Must be Oprah Winfrey firing up the cotton candy machine," Bo called out. A couple other staffers started to laugh.

"Nah, *People* magazine says she's on a diet again. Must be the treadmill sucking wind!"

Breedlove laughed along with them. He truly enjoyed his job as a staff engineer at the Folsom Control Center. He considered himself an integral part of a power grid that delivered 200 billion kilowatt-hours of electricity each year to more than 30 million Californians.

Working here at Cal-ISO's supersecret control center placed him on the forefront of America's infrastructure protection system. Like the guards, management, and other engineers, Breedlove had received training from state and federal crisis planners. In fact, the FBI had scheduled a scenario-based readiness exercise for the following week. He hoped the recent terror attacks would push it back a month so he could take that vacation his boss had just canceled.

"Hey, Bo, what position are you playing tonight?" Breedlove asked. They had a softball game after work, and the wife had given him the night to go out with the boys. It would be great to catch a couple brews down at Mulligan's.

"Second base," Bo answered. "Hey, anybody heard from San Onofre?"

The San Diego county nuclear power plant had scheduled to power down its reactor for routing maintenance later that night. The plant manager was supposed to call in with particulars.

"I hear the waves are breaking to the right on bitchin' three-foot swells with an offshore wind." Breedlove laughed. "They say it's *the kind.*"

Bo and Breedlove — both Orange County natives — had grown up surfing the shoreline between Richard Nixon's old home in San Clemente and the controversial San Onofre Nuclear Generating Station. The beach break there was known among locals as Trestles.

"You're a wiseass," Bo called back. He checked his monitors again and allowed himself a moment to reminisce about the old days. Southern California had been a very different place in the sixties, before the traffic and congestion got so ridiculous. The move to Folsom — a beautiful city of fifty-two thousand located halfway between San Francisco and Lake Tahoe — had given his kids the kind of youth he looked back on with such fondness.

And who could argue with the job? Bo worked as a high-tech traffic controller of sorts, monitoring a critical section of the Western Interconnect: 25,526 electrical circuit miles over 124,000 square miles of real estate, representing 40 percent of the Western Systems Coordinating Council's overall demand.

The tools Cal-ISO gave him made it all seem effortless. Bo sat in a command post any movie producer would have admired. In addition to the giant tracking board, four Electrohome video-projection screens displayed transmission data in sixteen interconnected western states. Televisions monitored cable and network news.

And anyone who thought about compromising the system had better think again. Armed guards patrolled the grounds topside, rivaling the nearby Folsom Prison for security. Palm readers and keypads prevented unauthorized access to the bunker, and its nondescript surroundings stifled inquiry. Most employees joked that anonymity was their best defense.

"Hey, boys and girls, it's Miller time!" a voice called out as Bo checked his computer screen.

He and his partner looked up to see the overnight shift filing in through an open door. One of the operators, a face they hadn't seen before, looked around with a little too much enthusiasm.

"How's the grid?" the man asked.

How's the grid? Breedlove thought. Who was this new kid?

"Did we hire somebody I don't know about?" Breedlove asked.

"Must have filled Sharon's spot." Bo shrugged. One of their coworkers had just landed a promotion to Sacramento.

"Must be. Who else would look so happy working the graveyard tour?"

Then something happened that changed both their minds. The new guy tossed his knapsack onto the half-moon-shaped console in the middle of the room and ran.

"What the hell?" Bo asked. But it was too late. He and his surfing buddy from the beach breaks of Orange County saw a steel cylinder roll out of the backpack and fall to the floor.

So much for softball, Breedlove sighed to himself. *So much for anything.*

■

A CRESCENT MOON hung just off the northern horizon, offering little light to spoil a cloudless sky of stars. Jeremy walked slowly alongside the colonel's last single daughter, wondering how in hell he was going to get himself out of this mess.

"So, you like Shakespeare?" Heidi asked.

The beautiful blonde wore a light-blue Navaho roper's jacket and a straw Stetson. She kept both hands in her pockets and kicked stones as she walked him down a gravel cow path.

"What I know about him, I guess," Jeremy said. He'd read the standards in high school — *Romeo and Juliet, Hamlet, Macbeth.* A girlfriend had played Rosalind in *As You Like It* during college.

"I thought you worked for a Shakespeare company?"

"I'm a stagehand," Jeremy explained. She smelled clean and warm in the thickening air. "I don't do any acting."

"But you hear the plays every night. Don't the words sink in? They're so pretty."

Heidi didn't say anything for a minute. They walked along through the quiet night, wondering what to make of each other's intentions.

"I played Juliet, one time, in high school. It was just a scene we did for senior English, but I liked it. Still remember my lines, want to hear?"

She jumped a couple steps ahead of him and yanked her hands out of her pockets. Jeremy had to smile at her instant and childlike enthusiasm. Her smile literally glowed in the still, crisp air.

"'What's in a name? That which we call a rose by any other name would smell as sweet; so Romeo would, were he not Romeo call'd, retain that dear perfection which he owes without that title. Romeo, doff thy name; and for that name, which is no part of thee, take all myself . . .'"

She waited as if for a prompter.

"That's your line."

"My line? I don't know it!"

"You say 'I take thee at thy word: Call me but love, and I'll be new baptiz'd; henceforth I never will be Romeo.'"

She stepped closer now, lost in fond recollection of words that had once taken her to a gentler place. Heidi reached out with both hands and gently cupped his face.

"I think that is the sweetest thing I ever heard. Don't you?"

Her words softened; then she leaned forward just enough to lay her lips against his. The kiss felt as natural as the scene around them, but he didn't return it. He was a prop in a play at this point. Nothing more.

"How cam'st thou hither, tell me, and wherefore? The orchard walls are high and hard to climb, and the place death, considering who thou art, if any of my kinsmen find thee here."

Heidi took Jeremy in her eyes for a long breath, and he wondered how much play there had been in her acting, after all.

"I'm a stagehand," he said. "Never been much good at acting."

Heidi leaned in and kissed him again. This time, the sentiment came not from some long-dead playwright, but from a young woman grown lonely in a soldier's life.

"Darn — you would have to be a good kisser, wouldn't you?" she asked. Heidi stepped back and crossed her arms. She thought it beautiful how the desert framed him at night.

"I'm not much of a ladies' man," Jeremy said. It was the truth, and she knew it.

"That's the best kind," she said.

Gunfire erupted behind them, out near the fifty-yard ranges. Then an explosion.

"What's that?" Jeremy asked. She shrugged her shoulders and kept staring.

"You think I'm too forward, don't you?"

"I think you're a beautiful woman trapped in the middle of nowhere." Jeremy smiled. He looked off behind her, trying to concentrate on anything besides her face. Then, when he knew there was nothing but this moment, he turned back. "Why else would you have any interest in walking around with the likes of me?"

Heidi moved back toward him — close enough to feel his warmth — her arms still crossed.

"The likes of you?" she purred. "Judgment is the Lord's, but I think 'cute' is my call to make. The likes of you suit me fine."

Heidi pushed herself up on the toes of her boots and kissed him again. This time she tested him with the tip of her tongue. Her lips touched his ever so lightly, timid but curious too.

Jeremy froze in the tumult of a grand misgiving.

You're married! a voice screamed in his head. *You can't be kissing this woman!*

But there was another voice, countering that he'd been sent here for a reason. People with more information than he believed Colonel Ellis responsible for attacks that had already killed thousands of people. If the best way inside his circle of Phineas priests was through his daughter's affections, who was Jeremy to deny her?

"Something's wrong, huh?" she said.

"No," Jeremy said. He put his hands on her arms, more like a coach than a hopeful lover. "Nothing's wrong."

Her eyebrows dipped just a bit as if she knew that wasn't so.

"I just didn't expect this," he said. "You're a beautiful woman. Stunning, really. And I . . . I don't really feel like I know what I'm supposed to do."

It was all he could think of. Killing was easy. Adultery was hard.

"Well, why didn't you say so, you silly boy?" Heidi giggled. The light twinkling in her eyes had nothing to do with the moon or stars. She bounced on her toes a couple times as if someone had just played her favorite song. "Follow me!"

Heidi wrapped her arms around Jeremy's waist and pressed her lips against his with a newfound confidence. There was nothing timid in her affections this time. She used her tongue to find his, moving tight against his weight, drinking him in with the danger and the delightful surprise of finding something wonderful in a landscape of cactus and stone.

■

"HOW IS HE?" Beechum asked. The president's secretary had worked for Venable since his first political campaign almost twenty years earlier. From the Connecticut legislature to the U.S. House of Representatives and then back to the statehouse in Hartford, the soft-spoken widow had devoted her career and, in many ways, her life to a man she revered.

"I'm getting worried about him," the secretary said. "He just won't sleep." A private door connected her desk to the Oval Office, and she had watched over him like a worried mother.

"I know," Beechum said. "Is he alone?"

"Yes. The secretary of state just left."

"Give us a couple of minutes, will you?" Beechum asked.

The secretary nodded her head and turned to an endlessly ringing phone.

The vice president knocked twice on an open door and found her boss sitting at the harmonium, hands in his lap, staring blankly at the keys. He looked every bit as torn and disheveled as the room around him.

"A word, David?" she asked.

"Umm, yes . . . Elizabeth. Please . . ."

The vice president walked in and sat on one of the two opposing couches.

"Is there news?" he asked.

"Nothing imminent," she lied. Financial markets were tanking around the globe. Americans were running stores dry of duct tape, bottled water, and ammunition. The FAA still hadn't untangled domestic flight schedules. Intelligence and law enforcement agencies were drowning in a sea of leads. Congress had gone into indefinite recess for fear of making themselves a target.

"How do you feel, David?"

The president nodded a little too enthusiastically.

"Good. Good." He shook his head as if trying to clear a daydream. "Do you hear that?"

The president stood up from his harmonium, ear cocked to one side, and crossed the room. "I can't seem to place it."

Beechum heard nothing.

"Place what?"

"That symphony," he said, wandering around the room, searching. "It sounds like Haydn, but I'm not. . . . Listen to the oboes; they're absolutely ethereal."

He shuffled around the Oval Office on unsteady feet.

"There, you hear it?" he asked again. The president reached out to the wall and ran his hand along the plaster as if the music were coming from invisible speakers.

"David, it's not Haydn," she blurted out. "It's your mind playing tricks on you. You need sleep."

Beechum held a vial of white powder in the palm of her sweaty right hand. The White House physician had agreed with her assessment but insisted on administering the proper dosage himself. She had argued that the president would not willingly take a sedative; the doctor's presence would do nothing but alarm him. Only the threat of allowing Venable access to TV cameras settled the argument. The physician agreed to wait outside in the Roosevelt Room until Venable nodded off.

"Sleep? Nonsense!" Venable barked, still cocking his ear toward the sound only he could hear. "We have a national crisis on our hands, in case you haven't noticed! What do you expect me to . . ."

He trailed off, searching again for the symphony.

"David, sit down and talk to me."

Beechum realized that dosing the president would not be easy. The powerful sedative in her hand was supposed to be odorless and tasteless, but getting it into his body might prove tricky. If her first attempt didn't work, someone would have to administer an injection, and that presented a whole new set of problems.

"Please, David, sit with me and have a sip of coffee." She waited until he turned toward the inaudible hum and poured the powder into a cup on the now ever-present service tray.

"Coffee?" he asked, as if the idea hadn't occurred to him. "No, I've . . ."

The symphony again.

"Here," she said. Beechum poured steaming liquid into the White

House china and mixed in a little cream, just the way he liked it. "We need to talk about the radioactive isotope theft."

"Where's Alred?" the president asked. "He's the only one of them who knows anything about . . ."

He lost his train of thought. The president wandered over to his second in command and sat. She handed him the drink.

Beechum poured herself a cup and sipped it with exaggerated interest.

"Very nice," the president said. He stared into the cup until he'd finished it.

"There's something I want to discuss with you, David. Please sit with me for a minute."

The president followed her suggestion like a man in a hypnotic trance.

"We have a source inside a group . . . ," she began. But there was no point in finishing. Before she could wonder if it had worked, the president of the United States slumped onto the center cushion. The cup fell from his hand and broke on the hardwood floor. His secretary heard it and hurried in.

"Oh, my . . ." The elderly woman gasped. She started toward the couch.

"It's all right, Millie," Beechum reassured her. "He's just decided to take a nap."

The doctor stepped in too, a stethoscope already around his neck.

"Tell the Secret Service we need to get the president to bed," Beechum ordered. "Quickly, please. We don't want to start any rumors."

■

JORDAN MITCHELL LOVED his country so much he had allowed it to hate him. From *USA Today* to *Imus in the Morning*, commentators, pundits, and unnamed government sources pointed to his Quantis phone as the facilitator of insurgent plots. Nothing could have been further from the truth of course. If not for information he had gathered through critical intercepts, America would have had to rely on bureaucrats at the FBI and CIA. What a tragedy that would have been.

"How close are we?" he asked.

"Just a couple of miles, Mr. Mitchell," Trask answered. They sat next to each other in the back of a month-old Maybach 62. The elegant 543 horsepower sedan — Mercedes's recent contribution to the handmade automobile market — smelled of grand napa leather, wool carpet, and French polished rosewood. A bottle of Pellegrino and two Waterford tumblers rested between them, untouched.

"Lovely in the snow, isn't it?" Mitchell asked. He held the prospectus of a successful biotech in his lap but let his eyes wander to scenery passing by his window. Borders Atlantic had never ventured into the life sciences, but from everything he had seen in recent months, biogenetic engineering looked like the newest frontier of venture capitalism.

"Just like James Taylor says," Trask observed. "'The Berkshires seemed dreamlike on account of that frosting . . .'"

"Who?" Mitchell asked.

"James Taylor. He's a singer. Wonderful, really."

Mitchell pushed the prospectus aside and picked up another folder that he had studied well during the past week. It held a half-inch stack of top secret military records and CIA after-action reports. The first document was a xeroxed copy of an Advanced Research Projects Agency file dated January 3, 1983. The title line read "Civil Defense Scenario 4: Project Megiddo." Beneath that someone had stamped TOP SECRET, then CODE WORD PROTECTED: ZORA.

"Odd that we settled so close to each other, isn't it?" Mitchell asked. He opened the folder to an army personnel file.

"Like you said, this part of the country looks lovely in the snow," Trask said. He typed away at a laptop — part of the car's business center, which included a fax, wireless Internet, and, of course, the company's secure Quantis communication system. Its electrotransparent rear roof, DVD player, and twin flat-screen televisions provided entertainment. A twenty-one-speaker Bose stereo offered music so powerful, its output was measured in terms of horsepower.

"That's it, there."

Trask pointed up the road to a modest but neatly kept gambrel-roofed house of 1970s vintage. The mustard-colored aluminum siding had faded unevenly, and the garage door looked ready for replacement, but the home fit nicely on its lot. The owner had parked his Ford F-150 in the driveway under a dusting of snow. His bright-yellow Fisher snowplow looked brand new from the dealer.

"I think I expected something a little more . . . a little nicer for this guy," Mitchell remarked. Most of the information in his file was two decades old, but his investigators had catalogued the basics. The man had made enough money to live larger than this.

"You know people and their money," Trask said, powering down his computer. "There's no accounting for taste."

The driver pulled in behind the pickup and hurried around to open Mitchell's door. Trask followed his boss up the concrete front steps and rang the bell.

"Yes?" the man of the house answered. He stood behind an aluminum storm door, clad in wide-wale corduroys and a threadbare cardigan. "May I help you?"

He looked at Mitchell, then at the car.

"Do you know who I am?" Mitchell asked.

"I read the papers," the man said. He showed no reaction one way or the other.

"Would you mind if we come in to speak with you for a moment?"

The man's knuckles tightened where he held the door. He looked up and down the street, then back at a man any of his neighbors would have recognized as well.

"What is it you want?" the man demanded. He craned his neck, peering up and down the street again. "Why should I let you in?"

"Because you were a patriot once," Mitchell told him. "And you have something I want."

This is a man who acquires billion-dollar corporations, the man in the cardigan thought. *Magazines reported about how Jordan Mitchell had spent years tracking heirlooms for his weapons collection. This man asks for things politely, but anyone can see in his face that "no" is just a waste of time.*

"What could I have that you would want?"

"Details about the Megiddo project," Mitchell said.

"The what?"

This man either had no idea what Mitchell was talking about or he was a damned good liar.

"This is very important," the Borders Atlantic CEO said. "I think you know I wouldn't be here otherwise."

Mitchell lifted the ARPA folder and held it up to the glass door. It was open to page twenty-two, a black-and-white photocopy of a man in OD fatigues and a green beret. The picture looked old and dated, but there was no mistaking the face.

"I'll be damned," the homeowner said. "They told me that guy had disappeared forever."

XIII

Friday, 18 February
02:10 GMT
Cabinet Room, The White House

FIRST NEWS OF the attack came via the U.S. government's principal intelligence-gathering agency: CNN. Andrea Chase was talking on an STU-III secure telephone to General Oshinski in the War Room at the Pentagon when Wolf Blitzer went live with footage of emergency crews in California.

"Havelock!" she yelled at the top of her lungs. The national security advisor's office was at the far end of the hall, down past the VP's suite. She didn't care who heard.

"Andrea have you seen . . ." The press secretary literally ran into her in the doorway as the chief of staff bolted from her desk.

"Assemble the cabinet," she said, ignoring the thought that the executive branch's spokesman would soon have his own problems to deal with. "I want the National Security Council in the SIT-ROOM. Now."

"TV is reporting power outages across the west," he said, running after her. "Seventeen states . . ."

"Where's the vice president?" Chase asked.

The president lay upstairs in a drug-induced coma, law enforcement and the intelligence community were already pushing the limits of their resources, Washington was just limping back into a city paralyzed by snow, and most of the White House staff was running on fumes.

"Where's the vice president?"

The press secretary knew he had ended up in the wrong place at the wrong moment, but there was no way out now.

"I don't know. It's getting late, she's probably in . . ."

"Andrea, the western grid is down," Havelock said, charging out of his office. Most of the staff had already gone for the day. The three senior officials stood in the white pall of overhead fluorescent lights and shuddered with dread.

"I want Alred and Vick over here as soon as possible," Chase said. She slapped fingers into her palm as she counted out directives. "We need to find the vice president and keep her here. Get the Secret Service shift commander and the military communications director to meet me downstairs right now."

She paused to run mental triage on the wave of political casualties flowing into her head.

"We'll run this out of the Oval Office, understood?" she said. "The West Wing will be crawling with press corps, and I don't want them asking why the lights aren't on in there. Go!"

The press secretary and the national security advisor hurried off in opposite directions to begin making calls.

Twenty-four hours, Chase yelled within her own head. *How could I have been so stupid?*

■

"SHHHHHH, HE'LL HEAR us," Heidi whispered. She dragged Jeremy by the hand, back behind the main house, toward a secret place where she knew no one would interrupt. "I swear that man can hear the sun rising."

"Are you sure this is a good idea?" Jeremy whispered back. "He said this area is off-limits."

The new moon had risen high above them, providing enough light to see but not enough to expose their movement.

"It's not off-limits to me." Heidi giggled. She watched the house as they scurried from one outbuilding to another, clinging to the shadows. A single lamp burned warmly in the living room windows, but the rest of the place looked dark.

"He's going to have my ass if he catches us," Jeremy thought out loud. He felt like a high school kid trying to find a place to park.

"Not if I have it first," she said. Heidi stopped to playfully kiss him again. Her nose felt cold against Jeremy's cheek, but there was no mistaking her heat.

Jeremy allowed her to drag him, still torn about how far this could go. He had lied for his government; he had killed for it. Would they really expect him to commit adultery too?

"In here," Heidi said. She stopped at a toolshed no more than six feet square.

"Oh, this is classy. Don't we at least get a couple bales of hay to lie on?"

"You want to talk or get lucky?" Heidi laughed. She reached into Jeremy's pants pocket. "'Cause I'm beginning to worry about you, Romeo."

She fished her hand around a bit, leaning closer and biting his top lip. Jeremy tried to control himself, but . . .

"Ohhhh," she cooed. "Is that for me?"

Heidi let her fingers roam just long enough to tease him, then pulled a Leatherman out of Jeremy's pocket.

"They lock this just to keep the students out. It's easy to pick."

Jeremy looked toward the house for signs of life as Heidi jimmied the door. It took seconds.

"Come on," she said, pulling him inside. "Watch the stairs."

Jeremy could see nothing in the inky blackness, but he knew by the smell and the way the air felt on his face that something was wrong. This was no toolshed.

"I can't turn the lights on until we get downstairs," Heidi whispered. She led him down concrete steps to what felt like a hallway. She held one of his hands in hers, but he used the other to guide himself along a wall. They passed two doors on the right, then stopped.

"In here," she said. Heidi tugged at his hand, then pushed a door closed behind them.

"Where in hell are we?" Jeremy asked.

"Not hell, sweetie," Heidi cooed. "If I get my way, you're gonna think you're in heaven."

She pulled his face down to hers and kissed him hard, hungrily, like a woman trapped in a life without affection. Heidi pulled open her jacket and guided his hand up under her shirt. She reached into his pocket again but found that things had changed.

"Don't worry, we're safe down here," she said.

Jeremy tried to return the desire, but a jackhammer of doubt pounded inside his head.

Never forget who you are inside, the UC coordinator had told him back at the Point. Many an undercover agent had failed worst when he failed himself.

What I am, Jeremy decided, *is married.* He loved his wife, and nothing he had learned in a couple days of role-playing at some CIA facility in North Carolina was going to help him act otherwise.

"Heidi," he said, pulling away from her. His lips felt moist with her lust. The impenetrable darkness exaggerated the sound of their breathing. "Heidi, I can't. Please, this isn't right."

Jeremy felt her hand slip out of his pocket. She stepped away from him.

"I'm sorry if I misled you," he said. "It's just that . . ."

"It's just that you seem to have trouble with the truth." A new voice filled the darkness. "Maybe that's why you have misled all of us."

Lights flashed on, red but still blinding. As Jeremy's eyes adjusted, he found six men standing in a semicircle around him. They wore robes that reached to the floor and hoods that covered all but their eyes. Jeremy heard the door slam shut behind him and knew that Heidi was gone.

"Now maybe you'd like to tell us your real name, Mr. Walker?" the man in the middle said.

There was no mistaking the accent, even through the mask — it belonged to the colonel.

■

SIRAD TURNED OFF the Merritt Parkway at Exit 37 and drove three miles along country roads to a business park distinguished by stone walls, manicured grounds, and shaded glass. Building 1100 looked no different from the others except for the satellite dishes atop its flat roof and the fact that security patrols at this Borders Atlantic off-site carried guns. Fog hovered above the now-melting snow, lending the place a Brigadoon-like hush.

"Malneaux; Quantis project," she told the man at the guardhouse. He checked her company ID, then found her name on a list of preapproved visitors.

"Suite twenty-two," he said. "You can park in lot A."

She did. A second security guard inside the front door escorted her through two cipher locks and a wave path like the one in the Rabbit Hole. Sirad found Ravi, I Can't Dunk, and a third man already hard at work.

"Slumming?" the systems engineer asked when she arrived.

"I should have stayed in the city," she said. "But I heard you needed some adult supervision."

Ravi laughed but didn't bother getting up from his terminal. He had surrounded himself with yellow legal pads, Red Bulls, and Twizzlers. I Can't Dunk stood over his left shoulder. He jotted notes on the palm of his hand but didn't acknowledge Sirad at all.

"Have you met our sound guy?" Ravi asked.

Sirad shook her head. The man sitting at Ravi's right smelled of cigarette smoke and well-ripened armpit. He wore about a week's worth of Bob Dylan scruff and a homemade T-shirt that read "E=MC Hammer."

"N-N-N-N-Nice to m-m-meet you," he said. Unlike I Can't Dunk, this guy stared shamelessly at Sirad's chest. "Fuck, Ravi, you d-d-din't tell me she w-w-was so g-g-goddamned hot!"

"Don't mind him, he's harmless," Ravi said. He pointed to a series of numbers and symbols on his monitor and turned to I Can't Dunk. "There's our anomaly."

"What are we working on?" Sirad asked as she pulled off her jacket and threw it on a vacant chair. The room around her looked different from the seventeenth-floor communications center at the Albemarle Building. This so-called mind lab looked more like a college computer classroom. A half dozen terminals rested quietly atop open work spaces. White boards covered two walls. There were a few cheap-looking landscape prints and a couch upholstered in earthtone plaid.

"Digital signature," Ravi said. "Our mole is using a pretty impressive cloaking algorithm designed to keep us from identifying him."

"F-f-f-fucker's smart," the sound guy said. He craned his head to check out Sirad's butt.

"Who are you, again?" Sirad asked. He held a Mountain Dew in one hand and a half-smoked Pall Mall in the other. Despite his hungover-frat-boy look, Sirad could sense a seething intellect.

"Wave theorist," I Can't Dunk spoke up. He seemed proud. "Sound waves."

"Why do we need a sound guy on an intrusion project?"

The Indian cryptographer pointed to another series of numbers and symbols. "You're right about those FORTRAN diversions," he said to I Can't Dunk; then he turned to look at Sirad as if annoyed with her ignorance.

"We need him to generate randomness. Remember the Nguyen cornerstone? We found it had specific application with regard to stochastic wave theory. Hammer Time, here, may look like roadkill, but he has found a way to uncover anomalous order coefficients. We just hired him away from a California tech firm."

"Yeah, I'm a real world fucking g-g-g-genius," he said.

"I thought we had already identified this mole," Sirad said.

"We have," I Can't Dunk said. "But we don't want them to know that. Hammer Time is helping us play possum until they make their move."

"K-k-k-kinda hot in h-h-here, ain't it?" the soundman asked. He sucked his filterless cigarette down to a stub and dropped it into the dregs of his Mountain Dew.

"You're going to have to stop that." Sirad scowled. "Smoke really bothers me."

"L-l-l-lighten up, sexy," Hammer Time said. "Those t-t-titties of yours are *killing* me, but I'm learning to c-c-cope."

Sirad had no time for this idiot's games. She pulled her shirt up with one hand and her bra down with the other, exposing two exquisitely formed, dark-nippled breasts.

"There," she said as if she'd just negotiated a trade. "Now you've seen them. So go take a cold shower and lose the fucking cigarettes. We've got a long night ahead of us, and I don't like the way you make me smell."

. . .

THE VICE PRESIDENT blew past two uniformed marines outside the main entrance to the Situation Room. Because of the heavy traffic now, she had ordered the doors propped open. Security had its place, but at this point, locks needlessly slowed things down.

"We've got everyone but the secretary of HHS," Andrea Chase told her. James trailed behind them with NSA flash traffic in one hand and Beechum's dry cleaning in the other. Everyone would need a change of clothes before this was over.

"They're upstairs?" she asked.

"In the Cabinet Room," Chase responded. "They'll wait."

Beechum hurried past the SITROOM's video teleconferencing center, down a hallway, through administrative cubicles, then right twice into the main conference room. Though called the Situation Room, this state-of-the art facility was actually a suite of offices designed to keep the president informed during times of emergency. Eisenhower had ordered it built under the West Wing in the 1950s, but no one ever intended it as a bomb shelter. That was over on the other side of the mansion and was referred to as PEOC: the Presidential Emergency Operations Center. The Pentagon claimed it could withstand all but a point-blank nuclear strike.

"Let's go. What have we got?" Beechum demanded.

"Shouldn't we wait for the president?" the FBI director suggested.

"The president is working with his cabinet," Beechum lied. Pulling this off would require the skill of a shell-game hustler, but with Havelock, the general, and Venable's own chief of staff in her corner, it might work. "Don't make me repeat myself!"

"Looks like a total loss of the Western Interconnect," Alred said. A satellite photo popped up on a recently installed flat screen behind him: the United States at night. Virtually everything west of the Rockies was black. "California is down."

"Details," Beechum said. She spoke firmly, with a laserlike focus no one had seen to this point in the crisis. The attitude of the room rose to meet her.

"Ten million households," Alred said. His back straightened, his voice grew louder. "Fourteen thousand hospitals, seventeen nuclear reactors, three of the country's busiest ports, both national laboratories. Between them and the university system, we're talking fifteen negative-pressure biohazard environments."

"What about our defense posture?"

"We have fifty-seven DoD facilities in the affected areas," Alred continued. "Those include the San Diego Naval Base — biggest in the country — NORAD, and Peterson Air Force Base in Colorado, as well as Fort Huachuca in Arizona. That covers JSOC assets, intelligence-gathering capabilities, conventional forces, and our Strategic Air Command. Our war-fighting posture has been significantly challenged."

"Do we know for sure what started it?" Beechum asked. She wrote nothing down. Her mind was enough.

"DOE says it started at a flow-monitoring center in Folsom, California. This country has three separate grids, and Cal-ISO manages the Western Interconnect — seventeen states with links to British Columbia and Mexico."

"How?"

"Conventional explosive in a backpack. Very small in size, but it was an RDD. DOE estimates one to two ounces of a gamma-emitting isotope, most likely cesium. The facility will take weeks to decontaminate."

"Connected to the Louisville theft?" Chase asked.

"We have to assume so," Alred responded.

"Who?" Beechum asked.

"The same group — Ansar ins Allah — claimed responsibility. Same audiotape delivery to local media markets concurrent with the attacks . . ."

"Attacks?" Beechum asked. "There was another?"

"We had a smaller, similar detonation at a backup station in Alhambra, California. That was also an RDD; also a complicated decon. Cal-ISO estimates that it could take weeks to reestablish the complex routing network that makes the grid work. We'll have some power restoration before then, but this has huge national security implications."

Beechum rubbed her eyes.

"There's something else."

"Of course," she said. "There's always something else."

"There were two survivors," Alred told her. "Well, they survived for almost an hour."

"Did we interview them?" Chase asked. "Did they see anything?"

"They saw the bomber. Male, white. An employee."

"What?" Havelock asked. "White? Maybe they were delirious. We're looking for Arabs."

"Not anymore," he said. Alred pointed to the same screen he had used for the satellite reconnaissance photo. The flat screen flashed with dull gray surveillance video from the Folsom Control Center.

"Does this guy look Arab to you?"

■

GI JANE HAD been taught the difference between right and wrong. Her father, a devoutly religious man, had shown her the power of a strong spirit and raised her with discipline. Parochial school had instilled a thirst for knowledge. Harvard had quenched it, offering the pristine realization that questions, not answers, provided the only true path to understanding. She had always led a life ordered by rules, savoring the symmetry of logic and the balance of an underlying truth.

Then she joined the army.

Deep breath, she told herself, trying to calm a pounding heart. *Stay back in traffic. Use the other cars for cover. Pick a spot and then make your move.*

No one could understand why an Ivy League–educated linguist would drop out of graduate school and trade academic robes for government-issued camouflage. But then, none of them had been approached the way she had. None of them had heard the calling.

Diplomatic license SA-227, she reminded herself. *Charcoal BMW Z4. Male driver. Arab. No passenger.*

They made it sound so intriguing. Hotel rooms in different cities. Plane tickets Saturday mornings to places she had never been. There was always a different face, someone offering just enough encouragement to string her along. It was more a chase than an employment process, she now knew. A delicate seduction.

There. She saw the sleek little sports car moving out of the fast lane, accelerating past eighty miles per hour to avoid a couple of black kids in a Toyota XRS. *Maintain a two-car buffer*, the Camp

Peary surveillance instructors had told her during the first phase of instruction. *Stay right or left whenever possible. Most drivers look there only when changing lanes.*

They had first approached her in the college library, between the stacks. A soft-spoken woman in a Burberry skirt and sandals had asked her something in Farsi. An innocuous question that she had answered without much thought. This was Harvard. People spoke in all kinds of tongues.

Move closer, instinct told her. *That car is faster than this one; don't let him get too far ahead.*

They shared common interests, common goals. This woman looked plain, like she did, and she liked to read. They met for coffee a couple times and became friends.

Damn that little thing is fast, she thought, pressing down on the accelerator. *Should have remembered that diplomatic immunity gives these assholes a get-out-of-jail-free card. Traffic laws are little more than a nuisance to them. Should have rented something a little more powerful.*

They went to New York for spring break and stayed with one of the woman's friends. There was a nice dinner, some wine. More wine. Then late at night, a question that ignited feelings she didn't know she had.

"Do you believe in anything strongly enough to die for it?" the woman had asked. They were in a bar. The woman's friend leaned back into his seat, watching her reaction.

Faster, she chided herself. Her speedometer read eighty-five, but the car was still pulling away. *That's the exit, less than a mile ahead.*

"Strongly enough to die for?" GI Jane had answered. "My family, I guess. Certain friends. Why?"

"What about your country?"

She remembered feeling the wine and the noise around her and the overwhelming sense that something was not what it seemed. First she felt strangely threatened, then excited, like the first time she'd stood on a diving board looking down. The moment prickled on her skin then settled between her thighs. It was the first real sense of thrill she had ever experienced.

Pull up behind him, she coached herself. *Anticipate, calculate, close the gate.*

It had gotten better from there. First the meetings with people who asked her questions like "How well do you think you can lie?" and "What's the largest thing you've ever killed?"

Some people would have recoiled and run, she thought at the time. But that was the whole point. They probably approached lots of candidates who had the basic smarts and background to do the job. The subterfuge helped weed out the posers.

Make it look like a pass, she told herself. *No sudden movements to draw attention. Wait until just before the exit and move with him.*

It had all been very calculated and professional. The woman in the Burberry skirt and sandals had made her from the start.

Right front bumper even with the Z4's left rear bumper, she thought. *Keep a decent standoff until . . . hold . . . hold . . . now!*

GI Jane eased the steering wheel right. The speedometer read seventy-nine miles per hour as her front bumper gently nudged the car in front of her. Traffic was heavy. It was a move Washington's busy I-495 beltway had seen a thousand times.

Sccccrrreeecchhh!

But this time, the bumpers touched. The Z4 broke traction just like the Camp Peary instructors had taught her it would. A PIT maneuver, they called it: pursuit intervention technique.

The Z4 began to spin in a slow, counterclockwise motion. The driver realized too late what had happened and tried to countersteer, but there was nothing he could do. The racy little convertible bolted back out into traffic, knocking a minivan into the path of a tractor trailer.

GI Jane saw the explosion in the rearview mirror as she pumped her brakes and disappeared around the exit circle.

All eyes focused on the carnage behind her, but even if they had managed to jot down her license plate, there would be no way to trace the rental car. Just as the CIA had transformed her life that day in the stacks of Harvard's Widener Library, the Burberry ladies had taken care of everything.

Hope you're satisfied, Mr. Mitchell, she thought, racing away from the accident scene. But of course he wouldn't be. This assignment was just another test of allegiance, another question mark in a tireless choreography of doubt.

. . .

"I LIVE BY myself," the homeowner said. "I don't keep much in the way of groceries."

"We're fine," Mitchell replied. He and Trask sat on a vinyl couch that had been covered with a macramé throw. An upright piano stood against the wall to their left; a wood fire in the scatter-brick fireplace to their right. There was a coffee table, some bric-a-brac on a wrought-iron bookshelf, and an oversized rocking chair in pine.

"You knew a lot of powerful people," Mitchell said. Framed photos covered flat spaces and most of the walls. They were pictures of a political life — rallies and fund-raisers, and ribbon-cutting ceremonies with Massachusetts luminaries: Tip O'Neill, Ted Kennedy, Michael Dukakis, Barney Frank, Silvio Conte.

"I served in the Massachusetts legislature for a number of years," the man said.

"From 1989 until two years ago," Trask spoke up. "Chairman of the Transportation Committee, member of Banking and Commerce as well as the Board of Regents for the university system, trustee at Fleet Bank. Married once; widowed in ninety-nine."

"What do you want?" the former politician asked. He was no stranger to negotiation.

"In the mid-1980s, the U.S. government developed an asynchronous warfare scenario code-named Civil Defense Scenario Four: Project Megiddo," Mitchell said. He tossed the folder of classified documents on the table, next to a backgammon board. "Twelve men with one mission: to get elected."

"Is that so?" The man shrugged. "Are you supposed to be telling me stuff like this? I mean, those papers, there, say 'top secret.'"

Mitchell continued as if he'd not even heard him.

"The project was run by a colonel named Buck Ellis, a former Special Forces soldier who found his way over to the wet side. MAC-V-SOG, Phoenix, Medal of Honor with a classified citation. He did time with the CIA and eventually ARPA."

"Sounds like an interesting guy," the politician said. Mitchell judged him a superb liar. "I was Special Forces, too, for a few years.

Got out to finish college and then went into politics, as you seem to know. What's ARPA?"

"There were twelve men, handpicked from half a million soldiers," Mitchell continued, ignoring the question. "West Pointers, Delta operators, War College instructors — the best-looking, fastest-thinking, most articulate candidates the U.S. Army could produce."

The politician crossed his legs, then his arms.

"Colonel Ellis groomed them. First an education: Harvard, Dartmouth, University of Virginia. Boston College in your case."

Mitchell stood and walked to the bookcase. He lifted one of the photos and studied it closely. It showed five men around a poker table. Two were former governors, one a former president.

"Then they went to charm school; acting lessons, public speaking classes, plastic surgery — just a touch-up here and there — instruction in how to shake hands, mnemonic name recall, civics and political science and grammar and sociology."

Mitchell looked over a picture of the man at ground breaking for the Big Dig.

"Two years later, the twelve soldiers received trumped-up military service records that would have made Wesley Clark envious. Then they got honorable discharges."

"And?" the man of the house asked. He seemed genuinely intrigued by the story.

"And then they simply vanished," Trask said. "All of them. Gone without a trace."

"All except one." Mitchell replaced the photo and turned toward his host. "One of them we happened to find. It wasn't easy, mind you, but I have formidable resources."

"Me?" the man asked. "You think I had something to do with this? To what end? You see what I've got: a bunch of old pictures and a couple dozen vacation houses I caretake to supplement my pension. What kind of conspiracy could I have a role in?"

He laughed a stiff, sarcastic huff.

Mitchell walked over to the file and turned to page thirty-two. Someone a long time ago had typed a curriculum vitae for a man identified only as Candidate Nine. Mitchell handed it to the man in the rocking chair.

"You say you read the papers; I assume you know that this country is under attack."

The politician read the dossier, holding his hands against his knees so his guests wouldn't see them shaking.

"There's talk of an operation called Jafar al Tayar, or Jafar the high flyer," Mitchell continued. "Sources say the bad guys have a mole in our government — somewhere high enough to accomplish devastating effect. We believe Jafar al Tayar may be one of your Megiddo project cronies."

The man receded into himself as if he'd just been told there was no God.

"I have a bad memory," the man all but whispered. "But let's say I could remember a different time in America, when the Cold War and airliner hijackings and kidnappings and suicide bombings made the government look for creative solutions. Let's say I played a role."

"Let's say we cut this bullshit and talk like soldiers!" Trask barked. "We need the names of the other eleven operatives."

"There are no names!" Candidate Nine erupted. He shook visibly now. A secret life of twenty years had just landed squarely on his chest. He could barely breathe.

"Don't you see? We never knew each other, just the mission. There could have been two of us or two hundred for all I know. The only Megiddo operative I ever heard about was me."

Mitchell was the one who crossed his arms this time.

"I had considered that possibility," he said. The chief executive looked disappointed but by no means defeated. "It will make things more difficult, but not impossible."

Mitchell thought silently for a time, then motioned to Trask. He stood, and the two men moved toward the door. They still had a busy day ahead and no time to dally.

"Don't forget your file," Candidate Nine said, surprised that they would go so quickly. He held up the folder with a trembling hand.

"Keep it," Mitchell said. "You deserve that much."

Candidate Nine let Mitchell get to the front step before deciding to stop him.

"Wait," he conceded. "There is something."

Trask kept walking, but Mitchell paused. Big flakes fell around him as he stood on the front step.

"I was at DLI in Monterey when they selected me. First they sent me to Boston College for a law degree, like you said; then they sent me down to the Farm for months of one-on-one instruction. Charm school. Lots of role-playing and video feedback. They would give me a tape after each scenario so I could study myself and learn from my mistakes."

Candidate Nine walked over to the fireplace and began feeding Mitchell's file into the flames.

"One evening, I was doing my homework. I slipped the day's videotape into a VCR to study my performance, but when I got to the end of the tape, there was more — more video of another student doing the same thing. I figured it had to be another candidate like myself, and that the instructors had just recycled the tape."

Mitchell stepped back inside. The fire flashed bright orange and yellow with the file of this lonely man's past.

"You recognized this person?" Mitchell asked.

"Not at the time, no," the man replied. "It was just a face. But later . . . yes, I know the person on that tape."

"They're a public figure now?" Mitchell asked. It was the only explanation.

"You could say that." The man nodded. He showed no reaction except a vague squint against the rising flames.

"Are you going to tell me who it is?"

Mitchell pulled the door closed behind him.

"I might" — the man nodded — "if you give me your word that you'll never come back here. And if you promise not to tell me I'm crazy."

XIV

Friday, 18 February
02:55 GMT
Council Bunker, The Homestead

"MY NAME IS Jeremy Walker." The FBI agent shielded his eyes, trying to focus better on his predicament. Two of the robed men carried long guns — a Ruger Mini-14 and some Eastern bloc AK variation. "Why are you doing this to me?"

"We ask the questions," the colonel said. His voice sounded firm and level, authoritative but not brash. "First of all, there's no record of any Jeremy Walker with your date of birth in the DC teamsters union. All stagehands have to belong. Second, the address you listed is rented in your name, but utilities are paid by someone named John L. Anderson."

Are they testing me? Jeremy wondered. Surely the FBI would have covered all this in their backstop.

"I had to use a different date of birth on the application," he said, trying to come up with something reasonable. "I've got a felony conviction, and that makes it illegal for me to own a gun. I figured you'd never let me in if you ran a background check and found out."

Jeremy knew his instructors had told him to stay close to the truth, but this was no classroom. Ellis and his thugs were going to kill him if he didn't come up with a convincing lie.

"What were you convicted of?" one of the men demanded.

"Firebombing an abortion clinic," Jeremy said. He tried to sound proud.

"Where?"

"Atlanta. 1998. I did five years as an accessory because all they had was one eyewitness who heard me talking at a pay phone. There was no physical evidence."

"Why, because you were innocent?" Ellis asked.

"No, because I was good," Jeremy bragged. "I'd do it again tomorrow, except I wouldn't talk on a pay phone."

Ellis and the others seemed interested in Jeremy's story.

"Why did you come here?" one of the men asked.

"To learn how to fight. You saw that I can shoot, but I need more knowledge of tactics if I'm going to stop these murderers from killing any more innocent babies."

Jeremy looked each of the hooded men in the eye.

"Judging from what I see here, I've come to the right place."

The colonel said nothing for a moment. He turned to the man on his right and exchanged something without words.

"What do you mean, the right place?" the colonel asked.

"I mean that what I'm seeing in front of me confirms everything I was told in prison. I'm a Phineas priest. I came here to find you."

Another exchange between the colonel and what had to be his second.

"What do you know about the Phineas Priesthood?" the man asked. He sounded younger than the colonel by a decade or more.

"I know what I needed to know when I committed my Phineas acts," Jeremy said. In the past week he had read everything Richard Kelly Hoskins had written. He had studied Christian Identity Movement dogma. He had committed to memory virtually everything the FBI had learned through a decade of white supremacist and fringe religion investigation.

"I'm a warrior for Christ, just like you," Jeremy proclaimed. "I came here to serve. And now I suppose we're going to get down to the business of proving it."

"Prep him," Ellis ordered. He motioned with his hand, and the sixth man in the circle produced a pair of three-bar handcuffs. One of the gunmen waved the muzzle of his rifle toward a chair, and Jeremy sat. He was no stranger to interrogation. They always seemed to start the same way — shackles, a seat to keep you upright, and a dull ache of foreboding.

"What can you tell me about Numbers?" the colonel wanted to know. The men held their semicircle, but the fifth man moved closer. Jeremy noticed that he looked different through the eyeholes of his hood. One eye was pink as a rabbit's; the other was covered by gauze. A black leather case in his left hand told Jeremy that this man would administer the encouragement.

"'And Israel abode in Shittim,'" Jeremy recited from memory. "'And the people began to commit whoredom with the daughters of Moab. And they called the people unto the sacrifices of their gods: and the people did eat, and bowed down to their gods. And Israel joined himself unto Baalpeor: and the anger of the Lord was kindled against Israel. And the Lord said unto Moses, take all the heads of the people, and hang them up before the Lord against the sun, that the fierce anger of the Lord may be turned away from Israel. And Moses said unto the judges of Israel, slay ye every one his men that were joined unto Baalpeor.'"

Jeremy held still as the fifth man moved closer. "Book of Numbers twenty-five, one through five," he said. "It's our motto."

"That proves nothing," Ellis said. "You could have read that in Hoskins's text. Memorizing the Bible doesn't make you a Phineas priest."

"No, it doesn't," Jeremy agreed. "But committing Phineas acts does."

The first blow came from an open hand. The fifth man's palm struck Jeremy squarely atop his left ear, popping the drum and leaving a slow rivulet of blood seeping down the side of his neck.

"The first real interrogation I ever witnessed took place in the back of a North Vietnamese deuce-and-a-half, two klicks inside Cambodia." Ellis talked with a certain nostalgia. "Nineteen sixty-five. I was the one-oh of a spike team out of an A base in the mountains north of Ben Het: two Americans and six Rhade Montagnard tribesmen. We had this kid named Yuk Ayun, claimed he was a sorcerer. Well, we got ahold of this Vietcong captain one evening, and our kid sorcerer set into him."

Jeremy thought back on HRT selection and the way they had beaten him, leading up to the "water board." It wasn't the pain he dreaded; it was the anticipation.

"I'm not going to be much good to you with a broken head," Jeremy said. He could feel the blood dripping onto his bare shoulder.

"'He got ghosts in him,' this sorcerer kept saying," Ellis remembered aloud. "'He got ghosts in him.' Well, this kid liked to work with electricity, and we had found this Soviet hand-crank dynamo in one of the hooches, so our sorcerer started to light this captain up. He'd give him a little juice, then bend over — real quiet like — and listen to the gook's heart. I guess he was trying to hear whether or not those ghosts were still in there."

The colonel nodded, and the fifth man turned toward his bag.

"I'm a spiritual man," the colonel said. "But I'm no sorcerer. And I've never been much interested in inquiring into a man's relationship with pain."

Jeremy watched as the fifth man opened the bag.

"That ear thing was for trying to take advantage of my daughter," Ellis said. "Heidi lured you down here for us, by the way. Don't read anything into her intentions."

The robed torture expert reached into the bag and pulled out two stainless-steel surgical instruments. One had a scissors joint and abraded tongs at the business end, some sort of retractor. The other looked like one of those probes dentists use to check for cavities.

"This is my way of listening to your heart," the fifth man said. He held the dental probe in the palm of his left hand and the retractors in his right. He carried the instruments gingerly, a professional who knew his way around trembling flesh.

"Do you have anything you want to tell me before we do this?" the colonel asked.

"I came here to offer myself for the one true and righteous God," Jeremy said. "I never thought it would be a bloodless fight."

"Well, you thought right." Ellis nodded.

The fifth man leaned in and held Jeremy's face still with a viselike grip.

"You have the most striking blue eyes," he said. "Let's see what they look like on the inside."

The torturer's free hand came forward with the forceps, but Jeremy saw no point in trying to wrestle free. Like he said, this wasn't going to be a bloodless fight.

■

"SORRY I'M LATE," Beechum apologized, hurrying into the West Wing Cabinet Room with Havelock and Alred in tow. James had run back to her office for the latest NSA updates. "General, what do we know?"

She pulled out a chair at the head of the table and poured herself a glass of water.

"Excuse me, Elizabeth, but shouldn't we wait for the president?" the secretary of state suggested.

"Ah, yes . . . the president," she said. "As you know, David has been working around the clock since this began. He finally decided to get some sleep and left orders not to be disturbed except in the case of dire emergency."

"And this would be what?" the secretary of agriculture asked. The former senator from Arizona didn't know Black Angus from ass backward, but that had never stopped him from speaking his mind.

"Albert, I understand we have fifty-seven DoD installations in the affected areas," Beechum said, turning to her secretary of defense. "How do we . . . ?"

"Elizabeth, I have to object," the agriculture secretary interjected. "Nearly half this country has been paralyzed by a terror-induced blackout. I think the president would want to know."

"Then you go up and wake him!" Beechum erupted. She had no interest in trying to placate the hollow concerns of a man who oversaw cheese subsidies. "The president has been on his feet for more than ninety hours, and these attacks may be long from over. He's a human being, goddammit. In order to remain effective, he's going to need a few hours of rest."

The secretary's lower lip drooped onto his chin.

"Now about those bases," Beechum continued. "I want to know exactly how much we're going to have to draw down the strategic oil reserves in order to keep them running on backup generators. Because if we keep taking hits like this, auxiliary power is about the only thing any of us are going to have."

■

CAROLINE WALLER LAY on the living room couch, watching cable news with Christopher in her arms and the channel changer in her right hand. Her parents lived in Buena Park, California, and after more than two hours of trying, she still hadn't contacted them.

Where the hell are you? she wondered about her husband. *Why is it that every time something happens, you run off to save the world but never get to help your own family?*

She had never been one to complain, but this was getting a little ridiculous. Life had been so different in Missouri. People there shared a sense of community that meant open doors and open arms in times of need. Many a night Jeremy had gone off to work a bank robbery or a kidnapping only to have one neighbor or another arrive with a covered dish and a comforting smile.

The Springfield FBI office had been great, too. With just six agents and two secretaries, everyone looked out for each other as if their lives depended upon it. Which they did. Men and women who carried guns for a living always knew the risk. In the best of times they laughed it off as an acceptable part of the job, but when tragedy struck, they shared a truly personal sense of loss.

Just a call, Caroline wished. *Just a few words to know that he's all right. Surely this assignment has something to do with the horrific series of attacks that has devastated the country. First the bombings, then the plane crashes, now this. Seventeen states, the news said. Radiological dispersion device — the dirty nuke everyone has talked about for so long.*

Well, it had finally come. Now what in the world would they do about it?

Ring . . . ring . . .

Caroline snatched up the cordless, trying to avoid waking Christopher. It had taken so long to get him to sleep.

"Hello?" she asked. Caroline knew it must be her parents, but she held a thin flicker of hope that it might be her husband.

"Hi, Mrs. Waller," someone answered. "This is Les Mason."

Oh my God. She silently gasped.

A knot the size of a golf ball rose in her throat. It was after midnight. The HRT commander had never even called her during the day. Why now, if not with terrible news?

■

"WE ARE EFFORTING to assess damage to operational readiness," the SECDEF advised his interim boss. It was the first time in history an American cabinet member had briefed a female commander in chief.

"Meaning, you don't know?"

"Communications are down in some areas," he said. "I can tell you that nuclear assets are secure and that our command and control staff is in contact with the War Room, but in terms of any actual damage assessment, we just don't have anything solid at this time."

Beechum turned toward her attorney general. "What about law enforcement?"

The former Iowa governor looked lost without his FBI chief.

"Well, ah . . . we have no real, uh, constitutional issues right now that I'm aware of," he stammered. Beechum dismissed him with poorly veiled disgust.

"Forgive my disinterest in our forefathers," Beechum said, "but we've got an acute national crisis on our hands. I want to know just what the hell we're doing to protect the integrity of our national infrastructure!"

"I, ah . . . I'll have to defer to our individual law enforcement heads," the attorney general said, writing ferociously on a yellow legal pad. "The Justice Department is . . ."

"What about our allies?" Beechum asked. She turned to Venable's secretary of state, a former ambassador to the United Nations.

"The Saudis are fully aware that we're looking at them," he said, much more confidently than his Justice Department counterpart. "The royal family believes that this administration wants to lay blame on them in order to leverage OPEC. The Crown Prince will announce tomorrow that he plans to roll back production by five million barrels a day unless we back down."

"Cost to us?" Beechum asked.

"We're talking twenty percent of daily consumption. That means five-dollar-a-gallon gas, maybe more. Same for heating oil, which could create real problems this time of year."

The interior secretary popped up.

"Anticipate widespread economic repercussions," he said. "The Saudis have about one trillion dollars in our financial institutions, and that doesn't include Saudi-friendly Mideast partners."

Beechum well knew the danger of a move against American markets.

"Treasury?" she asked.

A Brooks Brothers catalogue model tilted his head to one side.

"We're six months into the first recovery in five years," he said. "We anticipate substantial weakness in the dollar, a collapse in consumer confidence coupled with inflationary pressure as a result of rising energy prices. Transportation sectors have already been dealt crippling blows. Worker productivity will show significant decline as a result of . . ."

"All right, all right." Beechum stopped him.

"Excuse me . . ." The door swung open and the press secretary entered. He looked visibly shaken. "I'm sorry to interrupt, but there's something you need to know."

Beechum waved him in, knowing that an inquiry at this hour could only mean more trouble.

"I just got a call from the *Washington Post,*" he said. "They're citing a confidential source who says there are 'irregularities' in the president's military record."

"That's nothing new," Beechum huffed. "Tell them we dealt with that during the election and have a national crisis to address."

"I did, ma'am," the worried man told her. "They have been working this for a couple months and have found several people who say they do not recall him serving in their unit during his Vietnam tour."

"The president's military records were destroyed during the 1973 Military Personnel Records Center fire in St. Louis," Beechum said. "They know that."

"They claim the fire only affected personnel discharged prior to 1964. The president was discharged in 1972. They are going to run this up on their Web site, and MSNBC has already pushed it into heavy rotation."

Beechum pounded the table. *What else could happen?*

"Tell them . . . tell them a certain number of files were 'in transit' from one depot to another at the time of the fire." Which was true. "Tell them the army has already started looking into the matter but won't have an answer for six to eight weeks. Tell them we've got a goddamned *real* crisis to worry about!"

No one in the room offered a better answer. She hadn't expected any.

"Back to the real issue," she said, turning away from what at this point seemed a minor distraction. The press secretary disappeared without a good-bye. "Here's what I want to do."

The cabinet members sat straight in their chairs. All good bureaucrats responded well to a motivated leader.

"I want a total lockdown on information coming out of this administration. Until further notice, all directives, information, and consultations originating from the Oval Office will be considered matters of national security. Understood? I will consider leaks of any kind a direct abrogation of your sworn duties. Make sure your people know I mean to prosecute."

The cabinet nodded.

"Defense: I want the heads of CIA, DIA, NSA, National Imagery and Mapping, and all five branch intelligence agencies in my office . . . the Oval Office . . . by zero three hundred. They will bring individual readiness reports for all fifty-seven DoD installations in the affected areas and projections on collateral losses."

The SECDEF wrote down her orders.

"State: I want you face to face with the Saudi ambassador. Explain our position without making threats. Wave some intelligence in his face so he knows what has us so wound up. Stress our history of cooperation and mutual respect. Stroke him just enough that he doesn't panic."

She turned to the secretary of energy.

"I want a realistic time line for restoring power, broken down by state, city, and population density, and I want a detailed briefing by zero-five on the time lines for crisis site decon. I'll also need a damage assessment so we can figure out how much radioactive material might still be out there unaccounted for."

Turning last with a scowl to the attorney general, she said, "As for Justice, I want Alred and DHS down the hall as soon as you can get them here. Make sure they know I want the head of FEMA, too. We've batted around the continuity of government protocols. I want concrete recommendations. Finally, I want to pull the trigger on that group in Columbus, Ohio. No more waiting. I want HRT to hit the place and find out what we are dealing with."

Animated with the importance of matters at hand, the vice president stood up and leaned forward onto the conference table.

"I don't have to tell you how important these coming hours will be," she began. "It has been generations since this country faced a threat of this magnitude. I want you all to know . . ."

"Oh . . . my . . . God." The secretary of defense scowled.

All eyes followed his to a man nearly stumbling into the room. Andrea Chase held him by the arm. He wore gray-and-white pajamas unbuttoned to the navel. His hair looked like a rat's nest, his face a confused wriggle of stubble, worry lines, and rudely broken sleep. Only his navy blue robe bearing the seal of the President of the United States on the breast and flowing behind him gave up his identity.

"Somebody turn off that infernal music!" David Venable yelled out. "Turn off that music before I lose my mind!"

■

JORDAN MITCHELL MET his richly appointed Bell Jet Ranger on the pad at Longpath. The moon had risen brilliantly in a clear winter sky, but he took no time to notice.

"You've scheduled the meeting?" he asked.

"Eleven o'clock tonight," Trask answered. The chief of staff juggled two cell phones and a task list that would have challenged a Cirque du Soleil performer. He knew that Mitchell had purposely withheld any information about the meeting, but felt no slight. Trask worked at Jordan Mitchell's pleasure. There were lots of things he didn't care to know.

"Where's Sirad?" Mitchell asked.

Mitchell buckled his seat belt as the pilot pulled up on the cyclical and pointed the nose south toward New York.

"At the Mind Lab. Still nothing concrete."

"What about our friend GI Jane?"

The helicopter rose away from Longpath, up over Mount Greylock and the snow-draped playing fields of the Berkshire School.

"She took care of him about an hour ago. It's still local DC news at this point. Everyone thinks it was an accident."

Mitchell didn't bother offering congratulations. He had never taken death as cause for celebration.

"What about that biotech company?" he asked, turning back to the prospectus he had been studying earlier in the day. Few minds more effectively compartmented matters of such disparate importance.

"They have agreed to our terms. General counsel is working up the contract. We'll own them by this time next week."

"Good," Mitchell said, turning his attentions out the window. Things were finally starting to fall into place.

"Now, if we can just get a decent performance out of Waller."

Mitchell stared down into a landscape of moon shadows on melting snow. Trask had been right about the dreamlike nature of his Berkshire retreat. Too bad this job had stolen his interest in dreams.

KHALID MUHAMMAD SMILED broadly as the handsome Gulfstream private jet cleared the end of Guantánamo Bay's main runway and banked left. They flew just a few seconds before Camp Delta appeared in his window. The bright lights, barbed wire, chain-link fence; the guards looked like toy soldiers in a shoe box from one thousand feet up, but then the plane flew into a maritime squall and, as if by Allah's will, the interrogation center disappeared altogether.

The truth will set you free, Khalid thought to himself, remembering one of the posters on the wall in the infirmary. Well, maybe. *Then again, lies had worked pretty well, too.*

"Better sit down so you don't hurt yourself, sir," one of his fellow fliers cautioned. The man wore khakis and a safari vest like all the CIA people. It was a uniform they had adopted, trying to look worldly — like they really knew anything at all about Islam or what jihadists truly desired.

"Sir?" Khalid smiled cordially. "Five minutes off the ground and you call me sir? Amazing what a change of clothing will do, huh?"

A change of clothing, a change of attitude, a change of fortune. The information he had provided moved with great speed up the bureaucratic ladder. Within two days he had received an offer from the director himself. After another day of negotiating, he had gotten his deal. In exchange for details about Saudi agents inside the United States, he would get first-class air travel to Khartoum. The only things between him and freedom were a debriefing at some "undisclosed location" and about eight thousand frequent-flier miles.

"Would you like something to drink, Mr. Muhammad?" the other passenger asked. He was a much bigger man with thick body hair that would have grown all the way up his face if he hadn't shaved a big circle around his neck. The man looked Balkan, perhaps a Serb or Armenian. He sweated profusely.

"Yes, water."

Khalid looked out his window again, wondering how long it would take to fly back home. He had come here blindfolded and bound to a stretcher in the back of some lumbering military transport. What a wretched trip that had been!

Allah huakbar, he prayed beneath his breath. God had his own ways. How foolish for men to try to imagine where they fell within them.

"How high do you think we are?" the smaller man asked.

"I don't know," Khalid answered. "I'm no pilot."

The clouds had parted now, but there was no land in sight. A turquoise Caribbean floor rolled out below them, close enough that he could see whitecap reminders of the squall they'd just flown through.

"Neither were those fifteen countrymen of yours," the big man remarked, returning with Khalid's water.

"Fifteen countrymen?" Khalid asked. He took the glass and shook his head. It occurred to him that the plane should have been gaining altitude, but he turned to the big man. "What fifteen countrymen?"

"The spineless assholes who learned how to fly without worrying much about the landing," he said. "Remember them, Khalid?"

The smile was gone now. So was the *mister.*

"I wouldn't call men who gave their lives for their religion spineless," Khalid said. "You may disagree with their cause, but you can't argue their courage. Now how long before we arrive at this so-called undisclosed location?"

Neither American said anything. The smaller man stood and walked stoop-shouldered to the cockpit. He leaned his head in and said something, then returned.

"Better drink your water, asshole," the man said.

Khalid thought about correcting the man's language but saw no point in provoking him.

"Why drink my water? Are we there already?" Khalid asked. They had been flying no more than ten minutes.

"Short hop." The little man nodded. He shuffled to the fuselage door. "You know, I always wanted to ask one of you guys about that whole doe-eyed virgin thing."

"What?"

"Why you gotta have seventy-two of them when you die? I mean, you're dead a long time, right, so sooner or later you're gonna run outa virgins. Are you supposed to space 'em out over time or do you just get a nut every Wednesday night until you're out of 'em and then spend the rest of eternity banging the same old pussy?"

You rude American dogs, Khalid thought. *And you wonder why the rest of the world hates you?*

"Camel got your tongue, asshole?" the little man said. He pointed to his partner, who walked over and grabbed Khalid by the throat. The Saudi struggled to free himself, but the ape man held him with little effort.

"Well, you're gonna have plenty of time to figure it out," the little man said. "Coming open!" he shouted up front. Khalid felt the engines roll back to idle.

The ape man dragged him out of his seat as the partner in the safari vest opened the cabin door. A rush of wind filled the unpressurized space.

"Welcome to the undisclosed location, asshole," the big man said. "Mecca is that way."

Khalid didn't have time to look for directions. He was too busy falling.

. . .

"THERE IT IS again." Ravi pointed to what Sirad saw as a screen-sized paragraph of gibberish.

"Digital signature?" Sirad asked him. Hammer Time had calmed considerably after her last rebuke. He ogled her from time to time but made it less apparent.

"G-g-give the l-l-lady a Kewpie doll," he said. Sirad hated watching a man pout.

"How can you tell?" she wanted to know.

"Time-stamping," I Can't Dunk explained. "Time-stamping is a feature of hash function, which allows us to precisely document when a communication occurred in the data stream. Remember the zero knowledge proof we talked about before? Well, Hammer Time figured out how to use what is known as the Feine-Fiat-Shemir protocol to match time stamp with point of origin."

Ravi took over from there.

"Think of the Quantis data stream as a river of fluids flowing through a viaduct," he said. "And let's say this river contains effluent from hundreds of thousands of different tributaries, all uniquely stained with an identifying color. The river would look like a rainbow, but you could identify and track the source, destination, and volume of each current. Now, if you could also index the input time and color of each source, you could easily identify anything that stood out as an anomaly — something in the wrong place given when it entered the river and how it was supposed to move."

"Each Quantis transmission is identifiable because we know the source and destination of each call," Sirad deduced out loud.

"Exactly," Ravi said. "So we simply waded around in the data stream until we found a current that didn't fit."

"That's part of it," I Can't Dunk said. "That combined with some really confusing cryptanalysis mathematics."

"Save it."

"Right."

Ravi pointed to another series of characters on the screen.

"Once we discovered our intruder, we swam back upstream, following his current. When we got to the source, we ran into a check valve of sorts — a security firewall. See?" he said excitedly. "That's our intruder."

"If you ran into a firewall, how do you know what's behind it?" Sirad asked.

"Branding," I Can't Dunk explained. "There's a designer vestige here that their gatekeeper either forgot to hide or didn't think we were smart enough to figure out. It's like seeing a Picasso on the wall. You don't need a signature to know the artist."

Sirad pointed to the data stream.

"That's his digital signature?"

"Sure is, boss," Ravi said. "May look like a bunch of mumbo jumbo to you, but to the three of us it might as well be a neon sign."

"Plain and s-s-simple. Your mole is the president of the United g-g-goddamned States," Hammer Time said proudly. "And his name is bobbing up and down in our s-s-system like a hooker's p-p-panties."

■

JEREMY TRIED TO remain perfectly still as the fifth man reached out with the retractors and latched on to the tip of his left eyelid. The others in the circle moved closer, looking to see better in the muddy red light.

Phineas priests work on a system of leaderless resistance, Jeremy remembered his instructors telling him. *Because of this lack of a central organization, they rely heavily on symbolism and doctrine; no meetings, no addresses, no communications, no organization. They rely on methodology and mission. The members anoint themselves.*

The fifth man used the retractor to pull Jeremy's eyelid out and away from the socket. He rolled the probe from his palm to his fingers, the blunt end forward.

Jeremy's eyes darted nervously back and forth, searching for anything to focus on except for this hooded surgeon.

"And when Phineas, the son of Eleazar, the son of Aaron the priest saw it, Jeremy recited to himself, *he rose up from among the congregation and took a javelin in his hand; and he went after the man of Israel into the tent, and thrust both of them through, the man of Israel, and the woman through her belly. So the plague was stayed from the children of Israel."*

The fifth man laid the blunt probe against the top of Jeremy's eyelid and pulled the retractor up, rolling the eyelid back to expose the pink, mucus-lined membrane beneath.

Their identifying mark is a traditional Christian cross, modified with a P at the top of the staff, he remembered. *Two numbers are usually written beneath the cross: two and five: Numbers 25, their motto.*

"Do you see it?" Ellis asked. "Does he have the mark?"

This motherfucker is gonna hurt, Jeremy remembered the tattoo artist saying back at Harvey Point. He remembered how the huge, tea-sipping Redbeard had rolled Jeremy's eyelid back. He remembered the excruciating pain of the tattoo needle biting him over and over as the man inked a Phineas cross and the tiny numbers two and five beneath it.

"Well, Mr. Walker, I guess we owe you an apology," Colonel Ellis said. He motioned with his hand, and the fifth man released the pressure on the retractor. Jeremy's strained flesh snapped back down over his eyeball.

Thank you, Redbeard, Jeremy thought. The pain of the tattoo would have paled in comparison to what this session could have offered.

"Don't worry about it," Jeremy said, shaking his head like a swimmer, trying to clear the fluid out of his ruptured ear. "Like I told you, I never thought this would be a bloodless fight."

███

"IS IT JEREMY?" Caroline asked the HRT commander. She recognized a certain resignation in her own voice. Maybe it was the hour and the cold dark room around her.

"Yes, but nothing to worry about, Mrs. Waller," he assured her over the phone. "I just wanted to let you know that you might see stories about the team on the news in the next couple of days. Jeremy won't be involved, so don't worry."

There was a pause. Caroline didn't dare say what she was thinking. *Don't worry? How could I not?*

"I wanted you to know that he's a great patriot trying to save American lives," Mason added. "He's doing what he was trained to do."

Jeremy had always spoken highly of Mason, but the HRT commander struck Caroline as a callous, unapproachable man. *Of*

course he is a patriot doing what he was trained to do, but he is a hus-
band and a father, too. Don't any of these men ever admit to emotions
of the heart?

"I miss him," she said. Jeremy would have wanted her to say
something brave and selfless, but at this point, it was the best she
could muster.

"I know you do, ma'am," Mason said. "And we're going to get
him back just as soon as we can. Until then, I want you to know you
can call me personally at any time. I have team members all over
the world right now, but I recognize the sacrifice you wives are
making."

Christopher shifted in his mom's arms, and Caroline felt the
tears coming.

"Thanks," she said.

Then she hung up.

"Sacrifice," she whispered to herself, remembering the bodies of
innocent women and children destroyed in the terrorist attacks.
She caressed her son's dreaming face. How could she call this sacrifice compared to what other families had to endure? At least she
still had a husband to worry about.

Book III

EXECUTION

There are but two powers in the world, the sword and the mind. In the long run the sword is always beaten by the mind.

—Napoleon Bonaparte

XV

Friday, 18 February
05:07 GMT
Hillcrest Woods Mall, Columbus, Ohio

"ECHO ONE TO TOC," a voice whispered into a bone mike. "Have yellow, request compromise authority and permission to move to phase line green."

Ed Damon stood at the corner of a Payless Shoe Source in a suburban Midwestern strip mall. Light from a lone streetlamp had just been extinguished with the silenced burp of a 9mm MP-5SD. A low overcast of rain and sleet shrouded the crisis site in darkness perfectly suited to a midnight raid.

"Copy Echo One," Les Mason responded. "Stand by."

Stand by: *the toughest two words in this job,* Damon thought to himself. As leader of HRT's mobile assault team, he oversaw the lives of six other men. Now they were strung out in front of him like some deadly centipede awaiting orders to kill.

And kill they would. Contrary to what many believed, the FBI's Hostage Rescue Team was no SWAT crew. They were America's civilian counterterrorism asset, a fail-safe tactical team responsible for in-extremis action, which began when all other options had ended. They used explosive door breaches instead of "knock and announce" warrants, flashbang diversion grenades instead of fiberoptic entry cameras. They punctuated their intentions with submachine-gun bursts instead of orders to surrender. If a bad guy held a gun when HRT entered the breach, he died where he stood.

"You have compromise authority and permission to move to phase line green," Mason announced. The HRT commander sounded resolute but calm. He had stood in Ed Damon's boots a time or two himself.

The point man needed no further authorization. Once the HRT commander issued compromise authority, commitment became an eighth member of the team.

Speed, surprise, and violence of action, Damon thought to himself, mentally running a tally sheet of details he had seen to in the hours leading up to this assault.

They had arrived just before dark that evening, all fifty operators and the twenty-four-member support staff. The Columbus field office had cordoned off an area in the parking garage — typical road quarters for HRT.

After a team briefing in which the S-4 operations officer had read the five-paragraph warning order, Xray and Whiskey snipers had deployed to prearranged shooting positions. The objective was a former Golden Corral restaurant that had been converted to an Assemblies of God church, then sold to a group registered with the IRS as an Islamic charity. The sign outside still carried a Christian cross and the faded shadows of its former denomination, but the people inside were anything but pious.

Command initiated assault, Damon thought to himself. *Secure the door, set the explosive breach, enter dynamically in a standard SAS clear.*

Surveillance by the Columbus SOG had placed half a dozen men and two women inside the building. Investigation to date had shown financial transactions with a Saudi government funding mechanism that had been tied in several previous cases to suspected terror cells within the United States. Unfortunately, ties between the former White House and members of the Saudi royal family had foiled previous FBI and DHS efforts to take them down.

They are a legitimate religious group, tied to a close and vital Middle Eastern ally, the previous administration had argued. *Without concrete evidence of wrongdoing, they are not to be harassed.*

More political bullshit, the investigators had groused. Just about everything Saudi had been untouchable during the previous four years, from members of the bin Laden family who were whisked out of the country on U.S. government jets right after 9/11 to the highly questionable financial channels that threw government investigators into a tizzy. Whether you blamed it on oil or personal relationships between the president and the House of Saud, it just added to the cynicism that the war on terror often hinged more on money than justice.

Phase line green, Damon told himself as the point man held at the near edge of a plate-glass window. They had left "yellow," their last position of cover and concealment. Now the whole seven-man team was hung out in the open.

Without further prompting, the third man in line ducked under the window and scurried to the other side. Hunched over between the door and the expansive window, he pulled out an odd-looking device.

Damon watched as the Echo team breacher extended a collapsible aluminum pole with a one-gallon milk jug full of water at the end. An opaque tube the thickness of weed-eater cord ran the length of the pole to a trigger mechanism at its base.

Explosives worked in three ways, Damon had been taught — they pushed, blasted, or cut. HRT used them in all three ways, but in this case, they would use water — noncompressible, and thus instantaneously destructive — to "tamp" the explosive charge. On the command to execute, the breacher would lift the water bottle to the center of the eight-foot-wide window and set it off. The blast would clear the glass in a flash of overpressure, neutralizing anything on the inside and offering a much safer entry than the door.

"Echo at green," Damon whispered once he got a thumbs-up from his breacher.

The team waited for the countdown. Each man knew the objective: a computer room at the back of the storefront. There were no hostages to rescue tonight, but investigators believed information on the hard drive might save thousands.

"Hotel at green," another voice announced. A second group of assaulters had staged at the building's back door. Xray and Whiskey snipers covered the perimeter and any targets of opportunity from somewhere out there in the dark.

"HR-One to all units: stand by, I have control," Mason said.

Damon felt his heart rate slow, his mind clear, his breathing settle. A counterintuitive calm fell over him — the peace of conviction and ability that always led him into battle.

"Five, four, three, two . . ."

Rifle shots rang out behind Echo Team as snipers took their marks.

"One . . ."

BOOOOOM!

The water charge removed the glass window.

"Execute, execute, execute!" Mason called out, launching brave men into harm's way.

◼

"A BLACKOUT? WELL, just . . . just turn it back on!"

The president of the United States sat on an antique organ bench in the Oval Office, fumbling through a nineteenth-century arrangement of "Nearer, My God, to Thee." His beloved Estey harmonium groaned and squealed through a room restricted, now, to the vice president and just four of his closest advisors.

"David, we can't turn it back on," Beechum told him. She stood just off his left shoulder, trying to hide her pity. "There has been another attack. Two relay stations . . ."

"Terrorists?" the president yelled. He stopped for a moment, as if trying to place the word, then continued with the second verse.

"Do you understand what the vice president is telling you, David?" Andrea Chase asked. The chief of staff stood up from one of the couches and walked over to her boss. Venable sat in his blue robe, the belt hanging at his sides, its collar turned up around a tangle of salt-and-pepper hair, as if a new storm had blown in through open windows.

"Airliners." He nodded, suddenly breaking out in a hymn his mother had taught him in grade school. "O where, My Lord, shall the great horn blow . . . terrorists? Home Depot. Disneyland, that's the problem with Medicare, the OMB projects we can't fund it and Social Security, well . . . what I hope to offer the American people and the Democratic party is . . . we need your help to take the White House back from . . ."

He rubbed his fingers against his temples, as if his mind had cramped up and massaging it might restore proper function.

"I, uh, I hope you all . . ."

Venable pressed a key, then scrunched up his face at a mis-struck note and stopped altogether. The president sat at the antique organ, fingers still at the ivory but lost for a moment to the world around him.

"Mr. President," a third voice broke in. "It's Doctor Hernandez. Do you remember me?"

The White House physician looked appalled by what he had just seen. Sunken eyes, loss of fine motor skills, slurred speech, sallow skin, disorientation, even hallucinations. He had witnessed the effects of sleep deprivation — insomniac psychosis at this point — during his years in Vietnam. The battlefield had reduced perfectly capable men to babbling infants after as little as forty-eight hours with no rest. This man had been up for four days.

"Hernandez . . . S-S-Spanish . . . d-d-doctor . . . ," Venable stuttered. "Spineless cowards. They murdered innocent women and children. Barbaric. Evil in the name of religion . . . don't forget to tell Chase that this teleprompter just isn't keeping up with . . ."

"He thinks he's giving Monday night's speech, for God's sake, Doc," Oshinski said. The uniformed commander remained seated with Havelock on a couch. "He doesn't even know we're here."

The president started in again at the organ, but his fingers worked at odds with his mind, creating a cacophony of wheezing bellows and poorly orchestrated reeds.

"Doctor, a moment?"

The vice president took the White House physician by the arm and pulled him back to where Oshinski and the national security advisor sat. Andrea Chase followed them and huddled close.

"We have to do something," Beechum said. "I gave him the dose you prescribed and look — it barely fazed him. He's clearly breaking from reality."

"This is not atypical in moments of extreme stress, but it can be very dangerous," Doctor Hernandez said. "The human body can go weeks without food, days without water, but it breaks down quickly without sleep. He will be fine once his mind recalibrates, but clinically . . ."

"Mother! Mother, I've finished my lesson!" the president yelled. "I want to go out and play!"

"For God's sake, somebody get those reporters off the south lawn!" Oshinski called out.

Everyone looked up to see a FOX camera crew setting up a pre-arranged live feed. They appeared not to have noticed anything unusual in the Oval Office.

"I'll take care of it," Chase said. She hurried out.

"Doc, we need to sedate the president. We need to do it now." Beechum left no room for a second opinion.

"In medical terms, that's as simple as an injection," Hernandez said. "But this is no ordinary house call, Elizabeth. We're a country in crisis, and the medication I prescribe will render him virtually comatose. Are you sure you have the authority to make that decision?"

"If you don't, I will," Oshinski growled. "Look at him, Doc! He's a good and decent man. Do you really want history to remember him calling out for his mother? For Chrisakes, put the poor bastard down."

The fact that they were talking aloud in Venable's presence was lost on no one.

"Elizabeth, are you still here?" the president suddenly said. He stood up from the organ and walked over to them as if he'd just awoken from a pleasant nap.

"This is symptomatic," Hernandez said. He looked at Venable as if he were just another interesting case on morning rounds. "The mind can become lucid for minutes at a time, before lapsing back into dementia."

"Doctor Hernandez," the president said, surprised. "What brings you here?"

"Give him the injection," Beechum said.

"Injection?" Venable asked. Then his eyes glazed over again and his shoulders slumped. He stood there and disappeared back into his terribly confused mind.

■

SIRAD WOKE UP on a tabletop, covered with a topcoat she had found behind a copier. Hammer Time snored obnoxiously on the floor beside her. Ravi had taken the couch.

"How could you sleep through that?" I Can't Dunk asked, presumably referring to the stuttering wave theorist.

"You smell him?" she asked, pushing the coat off her and scrunching up her nose. "It's like week-old garbage."

"It's his breath," I Can't Dunk said. Sirad lowered herself off the table and walked over to him. He was playing Pac-Man on a PDA.

"Ugh." Sirad shivered. "How can you work with that?"

"No choice. He's brilliant. We need him."

Sirad shook her head, expressing her dismay, clearing the cobwebs, and remembering what lay ahead all in one jagged motion.

"I have to go back into the city and talk to Mitchell," she said. "Are you clear on what has to be done while I'm gone?"

The clock on the wall told her that she'd wasted entirely too much time.

"I've already started," I Can't Dunk said. "Just waiting for Ravi before I get too far ahead."

Good, Sirad thought. Steganographic alchemy would be the least of her concerns at this point. Ravi and his posse of quivering cerebrums knew just enough to take care of the detective work. Only she had all the information necessary, now, to put the whole thing together.

Borders Atlantic is full of secrets, and they're all mine, she remembered Mitchell telling her. The ruthless, arrogant CEO had spun her in circles, manipulating her role as a CIA nonofficial cover officer to an advantage she poorly understood all these months later.

Well, who has the secrets now? Sirad asked herself. She gathered her briefcase and hard-copy printouts of the digital signatures Ravi had shown her.

You may have the strongbox, Mitchell, she thought, *but I've got the keys.*

Now all Sirad had to do was decide which way to twist the tumblers.

■

JEREMY SAT AT a picnic table in the moonlight with the colonel on one side and an albino with a bandage over his eye on the other. Heidi stood behind him, tending his injured ear.

"I told you I'm not the farmer's daughter," she said, ignoring her father's disapproving scowl.

"We don't have time for this, Heidi," the colonel said.

"I never would have gotten you down there if I'd know they were gonna hurt you," she apologized to Jeremy. "The colonel said he wanted to ask you a few questions is all. I just thought it would be better if I took you down there instead of his men."

"Don't worry about it," Jeremy said. He winced as she used an eyedropper to administer some hydrogen peroxide.

"That's enough, Heidi," the colonel said impatiently. "You've got plenty to do seeing to tomorrow's classes. We've got two dozen other students, remember?"

"Yeah, but they're not nearly as cute as this one," she said, gathering up her first aid supplies. "That ear is gonna be a problem if you don't give it time to heal."

The colonel abided the way she ran her fingers through Jeremy's hair, then waited until she had gone.

"Are you sure you understand what we might ask of you?" Ellis asked. The interrogation had already satisfied most of his concerns about Jeremy's provenance, but the Phineas Priesthood was a small group that found its bedrock in the Christian Identity church. Like any movement, it held its share of secrets and pacts; offering them up to strangers always carried risk.

"I'm sure," Jeremy said. Heidi had packed his ear with cotton. That and the fizz of hydrogen peroxide bubbles left a bright ringing in his head.

"Death is all you need to understand," the colonel told him, just a little too melodramatically. He stared straight into Jeremy's eyes as if his Montagnard sorcerer had taught him a thing or two after all.

"Mine or theirs?" Jeremy smiled. It wasn't humor so much as conviction.

"Both. I think you know that."

"I do."

"That's why you came, isn't it?"

Jeremy shook his head. It wasn't really a lie.

"How did you know?" the albino asked. "How did you know you'd find us here?"

They were the first words he had spoken since the interrogation downstairs in the bunker.

"I didn't," Jeremy responded. "Not for sure; not until you took me down to the bunker."

Jeremy turned to his right and stared at Caleb. Ellis's son wore shuffleboard goggles — those giant sunglasses old people wear in Florida — and a wide-brimmed Panama hat. His skin looked lamb-skin pale, almost transparent.

"Caleb oversees Cell Six, our operations unit."

Ellis hadn't formally introduced his son, but Jeremy knew him well. Less than a week earlier he'd watched this man disappear into an Indonesian jungle.

"If we decide to accept you, you'll answer to me," Caleb said. His words sounded like a primer for some response.

"I answer to the one true and righteous God," Jeremy said. "I'll help you if you want, but you got to know where I stand."

Ellis nodded as if the answer impressed him. "Do you remember seeing this?" he asked.

Jeremy picked up a yellowed piece of newspaper someone had clipped from the *Washington Post*.

WHY IS THIS MAN IN THE WHITE HOUSE? it read. Someone had highlighted a quotation Jeremy well remembered — a state-ment about then president George W. Bush. *Why is this man in the White House? The majority of America did not vote for him. He's in the White House because God put him there for a time such as this.*

The name beneath it was General William "Jerry" Boykin, U.S. Army Special Forces.

"Are you saying Boykin is a Phineas priest?" Jeremy asked. He tried to sound more optimistic than incredulous.

"I wish," Ellis responded. "But no. My only point is that there are strong, well-minded patriots at all levels of government. You don't have to tattoo the back of your eyelid to support our cause."

The colonel took the clipping back and glanced over it admiringly.

"You've read the scripture," Caleb said. "You know what has to be done."

Jeremy nodded once. "I know the voice of the stranger; the gut-ter god. Muhammad of Islam. I know he has to be stopped."

"This country's leaders have left us in ruin," Caleb continued. "Homosexuals marrying. One race lying down with another. Mothers murdering their own unborn babies. Priests sodomizing the most innocent among their flocks. . . ." His voice trailed off into disgust so foul he could not lend it words.

"And two men against the world trying to stop it?"

A new voice rose behind them. It was a female voice, one Jeremy was not used to hearing in a situation like this. The hair on the back of his neck stood straight on end.

"I was just about to brief a new priest on how we might use him in our mission," Ellis said.

"Good," the woman responded, throwing a leg over the picnic table bench. She sat directly across from the man she had lain beside in the Jayawijaya Highlands. "Because according to the news, we seem to be running out of soldiers faster than we're running out of time."

"This is Sarah," Ellis said.

Jeremy saw no recognition in her eyes and tried to show none himself.

"Didn't expect a woman," he said.

"Neither do they," GI Jane answered. "Neither do they."

■

"CLEAR!" THE ECHO team leader heard one of his men call out from the back room. Behind them lay five dead terrorists amid a path of shattered glass, splintered wood, and empty shell casings.

"All clear," Damon repeated into his microphone. He walked from one room to another, visually checking to make sure none of the casualties wore American flags on their shoulders.

"Copy, Echo One," Mason responded through the dry chatter of the encrypted Motorola radio. "What's your down count?"

"Five bad guys dead, three captured," Damon responded. Smoke from the flashbang diversion grenades, "slap charge" door breaches, and submachine-gun fire burned in his lungs. "All HRT personnel accounted for. No injuries."

"What do we got?" Chuck Price, the Hotel team leader asked. He found Damon in a small office at the back of the building. A lone computer sat atop a cheap folding table.

"We got what we came for, I guess," was all he said.

Damon held a finger aside his nose and blew a gritty black string onto the floor. The Ensign-Bickford grenades provided excellent distraction, but the residue felt like beach sand between his teeth.

"All this for a fucking hard drive?" The Hotel leader shrugged. "Whatever happened to the days of search warrants?"

■

MITCHELL HAD JUST helicoptered in from his Longpath estate when Sirad found him in the War Room.

"May I come in?" she asked, knocking on the open double doors. It was late, but who slept anymore?

"Please," Mitchell answered. He stood between the red-oak conference table and his display cases. "I was just admiring my newest acquisitions."

He pointed toward the dueling pistols, mounted on velvet with their muzzles addressing each other, almost the way Alexander Hamilton had last seen them two hundred years earlier.

"So, what did you decide?" she asked, crossing to the windows. The lights of New York sparkled in the darkness.

"Decide about what?" he asked.

"About the Aaron Burr lucky shot controversy. I understood that you wanted to obtain these pistols so you could test the trigger yourself."

"Ah, yes. The triggers!" He looked relieved, almost playful. Sirad hadn't seen this mood before.

Mitchell opened a broad glass door and removed the pistol on the right.

"This is the one." He held it at a forty-five-degree angle to the floor and rested his left fist on his hip. "Hamilton lost his son to a .54 caliber ball from it in 1801, then lost his own life to a poor grasp of its idiosyncrasies three years later. Tricky thing, flintlocks."

Sirad watched as her boss adjusted his dueling stance and squared his shoulders perpendicular to where she stood.

"The controversy goes like this: in preparing his son for a duel of family honor in 1801, Hamilton opined that a gentleman always fired the first shot wide. If that failed to calm ruffled feathers, well, then the next volley would sound for keeps."

Mitchell stared at Sirad and pointed the pistol at her feet.

"You can imagine the pit in the young man's stomach as he stood across the river in New Jersey that fateful morning trying to decide whether he should follow his father's etiquette or do what instinct told him. He was a decent shot, by most accounts. He could have made the first ball count."

Sirad tried to look bored. She had come with her own information about presidential guile and predation.

"A light fog had rolled out over the Hudson as the seconds prepared the weapons. Philip must have felt the beads of perspiration rolling down the sides of his chest, sticking to his ruffled shirt and waistcoat."

Mitchell pulled back the hammer, filling the room with a two-stage, sharp metallic clank.

He loves this, Sirad thought to herself. *He loves the power of holding other lives in his hands.* This was the same expression he had worn that night six months earlier when the seventeenth-floor thugs had tied her down on a table and poured seltzer water down her throat. She remembered him standing over her as they asked her questions she couldn't answer, transfixed with her suffering and his authority to control it.

"They took their places, then 'Present!' his own second called out — Philip had won the toss. Then, by all accounts, both men raised and fired. Philip pointed wide at his father's urging; his opponent took dead aim, either unaware of noblesse oblige or all too aware of his desire to survive. Philip took a ball in the gut, severing his spine. It took a day and a half for him to die — more than enough time to ponder his father's advice, you'd think."

Sirad watched as Mitchell raised the pistol above and to the right of her shoulder. They stood about twenty feet apart, standard dueling distance.

"And this is the handicap Hamilton took to battle three years later," Mitchell continued. "Images of his dying son. A sense of code — the code that placed honor above all else. A torment of anger, duty, remorse, obligation."

"I came to tell you that we've identified the people trying to get into Quantis," Sirad said. This pantomime reminded her a little too keenly of Mitchell's taste for marking other people's weakness.

"And so, once again, the Hamilton family won advantage of second," he said. "'Present arms!' a man called out."

Mitchell swung the pistol directly at Sirad. She stared down the black hole it presented, a finger taut on the trigger, the hammer sprung back.

"Gun hands rose steadily," he said, as if reciting from a personal recollection. "Sun gleamed on gunmetal. Birds fell silent. The smells of pine and fresh-cut grass and black powder still unlit filled the air."

He looked sternly past the front bead sight, directly into Sirad's eyes.

"Shots rang out!"

CLACK . . . the hammer dropped as he pulled the muzzle away at the last moment.

"One man fell, mortally wounded. Hamilton."

Sirad thought he said the word a little too knowingly.

"A day and a half it took him to die, just like his son. A day and a half to reflect through the keen lens of agony on the value of honor."

Mitchell lowered the pistol and shook his head.

"Some have said these weapons had hair triggers, that Hamilton pulled prematurely out of stress or inexperience."

"It's the White House," Sirad said. She tried not to show how he bothered her.

"But it wasn't the trigger. That's too easy an explanation."

"Do you understand what I'm saying? The White House Communications Agency is behind this."

"Too easy an explanation for people who don't understand the way taking an oath can change a man."

It seemed that they were engaged in separate conversations.

"Because a man that would lay down the life of his own son out of honor," Mitchell said, "would never surrender it for himself. He would stare circumstance of almost laughable irony in the face and say, 'History take me for a dutiful servant more than a selfish ego. I would rather die an honorable man than live a villain.'"

And then Sirad realized that he was no longer talking about Alexander Hamilton or a duel that had ended tragically two hundred years ago. In the metaphor that seemed to frame his very existence, Jordan Mitchell had set her up once again.

"I have told you, Sirad, that Borders Atlantic is full of secrets and that they are all mine," he said. Mitchell leaned forward, hands on the table, one palm still wrapped around the dueling gun. "You've done an admirable job, but you're not there yet. You only think it is the president because you don't understand honor."

She felt his eyes on her. Not like other men, not lascivious; hard but hopeful.

"That's why I allowed them to hurt you. That's why I have kept you away from me these past few months. You're good, but you're still not ready for the role I have written for you."

Sirad began to tremble. Only Jordan Mitchell could do that to her.

"Go back and look deeper," he continued. "Reach beyond your gifts of physical beauty and psychopathy, and try to understand what would prompt a father to give his life and his son's for honor."

With that, Mitchell replaced the pistol in its case.

"We don't have a lot of time," he said. "But imperative can serve as a stern taskmaster."

He left the room.

"You sonofabitch," Sirad cursed under her breath, realizing full well the curse had nothing at all to do with Mitchell.

XVI

Friday, 18 February
06:09 GMT
President's Apartment, The White House

"HE'LL BE JUST fine," Doctor Hernandez assured the first lady. Victoria Venable tucked a down comforter under her husband's chin and brushed hair away from his face.

"Thank you, Elizabeth," she said, turning to the vice president. "This is the first time I've seen him at peace in days."

"I hope you understand that we had no choice," Beechum explained. "His behavior was beginning to show signs of . . ."

"Oh, I understand completely." The first lady pulled the blinds tight and unplugged the phone. "In fact, it took real courage to do what you did. God forbid that the American people would have seen him like that."

The doctor checked the president's pulse with two fingers on his wrist and a gold Rolex Daytona.

"Vitals are strong," he observed. "By this time tomorrow, he'll be back on his feet as if nothing ever happened."

"Thank you, Doctor," the first lady said. "Could I ask you to give the vice president and me a moment alone?"

The doctor closed his bag and walked out. He pulled the door shut behind him.

"What will happen if this leaks out?" Victoria asked Beechum once they were alone. She had lived a life at a politician's side and knew better than most how power could turn on a dime.

"No one will find out," Beechum said. "Only Andrea, Havelock, the general, and I know. The doctor, of course, and the Secret Service, too, but they are beyond reproach."

"The cabinet will ask questions, especially after what happened downstairs. Congress will look for direction; the country will expect some sort of public reassurance."

"You let me worry about that, Victoria." Beechum tried to comfort her. She reached out and held the concerned wife by her shoulders. "I know this town, and I know how to handle secrets. By the time David wakes up, we'll be ready to hand him a scenario that he will be proud of. No one will be the wiser."

"Thank you," the first lady whispered. "He's a good man, you know."

"I know," Beechum said as they leaned forward and held each other in a quiet embrace. *That's what's going to make what I have to do so much harder.*

■

JEREMY ARRIVED AT Washington's Reagan National Airport just before two o'clock Friday afternoon and rented a midsized Chevy using his undercover identity. Ellis had driven him and Caleb to Dallas, briefing them along the way.

Come on, come on! Jeremy yelled silently, frustrated at Fourteenth Street Bridge traffic, which had slowed down to little more than a trickle. At present, he was caught in this four-lane parking lot between a Lawn Doctor tank truck and a poorly tuned transit bus.

Though Ellis had revealed little of the larger operation, Jeremy knew its ultimate objective would be a catastrophic attack on the Washington area. Events of the past few days had been carefully orchestrated to lay blame on Islamic fundamentalists, but from what Jeremy had learned in Texas, that was merely a ruse. The real intention was to force a response by the United States government —

a response that would trigger widespread reprisals from not only networks like al Qaeda, but also smaller regional groups.

"Just like the Boston Tea Party," Caleb had bragged, comparing his father's brainchild to Samuel Adams's famous 1773 raid in which the Sons of Liberty dressed up as Mohawk Indians and tossed thousands of dollars worth of English Darjeeling into the harbor. "This will go down as one of the most creative and successful psychological operations in this country's history."

But that was tea Samuel Adams and his fellow saboteurs had splashed, not airliners.

"Let's go!" Jeremy yelled through his windshield. He honked his horn like everyone else around him and inched forward across the bridge. It was already almost two o'clock in the afternoon, and his instructions carried no room for excuses. By sunset, Jeremy had to "procure" a concrete mixing truck and drive it to a warehouse in Southeast DC. One of the other Phineas priests — a "cutout"— would meet him there with further instructions.

"That tattoo on the back of your eyelid buys you a tryout," Ellis had told him. "But if you really want to join our struggle, you will have to prove yourself."

This apparently was the first test.

"Get that piece of shit out of the road!" a passing motorist yelled.

Jeremy saw that the source of the traffic jam was a two-car fender bender that should have been settled at the other end of the bridge. The drivers involved seemed much more intent on returning obscene gestures to passing cars than they were with the slight damage to their own vehicles.

Where the hell am I going to find a cement mixer? Jeremy wondered to himself as traffic suddenly shot forward. Washington opened out in front of him, the top of the Washington Monument rising over the Lincoln Memorial.

A dozen questions filled his mind, half of them centered on GI Jane.

What was she doing at the Homestead? What possible ties could this woman have to the very men she had ordered killed in Indonesia? If she were simply an undercover player, why hadn't CIA or FBI briefers told him to expect her. If she was playing both sides against the middle, why hadn't she turned him in?

Jeremy stomped on the gas, racing toward a destination he hadn't even decided on. Somewhere out there among the city of monuments, Caleb was laying the groundwork for a cataclysm. The attacks of the previous days had been just a warmup, he bragged. What lay ahead would be taught to grade-school children for centuries to come.

Schoolchildren.

Jeremy's knuckles turned white around the steering wheel. In all the movement and confusion, he hadn't even thought about the possible consequences to his own family. Caroline and the kids lived just 42 miles south of the city, oblivious to potential danger.

"You sonofabitch," Jeremy cursed, wrapping Ellis and Caleb and their entire cabal of Phineas priests into one present evil.

Call Caroline, was the first thought that popped into his head. But that was impossible, right? What if this was just a test of his allegiance? What if Ellis had sent someone to follow him?

How's Ellis going to know? Jeremy wondered, allowing emotion to argue with professional logic. He and Caroline both carried the new Quantis phones, which only Borders Atlantic and Jordan Mitchell could listen in on. Mitchell knew about all of this anyway.

Jeremy pulled his cell phone out of a jacket pocket. Caroline would be at her office now. All he had to do was call the house and leave a message. Something simple, like "Get the hell out of town before the world goes to hell!"

He checked his rearview mirror for signs of surveillance. Nothing stood out. He changed lanes quickly, trying to "clean" himself — right on Independence Avenue, then right again toward L'Enfant Plaza. No one exposed themselves.

Do it! Jeremy prodded himself. Ethicists might argue that he had no right to save his own family and not those of his teammates and friends. But then again, ethicists seldom had to deal with the potential deaths of their wives and kids.

"Hello, you've reached the Wallers," Maddy's seven-year-old voice chirped in Jeremy's ear. Despite a mouthful of missing teeth she'd taken just two tries to lisp out the message. "We're all outthide playing right now, so leave uth a message after the beep."

"Hi guys, it's Dad," he said, trying to decide what to say. "Look honey . . . something's come up. I think you should go see your folks for a couple days. Tonight. Really . . . tonight, OK? I'll call when I can . . . but go NOW. Love you."

He hung up the phone.

"What kind of message was that?" Jeremy scolded himself. He'd never been much good with nuance.

But then a car drove slowly past him, and Jeremy turned his attentions to a different kind of subtlety. The driver had looked a little too long at the phone. His eyes showed a little too much concern.

You're just being paranoid, the emotional voice rang out in Jeremy's head, but then the professional logic took over. *Just because you're paranoid,* it said as Jeremy pulled a U-turn and raced toward Adams Morgan, *doesn't mean they're not after you.*

SIRAD DROVE NORTH again on the Merritt Parkway trying to sort through what Mitchell had told her. Though the CEO had assigned her oversight of the Quantis project, Mitchell kept her in the dark about many of its most important elements. On top of that, the enigmatic leader had known from the start about her real employer — the CIA. Borders Atlantic, like a surprisingly large number of U.S. corporations, had for years cooperated with the intelligence community, offering executive positions to case officers. Nonofficial cover, the Agency called it: NOC — an elite cadre of spies inserted into manufacturing, financial services, import/export, and communications sectors to gather information more traditional officers simply couldn't gain.

The downside felt steep at times. Traditional CIA covers were mostly diplomatic. The communications officer in a foreign embassy, for example, would carry a State Department credential and enjoy diplomatic immunity if exposed or "outed." An NOC would have no such immunity. If discovered as a spy, they could go to jail for life, or worse.

Despite the stakes — or perhaps because of them — elite case officers placed a premium on NOC duty. Foreign governments already watched diplomats with great scrutiny, limiting intelligence gathering to cocktail chats, open-source inquiries, and anecdotal observation. Business executives, however, came with promises of money. Since money tempted greed and greed trumped scrutiny even in the most suspicious countries, NOCs ended up free to cajole, proposition, and outright buy anyone they weren't clever enough to steal. In a world ruled, now, by multinational corporations worth more than the gross domestic products of many countries they did business in, money — not nationalism — had become the ultimate allegiance.

Sirad and her Agency controller — Mr. Hoch — had known all about this when Mitchell handed her the Quantis project, of course. But Mitchell's cooperation with the CIA had gone much deeper than she understood. Though no one had told her at first, the Borders Atlantic executive had earned his chops at the Farm, too. After graduating Dartmouth College in the late 1960s, he had been hired into a Cold War that took him first to an academic cover in Peru and then to a deeper cover running an import/export business in Chile.

Mitchell used $400,000 in ITT seed money to buy a Grumman Goose, hire a pilot and secretary, and move vital information in and out of the South American country. Working with multinational ITT, he had helped orchestrate the overthrow and eventual murder of Salvador Allende in 1972. ITT got the copper it needed for phone lines; the CIA got intelligence-gathering networks in a part of the world they desperately wanted to protect from Soviet expansion.

Thirty years and billions of dollars later, Borders Atlantic had grown into a diversified behemoth among international businesses. They had representatives in 117 countries and a network of spies who ranked second to none. Borders Atlantic's NOC cadre played both sides of the line, offering the company what it needed to build market share and the U.S. government what it needed to increase security.

Borders Atlantic is full of secrets, but they're all mine.

Mitchell had known all along that someone inside the White House — perhaps the president himself — was behind the attacks on Quantis. But how? And why had he wasted so much time and effort, dedicating his top programmers and cryptanalysts to the task?

What did he really want her to find? All that business about dueling and long-dead statesmen and honor had seemed like more of hubris, standing there in that dark-paneled conference room.

Borders Atlantic is full of secrets . . .

Something caught Sirad's eye as she drove. Just a reflection, a glint of light in the corner of her windshield, but it flashed in her head like a lightning bolt. Suddenly everything made sense — the beatings, all the talk of dueling and honor . . . even the attacks on Quantis.

Borders Atlantic may have lots of secrets — she smiled as she yanked the steering wheel and raced up to the security gate — *but it seems that Jordan Mitchell has finally cleared the way for me to keep a few for myself.*

■

NO ONE NOTICED the Montagne Mountain Goat STOL circling carelessly over a frozen stretch of tundra one hundred miles south of Prudhoe Bay, Alaska. These stout workhorses of Alaska's bush pilot trade were familiar sights in a state that boasted more aircraft per capita than any other. This was a particularly isolated geography, too — just north of the Arctic Circle and dozens of miles from any human habitation.

"How about that snowfield right down there?" the copilot suggested. He pointed to a shiny section of wind-matted snow that looked hard enough to support the plane's skis.

"You're the navigator," the pilot answered. He throttled back the lone engine and circled right, dropping the aircraft into a steep descent.

"You gotta love these buggers," the copilot said, impressed with the easy handling and responsive throttle. The Mountain Goat, a relative newcomer to Alaska Air, boasted heavy payload capacity, 160-mile-an-hour cruising, and a stall speed of just 25 knots. That made it the perfect craft for today's flight.

"Hang on," the pilot advised. "Ya never know what's under this crust."

But there was no need to worry. The plane landed softly, turned right, and stopped, facing into a giant steel snake that ran eight hundred miles from Prudhoe Bay to Valdez.

"Twenty minutes," the copilot said. The logistics cell had worked out every detail of this operation, from Alyeska Pipeline Service Company surveillance flight schedules to weather forecasts.

"I won't be late," the pilot answered, pulling the hood of his heavy parka up over his wool cap. "It's colder than a well digger's ass out there!"

The two men climbed out of the plane, shouldered eighty-pound backpacks, and started in opposite directions. Their job was pretty simple, actually. The Trans Alaska Pipeline may have been one of the engineering wonders of the twentieth century, but it lay dreadfully vulnerable to the simplest sabotage. Of its eight-hundred-mile length, more than four hundred miles lay aboveground, often propped atop ten-foot stilts designed to afford migrating elk and caribou a free range.

More than 9 million gallons of crude oil lay in the pipeline at any given time, flowing six miles per hour, pressurized at up to 1,180 pounds per square inch, heated and treated with additives to reduce drag. At forty-eight inches in diameter, each forty-foot section of concrete, steel, and insulation weighed some seventy-five thousand pounds.

First came the explosives.

Each man went to work on risers spaced about twenty-five yards apart. They wrapped two coils of lead sulfate flex linear shaped charge around each upright. The blasting caps had already been affixed, as had the detonation cord, which strung the whole thing together like a 750-foot length of pyrotechnic Christmas tree lights.

Attacking the pipeline would have been difficult if they had gone after the conduit itself, but the risers made everything much easier. All they had to do was cut the narrow legs out from under it and let its massive weight come crumbling down. By the time system engineers down in Valdez registered a flow disruption and shut down pump stations to the north and south, they would have lost a couple million barrels.

Next came the detonators — just one for each man's string. They were simple devices, radio activated with backup batteries and redundant firing mechanisms. Of military design, they were built with components that could quickly be linked to bombs used in other attacks during the previous week.

By the time the two men met back at the plane, their hands and faces were numb with cold. Fortunately, the plane came equipped with a more-than-adequate heater.

"Damn this weather," the pilot said, throttling up. "Can you imagine living out here?"

"Well, at least it's pretty," his partner said. He made sure the packs were stowed behind his seat and visually checked their work.

"Pretty for now," the pilot said. He pointed the nose into a twenty-mile-an-hour wind and fire-walled the engine. "But I'd hate to be an Eskimo in an hour."

■

COLONEL ELLIS WAS running students through CQB drills in the Kill House when Heidi found him with a cell phone. He knew when he saw her that it would be important. Everyone knew better than to bother him when there were firearms and tuition checks on the line.

"Excuse me, fellas," he said, stepping off to the side while one of the other instructors carried on as if nothing had happened.

He took the phone from his daughter without asking for clarification. He could tell by the look on her face that this was no courtesy call.

"Hello?" he answered.

"He placed a call," the voice said. Ellis recognized it as one of the Cell Six members, a former platoon leader with the Tenth Mountain Division. His new element had already moved into DC to help with logistics for the final stages of the operation.

"Is that a problem?" the colonel asked. He had expressed his concerns about operational security, but Jeremy had a life. It could have been anything.

"We think so," the man said. Ellis could hear children playing in the background as the man talked.

"And?"

"Caleb thinks this is a priority. He's broken off from planning to deal with it."

Ellis shook his head. Enemy infiltration had always been a possibility in his line of work, from Phoenix operations in the jungles of Indochina to compartmented projects at the Pentagon. He thought check valves built into the leaderless resistance model of the Phineas Priesthood had minimized the risk. Maybe he was wrong.

"To deal with what, exactly?" he asked.

"We tracked his call to a house in Stafford, Virginia," the man said. "The mailbox reads Waller, no *k*," the caller said. "We think that raises some serious questions. This guy is beginning to look like a real unknown."

Ellis barely took time to weigh the variables.

"Well, you know how I feel about unknowns," the colonel said. "Do what you have to do to get me some answers."

■

"ALL RIGHT" — THE vice president exhaled — "we've got less than twelve hours to pull this country back together. Where are we?"

Her immediate circle of advisors had distilled into three distinct groupings: law enforcement, intelligence, and politics. In addition to the chief of staff, who covered all the bases and kept the president's interests foremost in mind, that meant Alred, Havelock, and the general. CIA chief Vick and the DHS director had been cut out of the loop, as had the entire cabinet. The most dangerous thing in times of crisis was loss of control, and all of these agency heads represented redundancy.

"HRT hit the safe house in Columbus early this morning," Alred said. "It was our best hope of establishing a link between Ansar ins Allah and the Saudis."

"Was?" Beechum asked. "What did they find?"

The FBI chief shifted in his seat.

"Two assault teams hit the front and back, simultaneously," he said. "They encountered pretty stiff resistance but fought their way to the computer room, where they secured the hard drive. We flew it down to the lab in Quantico, and our cybercrimes division has pretty much concluded their exploitation efforts."

"Excellent!" Havelock blurted out.

"Not really." Alred scowled. "We killed five of them in the raid. There were three survivors who swore they thought HRT was a gang of anti-Arab street thugs. Seems they'd suffered a string of burglaries, death threats, and a couple assaults since the terror attacks started. As a security measure, they bought weapons and posted sentries inside the mosque. They said they were just trying to protect themselves."

"My God . . . ," Beechum said. "Are you telling me we never checked for gun permits?"

"We checked." Alred nodded. "So what? Legal or illegal — we couldn't read their minds. HRT had to consider the permits justification for use of deadly force."

"What about the hard drive?" Oshinski asked. All this talk of casualties didn't seem to bother him.

"Utility expenses, congregation addresses, fund-raising tallies . . . stuff you would expect to find on a business computer. There were some sermons the mullah kept, nothing really inflammatory. We're still running down leads, but we've got to be prepared for the possibility that this is a dry hole."

"Dry hole?" Chase exclaimed. "Are you telling me that all we've got after five days of investigation is five dead Muslims and a hard drive full of Excel spreadsheets?" She stood up and slammed her fist into the back of an empty chair. "Wait until the AP gets ahold of this!"

"We're a country under attack, Andrea," Havelock reminded her. "We're still pulling bodies out from under Space Mountain for Chrisakes. Five bucks says this won't even make the national news."

"What about ties to the Saudis?" Beechum asked, ignoring his assessment of the Fourth Estate. "This was the cornerstone of our case against them, wasn't it?"

"Hardly," Havelock said. He reached into a blue three-ring binder embossed with an Air Force logo and gold letters that said COMPARTMENTED MATERIAL ENCLOSED.

"I have assessments from the NSA, DIA, and CIA, everything from overhears — not chatter, but actual intercepts — to sole-source human intelligence and banking traffic. There's very little doubt that the Saudis are moving money to accounts we can track directly to al Qaeda sympathizers and Palestinian separatists."

"What am I going to do with bank transfers to al Qaeda sympathizers?" Beechum asked. "We need something concrete, something actionable."

"Let's not forget about the claims of responsibility," Alred noted. "We have videotapes: Arabs spouting off information only the actual bombers would have known."

"Hell, I can fake an Arab accent," Chase mocked him. "This could be anyone."

"Why?" Alred asked. "Why would anyone claim responsibility for barbarism like this unless they were responsible?"

"Look at the impact," Chase said. "More than three thousand dead; the western half of the country is dark and cold; the mayor of Los Angeles is threatening martial law to stop the looters; civil aviation is paralyzed; markets are crashing. We had a guy in Miami shoot a meter reader thinking he was a terrorist sneaking around his backyard, for God's sake! I never thought I'd live to say it, but we could be facing something cataclysmic here."

"That's enough," Beechum announced. "The citizens of this country didn't elect a government to throw their hands up and blame the referees."

"She has a point," Oshinski said, referring to Chase. "Our troops are spread very thin overseas, in Bosnia, Iraq, Afghanistan. Intelligence-gathering operations are strung to the breaking point watching North Korea, Iran, and China. We can't listen in on the Saudis because they have Jordan Mitchell's goddamned Quantis phones. The president can't even calm the American people because he's in a drug-induced . . ."

"Reminding me of things I can't control accomplishes nothing," Beechum barked. This time it was she who stood. "I don't need a council of briefers — I want to stop the next wave before it . . ."

"Excuse me, Elizabeth," Vick said, striding into the room. "But we're a little late for that."

He walked to the wall and turned on television coverage of the latest bad news.

"Three new incidents: a major disruption of the Alaska pipeline, two container ships sunk in the mouth of the Mississippi just north of New Orleans, and huge fires at natural gas storage facilities in Boston. Very few casualties, but these are economic and ecological disasters."

Blood rose brightly in Beechum's eyes.

"That pipeline represents fifteen percent of our domestic oil supply," Alred pointed out. More than 80 percent of America's infrastructure was privately owned, and he had memorized Bureau threat assessments on all of it. "The Port of New Orleans controls shipping to the Midwest via the Mississippi. Boston's natural gas reserves are . . ."

"Move the president down to the PEOC," Beechum ordered, dismissing his analysis. The Presidential Emergency Operations Center lay beneath the East Wing at the other end of the mansion and had been built as a Cold War bomb shelter. "I want National Guard and reserves activated in all fifty states. I want the Pentagon to shift operations to Raven Rock and to step up DEFCON INCONUS to its highest alert. I want financial markets closed, all civil aviation grounded, a call-up of all reserve units . . ."

She thought for a moment and then nodded as if agreeing with a crazy thought.

"And I want a press conference in twenty minutes."

"Press conference?" Chase blurted out. "You can't conduct a press conference without the president."

"The hell I can't!" Beechum yelled. "Until David wakes up, I'm the chief executive of a country under direct attack. That gives you two options, Andrea: either get the president out of bed to entertain us with some hymns or get your ass to work. It's time we fought back against these bastards and that is going to start with NBfuckingC!"

CHRISTOPHER WAS CHASING Maddy through what remained of the snow in front of their house when the blue Isuzu Trooper pulled slowly up Coopers Lane.

"I got you, Maddy!" he yelled, holding a long stick in front of him like a rifle. "Pow! Pow!"

"Missed me!" his sister yelled back, dodging imaginary bullets in their run-and-gun game of HRT tag. Their dad wouldn't let them play with real toy guns, so they used sticks instead.

"I did so get you!"

Christopher promptly slammed his imaginary gun on the ground, his cast hanging at his side, and began to pout.

"That's not fair, Maddy," he complained. It was late in the day, and he hadn't had a nap. "You always say I missed."

"That's because you're a bad shot," Maddy said, walking back toward her little brother. She turned to notice the Isuzu pulling even with where they stood on the snow-covered lawn.

"Am not," Christopher argued, still pouting, but angrily this time.

"OK, you got me," Maddy conceded. She picked up the stick and handed it back to him. "But now it's my turn to chase you. I get to use the fort."

She noticed that the Trooper had stopped. Its window was coming down.

"Hey, who's that?" she asked.

Christopher said nothing. All he could do was stare at the driver's odd-looking face.

"Hey, is this the Walker house?" the man called out.

Christopher stepped toward the truck, the imaginary gun firmly clenched in his one good hand. His mom had told him not to talk to strangers, but having proper protection made everything seem a lot safer.

"Not Walker; *Waller*," Christopher said. He raised the stick to eye level like his dad had showed him when Mom wasn't looking.

"Are you a pirate?" Maddy asked. She had seen men like him in books and movies — a black patch over one eye, a grin that made her skin prickle.

"Hey, how come your skin's so white?" Christopher asked. He kept walking closer to the truck, trying to get a better look.

"Is your daddy home?" the man asked.

"Don't get too close," Maddy said. "Mom said not to tell anybody nothing when dad's out of town. Especially pirates."

Neither of the children could see the 9mm automatic in the man's lap, but they sensed danger in his face.

"I don't like you," Christopher announced. Maybe it was the patch over the man's eye or the way his skin glowed whiter than the snow around them. Something struck the child as wrong. "You get away from here."

Christopher pointed his stick at the car.

"Get away or I'll shoot!"

The driver lifted his right hand and mimed a pistol of his own.

"Ay matey," the man growled, summoning his best Blackbeard impression. "I wouldn't want to fight a landlubber scalawag the likes of you!"

He pointed his index finger at the little boy, dropped his thumb, and smiled.

"But I'll come back when you're asleep, and then I'll snatch you away to my secret lair. Arrrggg!"

He sneered an exaggerated look of menace, then stepped on the gas and raced away down the street.

"Let's go," Maddy said as she watched tears well up in her little brother's eyes. She wanted to cry, too, but that was no way to act in a game of war.

XVII

Friday, 18 February
23:45 GMT
The Federal Mall, Washington DC

"KIND OF A cliché, isn't it?"

"What do you mean?"

"Meeting here in the shadows of the Lincoln Memorial, fog rising off the melting snow. Full moon. Two spies whispering amid the hint of treason. Feels like what I thought it would be when I first joined up. I was so naive back then."

Mr. Hoch wore a black North Face parka and a matching watch cap pulled down over his ears. GI Jane had dressed too lightly, anticipating a drive along the Rock Creek Parkway in some falsely registered car.

"Aren't you cold?" Hoch asked. The woman wore sneakers, jeans, and a fisherman's sweater that her grandfather had made for her in a retirement home knitting class.

"Have you heard from her?"

"Why is it that we always seem to talk at each other in two different conversations?" Hoch asked. He led her down a poorly shoveled walkway toward a copse of skeletal oak trees.

"Because no one in this business ever talks reality. I swear to God, I can't even have a normal conversation anymore. It's the lies, you know? Can't keep anything straight after a while . . . who you work for, what you do, your favorite color, what, if anything, you still give a shit about."

"She's tracked the intrusion to the White House Communications Agency," Hoch said. He reached his hands into the pockets of his jacket and hunched his shoulders, trying to close the collar around his neck.

The woman pondered what he said, walking just behind him. Her face pointed down, but her eyes searched incessantly among the surrounding sights.

"Does she know about Jafar al Tayar?"

"Of course not. She thinks she is backtracking intrusion software."

"That's all?"

"Yes."

GI Jane bent down and scooped up a handful of snow. She crafted it into a ball and tossed it up in the air a couple times, looking for a suitable target.

"What about Waller?" Hoch asked.

"He's here. They threw him a bone — a trial task to see how he'd handle it."

"And?"

"Haven't heard anything from Ellis, yet," GI Jane said. "Even omniscient, omnipotent, omnipresent spooks of my inimitable bearing occasionally have to wait."

Hoch cocked his head, not at her humor but at the inherent flaws in her theology.

"The CTC has come up with three working models," Hoch said, referring to the CIA's Langley-based Counterterrorism Center. He walked slowly through the dark, noting that the lights on the Capitol dome had been dimmed for security reasons. The entire downtown area — something he'd long considered a metaphor for America's eternal optimism — had fallen into half blacks and shadow.

"I'm getting cold."

"They're all radiological. The Bureau estimates that Ellis still has at least three kilos of gamma emitters, which is enough to make several decent-sized RDDs."

"It's here," she said, referring to the cesium and cobalt. "They'll go for high-profile sites. The real intent has nothing to do with casualties. He wants symbolic effect."

"Scenario one: he hits three or four different structures around the city. All soft targets. Places we wouldn't expect like the Georgetown Mall, L'Enfant Plaza, National Cathedral — he hates Catholics — Mormon temple, places like that."

GI Jane shook her head. She knew he was testing her. "Next?"

"Scenario two: he uses some conventional diversion — truck bomb, something like that — to focus attention away from harder targets. Once response crews move in, he launches a single, more devastating attack on the Capitol, the White House, or the Pentagon."

"Delivery mechanism is going to be a problem," the woman said. "We've locked down all level-one sites; he'll never get close enough to use an RDD."

"That's what we're briefing the White House," Hoch agreed. "Besides, any first response to a soft target diversion would be local; security at the big targets is all federal. Sending police, fire, and EMS to a bomb scene would not divert security from sensitive areas. In fact, it would probably have the opposite effect."

GI Jane threw her snowball at a shrub thirty feet away. "I hope you saved the best for last."

Hoch stopped and turned to her.

"There are a few of us who don't expect an explosion at all," he said. "Three kilos of radioactive isotope sounds like a lot, but in reality, any exterior exposure in this weather would be foolish. Melting snow would quickly dilute the contaminate and rob Ellis of symbolic effect. He obviously wants to close down America's seat of government. An RDD — even half a dozen of them — simply wouldn't do that."

"What's the alternative?" she asked. GI Jane never claimed to be a mind reader.

"Closed system contamination," Hoch answered.

"What? What kind of closed system could he . . ."

And then she understood. GI Jane, a woman who had always thought herself too smart and too tough to worry about the bogeyman, suddenly understood evil's genius.

"How are you going to stop him?" she asked.

"I'm not," Hoch answered. "And neither are you."

■

FINDING A CONCRETE truck had not been particularly difficult. Jeremy had simply driven around the city until he found one of its many new construction sites and followed a mixer back to its Arlington, Virginia, dispatch center. Once it got dark, he snuck onto the lot and popped the ignition. Most new cars had sophisticated anti theft devices, but the big Mack he selected could have been stolen by a grade-schooler.

A minimum-wage security guard logged the vehicle out but showed little interest in Jeremy's bona fides. The nation's capital had exploded in new construction, and concrete delivery had become an around-the-clock enterprise. Jeremy explained that it was a special last-minute order.

Maybe it would be best if they stopped me anyway, Jeremy thought to himself as he tried to look experienced behind the wheel of the house-sized road hog. *At least I wouldn't have to worry about helping Ellis kill innocent women and children in some horrific attack.*

But they didn't stop him. The guard noted Jeremy's departure on a clipboard and waved him through the gate.

1721 Thirteenth Street Southeast, Jeremy reminded himself, focusing on an address Ellis had given him back at the Homestead. He found the place in less than twenty minutes: a body shop, carved into the middle of a residential block — redbrick row houses across the street from what looked like a run-down school. The streets stood empty except for an odd pedestrian braving the cold air and a few people trying to dig their cars out of snowbanks.

Once Jeremy assured himself that he had found the correct address — Washington's wagon-wheel quadrants made navigation a risky enterprise — he pushed in the clutch, slipped the transmission into neutral, and set the air brake. He was just about to climb down and try to find his contact when the garage door opened. A man in new-looking denim coveralls waved him in. The man looked impatient but sure.

"You clean yourself good?" the man asked when Jeremy had shut down the big, clanking diesel. The garage looked bigger on the inside. Despite the low doorway, which he just barely cleared, the body shop rambled left and right with lifts, toolboxes, and vehicles in various stages of repair.

"Nobody followed me," he replied, climbing down from the cab. "Name's Jeremy." He reached out and shook the man's hand.

"Malachi," the man said. He stood about a foot shorter than Jeremy and moved as if he had worked at manual labor all his life. He could have been thirty or forty; the beard made it hard to tell.

Jeremy noticed two other men at the far end of the body shop, but Malachi didn't acknowledge them. They looked busy lugging heavy bags from the back of a Ryder box truck onto a forklift pallet. He couldn't see the writing on the bags, but there was no mistaking the smell: phosphate-based fertilizer, and lots of it.

"What do you want me to do now?" Jeremy asked, assuming none of these men had time for small talk. "They told me to deliver the truck. That's all they told me."

"And they told us to load it up," Malachi said. "By our own-selves."

"Should I wait?" Jeremy asked.

"Come back at eleven," the Phineas priest called out over his shoulder. "Somebody will be here when you get back to brief you on what's next."

Jeremy looked at his watch. That was three hours from now.

"There a place to get a cup of coffee around here?" he asked, but Malachi had already joined the others with their lifting.

Perfect, Jeremy groused to himself. He had three hours to sit and wait while Ellis and his men prepared for a devastating round of attacks. *Deep breath,* he told himself. *You're not the only one working this operation.*

The HRT sniper walked back out into the cold night hoping somebody else was making better progress.

. . .

SIRAD SMELLED HAMMER TIME even before she carded her way into the highly secure Mind Lab. He exuded a sharp, acrid odor that reminded her of Stilton cheese steeped in vinegar.

"For God's sake, isn't there a shower around here somewhere?" she asked.

"There's a w-w-washroom at the other end of the b-b-building," the wave theorist said, seemingly happy to see her. "But I wouldn't w-w-worry about it. You smell f-f-foxy."

She shivered at his compliment, then dropped her coat on a table near where Ravi worked at his terminal.

"Any news?" she asked.

"Some," he replied. "What did Mitchell say?"

Sirad caught herself before speaking. She had spent so much time wondering about Mitchell's intentions, she hadn't even considered what to tell her three partners.

"He wants us to go after them," she decided to say. "To go inside."

"Go inside the WHCA?" I Can't Dunk asked. "You must be kidding. It would be easier to explain the origins of the universe and provide three examples."

"Jordan Mitchell? Kidding?" Ravi responded.

"I guess he has confidence in you," Sirad told them.

"The WHCA holds the keys to the castle gates," I Can't Dunk pointed out. "They control all presidential communications, including launch-code encryption in the event of nuclear war. They have the most secure communications firewalls in the world."

"No, Borders Atlantic has the most secure firewalls in the world," Sirad corrected him. "And you have already demonstrated that you can identify White House tracking efforts. Why is it so hard to believe we can penetrate their defenses?"

"F-f-fucking A," Hammer Time said.

"I guess that means yes?" Sirad asked. Her nose wrinkled reflexively at his body odor.

"He's a wave theorist," Ravi countered. "What does he know?"

I Can't Dunk looked less optimistic.

"Getting in is one thing," he said. "Doing it without showing ourselves . . . that's another."

"Well, look on the bright side" — Sirad smiled — "we've got about eight hours to do it. After that, most estimates say it won't make a whole helluva lot of difference."

"F-f-fucking A," Hammer Time called out again. He seemed to come alive with the energy of a challenge. "I wanna r-r-rub up on some m-m-mathematics!"

"Tell you what, Hammer Time," Sirad said. "We'll get started on the math while you go rub up on a bar of soap. I don't want to sound rude, but you're starting to make my eyes water."

■

"IS IT YOUR arm, sweetie?" Caroline Waller asked. Bedtime had never been an issue for the little boy, particularly after a hard day playing outside, but tonight, he refused to go. "Is your arm bothering you?"

They sat on the living room couch in the soft glow of a table lamp. The sounds of *Kim Possible* drifted out of the family room television at the other end of the house. Maddy had insisted on watching one last cartoon.

"My tummy hurts," Christopher complained.

"That's probably from the medicine, honey," his mom assured him. "Remember? The doctor told you to eat it with your dinner so you wouldn't get a tummyache."

Caroline ran her fingers through the little boy's hair. He lay snuggled up in her lap, the smells of baby shampoo and freshly laundered SpongeBob pajamas filling the room with family warmth.

"I don't want to go to sleep," he started to cry, and Caroline hushed him.

"It's OK, baby," she whispered. "I'll hold you 'til you doze off."

She didn't mind. How could she? With Jeremy gone all the time, her children had become her only solace. No matter how hectic it got with work and bills and the demands of being a de facto single mom, she always looked forward to the last quiet cuddles before bedtime.

"I'm not going to sleep! Never, ever!" the little boy blurted out. Tears welled up in his eyes, and he buried his head in her arms.

"Hey, hey . . . ," she said. "What's the matter?"

This wasn't a little boy trying to con his mother into a few moments alone. This was fear. Something had disturbed him terribly.

"Christopher," she said, trying to calm him, "sweetie, what's wrong?"

Caroline tried to lift him away from her so she could look at his face, but he clung to her.

"It was the pirate," Maddy said. Caroline looked up to see her daughter standing in the hallway. "The pirate said he was going to come get us when we went to sleep."

"What?" Caroline asked. "I thought I told you kids not to watch cartoons like that."

"It wasn't a cartoon, Mom," Maddy said. The little girl crossed her arms, trying to act brave. She was the big sister, after all, and her dad had told her to watch over things while he was gone. "It was a real-life pirate."

Caroline sat up on the couch.

"Christopher, listen to me, honey," she said. The tone of her voice shifted instantly from gentle consolation to maternal concern. "What happened today? Did someone scare you?"

The little boy moved his head up and down against her chest, sobbing now but refusing to show his face.

"I told you, it was the pirate," Maddy insisted. She sounded resolute.

"What pirate?" Caroline asked. A child's imagination was a powerful thing. She had often seen it transform fantasy into real emotion. "There's no such thing as pirates anymore."

"The man in the truck. He drove up out front and asked if our name was Walker."

"When?" Caroline asked. Suddenly the dimly lit room seemed a little more menacing to her as well. "Tell me what happened."

"We were playing war and this truck stopped," Maddy said. Her voice began to crack, exposing the little girl behind the facade.

"Come here, baby," Caroline said, opening her lap. Christopher held on tightly. "I want you to tell me what happened."

Maddy climbed up onto her mom's leg. She had never been much of a cuddler.

"He had a pirate's patch on his eye, and he was all white like snow," Christopher said. "He said he was going to come back when we were sleeping and take us to his lair."

Maddy began to cry. Softly, trying to hide it.

"It's OK," Caroline assured them. "Nobody's going to take you anywhere."

She nuzzled them with her nose, trying to make this whole thing sound like some campfire ghost story.

"I bet he's waiting outside right now," Christopher argued. They lived in a subdivision, but the house backed up to a wooded area that often inspired frightened questions at bedtime. "He's just waiting for us to go to sleep."

"Not with me to protect you," Caroline said, summoning a voice like a Nickelodeon superhero. "Here, I'll prove it to you."

Her first impulse was to call Mason; HRT had a twenty-four-hour number designed just for occasions like this. If the kids were right, someone indeed may pose a very real threat.

"How?" Maddy asked. She was never an easy sell.

"Come with me."

Caroline wiped tears out of their eyes and scooted them out of her lap.

"There's snow all around the house, right?" she asked. They nodded, sniffling and following her as she led them by the hands to the back window.

"What if he sees us?" Maddy asked.

"There's no one out there, honey. See?" Caroline pointed outside to the snow-covered back lawn. "All the footprints are from little people's feet. Pirates have big feet. If anyone was out there, we'd see his tracks."

The logic reassured her a bit.

"But what if he comes after you go to bed?" Christopher asked.

"I'll stay up while you sleep. If I see any big footprints in the snow, I'll know the pirate is around."

Caroline coaxed the little boy right up to the window. Moonlight afforded them a clear view into the backyard.

"I wish Dad was home," Maddy said.

"I do too, sweetie, but your daddy taught me how to take care of silly old pirates. They are not allowed in my house, and they are not going to take you to any secret lair."

"You promise?" Christopher asked. His mother's assurances seemed to be working. He pressed his face against the glass, examining the footprints to make sure they were all small enough.

"I promise," Caroline said. She knelt down between her kids, confident that they felt safe, even if she no longer did. "I promise."

Christopher turned back from the window, a bit more sure of himself.

"Well, my tummy still hurts," he said. "But I think I can . . ."

"EEEEEEEE!"

Before he could finish, Maddy screamed as if Death himself had appeared in the window.

Crash!

A gloved hand smashed through the window and grabbed the little boy by the throat. Christopher tried to scream, but the hand choked his cries to a muffled wheeze.

Caroline fell over backward, then instinctively regained her balance, yanked Maddy behind her, and clawed at the fingers wrapped around her horrified son's throat.

"EEEEEEE!" Maddy yelled over and over, twisting and thrashing her hands up and down like a cat falling.

"No!" Caroline heard herself calling out. It was the desperate, detached voice of a woman who suddenly realized that as long as she lived, her children would never again believe her promises.

■

"I HAVE A prepared statement I'd like to read," the vice president announced to the forty-eight members of the White House press pool. She stood behind the famous Blue Goose podium and cleared West Wing phlegm from the back of her throat. "After that, I'll answer a few brief questions."

She tried to concentrate on the notes in front of her and the reporters in the room, but there was no way to overlook the fact that this hastily called press conference would beam instantaneously to the four corners of the earth.

"At three PM eastern standard time, terrorists struck at three critical aspects of our national infrastructure. These were just the latest attacks, of course, in a series of barbaric attempts by foreign enemies to thwart the will of the world's most powerful democracy."

Beechum adjusted her reading glasses, trying to make sense of handwritten notes she had scribbled down on two three-by-five cards.

"Within the past two hours, I have been advised that elements within our Department of Homeland Security and Federal Bureau of Investigation have made significant breakthroughs in identifying the people responsible for these attacks."

The room bustled from dead still to nearly uncontrollable excitement as four dozen of the world's most distinguished journalists smelled page-one print. They desperately wanted to call out questions, but this was the vice president of the United States and one renowned for toughness at that. Questions would have to wait.

"Because this is an ongoing investigation, I cannot offer many details, but I do want to say on behalf of President Venable, that the full faith of the American people will be justified. We feel cautiously optimistic that the murderous thugs behind these attacks will be brought to justice before they can strike again."

She looked up at what any politician would have viewed as maneating predators and removed her reading glasses.

Forty-eight hands shot up at the same instant. With almost a single voice, they called out, "Ms. Vice President."

"Harold," she said, pointing to the NBC correspondent. He caught her eye first.

"Where is the president and why is he not making this announcement himself?"

She had anticipated that, of course. America expected their commander in chief.

"As you can imagine, the president has taken an intensely personal interest in the welfare of the American people. He asked me to speak with you so he can attend to the more important business of leading our law enforcement and intelligence assets."

The language sounded canned, she knew, but the reason behind it made sense. Besides, this was a time for language of state, not personality and wit.

"Ms. Vice President, are you talking about the group Ansar ins Allah, the group that has repeatedly claimed responsibility for these attacks?"

Beechum turned toward the ABC reporter.

"As I said, national security prohibits further details. All I can say is that we feel confident that we have identified those responsible. And yes, it is safe to say that there is an element of support from foreign interests."

"Meaning the Saudis?" someone blurted out.

Beechum ignored the question and pointed to the *New York Times*.

"I'll ask the same thing," he said. "The Saudi government has taken great pains to deny involvement by the House of Saud. Are you looking directly at renegade members of the Saudi royal family? Prince Abdullah, perhaps?"

Beechum tried not to appear ruffled.

"We have longtime and proven ties with Saudi Arabia," Beechum said, walking a very fine line. "These are times of transition for the royal family, but they have been an important ally and we aim to maintain that relationship."

"But are they a target of your investigation?" another reporter called out. This among all press rooms understood protocol, but emotion was beginning to take over.

Beechum pointed to a reporter off to her right. She didn't recognize the woman's face.

"We have unconfirmed reports that an Islamic charity in Columbus, Ohio, was raided this morning by federal agents," the woman said. "Up to five suspects killed. Can you confirm this raid and tell us if this is the development you are referring to?"

Beechum glanced down at notes that held no answers to this one. It had only been a matter of time before the story leaked out.

"I came here this afternoon to reassure the American people that this White House is doing everything humanly possible to stop these terror attacks," she said. "I'm sure you and everyone else in this room understand the delicate nature of this investigation. You wouldn't want me to say anything that would place innocent lives at risk. I think I'll leave it there."

With that, the White House press secretary stepped up to Beechum's side and waved a hand, ending the press conference. The questions rose to crescendo, but the vice president excused herself and disappeared resolutely back into the West Wing.

"I trust you know something we don't," Andrea Chase said as she caught up to the vice president. She had not received any briefing that showed positive developments in the case.

"I know that two hundred and eighty million citizens need some reason to get out of bed tomorrow morning," Beechum responded. Even in times of calm she walked quicker than most. "I know that members of our press pool were starting to wonder what happened to the president, and I know that we need to keep these terrorist bastards guessing until we can catch a break. If you have a better plan, I suggest you spit it out."

Chase said nothing at first, then, "David is going to wake up in less than twelve hours with a lot of questions. I would rather not have the first be 'Where the hell do I round up the usual suspects?'"

Beechum left the chief of staff at the door to the Oval Office.

"You worry about tomorrow," the vice president called out. "I've got a country to run today."

■

DELTA FLIGHT 272 from Kansas City arrived ten minutes before nine into Reagan National.

The tall, distinguished-looking man in the port-side emergency row carried a canvas duffel and a copy of *Time* magazine. Its cover showed a split screen with President Venable on one side and Saudi prince Abdullah on the other. The caption read: *ALLIES OR AR-MAGEDDON?*

"Enjoy your stay," the flight attendant said as he followed the rest of the passengers into the terminal.

Not much enjoyment in any of this, he thought to himself as he walked out into a nearly deserted terminal. The clap of his cowboy boots on the marbled floors echoed through the beautifully renovated space. *But then again, duty and pleasure seldom share the same bunk.*

Colonel Ellis met his driver outside in a cold winter air that he well remembered from his Pentagon years. The Phineas priest behind the wheel drove a charcoal Ford with Virginia tags.

"Where are we?" he asked.

"Cell Six has pre-positioned in the Adams Morgan safe house. The intelligence unit has provided guard logs, shift rotations, and maintenance schedules at the McMillan Reservoir. We'll have the drop packs ready by nine tonight."

"What about the infidel?"

"Waller. Jeremy Andrew Waller. Thirty-one years old, married with three children, one hundred forty-five thousand dollar mortgage, partial plate upper front, subscriptions to *National Geographic*, *Popular Science*, and *McCall's*."

"He has a family?"

"He did. Now we've got them."

"FBI?" Ellis wondered aloud.

"Yes. Hostage Rescue Team sniper. I've put out feelers down at Bragg and Dam Neck, trying to dig up anyone who might have worked with him."

The former Special Forces spook turned to look out his window as the car pulled away from the arrivals ramp.

Hostage Rescue Team? he thought. This guy might prove to be more trouble than he was worth.

■

JEREMY RETURNED TO the body shop five minutes early. He'd spent most of the previous three hours reading a paperback over soggy French fries and microwaved McDonald's burgers. A sharp pain lingered just behind his sternum, some combination of gutter-food indigestion and apprehension.

"You ready for a driver?" he asked, knocking and entering with a confidence he hoped would sustain his cover.

"Hold it!" Malachi said. He stood near the back of the concrete mixer with a prohibitive hand in the air. The other two men stood behind him, wearing heavy rubber gloves and closed-circuit aspirators — the kind used by hazardous materials handlers.

"Smells like springtime on a dairy farm," Jeremy noticed aloud. He remembered working on his buddy Eric's farm as a kid. How could he ever forget getting up at the crack of dawn to hand crank diesel fuel into the big John Deere tractors as Eric loaded Agway phosphates into the "honey wagon"?

"Don't you worry about nothing besides the driving," Malachi scolded.

"Whatever you say," Jeremy told him.

He tried to assess the scene without looking overly curious. One of the masked men had climbed a ladder and was leaning into the mixing drum. A suitcase-sized black storage case rested on the ladder platform. It looked as if he had emptied its contents into the ANFO.

"How long before you're done?"

The other man bent over something near the truck's rear wheel well. Jeremy assumed it had to be the detonator.

"Five minutes," Malachi said, checking his watch. "Your contact should be here by now."

"I am," a voice announced. Jeremy recognized it immediately.

"Colonel?" he responded, turning toward Ellis and another man he had never met. "Didn't expect to see you again so soon."

"Well, I've learned that expectations can present serious liability," Ellis said. "Especially when dealing with strangers."

Jeremy thought he heard threat in the man's voice, but dismissed it as his own misgivings.

"We're all set, Colonel," the body shop foreman announced. He made no other attempt at conversation and came no closer.

"Thank you, men," Ellis said. "That will be all."

The three Phineas priests left through a side door — to decontaminate, Jeremy assumed. Ellis's bodyguard waited until they were gone, then caught his boss's eye and exited as well.

"So, are we still on schedule?" Jeremy asked when they were alone. He cocked his head toward the newly loaded concrete mixer. "Looks like everything is ready to go in here."

"That's what I understand," Ellis said. He talked through clenched teeth. "Our intelligence cell assures me that all elements are good to go."

Jeremy heard doubt, a sound he had learned to loathe in men of action.

"Do you have my orders, sir?" he asked.

But before the colonel could answer, the door opened and another man walked in.

"This is a busy place tonight," Jeremy remarked.

Caleb walked up beside his father. Jeremy saw that the albino had stripped off the gauze bandages and replaced them with a black eye patch. The man's pale, almost translucent skin glowed phosphorescent in the dimly lit garage.

"Your orders have changed," Ellis said sarcastically. He knew something. Both of them did.

Jeremy felt adrenaline surging into his chest, pumping like it had during the Yemen mission and the Puerto Rico hostage rescue and the Irian Jaya hit. This time, he had no rifle, no weapons at all except presence of mind.

"Changed? How?" Jeremy pushed his hands into his pockets to keep from showing nervous energy.

"We have your family," Caleb announced without further explanation. The words almost buckled Jeremy's knees, but he maintained a poker face.

"I don't have a family," Jeremy said. "What are you talking about?"

Caleb held up his right hand and showed Jeremy where blood had seeped through a bandage around his knuckles.

"You know how I got this?" he asked. "Dragging your son Christopher out of that nice little house down in Stafford. Your wife cried like a mongrel bitch when I took him, but then Satch got her and everything went real quiet."

Jeremy lunged at the albino. It was a reflex; a hammer blow to his head, which dropped the man in a rumpled heap.

"Stop or they're dead," Ellis said. His words came quietly, little more than a hiss. Jeremy might not have been able to restrain himself if the colonel had shouted, but the ease of his tone shocked him.

"What do you want?" Jeremy asked. He was talking to the colonel but standing just inches from Caleb as the albino regained his feet. Jeremy stared into the man's single remaining eye. It was pink.

"I want you to understand the commander's dilemma," Ellis told him. "I want you to know what it feels like to decide between those things you hold most dear and the greater good of people you swore to protect. Do you follow orders to save your wife and children, knowing that those orders will kill thousands of other people? Or do you deny this mission, knowing we'll kill your loved ones in the most brutal fashion?"

"You're a sick fuck," Jeremy said. Philosophy seemed beyond him at this point.

"No need to swear," Ellis scolded. "And I'm not sick: in fact, I'm blessed with an almost prescient clarity of mind."

Jeremy saw that Ellis held a Polaroid photograph in his hand.

"Thirty years ago in a bloody Asian rice paddy, I received an epiphany. My men were dying all around me. I had been shot several times, myself, bleeding, confused, scared, angry . . . raging against an enemy some politician defined for me. I knew I was going to die, never see my family again. I remember wondering about forgiveness — whether God would take me into heaven despite the numbers of people I'd killed."

Jeremy didn't care about the old soldier's justification. All he could concentrate on was the Polaroid.

"And he came to me. A soft voice. Just a presence, really."

Caleb stood motionless beside his father, ready to defend him at the least provocation.

"The Lord filled me up with a love I'd never felt before. Selfless, righteous love for something greater than my own desires. I had no idea what any of that meant, of course, except that I wasn't going to die there in that rice paddy. The truth in that epiphany wasn't revealed until later, once I'd gotten back to the world."

"You have a point?" Jeremy asked.

"In your unfailing love you will lead the people you have redeemed, scripture tells us," Ellis said. "In your strength you will guide them to your holy dwelling. The nations will hear and tremble; anguish will grip the people of Philistia."

His face seemed to glow with resolution.

"The Philistines — the gutter gods of Islam — will never rest until they have taken from us what God has given. It is our duty to defeat them. The Phineas Priesthood is Salvation's last defense."

Caleb handed Jeremy the photograph. It showed Caroline, folded over backward on a tiled floor, stripped to her panties with hands and feet duct taped together.

"One hundred Independence Avenue," Ellis said. He pointed to the truck. "You are going to make a delivery to the Capitol."

Jeremy felt an overwhelming desire to end this right there and then, but that was impossible. Ellis would have more of his priests at the safe house. They'd kill Caroline and the kids before he could find them.

"There's a big pour on the East Lawn," Ellis responded. "It's construction for a bunker they are building to protect the Congress against terrorist attack."

"You're going to kill them anyway, aren't you?" Jeremy countered. "You blow up the truck with me in it — make it look like some suicide bombing — then you kill my family, too."

"Not that quickly," Ellis said. "We have something much more productive in mind for you. I have expectations of great things, still."

"Yeah," Jeremy said, mustering a menacing smile. "Don't forget what you told me about the danger in expectation."

XVIII

"WHERE AM I?"

The man who one week earlier had shone presidential emerged from a sparse, military-style bunk room in a state of complete disarray. His once perfectly groomed hair was matted across his forehead. Heavy blue-black bags hung beneath his eyes. Two days of gray-and-black stubble covered his cheeks and chin. The navy-blue robe he'd found at the foot of his bed was drawn tightly at the waist, inside out.

"This is PEOC, sir," an Air Force communications sergeant said, jumping to his feet. Marine guards stood at either side of the bunk room doorway, but they seemed far less concerned.

"PEOC?" David Venable asked, stepping into a rude space full of whirring machines and artificial light. He looked well rested enough to understand these odd circumstances; sleep had humbled him. "I don't know what PEOC stands for."

"You're in a bunker beneath the East Wing, David," Andrea Chase said, walking toward him from a break-out room. She looked a little ragged herself.

"Presidential Emergency Operations Center, sir," the airman added. He had been asked a question by the president himself and didn't want to short the answer.

"What has happened?" Venable asked. He looked around the room at a staff of uniformed military personnel. All of them looked busy, none of them familiar.

"Airman, please call the vice president's office and advise Ms. Beechum that the president is up," Chase ordered.

"Yes, ma'am," he said.

Chase took the president's arm and spoke beneath the rattle of computer keyboards, telephones, and cable news reports.

"Are you all right, David?" she asked.

"I think so, yes," the president responded. He appeared to be conducting a personal inventory, rebooting his faculties. "How long have I been asleep?"

"In here," his chief of staff said. Chase led him into the break-out room she had just exited. "You've been down for twenty hours. It's Friday evening. The eighteenth."

"Friday?" he erupted. He tried to remember how he had gotten down here, then gave up, rummaging for the last memory of any kind. "The last I knew it was Monday."

"Well," Chase started to explain, but then she stopped. Nothing she could offer would sound reasonable at this point.

"Hello, David," Beechum interrupted. "How do you feel?"

"I wake up in some kind of bunker feeling like I got cotton between my ears and something dead in my mouth. I'm missing three days, and . . ." Venable noticed that his robe was inside out. "Look at me! I want to know what in the name of God is going on around here."

"There was another series of attacks while you slept — the Trans Alaska Pipeline, ships in the Mississippi, strategic natural gas reserves in Boston. The FBI is . . ."

"No, I mean with me!" The president slumped into a seat at a small conference table. "I want to know how I got here."

Beechum didn't miss a beat.

"You were sedated, David," she said. "I authorized it. The White House physician gave you an injection."

Venable nodded. He had suspected something like this.

"I took you on as vice president for the good of the party," he said, placing both palms flat on the table. His mind seemed to be re-gathering itself at lightning pace. "I knew it was wrong, but I felt that I had no choice."

"David . . ."

Andrea Chase tried to stop him, but he'd have none of it.

"I knew that you couldn't function as second in command," he said.

"You hadn't slept in more than ninety-six hours," Beechum ar-gued. There was no apology in her voice. She was an old lawyer lay-ing out an overwhelming case. "You were lapsing into what is called insomniac psychosis."

"So you lapsed into what is called treason?"

"No, David." Chase stopped him. "It wasn't like that. We did what we had to do in order to . . ."

"Excuse me, Mr. President." The Air Force sergeant knocked af-ter the fact. "You have flash traffic from Fort Meade."

"That's NSA," Beechum explained, reaching out for three pieces of paper in the sergeant's hand. "We've been waiting for word on anything linked to Prince Abdullah."

"This isn't your war anymore, Elizabeth," the president said, an-grily snatching the papers from her hands. He tried to read the doc-uments, then realized he had no glasses.

"Here, use mine," Chase said. She handed him pink-framed read-ing spectacles that looked absolutely ridiculous on his haggard face.

"DEST? NEST? More of those goddamned acronyms," he growled, trying to make sense of the National Security Agency missive.

"Domestic Emergency Support Team," Beechum explained. She'd read enough of the NSA summary to know these develop-ments had nothing to do with Abdullah. "DEST is a multiagency re-sponse element designed to coordinate large exotic attacks like what we're seeing. DOD, DOE, HHS, CIA, FBI, DHS. They are stag-ing out of a specially outfitted 737 called 'Gatekeeper.'"

Venable grudgingly handed the paper back to his VP.

"Translate this," he said. "Go ahead."

"DOE's Nuclear Emergency Search Team has identified a large radiological signature in Adams Morgan," Beechum read. "They deem it a qualifying anomaly inside the NACAP reaction cordon, meaning it may present a direct threat to White House personnel."

"Shit," Chase said.

"What's that mean?" Venable demanded.

"It means that FEMA is going to invoke the continuity of government protocols," Beechum said. She had seen this coming. "One of us is leaving town."

"Then pack your bags, Elizabeth," he said. The president's eyes cleared. He took off his robe and turned it right side out. "I don't have time to deal with the reasoning behind what you did. For now, I'm ordering you off to that *secure location* I keep hearing about. We'll see how easy it is for you to usurp my power from a concrete bunker deep inside some godforsaken mountain."

■

SATCH WAS A big man and strong, but the weight in his hands felt far more burdensome than anything he'd ever lifted.

"I hate this kinda stuff," he huffed. The black plastic road case bore no markings, but he felt all too familiar with its contents.

"You know what they used to say," his partner reassured him. "You ain't gotta like it, you just gotta do it."

"I ain't no SEAL no more," he argued. "And I never cared much for all those stupid sayings when I was in the teams, neither."

The other man stood half a foot and fifty pounds lighter than Satch, but he had trained hard for this mission. Nobody big or small was going to show him up.

"Yeah, well just don't drop that. I got all the fingers and toes I need, without growing extras."

Satch grunted half a laugh and followed his partner out of a modest row house toward a double-parked van.

"Good thing you already got four kids," Satch said. "I hear this stuff can make your balls pucker up like raisins."

"Then I guess the colonel picked the right man for this gig, didn't he? 'Cause the world ain't ready for offspring from the likes of you."

Both of them chuckled, lightening a troublesome moment. They walked down a long flight of stairs. Satch reached the van first. He held the box against the rear bumper with his thigh and unlocked the rear door.

"You hear a helicopter?" he asked. The other man looked up but couldn't see anything above the rooflines along the narrow city street.

"It's Washington DC," the partner said. "There's choppers everywhere."

"Right," Satch agreed. He hefted his box into the white Chevy Astro van and pushed the doors closed. "Can't be too careful."

"I'll drive, then," his partner said. "'Cause the most dangerous thing in this city right now ain't seven-point-five pounds of cesium — it's you behind the wheel."

■

"PLEASE, NOT THE children," Caroline begged. She could take the pain of physical abuse, but nothing could ever hurt like the fear she had seen in their once innocent eyes.

"Bring 'em in," one of the captors ordered. He was one of the men who had come through the window. And the pirate. The albino. Whiter than any man she'd ever seen, grotesquely scarred around the eye patch. Bloody from the broken glass.

"Mommy!" Christopher sobbed when he saw her lying there on the vacant cellar floor. The concrete had rubbed her skin raw where they had dragged her across it. Cruel welts and bruises covered her face and breasts.

"It's OK, baby," she said in the most soothing voice she could muster. The handcuffs ached around her wrists and ankles, but what hurt most was not being able to hold her kids.

Pull yourself together! she screamed at herself. So far, the injuries were superficial and would heal. *Stay strong for the kids*.

"What do you want from us?" she called out. They had asked so few questions. The beatings came for no apparent reason.

"We want you to keep these brats quiet," the captor said. He wore a flannel shirt and brown canvas Carhartt pants — the kind carpenters wore, and farmers.

"*Waahhhh*," Patrick cried. A second captor dragged the little boy in by his pajama collar.

"Especially this one. Little bastard hasn't shut up from the time we woke him up."

The carpenter pushed the child toward his mother, but there was no need for coaxing. Patrick ran to his mom and fell upon her.

Christopher, who had stood inside the door almost transfixed with fear, slowly followed his brother and knelt down, still trembling wildly.

"It's OK, sweetheart," Caroline reassured him. She tried to wipe the blood off her face with the back of her hand so her appearance wouldn't scare them. Her nose was probably broken; one blow had cut her above the left eye.

Goddamn the FBI. Caroline seethed beneath the surface. She fought futilely at the restraints and swore to herself that the children would not see her cry. It was bad enough that they had taken her husband. Now they had allowed these animals to take her family, too.

■

100 INDEPENDENCE AVENUE.

How perfectly ironic, Jeremy decided as he shifted up through the sixteen-gear transmission, slowly gaining speed with his load of fertilizer and number-two heating oil. His destination was the big, walled-off construction project obvious to anyone passing the Capitol's East Lawn. It had been under way for more than a year already: a secret project that hadn't stayed secret long. Sky-high cranes, excavators, and hard hats were just too hard to hide.

The *Washington Post* uncovered the $40 million congressional bunker first, but there had been little controversy outside the Beltway. In times like these, who could blame the nation's legislature for building a place to hide?

Twelve minutes, Jeremy reminded himself. It was just thirteen blocks from the body shop where he'd picked up the truck to the Capitol. Ellis's instructions had been concise and specific.

Enter through the security checkpoint at the East Gate, he had said. *They are running a thousand-yard pour tonight, meaning every concrete truck in the city has dropped off at least one load.*

How could the Bureau have overlooked it? Jeremy wondered, downshifting already for a stoplight. They knew terrorists sought symbolic targets and that there was no bigger target than that great domed People's House up there on the Hill.

Detonator, conduit, charge.

Jeremy let out the clutch and pulled into traffic, reminding himself of the simple, inalterable construction of any improvised explosive device. In this case, Ellis's men had rigged some kind of remote trigger. The detonator would fire a conduit — probably shock tube — which would deliver a lightning-fast spark to more than five tons of ANFO. Anyone who had seen Timothy McVeigh's handiwork in Oklahoma City would know what that could do.

Got to find some way to break the detonator-charge interface, Jeremy thought. And he had to do it in a way that would make a failure look plausible.

Honk!

Someone cut Jeremy off, causing him to lurch sideways, almost striking a bicycle courier.

"Watch where you're going!" Jeremy yelled back, understanding for the first time that people behind the wheels of big trucks had a very difficult job.

The man in the car flipped him the finger and raced off, leaving Jeremy's face flushed with anger.

Sonofabitch! he thought. If this idiot only knew what lay in the back of his truck. *If they only knew that the safety of my family and a city full of innocent citizens could be jeopardized because they were late for a hair appointment.*

Then he began to smile. He had an idea.

Jeremy stomped on the gas and shifted up. They'd be following him, of course; Ellis or one of his Phineas priests. He couldn't see any obvious tail in his rearview mirror, but they'd be smart enough to stay out of sight.

"So much for expectation," Jeremy said, believing he still might have a chance. His plan wasn't exactly genius, but the best plans seldom were.

■

SIRAD DIDN'T NEED to understand the Nguyen cornerstone or stochastic wave generation theory or Camus algorithms. All she needed to understand was that Ravi had found a way through White House Communications Agency firewalls without showing himself.

News of that came just after ten o'clock. Hammer Time had actually taken a shower, and I Can't Dunk had brewed a new pot of coffee.

"My God," Sirad remarked as her computer screen flickered

twice, then filled with prose in standard English. "This looks like a Web page."

"It is," Ravi bragged. "The WHCA's Sippernet interface with DISN's DSNET3."

"Ravi."

"Sorry. The Defense Information Systems Network has four packet-switching networks to handle military communications in-house and with other agencies. DSNET3 — referred to as the 'Y' side — is the most secure: Top Secret/SCI. It uses packet-switching nodes that work off international standard Disnet-three protocols."

"And this provides secure communications between the Penta-gon and the WHCA?" she asked.

"It allows what they believe to be secure information transfer from POTUS on down. Eyes-only access to the Y side."

"Brilliant, isn't he?" Ravi asked.

"What?" Sirad asked. "Who?"

"God."

"G-g-god?" Hammer Time jumped in. "What's God got to d-d-do with this?"

"Complexity. We just play at codes," Ravi said. "God dangles clues out in front of us, but when it comes right down to it, we can't even come up with decent questions."

"Come on, man," I Can't Dunk said. "How come you gotta get all misty every time we break into something?"

"God is the only great intelligence," Ravi responded. His words sounded reverent, prayerful. "The poet mechanic."

"Can we save the hallelujahs for a minute, fellas?" Sirad asked. "'Cause I've got a question."

She leaned into the computer screen and pointed to a line of text.

"If these intrusions really originated with WHCA, what's that?"

Hammer Time leaned in over her shoulder, trying to see where she was pointing. He felt more confident now that he smelled of Ivory soap and Head and Shoulders.

"'CAPSTONE3,'" he read aloud. "A d-d-dog-ear, maybe? A remote-access entry c-c-code."

"For what?" Sirad asked. She moved the mouse and double-clicked on something that looked particularly troubling.

"Let's say you wanted to read your own e-mails from somebody else's computer without knowing about it," Ravi explained. "Normally, you would sign in under your own name. But that leaves a trail. The better way would be to break in, clone your host's access protocols, and dog-ear your place so you could quickly move in and out. Hard to do, but it's a safer way to play hide-and-seek."

"A g-g-good way to fart and p-p-point your finger," Hammer Time stuttered.

"But this intruder thinks he's completely transparent," I Can't Dunk said. "Why would he need to cover himself with another layer of camouflage?"

"Because the downside in getting caught is too much to risk on a single backstop," Ravi suggested. "Because he is so high up, he can't take a chance that we will discover him."

"Who's that high up?" I Can't Dunk asked. "The president?"

Sirad said nothing, but her silence confirmed what they all had suspected.

"You can't be serious," I Can't Dunk argued. "Venable isn't smart enough to pull this off by himself. He'd need help from the NSA or DISA, and even then, he'd be vulnerable to time signature."

"Unless POTUS is just the dog-ear for CAPSTONE3," Sirad thought out loud. "What if someone knew the president was out of the loop? What if they used his signature, knowing he was too busy to pay attention?"

"Son of a bitch." Ravi nodded. "They wanted us to discover this all along."

"What are our limitations to on-site discovery?" Sirad asked, suddenly infused with energy. She scrolled up and down the screen, looking for something only she would recognize.

"There are none," I Can't Dunk assured her. "If it's in the WHCA or DISN system, we can access it."

"Incoming, outgoing communications?" Sirad asked.

"Yes. We have access to everything they do, say, and know."

"Domestic and international?"

"Yes."

"Civilian and military?"

"Yes, of course," Ravi answered. "We have free rein of every communication and conduit. What is it you want?"

"I want to access the fail-safe codes," she blurted out.

All three men stared at her.

"You m-m-mean the f-f-fucking football?"

"That's exactly what I mean," Sirad demanded. She reached for her coat and checked to make sure she had her keys. "Can you get them for me?"

"You bet we can," Ravi told her.

He leaned back and crossed his arms. All of a sudden, he understood, too.

THE PRESIDENT HAD showered and shaved, and now donned a traditional uniform of white shirt, red tie, and blue two-button suit by the time his cabinet arrived. They met in the Cabinet Room as usual, despite concern from the Secret Service, which had tried to keep him in PEOC.

"Good evening," he said, striding into the crowded space ahead of Andrea Chase and his press secretary. "I want to deal with the issue of my absence these last twenty-four hours."

No one else said a word. Some looked up at him, some stared into their briefing packages.

"I imagine there have been rumors, but I don't have time to deal with them right now. Whatever you have heard, I'm back in the Oval Office and well focused on the fact that we may not yet have seen the worst of this crisis."

Chase found a seat at the table. The press secretary stood along the east wall. Venable stood, as usual, behind his chair.

"Why don't we start with an investigative update," the president continued. He nodded to his attorney general then reached down for his glass of ice water.

"Should I, uh . . . shouldn't I wait for the vice president?" the empty suit asked.

"At the suggestion of FEMA, I have sent her to the Mountain," Venable said. His voice sounded firm and strong. "I would conference her in, but she's in a Marine Corps helicopter as we speak. Go ahead with your briefing."

The attorney general shuffled through briefing papers the FBI and DHS had prepared for him. Law enforcement had never been his thing, really. He was a jurist, an academic devoted to the letter of the law more than its application. Cops struck him as little more than a poorly educated, blue-collar cleanup crew assigned to the gutters of society. They were an occupational hazard.

"Where should I, uh . . . where should I start, sir?" he asked.

"Start with what I need to know," Venable answered. He had regretted this appointment since their first meeting, but it was too late to do anything now. "Have we learned anything more about the Saudis?"

The attorney general thumbed through his briefing package until he found a folder earmarked Saudi Arabia.

"Yes . . . ah, FBI investigation continues. Director Alred assures me that . . . the Saudis — yes — the Saudis . . ."

"Matthew, could you help us out, here," Venable said. As national security advisor, Havelock served as a one-stop-shopping update on everything that happened since Monday. Most thought the director of central intelligence or the new intelligence czar were America's top spooks, but in reality, the national security advisor had long been the president's chief intelligence officer.

"Three developments with the Saudis." Havelock jumped in with a confidence Venable hadn't seen in their first meetings. "NSA has picked up big increases in signals traffic with the Chinese. Most of these communications have involved Quantis phones so we can't listen in, but they parallel wire transfers out of several U.S. financial corporations. Real money. The FBI puts the number at a little under five hundred billion."

"Impact on markets?" the president asked.

"We anticipate a move on the dollar and sharp spikes in precious metals as soon as the news hits," Havelock told him. "I'm hearing speculation of a ten-percent hit on the Dow once it opens again . . . maybe more."

"What do the Chinese have to say?" Venable asked his secretary of state.

"They deny everything. It's oil, of course. We know that, but there's nothing we can do. The Saudis have cut production to pre-1976 levels, opened their southern quarter to every exploration company in the world but ours. Crude just topped seventy dollars a barrel. Our strategic reserves have dipped to their lowest levels since we started stockpiling."

"Why? How did we let our reserves run so low?"

"The previous administration," Havelock answered. "American oil companies reported record profits in the two years since Saddam Hussein was toppled. We're talking about a Texas oil family with very close ties to the House of Saud. You can draw your own conclusions."

"What's the bottom line?" Venable asked. He was an insurance man. He understood actuarials and stop-loss quotients.

"We have a legitimate national security exposure here, Mr. President," the chairman of the joint chiefs said. "Five-dollar-a-gallon gas may cause indigestion in Des Moines, but I've got jet aircraft and tanks that don't run well on diplomatic hot air. If we don't take hard, definitive action, and soon, we're not going to care much about a few thugs with pipe bombs."

The president tapped the back of his chair — that old nervous habit.

"You said three things," he reminded Havelock. "What else?"

The national security advisor folded his hands in front of himself and turned to the secretary of energy.

"Our Capitol region NEST team believes they have found the radioactive materials stolen from Kentucky," the energy secretary said. "Not all of it, but enough to initiate full-court surveillance."

"I was going to tell you that, Mr. President," the attorney general jumped in. He seemed thrilled with himself for having something to offer.

"We have coordinated with the FBI and DHS to maintain a safe standoff, but it is a hard perimeter," the energy secretary continued. "The good thing about radioactive isotopes is that they are hard to move without leaving a trail."

"They're here in Washington?" Venable asked. He had assumed they'd come, but not this quickly. "You're sure of that?"

"Yes, sir. CIA analysts say the best bet is several RDDs around the city. Remember, these terrorists want symbolic impact. We have to assume that this building will be a target."

"What else . . . locusts and plague?" Venable asked. If he'd known things were this bad, he might not have gotten up from his nap.

"There's a little good news, actually, depending on how you look at it," Havelock said. "That HRT raid on the group in Columbus? Well, it may have been a black hole in terms of terrorism, but hard drive exploitation turned up access codes for some of Prince Abdullah's close-hold accounts. The FBI and Treasury investigators may be able to freeze some of his assets. That could buy time."

"Abdullah would scream bloody murder," Venable rebuffed him.

"In private, maybe." Havelock nodded. "But not publicly. Remember, he's making a power play against his own family — trying to hoard enough of the royals' money to establish a power base once the Crown Prince dies. He doesn't want to see this story on Aljazeera."

"Excuse me," a uniformed marine interrupted. "Mr. President, the SITROOM has flash traffic for you, sir. A CRITIC message. Urgent."

"What the hell now?" he grumbled. Venable started toward the door. "Matthew and Andrea, I need you in on this. Richard, I want State's opinion on UN reaction to a military strike against Saudi Arabia. General Oshinski, I want a war plan on my desk by dinnertime."

"All options?" the chairman asked.

"All options."

Venable led his chief of staff and national security advisor out of the room, leaving the rest of his cabinet to ponder a grave possibility. "All options" was no code. In very open terms it meant that President David Venable had begun to consider launching the first proactive nuclear strike in more than sixty years.

■

JEREMY WATCHED THE light turn yellow ahead of him. A crowd of late-night barhoppers waited on the sidewalk to cross; taxis weaved back and forth, looking for fares.

This is gonna hurt, he decided, stomping down on the gas. The big diesel belched a cloud of black smoke and lurched ahead. The sparkly white Mercedes station wagon in front of him slowed for the light, but Jeremy kept his foot on the pedal, plowing into the back of it, pushing the car toward the crowded sidewalk.

Brakes screeched, horns honked, people screamed. The giant yellow concrete truck climbed up the back of the expensive German car like a car crusher at some redneck rodeo. Cars swerved in every direction, knocking into each other, dimpling, buckling, smashing — all burning rubber and broken glass.

By the time Jeremy realized no one had been seriously hurt, a DC Metro unit had raced up beside him, lights flashing. Capitol Hill was thick with marked units.

"License and registration," the first cop said, walking up to the driver's door.

Jeremy studied his mirror and the streets around him, trying to spot his tail. Had Ellis seen the accident himself? How long before he found out?

"Fuck you, asshole," Jeremy said. He spoke softly, from behind a humble, I'm-so-sorry-officer smile.

"What did you say?" the patrolman asked. He was thin, African American. A pencil-thin mustache adorned his upper lip.

"I said, fuck you." Jeremy smiled. He tried to look the model, obedient citizen. "I bet you like picking on white boys, don't you, you tar-colored stoop nigger."

The officer stood back and cocked his head, unable to believe what he was hearing. Sirens rose in the distance. Angry motorists were climbing out to assess the damage.

"Get out of the truck, sir," the officer said. Jeremy could hardly believe the man's resolute professionalism.

"You'd like that wouldn't you, you fucking doughnut gargler," Jeremy said, smiling as if talking about the weather. Anyone watching would have thought him a courteous, deeply regretful offender.

"What's that smell?" the second officer asked, arriving at his partner's side.

"Your mother, bitch," Jeremy responded.

"Say what?" The partner recoiled.

"Get the fuck out of the truck," the first responder ordered.

"Not until I use this gun I got to blow your black ass back to Rwanda."

The second officer reached down to his hip to cover his weapon while the man with the pencil-thin mustache climbed up and jammed his gun through the driver's-side window — its barrel pressed right up against Jeremy's nose.

"Now how 'bout you get your cracker ass out the truck so we can discuss race relations here in the District," the officer said. His eyes darted through the cabin, looking for the threatened gun.

"Happy to, officer." Jeremy nodded. Any tail would believe him the wronged party in this mishap. He hadn't defused the bomb yet, but he had certainly kept it from reaching the Capitol.

XIX

Saturday, 19 February
05:41 GMT
Mount Weather Special Facility, Clarke County, Virginia

ELIZABETH BEECHUM HAD seen site schematics and read off-budget funding requests but had never actually visited the so-called secure location. Referred to as Mount Weather, Site Seven, or just "that place out west," this unobtrusive collection of buildings and asphalt parking lots looked like any of a hundred military installations from the air.

Home to FEMA's Emergency Assistance Center, Mount Weather began life as a meteorological observation and research facility. It wasn't until the 1950s that anyone recognized its potential as a Cold War bunker. By the late 1990s, the 483-acre facility had become the federal government's top secret capital — home to a shadow government so highly classified, not even those chosen to staff it always knew exactly what to do.

"Please hold on, ma'am," the Marine Corps flight safety officer cautioned her as the big lumbering HMX-2 banked hard left and started to flare. "We get some pretty tricky crosswinds up here on the Blue Ridge. Hate for you to get bounced around."

Beechum did as she was told, craning her head to look out the aircraft's small round window. They had followed I-66 west, she knew, until it spilled into Route 50. Just the other side of Middleburg — where the mountains started to rise above the sprawling horse country mansions of Paris and Ashby's Gap — where Route 601 turned south, then back upon itself. The decrepit two-lane carriage path wound its way up Blue Ridge Mountain Road to where chain-link and barbed-wire fencing formed an ominous corridor of restriction.

The helipad sat next to a cluster of maintenance buildings. Even through the diffused glow of spotlights, Beechum could make out an entrance gate and a three-story brick building with tall stone pillars, which she had been told was just a facade built to cover ventilation shafts. Heavily armed military men guarded the helipad, but ordinary-looking rent-a-cops in unadorned blue uniforms stood at the perimeter like onlookers at a red-carpet star show.

Enjoy the view while you can, Elizabeth, the vice president told herself. *Might be a while before you feel the sun on your face again.*

The Shenandoah Mountains stretched out before her as the HMX-2 settled into its landing hover. A Brigadoon-like fog rose off a blanket of white, draping the distant valley in an almost mystical scene of moonlit beauty. They were just forty-eight air miles from her office on Pennsylvania Avenue, but Mount Weather might as well have been a different world.

◼

JORDAN MITCHELL HAD always been a man of action. Waiting bothered him on a fundamental level.

"Is she there yet?" he asked. The Borders Atlantic executive rarely visited the seventeenth floor, but everything he needed to begin the endgame lay within its electronically shielded walls.

"Just set down," Trask responded. The chief of staff stood at the other end of the room, trying to manage two phone conversations and an intemperate boss at the same time. There were just two other people in the room — a systems engineer who could help them navigate a daunting array of technology and Hamid, who had been in on the game from the start. He, better than anyone except Mitchell, understood the Swiss chronometer timing necessary to orchestrate the final hours of a delicately complex denouement.

"What about Waller?"

Jeremy Waller had turned out to be everything Mitchell had hoped for. And more. The HRT sniper presented a rare combination: a team player who functioned brilliantly alone, an intuitive thinker with the pragmatic mistrust of answers, a physical actor who understood the limitations of muscle. Any other man would have presented control problems, but Jeremy's blue-collar work ethic and deep-seated patriotism kept it well in check.

"Hang on a minute," Trask spoke into one of the phones. These calls were very important, but Mitchell remained his first priority.

"Jeremy has been arrested."

"Arrested?"

Mitchell hadn't foreseen this.

"He seems to have gotten himself involved in a car wreck," Trask said, trading attentions between Mitchell and the source on one of the Quantis phones.

"What about the truck?" Mitchell asked. "Where the hell is that truck?"

"Right here, sir," the systems engineer offered. He pressed a button, and Washington's Seward Square popped up on a wall-mounted flat-screen television. "Secret Service security camera mounted on a utility pole. I can get you three different angles."

The technician typed into his keyboard, and the screen broke into four isolation boxes: real-time video of cop cars, fire trucks, ambulances, and a crowd of curious bystanders.

The big yellow concrete truck sat perched atop the crumpled Mercedes like a rhinoceros tupping a hare.

"Do we know where they are taking him?" Mitchell asked.

Trask spoke into one of his phones and shook his head.

"It was DC Metro who arrested him. The precinct station is at Buzzard's Point, down on the Potomac. Probably take him there."

Mitchell tried to get inside Jeremy's head and figure out what his best tactical operator was up to. Had he planned this out or was this just another variable he'd have to overcome?

"Where is Ellis?" Mitchell asked. He pointed to a blank TV screen. "Bring him up on three."

The technician did as he was told. A street scene flashed on: point of view through a car windshield.

"That's him in the Navigator, headed north toward the safe house in Adams Morgan," Trask said. "We have a dozen people on him. Very low probability of evasion."

"Caleb?"

Trask spoke into his phone, then responded to his boss.

"Still on Capitol Hill. We're tracking him south on Independence. Appears that he is following Jeremy."

"Mr. Mitchell?" a female voice inquired over a sophisticated system designed to identify the target voice from a database of sound prints and filter out ambient noise.

"What is it?"

"You have a visitor, sir. Ms. Malneaux."

"Send her in," Mitchell said.

He caught Trask in a knowing glance.

"She knows," Mitchell said.

Trask just nodded and returned to his calls.

■

"I'M TELLING YOU, I was *trying* to get you to arrest me! Can't you figure that out?" Jeremy yelled. He had been trying to convince these two officers of his plan since they threw him unceremoniously into the back of their squad car.

"Nigger?" the cop with the mustache asked sarcastically. "Is there really a white man in America ignorant enough to use that word anymore?"

"I was sitting on twenty tons of high explosives with a bunch of murderous white supremacists on my tail," Jeremy rationalized. "What was I supposed to do?"

"You could have started with 'I need some help, officer,'" the driver said. He conjured up an Uncle Tom accent. "You'd be surprised what us colored folk can do if we puts our minds to it."

Jeremy craned his neck, trying to look back up Independence Avenue to where the ten-wheeled bomb sat, detonator intact. He had gambled on hopes that Ellis wouldn't want to waste the device on anything less than its intended target. If all went right, the colonel would wait until things settled down, then send another driver to pick it up.

"Look, I don't care what you do with me," Jeremy said. "But I'm telling you: that truck is filled with ammonium nitrate and fuel oil. ANFO. The same shit Tim . . ."

"How do you know about ANFO?" the driver asked. He had dropped the accent.

"I already told you! I'm an FBI agent working undercover, and I watched those assholes mix the stuff in a Thirteenth Street body shop."

"Want to call it in?" the man with the mustache suggested.

"What can it hurt?" Jeremy tried to reason with them. "Just tell one of your buddies to climb up and look in the drum. Anybody with a nose can tell that shit isn't concrete."

The cops sat in their seats trying to decide whether or not they wanted to trust the word of a flat-topped construction worker who felt no shame in dropping the *n* bomb.

"Your brother is up there," the cop with the mustache reminded his partner.

"Adam two-ten, Adam four . . . ," the driver spoke into his radio mike.

"Adam four," came the response.

Jeremy fell back into his seat, relieved. A quick look into the drum would confirm his story. Police could evacuate the area before disaster struck.

But it was too late.

The flash of light caught them first — brighter than sunshine in the car's mirror. It took a full two seconds before the shock of overpressure blew out the back window. And then came the sickening boom.

"Holy shit!" the driver yelled.

The squad car skidded right from the force of the blast. All three men felt their ears pop as if they were on a plane falling out of the sky.

"Holy shit!"

By the time the driver gained control and pulled to the side of the road, they all knew what had happened. The flood tide of terror they had seen on television and heard about in morning muster had finally washed into the nation's capital.

"Mothafucker!" The cop with the mustache gasped. He jumped out of his car to look back up toward the famous dome. Glass was falling from broken windows, but the superstructure looked intact.

Jeremy twisted in his seat, fighting the handcuffs and the smooth vinyl for a vantage on a tragedy he only thought he had averted.

"Adam two-ten, Adam four!" the driver called into his mike. His brother was up there in that mushroom cloud of gray-white smoke. "Adam two-ten, Adam four!"

But there was no response.

Traffic screeched to a halt all around them. People jumped out of their cars, gawking at a terrifying sight. Hundreds of late-working congressional staffers, local residents, bar drunks, and reception-bound lobbyists were already flowing down Independence Avenue like a raging stream of panicked animals.

"Holy shit," the cop said again.

Jeremy assumed he was referring to the explosion until he noticed the Chevy sedan. And the gun.

Caleb pulled up next to them and aimed a blue-steel pistol through the passenger window. He fired two shots as naturally as if asking directions. The cops fell dead.

Holy shit is right, Jeremy thought. Before he could decide what to do, Caleb had jumped out of his car, yanked open Jeremy's door, and pulled him into the idling Chevy.

"Thought you'd never get here," Jeremy said.

The one-eyed albino did not look interested in conversation.

■

"WELCOME TO MOUNT WEATHER, Madam Vice President," an Air Force colonel greeted Beechum, yelling over the prop wash of the HMX-2. Two Secret Service agents ushered her to a waiting limousine, black and armored. The younger of the agents carried her luggage: a prepacked overnight bag and her ancient leather briefcase.

"Thank you, Colonel," she hollered back. The helicopter's rotors had slowed considerably, but snow roiled in their downforce. "I'm hoping it's a whole lot warmer inside!"

It was. And more spectacular. Minutes after disappearing into the facility's ten-by-twenty-foot eastern portal, the vice president found herself inside an underground city that defied legitimate description. The facility's cavernous central tunnel descended into the mountain of smooth-cut rock, branching off like an ant farm into side tunnels filled with dozens of freestanding buildings — some three stories tall.

"Amazing," was all she could say as they drove along.

"Sure is, ma'am," the colonel said. "We're set up to support two hundred people for at least sixty days. We can sleep up to two thousand in shorter term. Full communications, medical, recreation, and data-assimilation facilities."

"Where are they?" she asked. "I mean all the people." She observed that despite signs of heavy activity, there was nary a soul to be seen.

"Locked down, ma'am. Protocol. Security plans go a lot deeper than what you're probably used to. During movement of principals — you or the president — we halt all activities and secure quarters."

"I've got to tell you, Colonel," she said, exiting the limo and following the uniformed man into a suite of offices. "I've been a lot of places, but I've never been to a place like this."

"It has its own charm, I suppose." He smiled. Marines in full combat gear stood at ready gun just inside the reception-area door. "We like to think of it as our silo away from home."

The man's attempt at humor surprised Beechum. With all the guards and machine guns and game faces, it came as a pleasant relief.

"This is Margaret, your secretary," the colonel said.

"Nice to meet you, ma'am," the woman responded. She wore civilian clothing — wool pants and a Fair Isle sweater with an American flag on the collar. Beechum guessed her to be about forty.

"Pleased to meet you, too, Margaret," Beechum answered.

"And this is your office." The colonel opened a side door. Inside was a desk, a couch, two end tables, and a credenza. Colors were limited to blue and gray. Lots of mahogany.

"There's a fridge in the credenza," he noted. "Three televisions with access to the networks and cable news service. Bathroom is through that door."

"What about HBO?" Beechum smiled. "You know, I hate to miss *The Sopranos*."

"HBO," the colonel agreed. "We've got our own TV and radio stations as well, just in case you feel inspired to come up with a series of your own."

"I'm surprised you haven't lined the walls with flat screens and piped-in scenes of Washington to make it feel more like the White House."

"Good idea," the colonel replied. "We do call this the White House, actually, but there's no mistaking one for the other. We wouldn't want to ruin our decorating scheme of Early Subterranean Bunker now, would we?"

Beechum chuckled.

"You'll have secure comms to the White House from this STU-III phone," the colonel said, lifting the receiver to demonstrate. "This second phone is a standard multiplex system like you have in your residence. It's a shielded seven-oh-three exchange, but it is not secure. This third phone is the JCSAN/COPAN system you're probably familiar with at the White House. This is your voice comms link to the NMCC at the Pentagon, the AJCC backup at Raven Rock, and the president wherever he may be worldwide."

"Thank you, Colonel," Beechum said. She looked around the room and suddenly felt terribly tired.

"You'll be getting a FEMA briefing on continuity of government protocols at half past the hour, and you'll meet with the cabinet shortly after that," he said.

"Cabinet?" she asked.

"Sorry, ma'am . . . I forgot. Yes, you'll get details during your FEMA briefing, but you should know that the COG protocols call for the existence of redundant wartime representation at each cabinet-level position."

"You mean backup secretaries of each department?"

"That's right, ma'am. They are appointed by the president, though not affirmed by the Senate for security reasons. We refer to them as Mr. and Madam Secretary. They have all the same authority as their aboveground counterparts during times of transition and acute augmentation."

Beechum didn't care to ask about acute augmentation, but one other thing bothered her.

"What about Congress and the Supreme Court?" she asked.

"Have you built redundancy into the legislative and judicial branches as well?"

"I'll leave that to your FEMA briefers." The colonel smiled. "It's a bit over my pay grade."

With that, Beechum's one-man transition committee disappeared, leaving the vice president to consider her options. Despite the novelty in this underground wonderland, Site Seven was a crypt that shut her off from the rest of the world and a mission only she could accomplish.

All right, Elizabeth, she told herself, trying to adjust to the flat fluorescent light. *You're buried beneath a quarter mile of solid rock while the president plans nuclear war against a threat he doesn't even understand. You think you're so smart. How are you going to get out of this?*

There was no time for an answer. Before she even sat down, the colonel stormed back in with news of yet another disaster. From what he said, the cozy little bomb shelter was about to get crowded.

■

WASHINGTON, DC GETS its raw drinking water from the Potomac River, filters it for harmful chemicals, bacteria, and trace elements, then treats it with additives such as chlorine, fluoride, and potassium permanganate before pumping it to consumers. It is a carefully monitored and scientifically controlled system that supplies the District's homes, offices, and federal buildings with almost 300 million gallons each day.

Colonel Ellis had become intimately aware of this process during his stint at the Pentagon. While working at DARPA, he had seen counterterrorism projections of aqueduct vulnerability. Though chemical and biological contamination seemed a distant possibility because of filtration and flow distribution checkpoints, experts feared one contaminate above all else: radiation. Anyone with the proper knowledge of plant operations could introduce dangerous isotopes post filtration, they decided. The impact of such closed-system contamination could be catastrophic.

Satch didn't care much about flocculation, clear-well dynamics, or pH controls as Ollie drove down MacArthur Boulevard toward the Dalecarlia Water Treatment Plant. All he cared about was meeting his contact — another Cell Six member — and getting the two remaining black boxes of "glow powder" inside without exposing himself.

"Whoa, whoa," his partner told him, pointing toward a security gate up ahead. A single rent-a-cop stood guard — female, fifty pounds overweight, and bored. "That's it."

Satch adjusted his tie and sat straight in his seat.

"Evening, officer," he said, rolling his window down and mustering his most officious smile.

She craned her neck to look inside the unmarked white van.

"Who you with, darlin'?" she asked.

"Corps," Satch responded. He held out an expertly forged ID card that read Army Corps of Engineers.

"Don't have any coffee in there do you, honey?" she asked. "Colder than a hooker's heart out here."

Satch shook his head.

"Shoulda thought of it on the way up," he apologized. "I'll get some inside and catch you on the way out."

"Cream and three sugars." She nodded, waving them in. "And tell that cute little partner of yours to smile once and a while. His face ain't gonna crack."

Satch could hear the woman laughing as he drove toward the water treatment plant.

"She's right, you know," Satch said. "A little humor once in a while wouldn't kill you."

■

CAROLINE WALLER FELT naked and alone lying on the concrete floor in the dark, empty cellar. Christopher had stopped crying now. Patrick was asleep on her stomach. Maddy sat off to the side somewhere, distant in many ways.

"Are you all right, sweetheart?" Caroline asked her daughter.

"Dad's going to come and save us," the little girl said.

"Honey . . ." — Caroline tried to sound optimistic, but there was no point in lying — "your daddy loves you very much. Remember that, OK? He's a very brave man, and he loves you with all his heart."

Maddy said nothing for a while, then, "I'm not a little girl anymore, Mom. I don't believe in Santa. I don't even believe in uni-corns or Batman or the Easter Bunny. But I know Dad is coming for us. He wouldn't let these bad men hurt us."

Caroline fought an overwhelming urge to cry. Innocence had fled them.

"You can tell Patrick and Chris that when they wake up," Maddy droned. "I know he's coming."

The overhead lights flashed on, but it was the sound of footsteps on open stairs that stilled them.

"You don't believe her, do you?" a man asked. Colonel Ellis descended into the cellar and walked toward the huddle of bodies.

"What kind of animal would do this to children?" Caroline asked. She aimed to make a poor hostage.

"Come now, Mrs. Waller," he said. "Do you ask your husband questions like this when he comes home from all those secret missions of his? You must wonder, though, don't you? In the back of your mind? You know he's a killer, too, but you don't want to think about it . . . to admit that good men do bad things."

Caroline thought about feigning ignorance, but this man seemed to know more about Jeremy than she did.

"You consider yourself a religious woman, Mrs. Waller?" His tone was soft, almost reverent. "Methodist from what I understand."

"What are you going to do with us?" Caroline asked.

Maddy stared at him through hate-filled eyes. The little girl wanted so badly to kill him but didn't know how.

"I want you to consider what the world would be like if you never had to worry again about getting on an airplane or a bus or a train. What if you never had to think about your babies growing up in a world where strangers meant them harm?"

The colonel walked close and squatted down like the Monta-gnard had taught him three decades earlier.

"What if names like al Qaeda and Al-Aksa Brigades and Jemaah Islamiya faded from public discussion? What if terrorism disap-peared from the airwaves, leaving MSNBC and FOX and CNN to concentrate on sex scandals and celebrity justice?"

The colonel reached down and gently brushed hair out of Christopher's face.

"What would you sacrifice to keep someone from coming after

your family, the people you hold most dear? I'm not asking a rhetorical question; I really want to know."

"Don't try to make me understand your sickness," Caroline said. She felt strength in having three children to protect.

"You would do anything, wouldn't you? You would kill or die to save them . . . gladly give up your life to save the one last thing worth believing."

Maddy climbed to her feet. They had taken her shoes, so she stood there in pink Powerpuff Girls socks.

"Well, that's what I want you to think about: a better world where gutter gods don't incite jihad. A world free of Muhammad and his false prophecies. No more suicide bombers and young minds stained with the promise of doe-eyed virgins."

"My dad's going to kill you," Maddy said. She had balled her fingers into fists. Both hands.

"Ah, don't hate me, darlin'," Ellis said. "It's an awful thing to bottle up inside a little girl's heart. Someday you'll understand."

He stood.

"I do this out of love, you know," he said. "Because only love will save us in the end. A Christian love. The love of a true and righteous God who would lay down the life of his only begotten son so that others might live. It's the love of a mother who would stand up and kill me to protect her children. It's a love so pure the devil himself would go to any lengths to stop it."

The colonel turned toward Maddy.

"It's a love that the lucky among us will die to save, sweetie," he said. "Me, you, that daddy of yours. It's a love for something better."

He turned and started up the stairs.

"He's still gonna kill you," Maddy said again. There were no tears in her eyes. Her voice did not waver.

The colonel paused a step but didn't respond. In a moment he was gone, leaving the Wallers with nothing but his words to haunt them.

■

"WE GOT THEM," Sirad said, marching into the seventeenth-floor operations center like a conquering warlord.

Mitchell turned toward her but then returned to something Trask had pulled up on the computer.

"I've got quite enough suspense already," he said. "What did you find?"

Sirad walked up beside him and noticed what looked like a script on his monitor.

"I'm not sure you're going to want to hear this in open forum," she said. Sirad noticed reference in the script to something called Jafar al Tayar. A fluent Arabic speaker, she immediately translated the phrase.

Jafar the pilot? she wondered. *Surely this has nothing to do with another airliner hijacking. Does it?*

"Everyone in this room is cleared and has a need to know," Mitchell said. He turned away from her to Trask, who remained at a workstation on the other side of the room. "Where's Waller?"

"Just turned left on Florida Avenue," the chief of staff responded. "Looks like they're headed to the safe house."

"Do you want this or not?" Sirad asked. She had come in with explosive news, news that would warrant Mitchell's full attention.

"I'm listening," he said. Mitchell, a man known for his ability to juggle complex issues, continued reading the script.

"We found a way through their firewalls," she said.

"The White House?" Hamid asked.

"The White House Communications Agency," Sirad clarified. "They control all remote and in-house links between the president and his staff."

"And the football," Mitchell pointed out.

"Yes," Sirad agreed. "They control continuity of nuclear launch codes as well as all command and control conduits linking the Pentagon, Langley's CTC, the FBI's SIOC, the White House Situation . . ."

"Come to the point," Mitchell demanded.

"The point is that we now have complete access to White House communications," Sirad bragged. "We went in to try and identify the mole, but we ended up with access to everything the president and his advisors say, write, and type."

Mitchell nodded approvingly. Sirad noticed that he did not seem surprised.

"And what have you learned so far?" he asked.

"The actual operator behind the intrusion is someone known as CAPSTONE3," Sirad told him. "But that's not really pertinent at this point. It's what he is trying to do and the authority behind him that we have to worry about."

"What do you mean?" Mitchell asked. "I would assume the authority for something like this would have to come from the president himself."

"That's the obvious assumption," Sirad agreed. "Until you look at what they are really trying to do."

"They're trying to tap our secure lines of communication. We know that," Trask pointed out.

"That's what they wanted us to believe," Sirad countered. "But that's just a mousetrap, a ploy to lure us in so we wouldn't discover their real intentions."

"And what is that?" Mitchell asked. She had his full attention. "What is it you think this CAPSTONE3 hopes to accomplish?"

Sirad looked around the room. Mitchell's story about the duel between Alexander Hamilton and Aaron Burr now made perfect sense. Despite its complexity, this whole thing really did boil down to an issue of honor.

"I'm sorry, but I can't tell you that," she said. "Not yet."

Everyone turned toward her. No one ever refused Jordan Mitchell's orders.

"Can't tell me?" Mitchell asked. "Surely you . . ."

"You told me long before this started that Borders Atlantic is full of secrets," she interrupted. "And that they are all yours."

Sirad knew she was taking a big gamble, but as Mitchell had said, sometimes the price for glory was sacrifice.

"Well, if you want to save this country from all-out holy war," she said, "you're going to have to trust me with one of my own."

■

"WHAT IN GOD'S name was that?" the president asked.

He was standing at his podium, strategizing with his chief of staff, his national security advisor, and the secretary of defense, when the explosion rattled the Oval Office windows.

Before anyone could answer, two Secret Service agents hurried in without knocking.

"We need to move you to the PEOC," the shift commander called out. He sounded urgent though calm.

"What happened?" Venable asked.

The agents physically took him by the arms and pulled him away from the podium.

"Wait a minute," he demanded, wrenching his arms free. "I'm not going back down into that godforsaken hole until we find out what just happened."

"Please, David," Chase argued. "They're here to protect you. I'll get your answers and meet you downstairs in ten minutes."

"This is not a matter for discussion, Mr. President," the shift commander said, resetting his grip on the chief executive's elbow. There was no hint of courtesy in his voice. "We need you to come with us. Now."

■

"WHY'D YOU COME for me?" Jeremy asked. Every blue light and siren in Washington looked to be converging on Capitol Hill by the time Caleb turned right on Eleventh Street Northwest.

"What did you think, that I was going to let them take you down to an interview room so you could ruin everything?"

Caleb drove north on Eleventh Street with his right hand and held the gun with his left hand resting in his lap.

"Ruin what? Everything I know about your operation just went up in smoke."

Caleb had to exaggerate the turn of his head to look at Jeremy. The loss of his right eye made side-by-side conversations difficult.

"You knew enough to get here in the first place," Caleb said in an accusing tone. "The tattoo, the doctrine, the fact that the colonel had pulled all the Phineas priests together."

"That you were working with the Indonesians?" Jeremy added.

Caleb twitched with surprise but offered nothing in response.

"Jungle clearing . . . Jayawijaya Highlands," Jeremy said. "Some Pygmy fuck with a gourd on his dick and a string of teeth around his neck riding herd on a bunch of wannabe terrorists."

The HRT sniper liked the fact that Caleb was the one rocking back on his heels now.

"I remember seeing you for the first time," Jeremy recalled. "My rifle crosshairs resting right between those little bunny eyes of yours. I remember the way that white trash with you called out your name as they ran around with bags over their heads and the D boys chopped them up with their Mark Fours."

BANG!

The pistol in Caleb's hand jumped as a 9mm bullet tore through the top of Jeremy's thigh. The copper-jacketed round barely grazed Jeremy's femur, exiting in a mist of blood and tissue before lodging in the door's plastic armrest.

Jeremy's mind froze for a moment with the searing, white-hot pain, but he choked it down, shook his head, and continued as if nothing had happened.

"Did those poor bastards you were with know you were going to live and they were going to die?" he asked, trying not to let his voice break. "You can probably still hear their voices, can't you? How's it feel to know you're still alive and people that trusted you are dead?"

"You'll know soon enough," Caleb replied. He focused on a passing driver who appeared to have heard the shot. The man drove alongside for a closer look.

It was Jeremy's turn to twist.

"You'd better kill me now," Jeremy said. HRT had taught him discipline, but every man had his margins. "Because if you don't, I'm sure as hell going to kill you."

"Like out there in that jungle?" Caleb said. "Who's got the bullet hole in him now?"

He ran a red light and turned left on Florida Avenue.

"No, I'm going to do this right," Caleb said. "I'm going to kill them in front of you so you can feel what it's like to lose the one last thing in life worth believing in."

Jeremy had passed the desire for comeback. He sat in the passenger seat, watching blood seep slowly down his pant leg.

There's a time for everything, he counseled himself. If he wanted to save his family and stop Ellis, he'd have to choke down ego and do things the best way he knew how: alone.

XX

COLONEL ELLIS HAD never shied from violence. From the neighborhood fights his uncle had matched him in for wagers to the military battles to the black operation sanctions he'd led all over the world — violence had followed him like a shadow.

Focus on your job, he scolded himself. *Only the one true and righteous God understands the course of man's vainglorious plottings. Only the one true and righteous God can guide his chosen people to the promised land.*

Ellis lay shivering in the snow, covered with white camouflage and a tangle of gathered brush. The chevron-shaped muzzle of a Barrett .50 caliber rifle poked out from his carefully constructed hide.

Soon it will all be over, he told himself. *Soon, the true impact of all our sacrifice will be revealed.*

He stared through his scope, down the length of Runway Two-three East. Somewhere down there beyond the carefully aligned C-141s, C-17s, jump-ready attack fighters, and heavily reinforced security stations, the Doomsday Plane would be getting its final run-through.

"Blessed be the peacemakers, for they shall be called the Sons of God," he whispered to no one but his own conscience.

Soon this would all be over. Soon it would all begin again.

■

"IT WAS A massive explosion with a radiological signature," Andrea Chase said. "Death toll is one hundred and thirty-seven at this point, but emergency response crews are still sorting things out. They expect it to go higher."

The chief of staff had followed the president into a corner of the PEOC's central chamber. Staff had filled most of the seats already, and additional personnel — everything from communications specialists to crisis-management logisticians and security experts — were crowding in.

"Dirty bomb?" he asked.

"That's the best bet at this point." She nodded. "DOE had a NEST team nearby, working the other cache in Adams Morgan. They broke off to assess exposure."

"And?"

"And, odd as it sounds, this exposure does not seem to pose a significant threat."

The president turned to television coverage on several large-screen TVs. How troubling, he decided, that the best intelligence he had received since the start of this whole nightmare had come from journalists and their cameras.

"No threat to whom?" the president exclaimed. "Iowa? Are you seeing what I am?"

The damage looked massive. Most of the shops along Independence Avenue had been leveled or severely damaged. The Supreme Court looked to have sustained structural damage. Car, bus, and truck carcasses littered the streets. Body parts could be seen hanging from trees eight blocks away.

"I was referring to the radiation," Chase explained. "It was obviously a horrific explosion, but the charge itself actually dispersed the radioactive material to less than lethal levels. DOE expects winds and snowmelt to effect decontamination naturally."

"Is that all of it, then?" the president asked. "Did they use everything they had?"

"Too early to tell," Chase explained. "The air force has a WC-135W called Constant Phoenix, which they are bringing in to measure the fallout."

Venable thought for a moment, then nodded as if agreeing with himself.

"I'm not waiting for the next attack, Andrea," Venable said. "It's time to hit back at these animals before they . . ."

"Hit back at whom?" she argued. Chase had seen this coming from the start. "You know the stakes here, David. We don't even know who's responsible yet."

"Local news stations just received claims of responsibility," a voice called out. It was Havelock, crossing from the door. He had the chairman of the joint chiefs in tow. "Same tape, same language. There's no doubt about it, Mr. President. These are the same murderous sonsofbitches we've been dealing with all along."

"We can't go to war on claims of responsibility," Chase objected. "We're talking about a potential World War Three, for God's sake!"

"There's more," Oshinski said. "NSA has picked up specific overhears of conversations between the Saudi foreign minister and Prince Abdullah. They talk in some detail about the attacks."

"What detail?" Chase asked incredulously. "I thought they were using the Quantis phones, that we couldn't intercept them."

"These were open-line conversations," Havelock said.

"Open line? Why?" Chase continued. "Why would they talk openly about something we've already threatened them over? What did they say? Did they admit responsibility?"

"No, not exactly," Havelock replied. "It was less specific than that. No smoking gun, but they had details that haven't made press reports yet."

"They have a world-class intelligence service," Chase argued. "They could have gotten this information from a dozen different sources."

Venable began to pace. The room hummed with activity around him.

"All right," he said finally. "I don't know the exact process, but I'm making the call. I want two strategic targets inside Saudi Arabia. Military installations with low probability of civilian casualties — don't want anyone playing up Middle Eastern sympathies."

"Al Qaeda training facilities," Havelock suggested.

"What al Qaeda training facilities?" Chase asked. "Do we know of any?"

"No, but that's the beauty of classified information," the national security advisor responded. "We can claim whatever we want. Who's going to prove different?"

Chase laughed indignantly, but Venable seemed to buy the suggestion. He stiffened with a confidence none of his advisors had seen since the crisis began.

"Four warheads," he ordered. "The smallest tactical weapons we have. We're going to end this right here and now."

"I'm afraid it's not exactly that easy, sir," Oshinski told him.

"What do you mean? As president I have full authority to . . ."

"We have our NATO allies to consider," Chase pointed out. "We have to make arrangements to notify them."

"And we have to move our delivery platforms into position," the general said. "We have the USS *Intrepid* moving south from the Suez Canal, but they can't launch until we assume a safe standoff in the Indian Ocean."

"There are homeland security considerations as well," Chase argued. "We've got to anticipate the possibility of an escalated response. That could lead to martial law — a mobilization of the DEST bird, Gatekeeper. We have to coordinate eighteen thousand local, state, and federal law enforcement agencies. We've got to give FEMA time to engage civil defense operations and prepare possible evacuation contingencies for NACAP as well as New York and Los Angeles. I imagine we're going to have to bring the Fed into this, too; we can pretty much guarantee a run on banks."

"We can't ignore our embassies and military stations overseas," the chairman added. "We have to change our war footing to DEFCON Four. That takes some time."

"And the Secret Service is not going to allow you to stay here, David," Havelock said. "Not now, especially."

"What do you mean?" Venable asked. "Beechum is already out at that Mount whatever it is. Where do you . . . they . . . propose I go?"

"Kneecap," Oshinski responded. "At least that's what we used to call it. It's an airborne command and control center designed to keep you above the fray during the initial stages of nuclear war."

"Nuclear war?" Venable asked. "What nuclear war? I'm talking about limited strikes against known al Qaeda targets."

"We have to anticipate a response," Havelock argued. "CIA analysts have modeled scenarios like this. They predict that the Arab world will view any unilateral strike as an attack on Mecca and react behind a unified front. We have to expect potential reciprocation from North Korea and Iran. The Palestinians will jump on this with both feet. Al Qaeda will whip up a holy war frenzy throughout the Pacific rim, Europe, and Africa."

Venable shook his head. He still hadn't been in office for a month, and he was ordering the first nuclear attacks since 1945.

"I can't just stand here idly by while they destroy us. Can I?"

No one responded. The overwhelming gravity of the president's question had rendered them numb.

■

SATCH, WHO HAD been a municipal engineer before he became a Phineas priest, had no trouble finding his way around Washington's Dalecarlia Water Treatment Plant. Though bigger than the one in his home city of Birmingham, this plant worked exactly the same way. Raw water from a natural source — in this case the Potomac River — flowed through massive induction aqueducts into sedimentation basins, which allowed gravity to settle particulate matter into sludge beds.

From there, water passed into multimillion-gallon clear wells, then through additional filters to a chemical treatment facility where everything from fluoride and hydrated lime to flavor-enhancing charcoal and sulfur dioxide was added. Only then was the final product stored in underground basins for distribution.

This, Satch knew, was where the system stood most vulnerable. Each year, the Army Corps of Engineers dumped almost four thousand tons of lime, eight thousand tons of alum, two thousand tons of chlorine, and forty tons of copper sulfate into the water supply. Dumping in two black boxes full of cesium powder and rice-sized cobalt surgical implants would take just moments.

Posing as water-quality inspectors, the Cell Six operator and his all-too-stoic partner bluffed their way into the automated chemical treatment facility. Everyone knew that inspectors worked alone to protect the integrity of their methods, and these two men had both the credentials and the jargon. In the time it took them to dump their deadly additives, the regular night crew made a fresh pot of coffee.

Good thing, Satch thought, as he poured himself a cup and an extra for the woman at the gate. There was cause for a congratulatory drink after months of preparation and a flawless execution.

"Cream and two sugars," was all he said. Caffeine was the one vice he allowed himself. He never had cared much for anything stronger.

■

ANY HOPES JEREMY had of quickly escaping died with the bullet wound in his thigh. He had managed to staunch the bleeding, but only while sitting down. He knew that once he got up and started moving, the wound would open again, and that was if he managed to get out of the car — an unlikely scenario. Caleb kept the semiautomatic pistol in his lap, out of sight to passersby but very deadly to his FBI passenger.

"How did you know about us?" Caleb asked after he had driven about ten minutes.

"Money," Jeremy responded. He stared out the window, trying to memorize landmarks. His familiarity with Washington was limited to the maps and addresses the FBI undercover briefers had given him. "You'd be amazed what turns up when you drag a five-dollar bill through a trailer park."

Caleb said nothing. The man's emotions seemed every bit as colorless as his skin.

"Do you think God really won't hold you accountable?" Jeremy asked. He felt no thirst for conversation, but it took his mind off the awful pain in his thigh.

"God?" Caleb said. Jeremy's suggestion struck him as absolutely ridiculous. "We are his warriors. His arm against the Philistines. He'll reward us with eternal salvation for what we do."

Jeremy tightened the pressure on his wound.

"You kill innocent women and children to get to heaven?"

"So that millions of others might live," Caleb argued. His tone changed noticeably. "War always has its casualties. Imagine how many will die if we allow the Muslim dogs to go on with their terror, massacring people in the street. How long will we last as a Christian people, allowing them to breed among us, to work their way into our communities? You think they care about the American way of life? They despise us, and they won't stop until we're all dead."

"So you align yourselves with them?" Jeremy asked. "You do their bidding here in your own country, where they can't work on their own?"

Caleb turned his eyes from the road. He looked at Jeremy more out of curiosity than animus.

"Is that what you think?" he asked. A smile broke out across his face. "Maybe we overestimated you. I guess we'll find out soon enough."

Caleb put on the brakes and turned left onto Everest, a street lined with freestanding single-story homes. It was a well-kept neighborhood defined by 1970s architecture, chain-link fences, and mirror-globed birdbaths.

"What's this?" Jeremy asked.

"You wanted to see your family, didn't you?"

Caleb punched a garage door opener and turned into a shallow driveway. The door opened and then closed behind them.

"My family?" Jeremy asked. The possibility seemed too good to be true. "You're bringing me to my family?"

"Of course," Caleb said, shutting down the motor. The door to the house opened, and another man emerged with a short-barreled shotgun. "It's the only way we can get you to tell us what we need to know."

THE SECRETARY OF DEFENSE had managed to escape Washington in a helicopter. He was a top military leader, after all, a man responsible for maintaining the national security in a time of crisis. He came and went by chopper all the time.

"What a cluster, huh?" the SECDEF spoke into his intercom. His administrative assistant sat beside him in the MD-530 "Little Bird," shaking his head. He was a former military man, but he had never seen anything like this.

Three hundred feet below them, a long string of vehicles wound their way west through the rolling hills of western Virginia. Black Town Cars and limousines, personal vehicles, and Humvees — anything big enough and fast enough to carry representatives of the legislative, judicial, and executive branches out of Washington. The nation's political elite was racing along Route 50 toward a future they still didn't understand.

"Looks like the OJ chase," the man responded. Black Secret Service Suburbans and police cars led the entourage, with CNN and FOX satellite trucks bringing up the rear. MSNBC wasn't far behind.

"I guess our unnamed secure location isn't going to be unnamed for long."

The SECDEF shook his head. Despite the hermetic seal around Mount Weather, there was no way to camouflage the rapid mobilization of Washington's designated survivors.

"We're two minutes out, sir," the MD-530 pilot advised. "We'll be going in hot."

The SECDEF looked ahead through the snow-covered hills as the highly maneuverable helicopter bobbed up and down, flying nap of the earth.

"What did you tell your family?" he asked.

"I told them I loved them," the aide responded.

"Yeah, me too," said the SECDEF. The sick feeling in his stomach told him that wouldn't be enough.

■

"DADDY! DADDY!"

Caroline looked up from the cellar floor and thought she was seeing some kind of hallucination. It couldn't be Jeremy.

But it was.

"Everything's gonna be all right, sweetie," the HRT sniper said in a calming voice as Caleb and the guy with the shotgun followed him down the cellar stairs. "Daddy's here."

Maddy stood up and ran to him, grabbing Jeremy around the legs as she had after so many previous missions. This time her hug sent shudders of pain through his body, though, and he almost buckled.

"Easy, baby," he said as the shotgunner pushed him forward. "You just wait over by Mommy for now, all right?"

Maddy backed away, stained with blood from where the wound had opened up and begun to trickle onto the concrete floor.

"You're bleeding, Daddy!" Maddy called out. "What did you do to my daddy, you ugly pirate?"

The little girl launched herself at Caleb, pounding at him with her fists, but the one-eyed albino simply swatted her away with the back of his hand. He hit the girl hard, knocking her to the cold cement floor.

"Maddy!" Caroline called out. "Come over here!"

Jeremy motioned with his head, and Maddy backed away, red in the face, with her little fists still balled in defiance.

"It's gonna be OK." Jeremy smiled. "But, honey, you've got to do what your mom says."

■

COLONEL ELLIS HAD waited thirty years for this day. All the planning, the sacrifice, the praying and soul-searching had led him to what his military comrades referred to as zero hour. This was the realization of a complex, audacious dream — a battlefield epiphany that even now he had no interest in questioning.

"Lead, follow, or get out of the way," his first drill instructor had beaten into his "brain housing group."

Well, he had never been one to follow.

Runway Two-three East, Ellis reminded himself, looking for signs of activity. Virtually every contingency had been checked and double-checked. As in any operation, there was potential for disaster, but precious little here. That was the beauty of the leaderless resistance model. Even if the enemy caught an individual member, they simply didn't know enough to compromise the larger organization.

The colonel checked and rechecked his equipment.

Take care of your gear and your gear will take care of you, the instructors had said all those years ago. It was the simple advice that stuck in the mind of an eighteen-year-old orphan who wanted nothing in the world more than a cause worth dying for.

Well, this was it. The battlefield revelation turned obsession. The final task.

"'Remember therefore how thou hast received and heard,'" he whispered in recitation from Revelation 3. "'He that overcometh, the same shall be clothed in white raiment; and I will not blot out his name out of the book of life, but I will confess his name before my Father, and before his angels.'"

White. Ellis nodded. *A new white: the color of good.*

■

"WHAT KIND OF piece of shit hits a little girl?" Jeremy asked. He had turned to Caleb and spoke in a voice his children wouldn't hear.

"The kind that wants information," Caleb said. He shoved Jeremy forward, almost dropping the wounded FBI agent.

"I told you he'd come back for us, didn't I, Mom?" Maddy asked. She stood above her mother but only because she had been told to. The little girl trained both eyes on her daddy and waited for an answer.

"Daddy?" Christopher asked. The second-oldest Waller child lifted his head off his mother's chest and sat up. "Daddy?"

"Hi, buddy," Jeremy said. Despite the pain in his leg and the anger in his heart, all he could do was smile. "You just stay right there with your mommy for now, OK?"

Christopher wanted to jump up and run to the man he considered superhuman, but then he saw Caleb. The terror he felt for the white pirate absolutely paralyzed him.

"This is all very touching," Caleb said once he had prodded Jeremy to within a few feet of his family. "But we don't have a lot of time."

He motioned with one hand, and the man with the shotgun knelt down to grab Christopher.

"No!" The little boy began to sob. He clung to his mother, tearing off the shirt that had been laid atop her. Caroline struggled to keep him, but the way they had tied her made any kind of intervention impossible.

"That's enough!" Jeremy hollered. He poked out with his free hand, trying to stop the shotgunner, but Caleb pushed him to the floor.

"You leave my daddy alone!" Maddy called out. She threw her body over Jeremy, trying to protect her father from these wicked men.

"How much do they know about the Megiddo project?" Caleb asked.

Jeremy tried not to show how much the pain bothered him.

"I've never heard of any Megiddo project," Jeremy answered. He pushed Maddy away, then used the wall to fight his way back up to his feet.

"Wrong answer number one," Caleb said.

The shotgunner slammed his hardwood stock down on Christopher's right foot.

"*EEEEaaaaahhhh!*" the little boy screamed. He fell to one side, unable to stand on the now-shattered limb.

Think! Jeremy howled to himself as the man raised his shotgun for another blow. *Emotion will not get you out of here alive. Use what you have around you to defeat your enemy.*

"There's nothing I can do to stop you from hurting my family," Jeremy told Caleb. He spoke in the calmest voice he could summon. "My orders were to stop you from carrying out further attacks. I never heard of any Megiddo project."

"Is that why you helped prepare the concrete truck?" Caleb sneered. He spoke in a normal voice until Christopher's agonized breath hold ran out. When the little boy began to wail again, Caleb shouted over him. "Is that how you stop further attacks?"

"I didn't know what you were planning," Jeremy reasoned. He tried not to look down at his tortured family. "You heard what Ellis told me! The only way I could figure out your plans was to go along until the last minute."

"You've never heard of Jafar al Tayar?"

Jeremy tried to look surprised.

"Sounds Arabic," he said. "Did you get that from the Indonesians or something?"

Caleb tried to make up his mind. Could a man of Jeremy's upbringing stand there and lie while his family suffered so? Only one way to find out.

The albino nodded, and the shotgunner brought the butt of his weapon down on Caroline's shin, snapping the tibia and splintering wood all over the concrete floor.

Caroline uttered a gasp but then choked down the vicious pain. *You've given birth three times,* she told herself. *Don't give this sadist the satisfaction.*

"Look what you've done!" Caleb yelled at the shotgunner, who held the broken gun by its foregrip. The man managed to finger the trigger, despite the damage, and pointed it menacingly at Caroline.

"Eeeeaaaahhh!" Christopher cried out again, unable to take the pain of his own wound. This was horror he had no way of understanding.

"Force suplex," Jeremy said.

The words popped out of his mouth involuntarily, like a burp or hiccup. They sounded ridiculous in the context of all this suffering. Force suplex was a child's game, something he and Maddy had shared in moments of laughter and love.

"Force suplex?" the little girl asked. Tears had spilled out of her eyes despite all her courage, but she wiped them away with the back of her hand. Maddy may have been a little girl, but she was her daddy's girl and that meant a genetic predisposition for action.

"Hell ya!" the third-grade terror cried out.

Caleb was too surprised by the outburst to react as Maddy left her feet two body lengths from the shotgunner and flew through the air like a WWE professional. The impact of her sixty-pound physique barely moved the shotgunner, but that wasn't the point.

Jeremy seized on the distraction. Standing to Caleb's right, he got a full step before the one-eyed thug knew what was coming. Jeremy's vengeful right fist caught the albino squarely on the chin and crumpled him to the floor.

BOOM!

The shotgunner fired a warning shot against the wall, spewing shrapnel into Caroline and Christopher. More screaming, more blood, more confusion. He worked the pump action, frantically trying to deal with the lack of a stock, the now deliriously violent Maddy, and, most important, the stunningly swift actions of an HRT operator trained in "immediate action" drills.

BOOM!

A second gunshot bounced off the wall, but this time it was from Jeremy. He lay on the floor with Caleb's pistol in one outstretched hand. Smoke drifted up from the barrel. Blood and shattered bone dripped down the fifth course of concrete block where the shotgunner's head had fractured against it.

"You're too late," someone said. The words sounded distant through the screaming and the echo of gunfire and the adrenaline and the pain. It was Caleb.

Jeremy turned the pistol on him.

"Not hardly," the HRT operator said. He knew exactly what he had to do. Despite the fact that the white pirate had been the first to gain his knees, there was no debating who had control.

■

NO ONE DENIED Jordan Mitchell access to anything.

"All right, you've got my attention," he said, fixing Sirad in a stare that left no room for equivocation. They stood in the women's bathroom, a one-stall closet lined with stainless steel and jade Ecuadorean tile. "Now what is this secret you think you can keep from me?"

"I told you, Mr. Mitchell — this is not something I can share at this point. You're going to have to trust me."

Mitchell caught his reflection in the vanity mirror. He looked composed considering the situation, but stress had begun to show around his eyes.

"Let's look back on our professional relationship these past two years, shall we?" he asked, watching her in reflection. "You came to Borders Atlantic as a promising junior executive, but that was just a cover. Your real role was to work as a CIA NOC — a government-trained con artist hell-bent on infiltrating not just foreign governments but the very corporation that hired you."

Mitchell paused to give her a chance to respond, but she crossed her arms to listen.

"I brought in the top experts in the field of deception," he said. "Polygraphers, voice stress analysts, profilers — and you made them all look like fools."

Sirad actually started to laugh.

"So I'm a good liar," she said. "That's one of the reasons you value me, isn't it? The only problem is that I may be too good. That's why you have kept me away from important assignments this past year. You wanted to find a way to test me, to see if you could build a framework of allegiance . . . something that would give you a measure of control."

This time, Mitchell was the one who listened.

"And you were right," she continued. "I understand the game better than I did that night in the War Room when you strapped me to a table and poured seltzer down my throat. I know, now, what you really want from me, and I am willing to give it."

Sirad, a master seductress who had almost forgotten what it felt like to make the kill, moved close to the one human being alive who could prove himself better. She leaned in to whisper in his ear.

"I know what you're up to," she said. "I know about Jafar al Tayar, and I know the stakes. You taught me the art of the duel and the difference between honor and victory."

"And?" Mitchell asked. He felt a chill run through his body. This woman was about to show herself worthy of everything he had once imagined.

Sirad touched his cheek with hers. She lingered there long enough for Mitchell to drink in her scent, to feel the heat of her breast, to taste the fruits of what he had planted and nurtured and grown.

"And it's time to face off at ten paces. I've got that big English horse pistol in my hand," she barely spoke. "Can't you hear the hammer cocking?"

■

JEREMY WOULD HAVE a lifetime to debate the justification of what he had to do next. Unable to walk and with a clock running on Colonel Ellis's Megiddo project, he decided to work his interrogation of Caleb in full view of his family. There was no way around it, he decided. They'd suffered unspeakable trauma already. What were a few more screams?

BOOM!

The first bullet took out Caleb's right knee. Jeremy held the muzzle against the patella, knowing that the contact shot would muffle the blast and spare his children's already tormented ears.

"Who is Jafar al Tayar?" Jeremy asked.

Caleb laughed out loud. The pain changed his expression but not in ways Jeremy expected. The albino enjoyed it.

BOOM!

The second round took out his other knee.

Jeremy asked again and got the same reaction. Blood spurted out of the ragged holes, arterial spurts that both men knew would kill within minutes.

BOOM!

The third bullet shattered Caleb's left elbow. He lay on the floor now, immobilized with horrible wounds.

"Who is Jafar al Tayar?" Jeremy demanded. He had never believed himself capable of torture, but then life had changed many perceptions in the past year.

"You can't stop them," Caleb said. The words slithered out of his mouth, and life spilled with them as blood pooled around the terribly injured man. His mind began to cloud. "It's too deep. Too . . ."

Jeremy knew there was no point in arguing. Pain would not work against this man, but there had to be something. There were just moments before the murderous freak bled to death, taking the secrets of the Megiddo project with him.

"Phineas priest," the FBI agent suddenly whispered. How could he have overlooked something so obvious?

Jeremy raced around the cluttered basement until he found what he needed: a razor-edged box cutter.

"Who is Jafar al Tayar?" Jeremy demanded. He reached down with his left hand and pulled Caleb's good eyelid away from the pink and white flesh beneath it.

"No!" the albino managed to gasp. He understood what his last moments held and that there was no way into heaven without the symbol of his service to God on earth.

"I need a name," Jeremy said.

He pulled the skin fold tight and pressed his blade against it.

"The president," Caleb said in a voice too soft to hear clearly.

Jeremy leaned close and demanded it again.

"It's the president who will save you." Caleb shuddered.

Jeremy twisted the blade and took the eyelid anyway.

Fuck him, he thought. *This man had no business anywhere but hell.*

XXI

Saturday, 19 February
07:07 GMT
HMX-1, airborne over Washington DC

"SO WHY DO they call that the football?" the president asked. He sat in the back of a CH-53E, one of fourteen HMX-1 "white side" airframes regularly tasked with executive airlifts. Beside him sat a navy captain with a black leather case, which unlike assertions of popular folklore was not chained to her wrist.

"President Kennedy came up with the idea during the Cuban missile crisis, but Eisenhower was the first to have direct access, sir," the captain said. She was a pretty blonde in dress whites, duty rigid yet personable. "The story goes that JFK was playing a touch football game in Hyannis when Bobby ran into one of their military aides. The attorney general dropped the ball, and the president joked that his brother juggled it like it was radioactive. After the game, Bobby joked that this was a nuclear football the president could never drop. The name stuck."

"Interesting," Venable said. He had been shown the contents of the suitcase but only briefly, during transition instruction by the White House Military Office. Inside the mysterious box lay a "black book" containing launch options as outlined in the Single Integrated

Operational Plan (SIOP-04), emergency action message "go codes," an emergency procedures White House booklet that listed suitable "off-sites," and a secure telephone. The White House Communications Agency had just added a Quantis cell.

"FEMA wants you to remain airborne for the first twelve hours after the strike," Chase said, leaning toward the commander in chief. General Oshinski sat opposite them, alongside Havelock. "We'll circle Midwestern states and land at Peterson Air Force Base in Colorado if conditions permit."

The president nodded his head.

"What about targeting options?"

"We have identified four remote villages in the southern quarter," the general told him. "Low population density, poor communications, Sunni hotbed. We can sell it as al Qaeda."

"What about the *Intrepid*?"

"Just cleared the straits of Yemen," Havelock answered. "The War Room says they'll have launch standoff in about two hours."

"Good." Venable nodded. "That will give everyone time to stand up to war footing at Raven Rock and Site Seven. I assume the vice president has come up to speed on COG protocols?"

He smiled gruffly, pleased with his new grasp of acronyms and esoteric terms of art.

"That's our understanding," Havelock responded. He looked out a side window at two other identical Marine Corps choppers flying in loose formation. They were decoys, he knew, designed to throw off attempts to shoot down their slow-moving and very visible "high value" target. One in three struck him as poor odds.

"David," Chase spoke up. "I think we need to talk about your decision here." The helicopter's interior was noisy but secure from eavesdropping. "We still don't have irrefutable evidence that the Saudis are behind this. There are several options available to us that fall short of nuclear weapons."

It was a losing argument, she knew, but one she felt compelled to make.

"This country is at war," Venable countered. "And my sworn duty as commander in chief is to protect it from all enemies foreign and domestic." He stared directly at the black suitcase, imagining what it would feel like to order it opened. "The only way we are going to stop further bloodshed is by sending a clear message."

"But a message to whom?" she asked. "To an Arab world that already thinks we're a threat to their very existence? This will only spur more resentment among moderate states. Saudi Arabia has been an ally, someone we . . ."

"I think you're going to want to hear this before digging your heels in," Havelock interrupted. The national security advisor closed his bifold cell phone. "DOE has detected high levels of radiation inside the White House, Capitol, and several other downtown buildings. DHS thinks it is a contamination of the public water supply."

"My God," Venable muttered. "The Louisville isotopes."

"Closed-system contamination," Havelock agreed. "Our worst fear."

Everyone in the chopper understood the implications. Every drop of water, from the Oval Office lavatory to FBI drinking fountains to showers in the Senate locker room had been poisoned. Terrorists had turned the nation's capital into a ghost town.

"How soon can we get airborne?" the president asked. His face glowed furious red.

"They're standing by with turbines spinning," Havelock said. "Twelve minutes."

"I want Great Britain, Russia, China, and NATO on the line as soon as we go wheels up," Venable demanded. "We launch as soon as the *Intrepid* gets into position."

■

"FREEZE, ASSHOLE!"

Jeremy had heard the upstairs door burst open and heavy footsteps storming through the house. He at first thought it had to be more of Ellis's Cell Six members, but there were too many of them.

"Police!" another voice shouted as flashlight beams shined down the stairs. A team of black-suited SWAT officers flowed down after them.

Jeremy dropped his gun and pushed his hands over his head, anticipating their tactics. They would key on weapons, assuming that anyone with a gun deserved killing.

"FBI!" Jeremy yelled. "I'm FBI!"

This seemed to cause a stutter step among the first two men in line, but not for long. The five-member team moved lightning quick to secure Caroline and the kids while knocking Jeremy to the floor and wrenching his hands behind his back.

"Holy shit," Jeremy heard one of the men say. It had to be a grisly sight. Caleb had bled out in a gallon-wide pool. The shotgunner's brains were splattered against the wall. Caroline lay almost naked, bound in an unnatural contortion. Patrick and Christopher huddled beside her, sobbing and moaning in torment.

"I know what you're thinking, but you're wrong," Jeremy tried to argue. "I'm an undercover FBI agent, and this is my family."

"Shut the fuck up," one of the SWAT members yelled. "We know you're the one who drove that concrete truck."

Another operator searched Jeremy for weapons then pulled his wallet out of his pants pocket. "This says his name is Walker," he called out, reading Jeremy's undercover license.

"That's my undercover ID!" Jeremy tried to explain. One of the men pressed his knee into the back of Jeremy's neck and wrenched his wrists up between his shoulder blades. It hurt so badly, he briefly forgot about his leg.

"Save your breath, asshole," the man who had cuffed him said. "My wife was on the Hill when your fucking bomb went off."

Patrick began to howl again, and one of the other officers tried to comfort him.

"It's OK, darlin'," he said. "We're gonna get you out of here."

"Bravo Two to CP, we need EMS with ALS," another man radioed. He reached down and re-covered Caroline with the ragged shirt.

"Don't you hurt my daddy!" Maddy yelled. She seemed to have rebounded quickly from the shock of another violent entry.

"Easy, darlin'," the team leader tried to calm her. "We're not hurtin' nobody."

"I need to reach the vice president," Jeremy pleaded. "We don't have time to . . ."

Before he could finish, another two-man team descended the cellar stairs.

"It's Ansar, no doubt about it," one of them advised. "You should see what we found upstairs: audiotapes, C-4, weapons, maps . . . the whole nine yards."

"Holy shit," the other said, aping an earlier observation. "What the hell happened down here?"

"I'm telling you . . . ," Jeremy tried to explain, but the man kneeling on his neck choked off further words.

"I don't know," the team leader said. "But we're sure as hell going to find out. Get the woman and kids to a hospital. Then take this piece of shit to Meade. We'll see what he's got to say with a cattle prod up his ass."

■

JORDAN MITCHELL HAD always considered variability his greatest enemy. It was the common lament of a control freak, he knew, but that didn't change his compulsion for order.

"Where are they?" he asked.

Trask pointed to a PowerPoint time line off to their left.

"Just touched down at Andrews," the chief of staff replied. "Kneecap is fueled and ready. Airspace is closed. They'll go with a vertical takeoff."

"They can do that?" Mitchell asked. Despite the crushing array of issues confronting him, the aerobatic abilities of a Boeing 747 suddenly seemed the most interesting.

"Yes," Trask said. "Bush did it right after 9/11."

"Got them!" Sirad spoke up. She sat at a terminal, alone.

Mitchell peered over her shoulder.

"Keystroke or voice transcripts?" he asked.

"Neither." Sirad pointed to a page of jumbled numbers, letters, and symbols. "This is the launch-code verification framework at Raven Rock. Even though WHCA handles all voice and data transmission, the NSA is responsible for verifying any attempt to use the football."

"Explain."

Sirad typed rapidly at the keyboard. She had done her homework well.

"As a fail-safe measure, the NSA changes launch codes — called gold codes — daily. These changes are wired via a secure Web-based conduit called DSNET3 to the White House, the Pentagon,

Strategic Air Command, and through burst comms to the Navy's TACAMO communications aircraft."

"This is their site you're looking at?"

"Not their site, their data stream," Sirad said. "We're tapped directly into the transmission conduit linking the National Command Authority — in this case, the president aboard Air Force One — and the Pentagon."

"Giving us immediate notification of any order to fire," Mitchell responded.

"More than that," Sirad said. "We have the ability to intercept. The NSA conduit has an automatic verification response fail-safe. The system is designed to ask for a redundant command, just like when you delete something on your computer. We can intercept the second response before it gets through. Think of it as having a pair of vise grips at one end of a garden hose."

"And we have access to Air Force One?" he asked.

"Same as the Pentagon." Sirad nodded. "They won't know the difference between us and some E-5 electronics tech."

"Excellent," Mitchell said in a rare exclamation of approval. "I have an urgent message from the FBI to the president. Prepare to copy."

■

ELLIS LAY IN his wooded sniper hide, knowing his part in the endgame was just minutes away.

Deep breath, he reminded himself. *Adrenaline is the shooter's scourge.*

His hands began to tremble as the three Marine Corps helicopters appeared from the northwest. He had lain in position for more than two hours now, but it wasn't cold that made him shiver.

Ammo, magazine, receiver, chamber, safety, trigger, scope, he silently recited. Each individual part of the process could fail, and there would be no second chance.

Ellis dropped the magazine and tapped it gently against his forearm to make sure the monstrous cartridges had properly seated. He pulled back the heavy spring-loaded bolt and checked the receiver group to make sure nothing had fallen in to contaminate it. Finally, he inserted the magazine, released the bolt, and listened for the first round to slam into battery.

Discipline, he coached himself. The colonel was a military man, born of violence and destined for delivery, but only God himself could guide what was to follow.

The Phineas priest settled behind the massive weapon's steel-and-plastic stock. He lowered his eye to the 10x Unertl scope and tested the swivel on his specially constructed bench rest. The stainless-steel device allowed free motion of the long black barrel.

United States of America, he read through his scope: four words written on an airplane. Four words that still represented his second strongest allegiance.

■

ELIZABETH BEECHUM HAD begun to assemble her shadow government as soon as the first armored Town Car arrived: forty members from each house of Congress; the secretaries of state, defense, interior; the attorney general; and three Supreme Court justices. Everyone gathered in a tiered 250-seat amphitheater fronted by a proscenium stage.

Members of Congress gravitated into predictable caucuses — Republicans on the right, Democrats on the left. The cabinet members sat down front, the Supreme Court justices nestled quietly off to the side.

"I'll dispense with formality," the vice president said. She spoke from a podium atop the stage. Her voice filled the room, courtesy of an ample PA, and conversation calmed to an almost palpable still.

"I don't know how much you have heard, but Washington's water supply has been contaminated with radioactive material," Beechum advised.

Voices erupted again. These people had families and friends in the District.

"Our experts tell us that it can be flushed out within days, but the president has ordered wholesale evacuation. His chopper just landed at Andrews Air Force Base. Kneecap should lift off within moments."

"Kneecap?" the junior senator from Rhode Island called out. "Isn't that the Doomsday Plane?"

"It's a mobile command and control center," she said in a clear, calm voice. "I have been authorized to tell you that the president plans to exercise his authority under the War Powers Act to launch retaliatory strikes against four strategic targets inside Saudi Arabia."

The group erupted again.

"What kinds of attacks?" the House's Republican whip called out. Rumors and speculation had already begun to spread.

"Tactical nuclear," Beechum announced to gasps and pockets of outrage. She stood at the podium, trying to present a visage of authority and calm.

"That will start a holy war!" someone called out.

"I know this comes as a shock to some of you," she said. "But that's the president's decision. If you have any objections, I suggest you take them up with him."

■

"SHUT THE FUCK up," the driver said.

Jeremy sat in the back seat of a blacked-out Suburban. Two marked units raced ahead of them, lights and sirens blazing a path through downtown DC traffic.

"I'm telling you, my name is Jeremy Waller. I'm an FBI agent assigned to the Hostage Rescue Team. I've been working a classified undercover operation in connection with this terrorism investigation."

They had restrained his feet and hands, but there was no way to silence his protests.

"Fuck you," the passenger said. "We've been surveilling you and your terrorist puke friends since you dropped off the concrete truck. So save the bullshit for your lawyer."

"All right, then, let me talk to him," Jeremy agreed. If Caleb had been telling the truth, he desperately needed to find Beechum. Only she could prevent the president from launching the world into Armageddon. "When can I talk to my lawyer?"

"Well, considering that you are an illegal enemy combatant, caught during the course of a national security investigation, and that we're under no obligation even to acknowledge that you exist, I'd say sometime around the end of the next century, you asshole."

Jeremy's heart actually hurt in his chest. *Think!* he screamed at himself. If he didn't find a way to Beechum, the identity of Jafar al Tayar would rot with him in his grave.

"Why don't you accept that you're busted, you traitor bastard?" the passenger said. He spun in his seat and jammed an accusatory finger in Jeremy's still-bloody face. "The only things I want to hear out of your mouth are the names of the people you're working with and the words *I'm sorry.*"

Jeremy wanted to fight back, but a sudden moment of revelation froze him in his seat. *That's it!* he thought. *That's the way out!*

"I'm sorry," he said with all the remorse he could fake. "OK, I've said it. Now take me to the vice president and I'll tell you everything I know."

■

"YOU'LL NEED TO take your seats immediately," the flight officer advised. It was the first time President Venable had seen any member of his military entourage wearing camouflage BDUs.

Andrea Chase led the way to the conference room, just behind the circular staircase leading to the upper deck. Dozens of people moved about inside the crowded wide-body, seeing to last-minute details of what could be a very long flight.

Though the 747-200, reconfigured as an Air Force E-4B, may have resembled peacetime sister ships, its inner workings looked very different. The National Airborne Operations Center held up to 114 people, offered nuclear and thermal effects shielding, electromagnetic pulse protection, electronic missile defense countermeasures, and state-of-the-art communications equipment.

"Hard to believe something this big could take off vertically," Havelock remarked. He had never been a fan of flying and did not relish the thought of what lay ahead.

"Four General Electric CF6-80C2B1 engines — generating fifty-six thousand seven hundred pounds of thrust each," Oshinski said. His staff oversaw NAOC operations. "Not only can we generate high-angle assent, we can maintain indefinite flight above forty thousand feet with in-air refuelings."

"Are we ready?" the flight officer asked. He bent over to help Havelock fasten his specially designed seat belt. The jet's monstrous engines cranked up, and the plane began to taxi out to the runway.

"We will be, airman," the general said. He motioned for the football, which the Air Force courier placed on the mahogany conference table. "I just want to make sure everything is in order should the president need to . . ."

His words trailed off as the briefcase opened, exposing the mechanism of World War Three. He pulled out the "black book," a seventy-five-page SIOP manual that divided military options into three categories: Major Attack Options, Selected Attack Options, and Limited Attack Options.

"You have two plan packages to choose from, Mr. President," Oshinski advised. He searched through the case to make sure everything was in proper order. "Launch on Warning or Launch Under Attack. I think it quite feasible that . . ."

"Excuse me, sir," an Air Force airman first class said, knocking simultaneously at the conference room door. "I have Yankee White traffic for the president."

The flight officer nodded, and the airman delivered his paper.

"What is it?" Chase asked as her boss read. It was her business to know everything that passed to him.

"I don't believe it," Venable said. He read the copy again just to make sure. "It's from the FBI's SIOC . . . says they have backed off their assessment of Saudi involvement. It says they have identified a white supremacist, Christian Identity Movement group called the Phineas . . ."

He turned to Havelock, his personal intelligence officer.

"For God's sake, they think this thing may be domestic."

■

BEECHUM AND HER on-scene administrator sat in the chief executive's suite — a trio of offices that hadn't seen duty since the weeks following 9/11.

"The president is about to lift off from Andrews Air Force base," FEMA's director of operations said. "Though he maintains ultimate authority, the government has ceased to exist outside these walls. For all intents and purposes, you are the de facto head of nonmilitary operations. In the event that something happens to Air Force One, you will assume complete control."

The vice president nodded her head. She had already played first chair once during this crisis. Responsibility and the call to lead had never intimidated her.

"I want to know the moment he goes wheels up," she said. "Have we established communications?"

"Yes, ma'am," the FEMA executive told her. "I just talked with . . ."

A bustle of activity in the reception area outside distracted him.

"She'll see me, dammit!" a voice called out.

An urgent knock on the door.

"Come," Beechum said.

The door swung open and a Marine Corps major stepped in with a Beretta 92F in his hand.

"Excuse me, ma'am," the marine said in a somewhat confused tone. "I know this sounds crazy, but the Department of Homeland Security is here with a man they have arrested. He claims to have critical, time-sensitive information about this investigation, but he'll only give it to you."

Beechum looked to the FEMA director and then at two Secret Service agents.

"My name is Jeremy Waller!" a voice called out. "Tell her my name is Jeremy Waller!"

■

"DOMESTIC?" HAVELOCK SAID. "What about all the Arab claims of responsibility?"

The president read from the FBI communication. It offered details in Bureau-speak, a language Venable was just beginning to understand.

"This says a domestic white supremacist group called the Phineas Priesthood used Muslim terrorists as a cover. This is a domestic operation intended to start a war between Christianity and Islam."

"That's ridiculous," Havelock bellowed. "Is this the same FBI that told me just hours ago that they had concrete ties between Prince Abdullah and radical cells inside this country?"

"Staged," the president read. "Analysts now believe these Phineas priests were trying to incite some kind of battle of the Apocalypse. Armageddon."

Oshinski put down the black book. Chase shook her head in dismay. Havelock rubbed his forehead, trying to make sense of a week that defied sensibility.

"Should I terminate the flight, sir?" the flight officer asked. His job included much more important tasks than buckling VIP seat belts.

Venable barely hesitated.

"Not on your life," he said. "This is the opinion of the FBI — the same FBI that has told me precisely nothing of value since the first bombing. If they think I'm going to risk national security based on some wild conspiracy theory about secret society priests, they're crazy."

President David Ray Venable pointed to the football.

"Pull out the launch codes," the commander in chief ordered. "The mission stands."

■

COLONEL ELLIS WATCHED as the massive blue-and-white plane turned right from the taxiway onto the main runway and began to gather speed. He knew that his timing would have to be flawless. He'd have just seconds between the time Kneecap lifted off and the point at which the airborne command post passed out of range. The best point to shoot would be at the seat of its rotation from level flight to vertical assent.

"'Blessed are the peacemakers,'" he whispered to himself, kneeling behind the ungainly bench rest, "'for they shall be called the Sons of God.'"

He was completely exposed now — a warm body in a field of snow — but that hardly mattered. It was too late for anyone to stop him. All he had to do was hit one engine at that critical point in full-power takeoff. His rifle magazine held ten rounds; he'd made tough shots before.

Hold . . . hold . . . hold . . . , he cautioned himself, laying his finger on the trigger. Air Force One came directly at him, the distinctive nose cone growing larger in his rifle scope.

Just one hit, he told himself. *Just one bullet to save the chosen.*

■

"WHAT IN HELL is going on here?" the vice president demanded.

Jeremy was led into her office in shackles. Blood seeped from the pressure dressing on his leg. His clothing was torn and soiled. Dried gore clung to his face and hair.

"I'm sorry, ma'am," the DHS agent apologized, "but he said . . ."

"I said I need to talk with you in private, Madam Vice President," Jeremy insisted. "We have no time to argue about this. I have information of critical national security importance. Extremely close hold. Your eyes only."

Beechum tried not to show that she recognized this man. It was outrageous that he had come — a direct violation of rules he had agreed to when they first met in Jordan Mitchell's office.

"Leave us," she ordered the others. "All of you."

"But ma'am . . . ," the Secret Service agent objected.

"Leave us!" she demanded. She had the authority, and they had no choice but to comply.

"You have no right to come here," the vice president said when they were alone. "You know that."

"I know about the Megiddo project," he blurted out. There was no time for arguing rules and decorum in a world that no longer seemed to recognize either. "I have identified Jafar al Tayar."

Beechum froze. Was it possible? she asked herself. Could this lowly FBI agent really have uncovered a secret that had been buried to the highest reaches of government for more than two decades?

"W-w-what?" she stammered. "What . . . who . . . ?"

"It's the president," Jeremy announced. He didn't care who heard. "He's going to use these terrorist attacks as justification to strike targets in Saudi Arabia, hoping to start a war with Islam. You have to stop him."

Beechum stood up from her chair. The look of apprehension suddenly disappeared from her face and gave way to a wry, ironic smile.

"You've lost a lot of blood, Agent Waller," she said. "I think you're getting delirious."

■

"MY GOD, IT'S not stopping." Sirad gasped as the Doomsday Plane rolled down the runway. Air force security camera video played the whole thing out on one of five main-console television screens.

"Did you really think he would?" Mitchell asked. If he felt any apprehension, he surely didn't show it.

"But what if . . ."

"Sirad." Mitchell stopped her. "Do you think I would have left a moment like this to the whims of a politician?"

The Borders Atlantic CEO picked up a channel changer and clicked away from the CNN broadcast of Capitol Hill carnage to an eerie scene on another channel — a broadcast that looked grainy black and white, like something from a closed-circuit camera. Everyone in the room noticed a small black figure — human — walking toward a stationary object of the same color.

"What's that, some kind of infrared imagery?" Sirad asked.

"That's death," he said, crossing his arms. "People call her GI Jane."

■

THE ROAR OF jet engines covered the CIA Special Activities Staff officer's final steps through the crusty snow. She moved fast toward the target as her mission planner in New York relayed GPS coordinates through a Quantis cell phone. The target knelt just ten yards in front of her, deeply focused on a shot of his own.

BOOM!

The unmerciful Barrett .50 caliber erupted, stunning her for half a breath with its report.

BOOM!

Fire leaped out the rifle's barrel as Kneecap's nose pointed skyward and began to climb.

BOOM!

The last shot sounded effete, more a *pop* than a concussion.

But the effect was unmistakable. GI Jane's .45 caliber pistol coughed just once, toppling Ellis right where Jordan Mitchell's satellites and their infrared sensors had discovered him.

"'And the seventh angel poured out his vial into the air; and there came a great voice out of the temple of heaven, from the throne, saying, It is done!'" she said. GI Jane had never considered herself a religious person, but the epitaph seemed fitting. He was a warrior, after all. She felt she owed him that.

The mysterious butterfly expert trudged off through the snow as Air Force One disappeared above her in the violent moan of a vertical takeoff. She had other work to do.

. . .

"WE'RE READY, MR. PRESIDENT," General Oshinski confirmed, once Air Force One had leveled off. He held the football's Quantis phone to his ear. An O-6 on the other end stood ready to launch nuclear-tipped cruise missiles from the USS *Intrepid* traveling 110 miles off the southern tip of Yemen.

"David, I want to try one last time to get you to reconsider," his chief of staff pleaded. She was first and foremost a policy advisor, but sometimes a woman's lack of testosterone facilitated reason beyond logic. "What if that FBI report is accurate?"

"Launch," the president ordered. The blood of righteous vengeance had reddened his face, but there was a look of apprehension, too.

"Missiles launched," Oshinski confirmed.

Well then, Chase thought, resigning herself to a future she had joined this government to prevent. *It really is done.*

■

MITCHELL RECOGNIZED THE launch codes that popped up on his computer monitor even before Ravi called them out.

"That's it," the Borders Atlantic CEO said. His voice sounded calm. Controlled. "Send the intercept to Mount Weather."

Sirad typed four quick keystrokes and punched Enter.

"Sent," she said.

Mitchell nodded.

Oh, how he loved to see a complex plan come to fruition.

■

"MADAM VICE PRESIDENT!" The FEMA administrator burst into her office without knocking. He sounded out of breath but not from running. "Madam Vice President, I have some devastating news."

Jeremy saw panic in the man's eyes. He was a career bureaucrat — one of those spineless empty suits who had risen to this position by escaping decisions, not making them. Well, now he had to face a big one.

"I'm afraid Air Force One has been shot down . . . ma'am, the president is dead."

No one said a word. It seemed more than anyone could imagine. But then the Secret Service and the armed marines entered again, and consequence became obvious.

"Dead. What does that mean for us?" she asked eventually.

"Under the continuity of government protocols, and according to Constitutional provisions, we will have to swear you in as president. Immediately."

"President . . . ," Beechum said. Her voice trailed off, leaving no clue as to whether she was mourning the untimely death of a political rival or trying out the new title.

"I have one of the justices on his way down," the FEMA man said. "We will have to convene a provisional Congress and establish this as the new seat of government." He stood at full attention. "I suppose this is no occasion for congratulations, ma'am, but I want to be the first to wish you luck."

Jeremy barely heard the man's shameful ramblings. All he could think about was Caleb's last words.

The president, the albino had whispered. *It's the president who will save you.*

And then, with a cold shudder of realization, Jeremy understood a truth that almost buckled his knees.

"Thank you . . . ," Beechum said in a loud, confident voice. She had anticipated this moment for so many years, it almost felt like deliverance. "I want to make the call to the first lady myself, and I want you to withhold any mention of this to anyone outside this room. Is that understood? Next I want you to connect me with the War Room at Raven Rock; then I want you to assemble the Congress or do whatever it is that you do to make this the provisional seat of government."

"Yes, ma'am," the FEMA officer said. His COG protocols outlined every link in the chain of governmental succession, but nothing had prepared him for a day like this. He turned, trying to stand erect, and nearly staggered out of the room.

"Jafar al Tayar," Jeremy said, oblivious to the president's immediate circle of guards. The words sounded thick and dirty in the dank air and fluorescent light of the underground bunker. "My God. You're the one?"

Beechum spun with a look of an almost transcendental conviction. She stared at Jeremy but motioned toward her guards.

"This man has nothing to offer our terror investigation," she said, nodding toward the head of her Secret Service element. "Get him out of my office before he bleeds on my rug."

■

"DO WE HAVE anything yet?" Mitchell asked. The room around him sizzled with apprehension, but years playing the pass line between financial ambition and patriotic duty had weaned him of any such weakness. It was his show at this point, and everyone in the room knew it.

"Nothing yet," Sirad said, reading the WHCA communications flowing across her computer monitor. The keyboard at her fingertips allowed direct communications between the U.S. government's highest officials and their most secure locations. The power of having tunneled into the WHCA's data streams made her fingertips tingle.

"She should have moved by now," Mitchell said. "Are you sure . . ."

"Wait, there it is," Sirad interrupted. "Someone at Site Seven just mobilized U.S. forces in Europe. I'm not really sure about all the acronyms, but it looks like a stand-up for all U.S. forces to war footing."

Sirad pointed to the screen, trying to find her place on a page of moving script.

"There's something else . . . looks like the USS *Intrepid* has been ordered back out into the Indian Ocean." She paused. "And there is another message — showing point of origin: POTUS. It's addressed to . . ."

"To me," Mitchell stated.

"Yes," was all Sirad could say. And then she understood the brilliance of Mitchell's plotting. She felt the chill of his power, how he had spun her in circles with the Quantis program and with the supposed intrusion and the links to the White House; how he had toyed with her, pushing her deeper and deeper into the encryption mechanics until Hammer Time and I Can't Dunk and the others had helped her pirate the president's own information pipeline.

Sirad turned from the screen and stared at a man powerful enough to seize the world.

"Read it to me," Mitchell said.

"It says, 'Project Megiddo complete,'" Sirad recited without looking back at her screen. "It says, 'All secure to you. Beechum.'"

No one said a word. Only Mitchell showed any particular understanding, nodding to himself and smiling with an almost painful shrug.

■

AIR FORCE ONE had leveled off at forty-one thousand feet before the president learned that because of as yet unidentified technical difficulties his command to level large chunks of Saudi desert had fallen on deaf ears. No cruise missiles had gone "over the horizon," his chairman of the joint chiefs told him. No supposed al Qaeda training sites had been destroyed as ordered.

Fortunately, the president also learned that the FBI report had been corroborated by sole-source CIA intelligence gathered from highly placed assets inside Arab governments. A former Special Forces colonel named Buck Ellis had been identified as the head of a little-known group known as the Phineas Priesthood. FBI and DHS investigators were searching his Homestead Ranch outside Kerrville, Texas. Records there revealed the names of eighteen cell members — white separatists responsible for the worst wave of violence in American history.

Within an hour, the president had returned to Andrews Air Force Base to try to spin the all-too-visible launch of the Doomsday Plane and to begin rebuilding a battered nation.

"There's one other issue," Andrea Chase told him as Marine One met them on the tarmac for the next leg of their journey. With Washington's federal buildings closed because of radiation contamination, all executive operations were being relocated to Site Seven at Mount Weather.

"To be perfectly honest with you, I'm not sure I can handle another issue at this juncture," Venable said. As with any crisis, the ache of acute loss was giving way to a uniquely human hope for recovery.

"It's about Elizabeth," Chase continued. They fastened their seat belts inside the big Marine Corps helicopter and felt it lift off, nose dipping to the northwest. "There's something about her that you need to know."

■

THE VICE PRESIDENT of the United States was sitting quietly behind her desk when the door opened and two Secret Service agents led Jeremy Waller back into the room. The clock on the wall read 12:04 Zulu — less than ten minutes until the president's helicopter arrived at Site Seven.

"You know, it's the windows I miss down here," she said, standing and motioning for the guards to leave. "I like having a reminder that there is something out there still worth believing in."

Jeremy stood before her, hands cuffed behind his back. The scene felt surreal, hard to grasp even within the framework of his own experiences.

"Windows . . . ," he muttered. Better words failed him.

"I know what you're thinking." Beechum nodded. She reached into her top drawer and retrieved an object that Jeremy could not see. "You think I'm a traitor. You think I have betrayed this country . . . everything you have almost given your life to protect."

"They tried to kill my wife and kids," Jeremy seethed. Traitor hardly sounded strong enough. This woman was a mass murderer. She represented evil.

"Turn around," she said.

Jeremy watched Beechum stand up and step out from behind her desk. She held something in her right hand, something small enough to fit inside a clenched fist.

"They'll stop you," he said, watching her, trying to decide what to do next. "Mitchell will figure it out. He'll find a way to . . . ."

"Turn around!" Beechum ordered. This time, she stepped close . . . close enough that Jeremy could see the torment in her bloodshot eyes. This was not the look of a politician but the conviction of a true believer — someone capable of doing anything.

"I don't think so." Jeremy shook his head. "If you're going to kill me, you're going to have to do it face-to-face."

Beechum started to laugh. It was a nervous growl, more the product of irony than humor.

"Kill you?" she answered. "I'm not going to kill you. I'm going to set you free."

With that, she stepped around behind him and used a handcuff key to release his ligature.

"I am Jafar al Tayar," she said. "You're right about that, but not in ways you understand."

Jeremy rubbed his wrists as she pulled off the cuffs and tossed them onto her desk. He stood still and waited for her to move back in front of him.

"Twenty-five years ago, an army colonel approached an idealistic young lieutenant with a bold and intriguing idea. This country faced a threat from Communism, he said, a threat that reached beyond nuclear weapons and Cold War skirmishes in Third World countries. America faced the very real possibility that someone could infiltrate its government through the very democracy that defined it. What if someone rose to power through election? he asked. What if they . . ."

"I know the story," Jeremy interrupted. "How the hell do you think I found you?"

"What if they worked within the system to bring it down?" Beechum walked to her desk and leaned against it. She seemed lost in thought, transfixed with another time and place. "What if our enemies came to realize that the greatest weakness of a democratic society is its own preoccupation with freedom?"

"How could it have gone so wrong?" Jeremy asked. "That's what I don't understand. How could the military's best and brightest have gone so . . . how could *you* have done something so horrible?"

"She didn't," a voice interrupted. Jeremy recognized it without turning.

It was the president.

"Good to see you, David," Beechum said. She walked toward the commander in chief and embraced him. "I imagine they've briefed you by now."

"They have," he said. "But someone apparently owes Mr. Waller, here, a bit of an explanation."

Jeremy shook his head at first, but then he began to understand.

"You hadn't identified the others." He nodded, staring at Beechum. It seemed obvious now. "You didn't know who else Ellis had recruited. It could have been the president, so you had to try to expose him."

"Unfortunate for me, under the circumstances," Venable said. He walked over to the desk and rearranged some of Beechum's things atop it. "But I see, now, that there was no other way. There was no way to stop the terror attacks without jeopardizing the larger investigation. Millions could have died if we had degenerated into war with Islam."

"When did you know?" Jeremy asked. He probably had no right to ask, but then again, he'd gotten this far.

"Not until Ellis actually tried to shoot down Air Force One," Beechum said. "It wasn't until then that we knew for sure that I was the highest-ranking candidate from the Megiddo project."

"But why tell everyone that the president was dead?" Jeremy asked. "Why swear you in as president?"

"Fail-safe," Venable said. "Once I learned of the whole plot, I decided not to take any chances. If any other of Ellis's recruits had worked their way up through the Congress, they would have surfaced once Elizabeth seized control of the government."

Jeremy shook his head in disbelief.

"Now if you'll excuse us, Agent Waller," the president said, "I'd love to stay and chat, but we've got a country to rebuild. I'm sure you understand."

EPILOGUE

Six Months Later
Hurkamp Park, Stafford County, Virginia

"DADDY! DADDY! LOOK at me!"

Jeremy turned his eyes into the sun and squinted to find his daughter, Maddy, among the crowd of swimmers. The county pool had swelled to capacity in what weather forecasters called the hottest summer in twenty years.

"I'm watching, sweetie!" Jeremy called out.

His little girl stood with her toes over the edge of a one-meter springboard, bright as a lightning bug in her fluorescent-yellow bikini.

"Here I go!"

Maddy clasped her hands together above her head, checked one more time to see that her daddy was watching, then fell forward in what any Olympic judge would have rewarded with an ear-to-ear smile.

"Nice one, cute stuff!" Jeremy called out.

"My turn, Dad!" Christopher hollered.

It was good to see him happy, Jeremy thought. The nightmares had taken even longer to heal than the broken bones.

"Do you miss it?" Caroline asked. His wife sat next to him on a park bench with Patrick in her lap — the little boy didn't seem interested in much else since the kidnapping.

"What?" he said, turning back to her from the diving exhibition.

"Do you miss the team? HRT?"

What could he say? Jeremy had agreed to leave only when the alternative threatened to destroy his family.

"Nah," he lied. "I'm just glad to have my life back."

Jeremy didn't immediately recognize what turned his head. Perhaps it was sun glint on a windshield or a tree branch moving in the wind. But then he looked closer and knew. It was a familiar face, not just to him but to every American. The woman wore sunglasses and a broad sun hat and a pretty madras sundress. She sat in the back of a Town Car, glimmering in the hundred-degree heat like a desert mirage.

"Look, butterfly, Daddy," Patrick said as a bright-winged monarch fluttered through the humid air and came to rest just a foot or two from his outstretched hand.

"Yeah, that's a beauty," Jeremy said, but his eyes held the car instead. There was another passenger in the back. A man almost equally recognizable.

"Honey, I'm going to run out to the car for a minute," Jeremy said. He felt that dull ache in his stomach — the one he got the first time he stayed over at a friend's house as a kid or when a teacher called on him in math class or at the start of a long competitive run. "Can I get you something to drink?"

"No, I'm fine. Get the kids some water, though, will you?" She smiled. "It's so hot, I worry about them."

"Be right back." Jeremy stood up, sending the monarch off toward the sounds of children playing.

It was the man in the car who first saw Jeremy approaching. The woman in the sun hat and shades sat quietly beside him. She may have been the vice president of the United States, after all, but it was Jordan Mitchell who ruled the world.

ACKNOWLEDGMENTS

I would like to thank all my friends and colleagues at Little, Brown, particularly Michael Pietsch, who gave me the opportunity to publish fiction, and Geoff Shandler, who turned it into something I feel proud of. You have treated me like family and I will always appreciate that.

Thank you, Suzanne Gluck, for sticking with me despite my shortcomings. You are a loyal friend and an extraordinary agent. None of this would have happened without you.

A great debt of thanks to my family, which puts up with far too much, and to all the friends who have offered encouragement. The writer's life, for all its magic, can be a lonely ride. You add music, laughter, and a smack in the head when I need it most.

Finally, I want to acknowledge all the faceless warriors out there fighting to keep us safe. The world has become a complicated place these days. Thank God there are still heroes brave enough to scout it.

ABOUT THE AUTHOR

Christopher Whitcomb is the author of *Black* and *Cold Zero,* a memoir of his fifteen-year tenure in the FBI, where he served as a Hostage Rescue Team sniper, an interrogation instructor, and, most recently, the director of intelligence and strategic information for the Critical Incident Response Group. A recipient of the FBI's Medal of Bravery for exceptional courage in the line of duty, he left the FBI in 2002 to become a novelist.